THE FACE OF CHAOS

The nightmare was beginning again.

Remember . . . Come back . . .

Tarod gasped, trying to turn away as the whisper echoed from the silver door at the end of the passage. But his body refused to respond.

Remember . . .

Something was coming along the corridor, moving inexorably toward him. It neither walked nor ran, but seemed to shift without motive power of its own, dreamlike, drifting. The face—his own face—smiled, but the smile was an illusion, a human mask hiding something far more terrible. The long, narrow eyes changed color constantly, and the gold hair flowed in a rising current of air as the apparition raised its arm, holding out gaunt, long-fingered hands toward him. . . .

THE INITIATE

BOOK I of the TIME MASTER TRILOGY
by Louise Cooper

A powerful saga of the ancient battle of Light and Darkness, Louise Cooper's TIME MASTER TRILOGY is a major fantasy masterwork by an exceptional new writer.

BOOK ONE IN THE *TIME MASTER* TRILOGY

LOUISE·COOPER
THE INITIATE

A TOM DOHERTY ASSOCIATES BOOK

THE INITIATE

Copyright © 1985 by Louise Cooper

First printing: December 1985

A TOR Book

Published by Tom Doherty Associates
49 West 24 Street
New York, N.Y. 10010

Cover art by Robert Gould

ISBN: 0-812-53392-5

Printed in the United States of America

0 9 8 7 6 5 4 3 2 1

Sign of the Southern Cross started it . . .
Zero the Hero added fuel to the fire . . .
Born Again set the seal on it.
Thanks, Tony and Geezer.

N
W — E
S

GREAT EASTERN
FLATLANDS

MARGRAVATE

MARGRAVATE

KENNET
HEAD
(Cyllan's
Birthplace)

WHITESHOALS SOUND

FOREST

EAST
HAN

MARGRAVATE

WISHET
PROVINCE

MAIN DROVE ROADS
RIVERS
SISTERHOOD COTS
PROVINCE CAPITALS

PORT SUMMER
(Margravate)

SHU
PROVINCE

SHU-NHADEK
(Margravate)

SUMMER ISLE STRAITS

SUMMER
ISLE

High Margrave's Court

BAY OF ILLUSIONS

WHITE ISLE (Shrine of the Casket)

Throughout history, the twin powers of Light and Darkness have appeared in many guises. Day and Night, Good and Evil, Order and Chaos—and, in many of the ancient religions of our world, personified in the forms, sometimes human, sometimes beyond humanity, of warring deities—Osiris and Set, Ahura-Mazda and Ahriman, Marduk and Tiamat, and many more. Each personification has its followers, and each personification is unique—but all draw their true nature from the same universal source; the eternally conflicting forces of manifest duality.

The Lords of these twin realms—whatever the names under which they are worshipped or reviled—are masters of the forces of Nature; those powers that mere humans have called "magic." Manipulators of Time and Space, their influence pervades every mortal world, and their eternal battle for supremacy maintains an uneasy balance in the many dimensions which form the fabric of our Universe. But there can be times in any one of those dimensions when the balance tilts too far, and one power triumphs to reign at the expense of the other. And without its opposite to counter it, neither force can perpetuate; the relationship is symbiotic, and Order without Chaos, or Chaos without Order, must finally result in entropy.

Somewhere, far beyond the Earth we know, is a world where the balance has slipped out of true. The Lords of Order are victorious, and have banished every manifestation of Chaos from the land . . . or almost every manifestation. Perhaps, somewhere, a single spark still remains—and if it can be found, and nurtured, then a day must surely come when the Lords of Chaos will return to challenge their ancient enemy once again . . .

Prologue

"There is little time left to me to write this account. Even as the ink dries on my parchment I feel the fate that hangs over us drawing closer, and though the insights of a Magus are beyond my skills I know I mistake neither its cause nor its intent. Our time can be reckoned in mere hours; but as senior historian to the Lords of the Star Peninsula, it is my duty to commit to posterity all I can of the events that will bring about our final demise. This duty I will not shirk, if the gods of Chaos can grant me sufficient respite.

"The power of this Castle, so long a focus for the forces that our Magi have called through the gates of Chaos itself, is rapidly crumbling. Another Moonrise will see the horde at our portal, baying for their masters' triumph, and a sure instinct tells me that before the Sun breaks in the East we will look on the accursed face of Aeoris, and die.

"We have served Chaos truly and loyally for generation upon generation; now though even those seven great Lords cannot save us, for their sway has been broken. Through the treachery of those whom we ruled the demon Aeoris and his six brethren have returned to the world; the eternal enemy, Order, has challenged Chaos and prevailed. Our gods are retreating and cannot save us. We have called upon the greatest occult forces known to our race, and cannot aid them. And though we might destroy one or ten or a hundred mortal armies, against the full might of Order we are powerless.

"And so we prepare to leave this world for whatever fate awaits us in the afterlife. Those who succeed us, those blind followers of Order, will destroy or abuse the skill and wisdom that we have gleaned over the many centuries of our rule. They will revel in the overthrow of our sorcery, praise the annihilation of our knowledge. They will dwell within our stronghold and deem themselves leaders, and they will think themselves our equals. We, who owe our origins to something above and beyond their mortality, might almost find it in our hearts to pity the ignorance and fear which will bring about their own ruin as surely as it has brought about ours. But there can be no pity for these human traitors who have turned their backs on the true ways, to follow false gods. There will be bloodshed; there will be terror; there will be death . . . but our sorcery alone cannot stand against the Lords of Order, called from their long banishment to challenge the rule of Chaos. They will prevail, and our day is done.

"Our gods go into exile; we go to destruction. But we have solace in the certainty that the rigid and stagnant reign of Order cannot endure for all time. Let it take five generations or five thousand, the circle will come about once more. Our gods are patient, but in time the challenge will be issued. Chaos will return.

"This last document by my hand on the day of our fall; Savrinor, Historian."

"This manuscript is one of the few fragments to have survived the Scourge carried out in the Castle of the Star Peninsula this five years past, after the final fall and annihilation of the race known to us as the Old Ones.

"Those of us who, by the grace of Aeoris, survived the War of Just Retribution (as it has come to be known) and have since lived on to prosper and flourish in the very seat of the tyrants' power, are aware of the great responsibility laid upon us by the Gods whose hands have elevated us from the realm of serfdom to the realm of rulership. The wrongs done to the people of our land by the Lords of Chaos and the sorcerers who followed their evil doctrines are manifold; there has been suffering and terror and oppression. Now it is our holy duty, in the name of Light and Sanity under the bright banner of Aeoris, to put our world to rights and to eradicate the name of Chaos from all hearts and minds.

"To this end, the first Great Conclave of Three has taken place upon the White Isle, in the very place where Aeoris himself adopted human incarnation to answer our prayers for salvation. While he trod our earth in mortal guise, the great God charged us to rule wisely, to uphold his laws, and he has placed in our safekeeping a golden casket to be enshrined and guarded upon the Isle. Should our land ever again face the dire peril of Chaos we are pledged to open the casket, and in doing so call great Aeoris back to our land.

"I hope and pray with all my heart that such a day will never come. Chaos is banished utterly from the world; we are charged with the task of ensuring that it cannot return. Three we are, empowered to tend to our people and bring the Light of Order back to this torn land; and I give humble thanks each day for the honor done me in elevating me to that great triad.

"Far in the South in his new palace on the Summer Isle dwells our High Margrave, to whom all honor and homage. Benetan Liss fought at the side of Aeoris himself in our last great battle and proved himself a warrior and conqueror worthy to become the First Ruler of all the land. He it is who shall dispense the justice due his people, and I pray that his descendants will flourish to continue the noble line. And our Lady Matriarch, Shammana Oskia Mantrel, is mistress of the newly endowed Sisterhood of Aeoris, that body of good and devout women who will forevermore keep the flame of Aeoris's love burning in all our hearts. And I, Simbrian Lowwe Tarkran . . . as first High Initiate of the Circle, charged by Aeoris himself to cleanse the taint of evil sorcery from this Castle and from the world, I am aware from dawn to dusk of the magnitude of my task. The Old Ones have left us a legacy of darkness and mystery; much remains to be unravelled and only a fool would deny that their black skills surpassed those of even our greatest Adepts. But we will prevail: we draw strength from righteousness, and the wisdom of Order will sustain us in our task. The Circle—a small but growing body of magicians and philosophers, of which I believe I am justly proud—has pledged itself to the pursuit of knowledge and justice in all matters of our religion and our creed. While we stand as upholders of the divine laws laid down for us by Aeoris, the minions of Chaos will never again gain a foothold in this land, and the nightmare of the past will one day be forgotten in the purity and peace of Order.

"The road ahead of us is long and arduous; our accomplishments as yet are relatively few. But my dreams are full of hope. Dawn has finally broken; mayhem and madness are no more a part of our lives and we have emerged from the blackness of enslaved terror into the light. The hand which recorded and railed against the death of Chaos is dead also; we live, and shall grow and prosper. And for that I give my undying thanks.

"Written this Spring Quarter-Day in the fifth year of peace, the hand of Simbrian Lowwe Tarkran, by consent of Aeoris First High Initiate of the Circle."

But Chaos will return. . . .

Chapter 1

With the dawning of the Spring Quarter-Day, the wet weather which had plagued Wishet Province since midwinter abated. Self-appointed sages, who claimed to have predicted the change, pronounced it a good omen, and the more pious inhabitants of the province gave thanks to Aeoris, greatest of the Seven Gods, in the privacy of their homes.

Today, following a centuries-old tradition, every town and village in the land would be celebrating the arrival of Spring and one small Wishet district, some seven miles inland from the province capital, Port Summer, had prepared well in advance for the lengthy ceremonies. As always a mass procession, headed by the Provincial Margrave with a train of local elders and dignitaries, would parade through the town to the river where a ritual dressing and revering of wooden statues of the Seven Gods would take place. The Quarter-Day Rites were an occasion for the entire populace to attend, from the highest to the lowest—even the household of Estenya, an impoverished woman who lived with her illegitimate son in the poorest part of the town and depended on the grudging charity of more fortunate members of her clan.

Today, Estenya was more acutely aware than usual of her lowly status as she looked at her reflection in the fly-specked mirror. Her dress—the best she possessed—was old, and hadn't been new when it came to her; washing had shrunk the fabric so that the hem was barely below her calves. And the embroidered shawl that she wore in an attempt to brighten the dress's drabness was thin and would do little to keep out the bite of the Easterly wind. But today, appearances mattered more than comfort; she would simply have to put up with the cold, if she didn't want to disgrace her relatives . . . not, she reflected bitterly, that they were likely to do more than curtly acknowledge her during the festivities. She was the blot on their immaculate record, the pretty and promising girl who had inexplicably fallen from grace and had been paying the price ever since. . . .

Estenya worked her face into an expression that she hoped would disguise the lines which, at thirty, were now beginning to mar her skin, and silently railed against the events that, twelve years ago, had set her on this road. Then, exhausted by the birth, overemotional, she had pleaded to keep her son against family pressure to pass him off as a servant's child, and she had won—at the price of her own prospects. The boy had no father from whom to take a clan name, as was traditional for male children, and her family had flatly refused to bend the rules and grant the baby the privilege of their own name. So from birth he was clanless—and Estenya became, in effect, outcast. She had submitted willingly enough to the strictures at first, but as time went by and the first bloom of her youth faded while the boy, growing, seemed to become less and less a part of herself, she began to bitterly regret the decision she had made.

But even if she could have been freed from the burden of the boy, she doubted that any man would think her worth marrying now. There were too many younger, fairer women; women without a shameful past to hamper their chances. If only, she thought to herself, if only I hadn't been such a fool!

A faint sound suddenly impinged on her and she turned, then started with shock.

The boy had opened the door and come into her bedroom so silently that she hadn't had the least inkling of his presence. For all she knew, he might have been standing there watching her in that inscrutable, unnerving way for ten minutes or more, and as always his look suggested that he knew precisely what she was thinking.

Angrily, she snapped at him. "How many times have I told you never to enter my room in that way? Do you want to make me die of fright?"

"I'm sorry." The brilliance of the boy's strange, green eyes was masked momentarily as he lowered his gaze. Looking at him, Estenya wondered how she could have given birth to such a boy. The established clans of Wishet shared certain similarities of build and coloring, typified by the stockiness and sallow skin that Estenya had inherited from both father and mother. But the boy . . . already he outstripped her in height, and his was a rangy, harsh-boned frame. His hair—jet-black—curled in wild tangles to his shoulders, and the green eyes against his pale, thin face gave him a disturbingly feline look. Perhaps he drew his genetic heritage solely from his father—and always on the heels of that thought came its unpleasant corollary: if she had known who his father was! There lay the unhappy root of this whole unhappy affair; the fact that the identity of the stranger whose ardent advances at a long ago Quarter-Day celebration she had been unable to resist was, and still remained, a mystery. One mistake had caused her so much misery . . . and she couldn't even remember his face.

Now she looked critically at her son. She didn't mean to

be irritable and impatient with him, she told herself; he could hardly be held to blame for her circumstances. But nonetheless the resentment was there, and surely anyone with any heart could understand it.

"You haven't combed your hair," she accused. "You know how important it is to look your best today. If you disgrace me . . ." She let the threat hang in the air unspoken.

"Yes, Mother." A flicker of near rebellion in the odd green eyes, but it was gone almost before she could register it. As he turned to leave the room she called after him, "And you are not to associate with Coran. Don't forget!"

Privately, Estenya hated having to impose that restriction. Coran, her cousin's son, was of an age with her own boy and the only good friend he had. But Coran's parents disapproved of more contact than was necessary with a bastard child, whatever the blood relationship, and she dared not cross them. The boy didn't answer her though she knew he had heard, and a minute later his footsteps clattered down the uncarpeted stairs of the shabby and cramped house.

Estenya sighed. She didn't know whether he would heed her warning; he had always been secretive, but lately his mind had become a closed book to her. All she could do was hope, and try to get through the day as best she could.

A large crowd was already gathering in and around the streets of the town as the boy made his way towards the main square. He was glad to be free from the stifling confines of his home, where he never seemed able to do anything right, but at the same time he felt no enthusiasm for the day ahead. Despite the supposed festivity of the occasion, a Quarter-Day tended to be a solemn and dull affair. People were so preoccupied with their status and dignity that it seemed that the true nature of the celebrations was lost. And today, with the Sun tracing a low arc in the sky and the last of the heavy-bellied clouds still hanging far away inland, the Rite promised to be gloomier than ever.

The procession itself was just forming up as he reached

the square, and the ritual drums had begun their funereally slow and grave beat. The long crocodile of Province Councillors, religiouses and elders, with the portly figure of the Provincial Margrave at their head, was bathed in a dull red radiance that was the best the heavens could provide at this time of year, and even in this prosperous sector of the town everything looked mean and small. Even the seven garlanded statues of the gods, swaying on their litters above the heads of the procession, seemed grotesque and tawdry, showing the wear and tear of age through the touched-up glory. The boy moved slowly among the crowd, aware of his mother's earlier admonition not to make himself conspicuous, and took up a stance at the entrance to a narrow alley that led into a maze of back streets. Restless and uninterested in the proceedings, he was relieved when, as he had half hoped, a voice hailed him.

"Cousin!"

The boy's face broke into a smile. "Coran—" Instantly Estenya's warning was forgotten as he shouldered his way through the press of people to join the auburn-haired boy. The contrast between Coran's fine clothes and the handed-down shirt, jerkin and trousers of his cousin was something that the boy tried—usually with success—not to notice. The differences had never been a barrier to friendship, and now Coran stood on tiptoe to whisper in his taller cousin's ear.

"Dull as ever, isn't it? I tried to find some excuse for staying away, but Father wouldn't hear of it."

The green eyes narrowed, and he smiled a wolfish smile. "We've attended, as we were bidden. Isn't that enough?"

Coran looked round hastily to see if anyone had overheard this invitation to rank disobedience. "We'll both be for a whipping if anyone finds out," he said uneasily.

The other boy shrugged. "A whipping's soon over," he pointed out. He had suffered enough such punishments for them to mean little to him now. "And if we go to the river, no one will ever know we didn't follow the procession all the way."

"Well . . ." Coran hesitated, less inclined to flout authority, but the temptation was too great to resist. Together they slipped into the alley, weaving their way through the narrow lanes until they reached the river jetty at the eastern end of the town. Here the main Rite would take place; the statues would be ceremonially washed in the sluggish current to symbolize the rebirth of life within the land, and interminable speeches would be made before the celebrations ended with music and stiff, formal dancing.

Now though, the jetty was deserted. Several small cargo boats, newly come upriver from Port Summer, bobbed on the ebbing tide, and the black-haired boy squatted near the water's edge gazing speculatively at the craft. He had often dreamed of escaping from his present life, secretly boarding such a boat and sailing away to another part of the world where no stigma would attach to his existence. No one would miss him, for no one cared about him. He was an embarrassment, unwanted even by his mother; so much so that he had no clan name and the forename Estenya had given him was rarely used. In the solitude of his room he had invented another name for himself, but no one knew of it, for he never spoke it aloud lest it should be discovered and taken away. And yet the boy felt in his bones that he was, somehow, special. It was the one lifeline that had kept up his lonely spirits as he grew towards adolescence, and lately it had begun to goad him more and more towards a half-formed idea of running away.

He would have given much to see the world. He often walked the seven miles to Port Summer on errands, and had been told that from the Port's high cliffs, if he strained his eyes hard enough, he might just see the Summer Isle, home of the High Margrave himself, ruler of all the land, lying in the hazy distance offshore. He had tried, but he had never glimpsed it. Nor had he ever seen what was said to be the most breathtaking sight in all the world—the White Isle, far to the south, where legend had it Aeoris himself, highest of the gods, had taken human incarnation to save his worshippers from the forces of Chaos.

The boy had an insatiable appetite for the mythology of his land; an appetite frustrated by the fact that no one ever had the time or the patience to tell him what he wanted to know. Oh, he had been taught to worship his deities, learned his catechisms, said his prayers each night. But there was so much more he wanted to know, needed to know. Sometimes the Quarter-Day festivities were attended by Sisters of Aeoris, the religious women who were responsible for maintaining all the traditions of worship, but he had never spoken to one of them, and anyway they could not fulfill his hunger for knowledge. What he truly longed for was to meet an Initiate.

The very word Initiate sent a shiver of excitement through the boy. Those men and women were, he knew, the very embodiment of power in the world; mysterious, unreachable, occult. They lived in an impenetrable stronghold on the Star Peninsula, far to the north at the very edge of the world, and any man who defied their word brought upon himself the full wrath of the gods. The Initiates were philosophers and sorcerers, but fact was clouded by rumor and hearsay—stories, he had been told, not fit for a child's ears. But whatever the truth, the Initiates commanded respect and fear. Respect because they served the Seven; fear because of the manner in which they served them. It was said that the Initiates communed with Aeoris himself, and from him took powers that no ordinary mortal could comprehend, let alone wield. A cauldron of speculation and half-truth and fable . . . but the little he had learned made the boy hunger for more. Fancifully, he imagined running away and away, over plains and through forests and across mountains, until he found the Initiates in their stronghold. . . .

It was that thought that first put the idea into his head. He and Coran had been idly skimming stones into the river current while in the distance the clamor of the procession drew slowly nearer. The spearhead would not arrive for some while; there was time enough to give rein to the idea that had suddenly fired his imagination.

When he suggested the game to Coran, his cousin was appalled.

"Pretend that we're Initiates?" Coran's voice was a whisper. "We can't! It's—it's heresy!"

Even to speak of Initiates without due reverence invited ill luck, but the black-haired boy had no such fears. The knowledge that he was breaking taboos excited something deep within him, added spice to a feeling already half-formed and half-recognized. He knew nothing of what powers Initiates possessed, but he had a free and ferocious imagination. Coran was less adventurous, but malleable to his cousin's stronger will, and at last—though in trepidation—he agreed.

"We'll be rival sorcerers," the black-haired boy said. "And we'll battle, using our powers against each other!"

Coran licked his lips and hesitantly nodded. But even his timid spirit entered into the game as imagination began to take over.

And then, it happened.

The boys were so intent on their play that they were unaware of the vanguard of the procession as it rounded a corner and came into full view of the jetty. Leading the long human chain came the Margrave; behind him the statue of Aeoris towered—and the god and his bearers saw everything.

Coran, by now as caught up in their fantasy world as his cousin, had called down a thousand curses on the head of his rival. Not to be outdone, his rival raised a hand, pointed with a dramatic gesture; as he did so, a stray shaft of watery sunlight glinted with shocking brilliance on the colorless stone of a ring on the boy's left hand. An ornate ring, a strange possession for a child to own . . . for an instant, as the sun struck it, the stone seemed to come to ferocious, blazing life—

And, with no warning, a bolt of blood-red fire smashed from the pointing finger with a crack that momentarily deafened him. For an instant only Coran's face was frozen in a mask of astonishment and disbelief . . . then his charred, broken body keeled sideways and fell with a sickening thud to the flagstones.

The black-haired boy reeled back as violently as though struck by a monstrous, invisible hand, and though he tried to scream, not the smallest sound came from his throat. For a moment as the procession ground to a chaotic halt there was utter silence—then pandemonium broke out. Rough hands took hold of him, spinning him around, punching and slapping and kicking him in a rising tide of horror and outrage. Women shrieked, men shouted, and at last the cacophony resolved into words that beat like waves in his ears, cursing him, damning him, naming him blasphemer and desecrator, unfit to live. In a matter of moments the veneer of civilization fell away to reveal the ugly face of naked fear in full, primitive flood, and amid the mayhem the boy cowered, hands over his head, too shocked and numbed to understand what was happening to him, what he had done. As if in a waking nightmare he felt his hands being bound, the cords cutting deep, and he was manhandled into the middle of a circle of hostile, shouting faces. *Stone him!* they said; *hang him!* they cried, and he could only stare back, uncomprehending.

The Provincial Margrave, white-faced and shaking, moved unsteadily forward. Somewhere behind him a woman was screaming hysterically; Coran's mother, who refused to be dragged away from her son's corpse. As the Margrave approached the boy, seemingly afraid to come too close, the town elders set up a fresh clamor. Heresy and blasphemy—a demonic power at work—possession—the bastard son of the woman Estenya; unfit to live . . . And the Margrave, spurred on by his councillors, pointed accusingly at the black-haired child who had brought such horror to the celebrations.

"He must die," he said in a voice that quavered. "Now—before he can do even worse!"

As if in anticipation, a stone flung by someone in the crowd missed the boy's head by a hairsbreadth. Some semblance of reason was beginning to return to him after the initial shock, and he thought he was going to be sick as an image of Coran's face, before he fell, flashed into his mind. *What had he done? How had it happened? He wasn't a sorcerer!*

"Stone him!" a voice yelled, and the cry was taken up again.

He tried to protest, tell them he hadn't meant to harm Coran, they'd been playing a game, he had no power to kill anyone. But the words would mean nothing to the mob. They had seen what they had seen, and in their fear were determined to stamp it out without mercy. And without understanding what had happened to him, he was going to die. . . .

Though always a solitary child, he nonetheless felt more alone than he ever had in his life. Even Estenya couldn't help him now; he had seen men carrying away a woman who had fainted, and had recognized the color of his mother's shawl. There was no hope of reprieve. For a moment his gaze locked with the dead, wooden stare of the statue of Aeoris, then he shut his eyes tightly, praying in silent hopelessness that the god, who alone must know the nature of the appalling power that had struck his cousin down from nowhere, would come to his aid.

The men holding him had moved back, and the boy saw the stones that even now were being gathered from the detritus around the jetty. Every muscle in his body tensed— then suddenly a lone voice among the mob called out in horror.

"Aeoris preserve us!"

A hand was pointing northwards, far beyond the town, and as one the crowd all looked. In the distance, the sky was changing. Slow bands of faint color were marching across the empty bowl of the heavens, and, fascinated, the boy had counted green, scarlet, orange, grey and an eerie blue-black before common sense returned and he realized what he was witnessing.

"A Warp . . ." There was naked fear in the Margrave's voice.

The boy felt a faint tingling from the earth, transmitted through the cold stone of the jetty. He sensed an electric tension in the air, and his nerves began to crawl with something that terrified him far more than his impending fate; something that evoked the worst nightmares any human being could experience. A Warp—and the town was directly in its path!

Warp storms—the eerie, horrifying forces which racked the land at unpredictable intervals—were the deadliest phenomenon known to man. Some said that Warps were a manifestation of Time itself; that the powers unleashed could shift and change the very fabric of the world. When a Warp struck the wise shuttered themselves in their homes and covered their heads until the rage was past and the elemental forces exhausted, and no one knew for certain the consequences of being caught in such a storm, for no one had ever returned to tell the tale. The boy recalled a neighbor who had braved the full fury of a Warp, and vanished. They had searched for some trace of him for a full seven days, but had found nothing. He had simply ceased to exist. . . .

The weird aurora marching towards them out of the north was coming rapidly; now it had all but eclipsed the sun, and some refraction was distorting the solar orb so that it looked like a squeezed, overripe fruit, sickly and aged. Strange colors swept across the buildings and the faces of the throng; people looked bizarrely unhuman and two-dimensional, and to the boy's fevered imagination it seemed that the statue of Aeoris had come to a terrible semblance of life.

From the sky a harsh singing note now emanated, drowning the frightened shouts of the townspeople, as if something unhuman rode high and fast above the wind and cried out in torment. The boy remembered tales of damned souls lost to the Warps and doomed to fly with them forever, and for a wild moment he thought: better that than an agonizing death at the hands of his human judges!

But the death promised him wasn't to be, yet. Already people were scattering, running for shelter as the weird, ululating sound in the sky drew inexorably closer. Someone snatched at his bound arm, almost pulling him off balance, and he found himself being towed along in the midst of a group of Councillors who were making towards the House of Justice a short distance away. This building, which combined court of law with counting house and a bargaining center for out-province traders, was the most secure structure in the town with its massive doors and shuttered windows, and as the boy was hustled up the steps and under the great portal, he saw that half the townspeople had chosen it for their haven.

"Bolt the doors—hurry! It's nearly upon us!" The Margrave had lost his dignity and was on the verge of panic. Still more people were pouring in, and in the huge reception hall some had already fallen to their knees and were earnestly praying to Aeoris for their souls. The boy, now trembling violently from shock, wondered why they should pray, when surely Aeoris himself must have sent the Warp in the first place.

Aeoris himself . . . *and the Warp had come mere moments after he had sent his last, desperate plea silently heavenwards . . .*

It wasn't possible, he told himself. He was a murderer—the gods would have no reason to save him—

But the Warp had come from nowhere, with no warning . . .

Deep down, he knew that his sanity must have deserted him. But it was a chance, the only chance he would have before punishment was meted out and he died the ugly death he had been promised. Better that . . . If he worked his hands surreptitiously behind his back he thought he could free them; whoever had tied the cords had failed to fix the knot properly, and it was coming loose. . . . The last stragglers were entering the House of Justice now, and in the confusion no one was paying him any attention. One more effort . . . and his left hand came free. The doors were closing, he had only moments—

With a speed and agility that took his captors by surprise, the boy dived for the doors. He heard someone shouting at him, a hand reached to stop him but he evaded it and half stumbled, half fell out onto the steps. His headlong rush carried him down—and as he emerged, the Warp came screaming overhead.

The outlines of houses, boats, the jetty, twisted into an impossible chaos of howling color and noise. The ground was falling away beneath his feet, the sky crashing down to meet him, spitting tongues of black brilliance. Then, with a deafening crack, the world exploded into the image of a seven-rayed star that seared into his mind, before—

Nothing.

Chapter 2

Tarod . . .

He heard the word in his head, and clung to it. It was his secret name, and while he held it he knew that he still existed.

Tarod . . .

He was lying face downward on a surface that felt harsh. Something—a stone, he thought—pressed cruelly against his right cheek, and when he breathed in his mouth and nostrils clogged with dust. He tried to move and a searing pain shot through his right shoulder, so that he had to bite savagely into his tongue to stop himself from crying out.

Slowly consciousness returned, and with it some semblance of memory. Faintly, he recalled the last moment before the Warp had struck; the image that had smashed into his brain before the full fury of the storm swept over him. Was he dead? Had the Warp taken him to some unimaginable after-life? He tried to remember what had happened, but his mind was cloudy and he couldn't rally his thoughts. And besides, he felt alive; painfully alive. . . .

Again he attempted to move, and this time succeeded in fighting off the pain enough to raise himself on his undamaged arm, though it took a tremendous effort of will. Something clogged in his eyes, making it impossible to open them, and only after he had rubbed and rubbed at them could he finally part the lids.

He was surrounded by a darkness so intense that it was almost suffocating. And yet his senses told him that he was in the open, for he had the sensation of space, and it was cold. An insidious breeze licked at his black hair, lifting it from his face, chilling a dampness on his cheeks.

16

He blinked the dampness away—it might be water, blood, sweat; he didn't know, and was beyond caring—and began to grope cautiously with his hands to gain some idea of where he was.

His fingers found rock; a slope of rough scree littered with stones and vicious pieces of shale. Doubly afraid now, the boy tried his voice. It came dry and cracking from his throat and he was unable to form words, yet it was at least a sound, physical and real. But he was unprepared for the answer of a myriad soft echoes that came whispering back to him, seeming to emerge from solid rock that stretched immensely in every direction. *Solid rock* . . . with a shock he realized that he must be among high hills, perhaps even mountains. But there were no mountains in Wishet province; the nearest range lay far, far to the north and west, an unimaginable distance! He shivered violently. If he was still in the world, then it was no part of the world he had ever known . . .

Mustering courage, he called out again, and again the rocks answered, mocking him. And among their voices he heard one that was not his own, and it whispered the name that had sounded in his mind as he regained consciousness.

Tarod . . .

Suddenly the boy was overwhelmed by terror and a frantic, almost physical need for comfort. He wanted to cry out for someone to come to his aid, but even as the need surged another memory hit home. *Coran—Coran was dead, and he had killed him!* No one would help him now—for he had already been condemned.

Suddenly the shock of what he had done, however unwittingly, overtook him, and he shut his eyes again in a desperate and futile attempt to blot it out. Helpless, he began to retch violently, and when the spasm passed his head was spinning. Tears started at the back of his eyes, forcing their way between his dark lashes and flowing unchecked down his cheeks. He didn't understand what had happened to him, and no amount of bravado could combat the fear and grief he felt. Somewhere deep down a small voice was trying to comfort him, reminding him that at least he had survived this ordeal—but now, as the tears

began to flow more copiously, he felt that for all the hope
he had he might as well have died alongside Coran.

Later he believed he must have lost consciousness again,
for when he woke there was light. Little enough, true, but
a faint, bloody crimson glow was tingeing the air around
him; and for the first time he was able to make out his
surroundings.

There were mountains—vast, towering crags of granite
that humped into a frightening distance overhead and seemed
to topple towards him, making him reel with vertigo.
Though from this vantage point he couldn't see the sun,
the sky above the peaks had paled to an unhealthy hue like
old, worn brass, and the crags were stained with its gory
reflection. Dawn . . . so he had been lying here all night.
And "here" was a narrow gulley half-filled with the detritus of innumerable landslips; loose shale, a massive boulder with one jagged edge showing where it had broken
away from the rock face. When he turned painfully to look
about him he saw that the gulley ended just beyond his
feet, falling away in a shallow but sharp drop to what
appeared to be a track of some sort at its base. A pass
. . . ? He shook his head, trying to clear his mind. His
shoulder and arm felt as though they were on fire, and he
knew that at least one bone was broken, maybe more.
Trying to combat the pain, he scrabbled for a foothold on
the shale and after a protracted effort succeeded in hauling
himself to his feet, using the sharp-edged boulder for
support. The movement brought on a concussive spinning
and thundering in his head; his stomach reacted and another spasm of retching bent him double, so that for a
while he forgot everything but the sheer misery of his
predicament. In the wake of the spasm he began to shiver
afresh, aware that his body's defenses were dangerously
weak. He was by this time on his knees again, unable to
stand upright—if he was to survive, he must find help. But
the concept seemed meaningless—his control was deterio-
rating and he couldn't think clearly enough to decide what
he should do.

The boy turned about until he was facing, as nearly as

he could judge, the direction of the rising sun. Then, by slow and painful degrees, he began to half stagger and half crawl along the ridge that ran beside the twisting mountain track.

By the time the brief day ended, he knew he was going to die. For endless hours he had crawled like a wounded animal, parallel to the track along a shale ridge, always hoping that the pass would end around the next outcrop to reveal a village and always suffering bitter disappointment. Far above him the Sun had climbed aloofly into the sky, reached a weak meridian and slipped down again, and never once had a single ray of warmth penetrated the shadows. Eventually he had lost touch with reality, and the narrow world of the mountain pass seemed like an eternal dream, with no beginning and no end. Each twist and turn looked the same as the last, every bare, hostile crag above him the same as its fellows. But he kept moving, knowing that once he stopped, once he admitted defeat, then death would come swiftly and inexorably. And he didn't want to die.

He became aware at last that his vista was darkening once more, and as the grim day deepened into twilight the rocks seemed to close in on him, as though trying to enfold him in a final embrace from which he would never wake. By now he was murmuring wordlessly to himself, sometimes trying to laugh through parched lips, once even shouting some confused challenge to the crags. And as he crawled, the name, his one lifeline, reverberated over and over in his mind.

Tarod . . . Tarod . . . Tarod . . .

Finally the moment came when he knew he could go no further. The last of the light had all but fled, and when he raised one hand in front of his face he could barely make out the pale outlines of his fingers. A boulder loomed in his path and, reaching it, he huddled at its foot, pressing his face against the rock and listening to the pounding of blood in his ears. He had tried to save himself, and he had failed. There was no more he could do. . . .

And then, through the roaring of his own pulse, he heard another sound.

It was slight—nothing more than the faint rattle of a stone dislodged and sliding on the shale. But he was instantly alert, for the noise could mean only one thing—someone, or something, was moving nearby.

Heart hammering, he shifted his position until he could look in the direction from which the sound had come, and his eyes strained to see into the deepening darkness. And just when he was beginning to think he must have imagined it, he heard another soft, slithering rattle of stone on stone, this time from a little further away.

Then he saw them. Three silhouettes, only slightly darker than the surrounding terrain, moving with careful stealth across his field of view. They stood upright, and although their heads seemed to be shrouded in caps or hoods of some kind, they were recognizably, unmistakably human.

The shock of encountering human beings at the very moment when he had given up all hope was indescribable, and only self-discipline stopped him from screaming aloud with what little strength he had left. He lurched forward, trying to rise . . . until an instinct warned him to hold back.

Something in the way the silhouetted figures were moving had sounded a warning bell in his mind, telling him not to reveal his presence. The figures were making their way cautiously along the ridge; he saw an arm raised, darker against the backdrop of the crags; heard a muffled curse as someone slipped. The accent was unfamiliar . . . Then abruptly, at a signal from one who appeared to be their leader, more figures emerged from the dark. Holding his breath and trying to ignore the painful pounding of his heart, the boy began to count their numbers—but almost before he could begin, a new disturbance diverted his attention.

Hoofbeats. Far away as yet, but as his ears strained the sounds resolved into greater clarity. Several horses—it was hard to judge the numbers, as the sounds echoed and re-echoed in the pass—and they were approaching rapidly. The men, too, had heard them, and the scattered silhouettes tensed. Something glinted in the hand of one of them; dully gleaming metal . . .

The boy saw the lights before he saw the horses and their riders; small, bobbing pinpoints approaching like fire-flies along the pass. Three lanterns, borne on long poles, and as they drew closer their flaring glow illuminated the faces of the riders.

Almost all the travellers were women.

Women, riding through a forsaken place like this? Before he could muster his thoughts the shadowed figures on the ridge moved. The boy saw their plan immediately, and realized that these men were nothing less than brigands—he was about to witness an ambush! The women wouldn't stand a chance . . . A cold deeper than the chill of pain and exhaustion and the bitter night penetrated to the boy's marrow and he shrank further back against the boulder as the first of the riders clattered by a mere few feet below him.

The attack was swift, and shockingly efficient. The brigands gave no warning; they simply sprang from their vantage point like phantoms materializing out of the night, and three riders and two lanterns went crashing to the ground as the leading horses reared whinnying in terror. Women screamed, a man's voice bellowed raucously, the sounds echoing back from the peaks, and pandemonium erupted in a matter of moments.

The boy watched, unable to move, unable to tear his appalled gaze from the mayhem below. By the light of a wildly swinging lantern he saw the bandits' long knives, saw a horse go down, blood fountaining from its throat and a hideous, thin shriek bubbling from its mouth. A woman, vulnerably visible in a long and cumbersome white robe, was trying to crawl from under the flailing hooves; a hooded figure shadowed her suddenly; he saw a knife flash, but her cry—if she cried out—was lost in the uproar.

To attack a woman . . . she was defenseless! The boy's stomach churned suddenly as a terrible emotion rose in him, and seemed to flood his whole being. His fists—even the fist of the shattered arm—clenched convulsively, and

rage and bitterness surged to the surface. The feeling made
him want to hurt, to kill, to avenge the brigands' victims,
and as the desire formed, an exhilarating sense of power
swept through him and took control, fuelled by his anger
and blotting out all other forms of consciousness. Had he
had time to reason, he would have realized that that power
was twin to the force that had struck down Coran—but
reason was beyond him. Without knowing it he was on his
feet, the strength of pent-up fury filling his body. He
raised an arm high above his head, and the world about
him seemed to turn crimson—for an instant the upturned
face of the brigands' leader was caught and held with
terrible clarity in his field of vision; disbelief registered on
the broken-nosed features, then was frozen forever as a
single bolt of livid crimson brilliance seared with a deafening crack from the boy's fingers. The bolt struck the
brigand full on, and his body seemed to erupt in a second,
lesser flash before the scene was plunged into a stunning
darkness and silence.

The boy rocked dangerously on his feet. *What had he
done? What had happened to him?* The flood of power had
taken him over totally, but now, expended in a single
moment, it had gone, leaving only a hideous aftertaste. He
wanted to be sick, but his stomach was empty; he could no
longer control his muscles. . . . For a moment he saw the
faces below him, stunned into immobility by what they
had witnessed. Somewhere, far away he thought, men
were yelling, footsteps scrabbling and stumbling as someone fled. Then a wave of nauseous darkness rose, ebbed,
rose again, stronger this time; he felt his legs giving way—

Thankfully, there were hands waiting to catch him as he
pitched forward from the ledge into the pass below.

Tarod . . . Tarod . . . Tarod . . .

The name was calling him back to consciousness. He
tried to open his eyes, but pain filled him at the smallest
movement and he gave up the attempt.

His tongue was swollen and leaden in his mouth, his
throat raw, but he couldn't find his voice to ask for water.
If, indeed, there was anyone to hear him. . . .

But there *was* a presence. He could sense it—or, rather, them—moving quietly about him. And he was no longer lying on the cold shale but on rough fabric, warm against his flesh. A sense of being closed in . . . a shadow passed across his lids and again he tried to open them, but again was incapable.

Tarod . . . Tarod . . . Tarod . . . This time the word in his mind resolved into other words; low-pitched voices, physical, real . . .

"And I tell you, Taunan, that the boy is badly injured! Would you have him die on the journey? My Cot is no more than half a day on—"

"Lady, I appreciate your concern; I share it." A man's voice, this. "But you saw what happened with your own eyes! Evidence of such a power is—is—" words seemed to fail the speaker momentarily, "unheard of! No; if he can be mended, our physician can mend him. He must be taken to the Peninsula."

The woman stood firm. "He shall be brought to you when he's healed. Unless, of course, his clan should claim him in the meantime."

Horrified, the boy wanted to protest, to tell them that he had no clan and nothing in the world could induce him to return to Wishet. He was desperately relieved when the man replied, "He shall come with me now! And damn his clan—no one can spawn such a prodigy and expect the Circle to shrug its shoulders and ignore the fact! Aeoris preserve us, when Jehrek hears of this—"

"He will quite probably have your addled brains on a silver dish for your carelessness, if I know the High Initiate!" the woman retorted tartly.

Initiate! The boy managed this time to gasp, and immediately another female voice, lighter and younger, spoke close by his ear. "Madam—Taunan—I believe he is stirring!"

The man swore roundly under his breath.

"Thank you, Taunan, I would remind you that there are novitiates present," the older woman chided him. "There now, Ulmara, let me see the boy; ah yes, he's regaining his senses even if he tries to hide it." A rustle of clothing and he felt a second presence at his side, smelled a faint, unfamiliar herbal scent. "To think that without him, we might all now be dead . . . child, can you hear me?"

Something in her voice, firm but kind, made the boy want desperately to respond, but his vocal cords would not obey his will.

"Water, Ulmara. There's a flask over there; I think it's undamaged."

Something cold was put to his lips and he swallowed convulsively. The water was stale but welcome, and at last he felt throat and tongue beginning to unlock.

"That's better," the older woman said with satisfaction. "Now, can you speak? Can you tell us your name?"

Name? He had no name, not any more, and with that thought the fear resurged. Without thinking he tried to move, and the pain it brought to his shoulder and arm was so great that he moaned aloud and fell back.

"Sweet Aeoris, Taunan, the wound's opened again. Fetch me a cloth, Ulmara, quickly. Yes, yes, that will do; no matter if it soils!" A pad was applied to his shoulder, and the coldness of it was a balm to the fire that seemed to be trying to sear his flesh. Calmed, he wondered what he could tell them, and at last, goaded by confusion, he found his voice. But he couldn't form the word he wanted to say, and instead whispered, "Brigands . . . "

The man made a sound that might have been surprise or amusement. "The brigands? They're gone, lad. Scattered like babes before a Warp; all except the leader they left behind, thanks to you—"

"Taunan!" said the woman warningly.

Taunan brushed her protest aside. "He knows what he did to that piece of offal, or what's left of it, and he should know, too, that he saved all our lives by doing it!"

"Nonetheless, he might be in shock and it'll do no good to remind him—"

"No, not this one." A hand touched the boy's forehead. "He's strong, lady—stronger, I suspect, than you or I or anyone we know. A strange fish, and no mistake."

Something in the boy's consciousness rebelled at their talk; they spoke as though he were some inanimate piece of meat to be discussed and dissected at their leisure. What had he done? He couldn't remember now . . . He clenched his teeth, made a tremendous effort to combat the pain, and forced his eyelids to open.

At first the scene before him wouldn't focus, but remained a blur of shapeless shapes, colorless colors. Then he saw that just a pace away from him was a cloth wall; above his head a cloth ceiling. He was in a tent, or at least a crude and hastily constructed shelter. The small, cocoon-like world it formed was comforting; he felt—however illogically—safe from the night that lurked beyond. He blinked crusted lashes, and someone dabbed gently at his eyes with a wet cloth, so that at last his vision cleared and for the first time he saw the faces of his companions.

The woman who knelt beside him was older than her vigorous voice had implied, her face long and strong-boned, the skin pale, the eyes a faded blue. Her hair was invisible, drawn back under a wide, white linen band that circled her head, and she wore the distinctive white robe of a Sister of Aeoris over what appeared to be coarse travelling clothes. When she smiled she showed several missing teeth, although the lantern-light, casting a soft glow over the scene, mellowed the deep lines on her face. Other figures moved and he saw a girl only a few years older than himself, rounder and snubber of feature, her eyes staring widely at him. Two more women sat gazing at him from a distance; they too wore white robes, torn and stained after their ordeal, and one held her bandaged arm at an awkward angle. Intuition told him that she was the one he had seen trying to crawl away, the one the brigand had struck. So she had survived without too much injury . . . he was glad. The boy tried to smile at her, but before she could respond, the man whose voice he had heard interposed his body between them. He was tall and spare, the hair light brown, cut roughly to lie on his shoulders. His eyes, too, were light, framing a sharp, high-bridged nose, and something in their look told the boy that there was a good deal more to Taunan than first impressions suggested.

Now Taunan squatted on his haunches and leaned forward. "Can you see me, lad?" he asked.

The boy nodded with an effort, then bit his lip hard as pain shot through him again.

"Don't move more than necessary," the old woman admonished. "You've lost a good deal of blood, child, and you are weak. But you're safe with us. The brigands are long gone." And she stared down any further comment Taunan might have made on that score.

Taunan's gaze flicked from the woman to the boy once more. "We owe you a debt, lad," he said seriously. "And we'll repay it, if we can. What is your name, and your clan?"

The boy would dearly have loved to tell Taunan the truth, but wariness made him hold his tongue.

"Either he doesn't know, or he doesn't want us to know," Taunan murmured. The words were not intended for the boy's ears, but he heard them nonetheless. "Or he could be a stray—he's nothing but skin and bone."

The old woman sighed. "Yes . . . and that's an added danger, with the injury he's suffered. If only we had something to nourish him; some milk—"

"Milk?" Taunan gave a short, sharp bark of a laugh. "Lady, you'll not find any milk within a day's ride of this hellhole! The best we can do for him is brackish water and a bite or two of whatever provisions any of us are carrying, if he can stomach it, which I doubt."

The boy felt his mind beginning to drift away, detach itself from the quiet scene in the shelter. It was a peculiar sensation, like floating on a cloud of damp air, and he relaxed his grip on his senses enough to indulge it a little—until Taunan leaned over him again. As the man moved something glinted at his right shoulder, catching the boy's attention, and when he looked at it his pulse quickened. It was a gold brooch, an insignia that formed a perfect circle bisected by a single, jagged lightning-flash. He had seen such a brooch once, in a picture . . . it was the badge of an Initiate!

Against all odds it seemed that his saviors were the servants of Aeoris himself! If only he could—

Agony flooded him when, without thinking, he tried to sit up. Taunan caught him as he started to retch in reaction to the pain, and when he was laid back on the pile of cloaks and coats that formed his bed he felt as though the whole world were a single scarlet vortex of torture, twisting and tumbling around him. Taunan swore again and they gave him more water to drink, but this time when the pain decreased it left behind a sick, throbbing pulse that wouldn't be quieted. When he opened his eyes once more, everything he saw—the shelter, the two women, Taunan— was surrounded by an unsteady and garish aura.

"He can't stand much more, Taunan," the old woman said worriedly. She seemed to be speaking out of a vast, empty distance. "However strong his constitution may be, he has suffered a great deal. And he's only a child! If we delay much longer, then any decision as to where he should be taken will be academic."

Was he going to die? He didn't want to die. . . .

Tarod . . . Tarod . . . Tarod The secret name came back unexpectedly, catching him off guard. Delirium was beckoning although he tried to fight it; he was on the borderline between consciousness and illusion, and finding it harder each moment to distinguish between them.

Tarod . . . Tarod . . .

The old woman stood, brushing down the skirt of her robe and flexing numb toes inside her heavy leather boots. "I'm afraid I must give you best, Taunan. The child is in poor shape and, as you said earlier, if he can be mended, your physician can mend him. We haven't Grevard's skills at the Cot. If he's to be saved, the Castle must save him."

Castle? The word triggered off something deep within the boy, something he needed to articulate. He was only half conscious, close to the borders of an uncertain nightmare, but he had to find the strength to say it, before the world of delusion stole the chance away.

"Tarod." He surprised himself with the clarity of his own voice, and was gratified by the momentary stunned silence that followed.

"What did he say?" Taunan hissed.

"I don't know . . . it sounded like a name. His name,

perhaps?'' The boy felt the old woman coming closer.
"Child, what was it you said? Your name? Can you say it
again?''

"Tarod . . ."

They heard him better this time, and the word was
echoed on Taunan's lips. "Tarod . . . it's unfamiliar to
me, but . . ."

"His name," the old woman agreed. "It must be. His
name is Tarod."

The boy was slipping away, across the chasm that di-
vided him from reality. But as his eyes closed he smiled a
confirmation, and in the confirmation were satisfaction and
relief.

The early spring dusk was cold and silent. In these far
northern latitudes the sun never climbed high, and at
setting it was a bloated crimson orb, old and jaded and
gloomy. As she and Taunan emerged from the mountain
pass that isolated the Star Peninsula from the rest of the
world, the Lady Kael Amion, Senior and seer of the
Sisterhood of Aeoris, looked down at the roughly constructed litter which the animals drew between them. It
was a thoroughly unsatisfactory way to transport an injured
child, but there had been no other choice if they were to
make good speed to the Star Peninsula. And by the grace
of Aeoris, she thought, at least the boy was still alive.
Shivering, she recalled the way he had raved as they
prepared for this ride; the unease on the faces of Ulmara
and the other women when she had packed them off to
finish their journey to the Sisterhood Cot in West High
Land. She had reminded them forcibly that the story of the
child with mysterious powers would spread like a southern
grass-fire in high summer, and no brigand would dare set
foot in the district for many a day to come, but still she
prayed silently that her charges would reach their destina-
tion without incident. While she rode back to the Castle on
a bizarre mission, still not certain in her mind why she had
agreed to it at all. . . .

Taunan, sensing her unease, also looked down at the
boy. He too had had doubts about allowing the other

women to continue on alone, but felt there was no option open to him. After what he had witnessed in the mountain pass his priority was clear, and the last thing he needed was a gaggle of chattering Novitiates to impede progress.

The mountains lay behind them now, dark and titanic, defying the sun and casting a grim shadow over the two riders as they reined in. The horses had picked their way through the rough scree that littered the lowest slopes, and ahead of them was the final stage of their journey—the Star Peninsula.

The Star Peninsula was the most northerly point of land in the entire world; a small but spectacular buttress of granite cliffs that reached out into a cold, hostile sea. Not even the hardiest fishermen sailed that ocean, and Taunan doubted if its unknown reaches would ever be explored by men. Born and brought up with the sea as a close neighbor he could empathize with the mingling of fear and love that the fishermen felt toward the element that controlled their lives. If matters had turned out differently he might himself have been a fisherman, braving the sea's power to grant life or death at a whim. . . .

He mentally shook himself. The Peninsula always affected him like this when he returned after an absence of more than a day or two; his first sight of the grey-green finger of land stretching away from the mountains' feet, the heavy breakers rolling in from the north to crash and spend themselves on the rocks hundreds of feet below, still had a power to entrall him that no amount of familiarity could dispel. From here it was difficult to make out the single stack of rock that stood out beyond the Peninsula's tip; evening mist and the angle of the sun obscured it. But he felt the familiar sensation of coming home. And the knowledge that home was the most widely known and respected—yes, even feared, he told himself—structure in the entire world, still gave him a frisson of pride when he stopped to consider it.

Kael Amion had taken advantage of Taunan's reverie to dismount from her horse and kneel on the damp grass to look more closely at their young charge. At first glance the boy seemed to be asleep, but tell-tale signs warned her that this was no normal slumber. Sweat beaded the child's face; his cheeks were flushed and his breathing shallow and uneven. He had fallen into a coma, she suspected, and he silently prayed to Aeoris that Grevard, the Castle's senior physician, would be able to help him.

Taunan twisted round in his saddle to observe the child. "How is he?" he asked.

Kael Amion shook her head as she remounted her horse. "Not good. And the longer we delay here, the less I like his chances."

A north-westerly wind caught them as they left the mountains' shelter and began to ride across the short, springy turf of the Peninsula. Never having had a good head for heights, Kael kept her gaze firmly on the ground a few paces ahead, only glancing behind her occasionally to check on the bumping litter. The Peninsula was a barren, empty stretch of land, unbroken by even a single bush or tree, a forsaken piece of clifftop; and not for the first time she wondered what kind of disturbed mind could have chosen to build a fortress here, when they had an entire world to choose from. But then, the Castle had been created before known history began—if the records spoke truth, no sane man or woman could or would wish to fathom the dark motivations of the Old Ones. . . .

They had no more than half a mile to go, on a gently descending slope, before the Peninsula came to an abrupt end. Here lay the final part of their journey and the part Kael dreaded most: the crossing of the causeway that would take them to the Castle. Long ago, the ground on which the Castle stood had been an integral part of the Peninsula, but over the centuries the sea had taken advantage of a fault in the rock strata, eating at the granite until finally the cliff had given way to the ceaseless battering of the tides. Now the stack was joined to the mainland only by a perilously narrow natural bridge of rock that formed a great arch between the two. Each time she rode across that arch Kael's stomach turned over at the thought of the thin, worn span which alone separated her from a plummeting drop of nearly a thousand feet to the ever-hungry sea.

Swallowing her fear she forced herself to look ahead to

where the causeway's beginning was marked by two stone cairns. Raising her voice to be heard above the wind and the sea she called to Taunan, "Is the bridge wide enough to take us side by side, with the litter?"

"It's wide enough for four, lady—just."

Shading her eyes against the slanting sun she peered across the bridge, trying not to think about how narrow and how precarious it looked. Now she could see the stack with greater clarity, and as always it gave her a momentary frisson when, even at this close range, there was no visible trace of the Castle. No one knew the full secret of the formless barrier that separated the Castle of the Star Peninsula from the rest of the land; it was believed that the Castle's structure encompassed an extra dimension, but since the final fall of the Old Ones no Adept had succeeded in unravelling the conundrum. They used the Maze—as it was known—to hold themselves aloof from idle scrutiny, but they did not fully understand what they used.

Kael smiled wryly. The crossing had to be faced—better to face it now, and have it over and done with the sooner. Touching light heels to her mount's flanks she urged it forward in line with Taunan, felt the slight drag on the improvised harness as the litter began to move. The entire sky was a bowl of blood-red light now as the sun set, and the glow on the sea made it look like an endless, heaving surface of molten steel. If she looked westward she might glimpse the stacks and islets off the mainland of West High Land Province as tiny black coals in the vista of crimson fire; while eastward the vast coastline reached away into gathering darkness.

Kael Amion did not so much as glance to either the east or the west. Gripping the reins more firmly in one hand, and taking a surreptitious hold on the pommel of her saddle with the other, she drew a deep breath as the two horses stepped, side by side, onto the dizzying causeway.

Chapter 3

Arriving without mishap on the Castle side of the causeway, Kael Amion and Taunan urged their horses on to the expanse of greensward that spread away before them. For a newcomer, Kael thought, this was usually the worst moment of all, to reach the stack safely and yet still find no trace of the Castle, and she was thankful that the boy had not regained consciousness.

Taunan pointed towards a familiar dark patch in the sward ahead, and carefully the two riders guided their horses over it, making sure that not one hoof strayed beyond its boundaries. And as they crossed it, the change began.

It was gradual, subtle, but sure. The grass below shifted sideways, or seemed to, making Kael blink with momentary disorientation. And then directly ahead she saw something that a moment ago, it seemed, had not existed.

It rose huge and dominant out of the ground, so black that it absorbed what little light now remained—a vast silhouette of a place, silent and chill. At each of the four cardinal points a titanic spire soared skywards, and an archway had been cut into the black stone to make an entrance, shielded by a vast wooden gate. Kael knew what would follow, and held her breath as, with a soft and barely audible sound at their backs, the outside world—road, mountain pass, causeway—vanished, as though an invisible door had been closed on it, and only the stack itself and the restless, surrounding sea remained.

Silence enveloped them. Even the roar of the tide had been swallowed into nothing, and as the eastern sky turned pewter-dark the distant horizon was blurring into night. Kael forcibly reminded herself that they were still in the world as she knew it; the Castle's peculiarities had simply altered time and space by a fraction. A useful precaution, under some circumstances . . .

Tarod twisted suddenly on the litter, and moaned as though disturbed by the changes. Alerted by the sound Kael nodded to Taunan, and the two spurred their horses on.

As they rode towards the towering bulk of the Castle, a small shape, only dimly visible in the deepening twilight, detached itself from the shadows by the gateway and came streaking across the grass towards them. Taunan smiled as he recognized it.

"Our arrival hasn't gone unnoticed," he said. "That's Grevard's cat."

The shape now resolved into that of a small, grey feline with brilliant gold eyes, which turned about as it reached them and ran alongside Taunan's horse. These cats were native to the Northern regions, and though they tended to be feral they were nonetheless great opportunists, often inveigling their way into human settlements. Several dozen of them—almost, but not quite, domesticated—lived in and around the Castle, and Grevard the physician, among others, had adopted one as his own pet. The cats were telepathic, and with patience could make useful messengers, although the differences between human and feline consciousness made communication a haphazard affair. Now Kael felt the creature tentatively probing her own mind for a moment before it turned its attention to Taunan.

"Can you persuade it to warn Grevard that we need him?" she asked hopefully.

"I can but try." Taunan caught the cat's eye; it hesitated, holding up one paw—then a second later it was racing away back in the direction of the Castle. Taunan watched it go, and shrugged expressively.

It seemed that the cat had delivered its message, though, for as they neared the entrance the huge gate began to swing open. Light glimmered faintly from within; the arch yawned overhead, then the thump and rustle of hooves in the grass changed abruptly to a raucous, echoing clatter as they rode into the main courtyard.

The Castle's grim exterior was in complete contrast to the sight that greeted them now. The courtyard, a huge flagstoned square, was surrounded on all sides by the sheer walls over which vines and creepers rambled unchecked. Here there was light; a soft amber glow from hundreds of windows that studded the walls' blackness, giving the scene an ethereal air. In the courtyard's very center an ornate fountain played, water catching the light and shattering it into cascades of tiny starpoints, and beyond the fountain, flanked on either side by colonnaded walks, a flight of steps led up to the main door. The peace, the tranquility, the stability of the scene moved Kael, as it always did, and she felt a familiar surge of pride at being welcome in this incredible place.

Suddenly the spell was broken as people emerged to greet them, and among them Kael recognized a small, slight, fair-haired woman in middle age.

"Themila!" The Sister slid gratefully from her saddle and returned the small woman's embrace.

Themila Gan Lin, Initiate of the Circle, kissed her old friend on both cheeks. "My dear, what brings you back to us so quickly? Is there some trouble?" And then she saw the litter.

Kael explained in as few words as possible, and Themila bent over the unconscious boy. "Poor child! You did right to bring him directly to us, Kael."

"Here's Grevard," Taunan said with relief.

The physician shouldered his way through the knot of curious Castle-dwellers which had gathered, greeted Kael and Taunan with absent-minded courtesy, then crouched beside the litter and looked down at the boy, probing lightly at his arm with practiced fingers. "Badly fractured bone and a high fever," he said. "The cat warned me he was in a poor way—it seems the creature was right."

"The cat told you that much?"

"They're useful creatures at times like these, lady!" Grevard smiled at Kael's surprise. "And thanks to mine, a fire's being lit in one of the spare chambers at this very moment. Here now; let's see if we can move him litter and all—no sense in disturbing him more than necessary." The physician's brisk, efficient manner reassured Kael, and she watched as two men, under Grevard's direction, hefted the litter and bore it away towards the main door. As it disappeared she was surrounded by people curious to know the identity of the stranger in their midst. Outsiders at the Castle were a rarity unless some formal celebration was in progress, and Themila's efforts to stem the questions and lead Kael away from the crowd were in vain—until at last the hubbub was quieted by the arrival of a newcomer.

The man had a hawklike face, shrewd eyes, hair sweeping back and greying at the temples, and at the sound of his voice everyone else fell deferentially silent. Like Taunan and Themila he wore an insignia on his shoulder, but his was a double circle, concentric and bisected by the same lightning-flash. Jehrek Banamen Toln, the High Initiate in person, head of the Circle.

"Kael—this is an unexpected surprise!" Jehrek's smile was warm, softening the sharp contours of his face. "Grevard tells me you've found a child in need of his attention."

Taunan, who had been standing uncomfortably by with the horses, spoke up. "There's rather more to it than that, sir. If I might speak with you . . ."

The High Initiate frowned. "Certainly, Taunan, if there's something I should know. But—"

Before he could say more, they were interrupted by a long-legged lad who came flying down the steps and all but cannoned into the High Initiate. Jehrek turned on him. "Keridil, where are your manners? I've told you before—"

The boy—who was about the same age as Tarod—grinned, unabashed. "I'm sorry, Father. But I saw the litter, and I wanted to know what happened."

There were distinct echoes of Jehrek as a younger man in Keridil's light brown hair and tawny eyes, and Taunan hid a smile, wondering irreverently if the High Initiate had been equally ingenuous at the same age.

"Whatever it is, it's no concern of yours at present," Jehrek told his son sternly. "Taunan and I have matters to discuss."

"Then may I help Grevard with the newcomer?"

"Certainly not! Grevard has enough on his hands without the meddling of small boys. If you wish to be useful, you may escort the Lady Kael Amion to the dining hall and find food for her." And, as Keridil tried to hide his disappointment, the High Initiate bowed to Kael. "If you'll pardon us . . ."

Kael smiled and nodded, allowing Themila to take her arm, and watched as the two men moved away across the courtyard.

Jehrek Banamen Toln leaned back in his upholstered chair and stared into the small votive flame that burned constantly on a table by his window. In the low light of the room Taunan thought that he looked strained.

"It's not a pretty tale, Taunan," Jehrek said slowly. "A child who can command power such as that—"

"I don't believe he was even aware that he summoned anything at all, sir. Certainly he had no idea of what it was."

Jehrek smiled thinly. "He's not alone in that."

"Indeed not." Taunan shifted uncomfortably. "But there's no doubt the boy has power, and an innate talent for using it."

"And you're about to tell me that we need such power as never before. I know, Taunan; I know."

"The Warps are growing more frequent, more unpredictable. There's something afoot in the world; something that threatens us. And we're no closer than we've ever been to discovering its cause."

Jehrek gave the younger man a sharp look and Taunan flushed, realizing that he'd made the mistake of trying to tell the High Initiate what he knew all too well. "For the time being that's irrelevant," Jehrek said. "My present concern is the boy. What, by all the powers, was he doing in that hellhole to begin with?"

"He hasn't yet spoken of it," Taunan said, "but I have a suspicion. We've learned nothing of his clan, or where in the world he comes from. If he has exhibited such—talents—before, which seems likely enough, then—well, people are superstitious. His clanfolk might have reacted unfavorably . . .''

"And preferred to quietly dispose of anything that smacked of trouble? Yes, perhaps. When he recovers, we must see where the truth lies. Meanwhile, Taunan, you acted rightly in saving the lad. And we *do* need new blood . . . just so long as it's clean blood.''

"He didn't know what he was doing, Jehrek. I'm sure of that!''

The High Initiate made a placatory gesture. "Of course, of course; I'm not disputing it. Only . . .''

"Sir?''

"Ah, nothing. Just put it down to the peculiar fancies of an old man who has spent too long within these four walls.'' Jehrek rose, indicating that the interview was coming to an end. "I trust your judgment, Taunan—in some ways, maybe better than I trust my own these days. I think I'm growing jaded. But—watch that boy, my friend.''

"I shall.'' Taunan moved towards the door, opened it, then turned back with a slight smile on his face. "We'll spare no pains to tap whatever potential he has, Jehrek. And if I'm right, it'll be the making of him.''

He went out, the door closed behind him, and Jehrek Banamen Toln spoke softly into the empty air.

"Or the ruin of us all . . .''

"Tarod . . . Tarod, can you hear me?''

Tarod turned over in the bed, surprised by the low pitch of the woman's voice. His mother's tone was high, almost shrill. She rarely spoke so gently to him—and she didn't know his secret name. . . .

He opened his green eyes and almost cried aloud in shock as the unfamiliar room swam into focus. Dark walls, rich furnishings, the strange, reddish light filtering in at the window and casting disturbing shadows—this wasn't his home!

And then, as the last vestiges of sleep faded, he remembered.

Themila Gan Lin smiled as the boy met her gaze. He was a strange child to be sure; an intriguing conundrum.

Through the past seven days he had muttered in his delirium about three topics; a Warp, brigands and someone
called Coran. Now though, his shoulder was mending and
the fever gone. Perhaps at last the mystery would be
unravelled.

"Well, now." She settled herself more comfortably on
the bed and took Tarod's hand. "I am Themila Gan Lin,
and I am here to look after you. We know your forename
is Tarod, but what of your clan name?"

A peculiar, hard look crept into the boy's eyes and he
said, "I have no clan."

"No clan? But surely your mother—"

His mother? She believed him dead, lost to the Warp,
and that was safer. Besides, she would be better off without him . . .

"I have no mother," he said.

There was more to this, Themila realized, than perhaps
anyone would ever know. Recalling the talk she had had
with Jehrek a few days previously, when they had discussed the bizarre circumstances of the boy's discovery,
she decided against pressing the point. She was about to
ask the child if he was hungry when a thin hand took her
arm with surprising strength.

"Is this the Castle?"

"The Castle of the Star Peninsula? Yes, indeed it is."

Some inner fire lit up the green eyes. "I saw a man—he
was an Initiate . . ."

Themila thought she was beginning to understand. And
if Jehrek's suspicions were right, it fitted the small picture
she had already begun to form of the boy.

Gently, she said, "This is the home of the Circle,
Tarod. Many of our number are Adepts—look." And with
her free hand she pointed to her own shoulder.

Tarod drew a sharp breath as he saw the now familiar
insignia on Themila Gan Lin's light, woven shawl. So it
hadn't been part of the delirium . . . He remembered the
hints and rumors he had gleaned about the Castle and what
went on here; sorcery and dark practices, secret knowledge
and power. In his homeland people feared the Castle, but
Tarod was not afraid. Impossible though it seemed, the

wild dream he had had of fleeing from his old life and finding the stronghold of the Initiates had come true. He wasn't dead, his soul doomed to ride the Warp forever— instead, the storm had brought him here, as if, somehow, it had been predestined. And this woman, herself an Initiate—he trusted her, knew that if he should reach out to her she would not spurn him as others had done. He was home.

Suddenly, tentatively, he let his hand slide down to touch her fingers. "Can I stay here?"

Themila squeezed his hand. "Child, you may stay as long as you please!" And she thought, suddenly disturbed: *oh, yes; you must stay . . . whether you wish it or no. . . .*

That evening, Tarod had another, unexpected visitor. Keridil Toln, son of the High Initiate, had used all his charm to persuade Themila to allow him to take food to the stranger, and she, aware that the boys could benefit from each other's friendship, agreed. Tarod was unused to having a companion of his own age without incurring disapproval, and was disconcerted at first by the other boy's arrival, but Keridil's open enthusiasm soon began to break down the first barriers.

"I've been waiting days for a chance to see you," Keridil told him, then added without a shred of tact, "Everyone in the Castle's talking about you."

Tarod felt unease constrict him. "Why?" he demanded.

Keridil took a slice of meat from Tarod's plate without asking and began to wolf it. "For one thing, it's rare for someone to enter our community from outside. But mainly it's because of what you did."

"You mean . . . the brigands?" Even now the memory was hazy, and Tarod was suddenly cautious. "What did they tell you?"

Keridil shook his head. "They didn't tell me anything. In spite of the fact that I'm *supposed* to be important, because I'm *supposed* to be groomed to succeed Father as High Initiate one day, I'm also *supposed* to be too young to understand a lot of things." He hesitated, then grinned. "But I understand a lot more than they think I do, and I have my own ways of finding out. You killed a brigand when Taunan and the Lady were attacked. But you didn't use a sword or a knife or anything. You killed him with sorcery!''

Sorcery? The word sent a shiver through Tarod. So that feeling, the force that had taken over his mind and body—that had been sorcery? But he knew nothing of magic . . .

"They say you didn't know what you were doing," Keridil went on, clearly impressed. "And that's why you're to stay here. Father has been making all kinds of enquiries about your clan, but—"

"*No*—" Tarod's sudden vehemence startled the fair-haired boy into a momentary silence. Then he said: "Why not?"

For a moment they stared at each other, then Tarod decided to risk telling Keridil the truth. Slowly, quietly, he replied, "Because I was . . . condemned. For killing someone else. Just the same way as—they said—I killed the brigand."

"Aeoris!" Keridil was adult enough to be shocked rather than impressed. "Who? I mean—was it an accident?"

No one in Wishet had once troubled to ask that question, Tarod thought with a sudden constriction in his throat. And he realized that, with Keridil, he was able to talk about Coran without the nightmare of fear and revulsion. As though, in crossing the invisible barrier between the Castle and the outside world, he had put the past behind him. . . .

Keridil listened gravely to the story, then whistled through his teeth.

"Gods! Little wonder the Circle want you!"

Suspicion again rose in Tarod. "Want me . . . ?"

"Yes!" Keridil stared at him, then realization dawned. "Hasn't anyone bothered to explain? You're to be trained as an Initiate."

Tarod felt as if the ground were falling away beneath him. "I am—?" He tried to express what he felt, but words were beyond him.

Keridil's eyes narrowed abruptly. "You don't understand, do you? Firstly, you've faced a Warp and you've survived. That's an incredible omen! And secondly—look, dont't you realize that there's probably not a single man or woman within these walls who could do what you did just by snapping their fingers?''

Tarod was nonplussed, and alarmed. ''But the Initiates—their power—''

''Oh, it exists, yes, and there are people who can wield it. I could tell you some of the things I've seen, and I'm only allowed to witness Lower Rites. But what you did—maybe the Old Ones could have drawn on power as easily as that, but they're all long dead and gone!''

''The Old Ones?'' Tarod felt a peculiar stirring in some dark, unreachable corner of his mind, but it was gone before he could grasp it.

Keridil made an expressively helpless gesture. ''We call them the Old Ones because we know of no better name. They were the race who lived here before us, who built this Castle. You must know your catechisms, about how Aeoris''—here Keridil made a quick, reflexive sign in front of his own face—''brought the gods to our world, to destroy the followers of Chaos?''

''Oh . . . yes.''

''Well, from the few writings the Old Ones left—those historians like Themila have been able to decipher, anyway—it would seem that, to them, our skills would be little better than the gurglings of a babe in arms!''

Tarod said nothing, but his private thoughts were moving rapidly down an unexpected path. So the Initiates of the Circle, these half-legendary folk of whom outsiders spoke in trepidation, had no claim to invincibility . . . he felt oddly disappointed. And yet . . . they said he had power. Greater power, possibly—unless Keridil exaggerated—than even their highest Adepts. It was a chilling concept, and suddenly he ached to know more.

But before he could form a question, Keridil saw something he had not noticed before, and pounced.

''What's that?'' He had grabbed Tarod's left hand and his fingers closed over a ring on the index finger. ''I've never seen a gem like it—is it yours?''

Tarod snatched his hand away and stared jealously at the

ring. It was a single, utterly clear stone, set in a heavy and
ornate silver base. Since they had taken away his ruined
clothes and furnished him with new ones, this was the sole
artifact that linked him with the past.

"Yes, it's mine." He offered no further comment.

"Wherever did you get it?"

"My—" and Tarod hesitated. He was about to say it
was a gift from his mother, but, in truth, it was something
beyond that. Granted she had given it to him, on his
seventh birthday, but he remembered her saying that it was
his legacy—his one legacy—from the father whose identity neither she nor he had ever known. Since then it had
never once left his finger and, strangely, as he grew the
ring itself seemed to grow also, so that it always fitted him
perfectly.

"If you ever want to swop it," Keridil said enviously,
"I have a sapphire that—"

"*No.*" The refusal was instant and ferocious, and the
fair boy blanched. "I'm sorry, I didn't mean . . ." his
voice trailed off.

Tarod didn't answer him. He was gazing out of the
window, green eyes narrowed as if behind the mask of his
face he was lost in thought. There was something unreal
about the courtyard with its playing fountain, something
dreamlike; and for a moment he caught himself wondering
if he might at any moment wake and find himself back in
Wishet, facing a death sentence. But he dismissed the
idea. However strange his surroundings, the tireless, talk-
ative Keridil was real enough. And despite his innate
mistrust of people, he felt an affinity with the other boy.

"No," he said, "I'm sorry, Keridil. I didn't mean to
take offense."

Keridil breathed out. "Then I'm glad, because I wouldn't
want to lose your friendship when I've only just found it. I
haven't had a friend of my own age before. All the other
boys seem to think I'm above them or something, because
of who my father is."

It hadn't occurred to Tarod that Keridil, brought up in
such a close community, might be lonely, and he was
oddly gratified—this made them two of a kind.

"But we will be friends, won't we?" Keridil went on. His fresh, open face was suddenly serious. "I'd like to think we will, because—well, I'm no seer, but I'll prophesy this: one day, I'm destined to be High Initiate of this community, unless I fail the test, which I believe I shan't do. But whatever my achievements, whatever my power, I believe that I shall never be your equal."

For a fleeting instant something in his voice seemed to transcend youth and immaturity, a pre-echo of an unimaginable future, a truth Tarod couldn't understand, yet which he felt acutely in the marrow of his bones. But before he could speak, the door of the chamber opened to reveal Themila.

"Keridil, did I not tell you you mustn't tire Tarod with your chatter?" she said sternly.

Keridil stood up. "I haven't tired him, Themila," he replied with dignity. "We were merely becoming acquainted."

Themila laughed. "Get along with you! It's a wonder the lad's brains aren't addled from your prating! You should be asleep, both of you! There'll be time enough for talking yourself hoarse tomorrow."

Keridil raised his eyebrows at Tarod, shrugged a wry apology and paused at the door to kiss Themila soundly on the cheek. When his loud footsteps had diminished away down the passage Themila crossed to where a torch flickered in an iron bracket on the wall.

"You're not afraid of the dark, Tarod?" Her tone was kindly.

Tarod shook his head. "Thank you. I like the night."

"Then I'll wish you good rest. Sleep is the best healer for you now." She took the torch, her shadow twisting and looming grotesquely as the angle of the light changed, then after a hesitation added, "Take heart, child. There's nothing for you to fear here."

She might have imagined it, Themila thought later, but there seemed something faintly disturbing about Tarod's answering smile in the gloom. For a moment the green eyes glowed like lamps.

"I am not afraid," said Tarod softly.

Chapter 4

"**A**nd so it was that Aeoris, greatest of the Seven Lords of the White Isle, gave a casket into the safe-keeping of those whom he had saved from the demons of Chaos. And Aeoris decreed that the casket should be a symbol of his protection, and that, should Chaos ever return to the world, the casket might be opened by one appointed as the gods' representative upon the land, to bring back the full might of the Lords of Order, once again to save their people."

As Jehrek Banamen Toln's well-modulated voice spoke the final words of the ancient, formalized myth, the crowd that thronged the Castle courtyard breathed out in a single, soft hush of sound. Stiff in their ceremonial robes, the patterns of gold and silver thread reflecting in the scarlet-tinged sunlight, the Council of Adepts moved slowly down the steps and through the aisle that was formed as the crowd parted to allow them passage. Jehrek led the procession, still an imposing figure despite the fact that he was beginning to stoop with age and his hands were a little arthritic; behind him the visiting dignitaries took pride of place—the Margrave of West High Land Province, several Seniors of the Sisterhood of Aeoris—and following them the Council members in order of rank, including Themila Gan Lin and beside her the tall, muscular figure of the High Initiate's only son and heir apparent to his position. At the far end of the aisle near the Castle gateway seven wooden statues had been positioned, twice life size, their painted faces staring impassively out over the gathering. Jehrek stopped before the first and largest, gazed up for a moment at the carved, ascetic features, then knelt, with difficulty, and touched his forehead to the statue's feet.

The dignitaries followed his example and the orderly crowd began to close in, waiting to take their turns behind the Council.

Near the back of the gathering—further back, in fact, than his rank would have allowed—one man watched the proceedings with an expression as enigmatic as those of the statues. Soon enough he too would have to make the ritual obeisance to the effigies, but he preferred to postpone the moment for as long as possible. Not that he felt less reverence for the Seven Gods than did any of his peers, far from it; but he couldn't help the small, rankling conviction that these formal occasions, the pomp, the endless ceremonial, served more to satisfy the conceits of the visitors than to further any deeper purpose. Besides, at this moment he badly needed time to think.

Any one-time acquaintance who hadn't seen Tarod during his ten years at the Castle of the Star Peninsula would almost certainly have failed to recognize him. Taller even than Keridil, who outstripped most men, his was a powerful, long-boned but almost gaunt frame. His face had long since lost its boyish traces to become a sculpture of high cheekbones and fine jawline with a narrow, aquiline nose, setting off the oddly feline green eyes; and his black hair—which, carelessly, he never took the trouble to clip— was by now an unchecked tangle. It was as if, remembering his old childhood belief that he was different, he had chosen to emphasize rather than mask the differences, and stand deliberately apart from the norm.

And the changes went far deeper than mere outward appearance. The half-terrified, half-defiant child who had been brought like some unfledged waif to the Castle more than a decade ago was nothing more than a pale ghost. The clan which had grudgingly succoured him for the first thirteen years of his life believed him long dead and gone—the High Initiate's enquiries into his past had produced no one ready to claim him—and so he had sloughed off his old identity and taken up a new life without a moment's regret. Now, there was knowledge and understanding far beyond his years in the green gaze; a confidence that the old existence in Wishet could never have imparted. He had progressed rapidly, learned much that was hidden from all but a chosen few; found friendships that transcended any claims of blood kin. Even those who disliked or envied him—and there were a small number—couldn't deny that he had more than fulfilled the promise which both Jehrek and Taunan had seen in him so long ago.

He sighed, seeing that his own section of the crowd was moving towards the statues. There were too many unwanted influences here to allow for coherent thought, and reluctantly he gave himself up to the demands of the ceremony. The stiff collar of his formal cloak—the green of a seventh-rank sorcerer—itched abominably; irritated, he cast it back, revealing the close-fitting black shirt and trousers that he tended to favor over any other color, and noticed a man near to him—a visitor—draw hastily away at the sight of the wicked-looking knife in its sheath at Tarod's right hip. He smiled thinly. Tales about the Initiates which circulated in the outside world still tended to be laced with speculation and rhetoric, and although he shouldn't have been amused by the man's obvious discomfort, the temptation was hard to resist.

The crowd shuffled forward; Tarod found himself before the statue of Aeoris. And in the moment that he dropped to one knee, a sharp sensation of déjà vu snatched at him.

The dream—it was something to do with the dream—

Sweat broke out on his forehead; people behind him were waiting . . . Hastily, and hoping no one had noticed the momentary loss of composure, Tarod bent his head briefly to the carved feet of Aeoris before rising and making his way quickly towards the main door.

Themila Gan Lin adjusted her Councillor's circlet and slid between two of the long tables to reach the bench where Tarod sat alone. The banquet was over, the speeches completed, and now the Circle and their guests were relaxing in the enormous dining hall while wine circulated freely. It was late, but outside the sun still hung sullenly on the horizon and all the hall's windows glowed with the gory light of a northern summer evening.

"So this is where you've been hiding yourself," Themila said in mock accusation as she sat gratefully down.

Tarod's smile was warm. "Not hiding, Themila. Simply—not joining in."

"Don't try and blind me with semantics." She held out her wine-cup for him to fill. "You have the distinction, I'd remind you, of being the worst philosophy student it has ever been my displeasure to try to teach!"

Tarod laughed immoderately, and Themila wondered how much wine he had drunk. It wasn't like him to be in his cups, and the departure puzzled her. Over the years he had become, in a sense, the son she had never borne, and she was correspondingly alert to his moods. This mood didn't fit any of the known patterns.

"Philosophy," Tarod said at last. "Yes . . . you're right. Perhaps I should have studied it more thoroughly after all. Or history."

Themila frowned. "Tarod, you're speaking in riddles. Either this is some game you're playing with me, or—"

"Oh, no." He interrupted her. "It's no game. And I'm not drunk, either, if that's what you're thinking."

As though to prove the point he refilled his cup, and she said, "Then the third possibility is that something's troubling you."

Tarod looked out across the hall, where the multiple colors of cloaks and skirts moved as the guests mixed. "Yes, Themila. Something is troubling me."

"Can you tell me about it?"

"No. Or at least . . ." Tarod seemed to debate silently with himself, one thin, restless hand tapping the side of his cup. Then, abruptly, he said, "Themila, are you a dream-interpreter?"

"You know full well I'm not. But if it's a dream that troubles you, I would have thought that for a seventh-rank sorcerer—"

He cut in with a contemptuous snort. "*That*—"

"Speaking as one who has never progressed beyond third rank, I'm a little less dismissive about the accolade," Themila said with some acerbity.

"I'm sorry; I didn't mean to give offense. But I think perhaps that's at the root of the whole problem."

"Your rank?" She was nonplussed.

"In a sense . . ." Suddenly he looked directly at her, and she was taken aback by the light in his green eyes. For an instant, he looked dangerous. "Themila—how closely do you believe in following the doctrines of the Circle?"

Themila tried to interpret the motive behind the question, and failed. Cautiously she said; "That's not an easy question, Tarod. If you mean, do I accept all I am told without comment, then my answer is no. But the wisdom inherent in our teachings has an impeccable source."

"Aeoris himself . . . yes." Tarod made the small gesture that by tradition always accompanied the utterance of the god's name. It was a habit ingrained into all Initiates, but she had the discomforting impression that, for him, it was no more than a casual reflex. "But can we be sure that we interpret that wisdom rightly? Sometimes I feel that the rituals, the rigmarole, the mass participations, are blinding us. The power of the Circle isn't in dispute. But it's a grossly limited power."

Themila began to see what he was leading up to, and her heart sank. She had been awaiting this development—dreading it—ever since the boy Tarod had first begun his studies under the Circle's tutelage. From the start it had been obvious that his innate talent for sorcery would soon leave his tutors far behind, and as he developed the Initiates' chief concern was with schooling him to control the powers that he could all too easily command. In this they had succeeded, although an independent, rebellious streak in Tarod had sometimes been a stumbling-block. But Themila, who knew him better than anyone save Keridil, believed that eventually Tarod would want more than the Circle could provide. He held seventh rank simply because no higher status existed, and he was at an impasse, for unless he chose to involve himself in the more exoteric duties of an Initiate—which, knowing Tarod, Themila realized he would not do—then the Circle had little more to offer him.

Choosing her words carefully she said, "You're thinking, then, about the potential power of the individual mind, without the protection of established ceremony?''

"Protection?" Tarod asked. "Or restriction?"

Despite the fact that she had been expecting something like this, Themila was shocked. "What you're suggesting goes entirely against all our teaching!" she protested. "It's nothing short of heresy!"

"According to our sages, yes. What the gods would have to say about it might be another matter."

This was going too far. Realizing that such a train of thought must be stopped before it got out of hand, Themila reached to take hold of Tarod's fingers as he was about to refill their wine-cups. He paused.

"Tarod, I think we would be wiser not to pursue this, not now. Earlier, you asked me if I could interpret dreams. If it's a seer you need, perhaps you should speak to Kael Amion."

Tarod looked surprised. "The Lady Kael? Is she here today? I didn't realize—"

"She is here, although she felt unable to take her place with the dignitaries. These days her stamina isn't what it was."

Kael Amion might provide the answer he so desperately needed, Tarod thought. He was too close to the dream, and needed the balance of an outside view.

Themila nodded across the hall. "If you want an omen," she said, "Kael is approaching us at this very moment."

Tarod looked up quickly and saw the frail, white-robed figure of the old seer moving slowly but surely towards the bench where they sat. He was, however, disappointed to realize that she was not alone. Walking deferentially beside her, one hand steadying her arm, was Keridil. And beyond Keridil and doggedly tagging him came a plump, pretty girl with shocking red hair, dressed in clothes that exhibited wealth rather than good taste.

"Inista Jair, from Chaun Province," Themila commented in an undertone to Tarod. "Her father is the man who has been monopolizing our High Initiate since the banquet ended, and I think he has a match in mind."

"With Keridil?" Tarod raised his dark eyebrows, amused. "I hardly see it as a likely pairing!"

"Nor I. But the son of the High Initiate is a valuable prize."

Tarod snorted with laughter, which he quickly disguised in a cough, rising as the trio joined them.

Tarod bowed over Kael Amion's hand, and the old Sister scanned his face shrewdly. She had seen little, lately, of the one-time waif she had succoured, and was surprised and not altogether pleased by the changes in him. Inista Jair was less tactful; she simply goggled as the black-haired sorcerer was introduced, overawed by the stare of the peculiar green eyes, and took a seat as far from his as she could. They all talked inconsequentially for a while, but Tarod was restless. He couldn't approach Kael with the others present, yet the need to speak to someone who might help him was weighing urgently on his mind, and finally he couldn't tolerate the prevarication any longer. He stood.

"Lady—Themila—forgive me, but I must leave you." He looked at Themila for a long moment, hoping she understood the silent appeal in his eyes. Before anyone could speak, he had bowed in turn to them all and was moving quickly away towards the double doors at the far end of the hall.

Inista Jair turned to Keridil. "He is your friend?" she queried, her confidence returning now that the source of discomfiture had gone. "I find that hard to believe! You are as unlike as—as—" Analogy failed her.

Keridil wished privately that his duty didn't extend to entertaining pretty but empty-headed eligible girls such as Inista. But since his election to junior membership of the Council his father had insisted that he should take more responsibility onto his shoulders. It was all part of the grooming for his eventual rise to High Initiate, but at times Keridil found the burden onerous. In a wryly good-natured way he envied Tarod's comparative freedom to do as he pleased. But at this moment—if the look on his friend's face had been any indication—he didn't envy Tarod his thoughts.

The girl was still staring at him, and he smiled with exquisite politeness. "I wouldn't be so sure, Inista," he said. "In many ways, Tarod and I are more similar than you might think."

The outer door of his rooms slammed echoingly behind Tarod as he strode through to his bedchamber. Another crash—the inner door this time—and he hurled his cloak aside before savagely pulling the velvet curtain across the window and throwing himself at full length on the bed.

He couldn't have stayed in the hall a moment longer. The pressure had been building up in his mind all day, without release, and finally his self-control had snapped. That in itself was a bad sign, for where self-discipline lapsed, will power was sure to follow. And if he didn't resolve the conundrum of the dream that had been haunting him for the past eleven nights, Tarod was beginning to wonder if he might not also lose his sanity. . . .

Every night it began in the same way. He opened his eyes to the darkness and silence of his room and for a moment thought himself awake, until a tell-tale edge of unreality told his mind that he was asleep, and dreaming. And there was a sound in the room—a muffled, half-heard humming that impinged on his consciousness and, unexpectedly, worried him. In the dream he slid from his bed and padded across to the window. A new sensation was rising within him; some forgotten feeling that dragged at the deepest levels of his mind and called, incessantly called.

Come . . . Come back . . . Remember . . .

It was as insidious as the rustle of grass in the wind that heralded a Warp. There were no words.

Come . . . Come . . .

No, he told his dreaming mind, there were no words!

Come back . . .

Tarod was a sorcerer with a will and control matched by no man in the Circle; but now, as the dream grew more nightmarish, he was frightened. And despite his efforts he couldn't wake himself, but instead pulled back the curtain and looked down into the courtyard, which was bathed in

the chilly light of the smaller of the two Moons. Its thin
crescent threw sharp contrasts of silver and shadow across
the empty square, yet Tarod couldn't see clearly; a faint
haze seemed to cloud his vision. And then, by the colonnaded walkway, something moved.

It was no more than a shadow, and it glided between the
sculptured pillars of the colonnades. Human or something
beyond, he couldn't tell, but he felt drawn to it as a moth
to a candle-flame. Involuntarily, the fingers of his right
hand touched his silver ring, and suddenly the voice was
back in his mind, whispering a sibilant, insidious lure.

Remember . . . Come back . . .

Back to what? Tarod's mind asked in silent desperation.

Back . . . Back . . .

And shockingly, he was awake in the darkness of his
room, and the voice had gone. . . .

Tarod closed his eyes, shutting out the memory of the
dream. After the third recurrence he had called on the
resources of his considerable will to banish it, but, to his
alarm, the efforts had failed. And throughout his waking
hours the dream was haunting him, for it rang disturbing
bells in the depths of his mind, raising questions that might
be better left unasked.

Why was it that he seemed to possess an innate talent
for sorcery that was unheard-of in the Circle's history? He
himself had known it since he began his studies here; now
it was acknowledged—albeit reluctantly—by even the highest Adepts. His command of Circle ritual was unsurpassed,
yet unlike his peers he had no true need of ritual; he could,
if he chose, kill with nothing more than a single thought.
Twice in his life he had killed in such a way—and that, as
perhaps he had always known, set him apart. Lately he
had begun to grow more and more impatient with the
Circle's accepted doctrines and practices—as tonight he
had tried to explain to Themila—and he was conscious of
a growing sense of disappointment that harked back to his
earliest days here. His belief that the Initiates were all-
powerful had soon crumbled as they proved instead to be
very fallible human beings. And now that he was privy to

the powers which the rest of the world held in awe, he found those powers lacking.

Yet however hard he strove to look into the deep recesses of his consciousness and his motivations, he was no nearer to answering the all-important question, why. It was as if something was calling to him, something which had always been a part of him yet which he couldn't comprehend, and the recurring dream was bringing it into focus.

Suddenly goaded by a wave of frustration, Tarod rose from his bed and paced across the room to where a pile of books, musty and yellowed, lay on a small table. In his efforts to find the elusive answers he needed he had spent a good deal of time in the Castle's extensive library, in a separate wing. Here were all the records of known history, some written so many centuries ago that the script was faded and all but illegible. The Castle was the world's sole repository for such knowledge, the Circle its sole guardians—and to a scholar from beyond the Castle's boundaries, the privilege of being granted access to these volumes for study was beyond price. Until recently Tarod had barely ever troubled to make use of the library himself, but now, fascinated in spite of his preoccupations, he had found accounts of the earliest days of the Circle's existence, when the world was newly emerged from the dark age of the Old Ones after Aeoris himself had vanquished the tyranny of Chaos and restored the Lords of Order to rule in its stead. So little was known about the ancients and their skills; many of the strange properties of this very Castle were still hidden territory to the Circle which had inhabited it now for so many generations, and Tarod would have given much to unravel some of those old mysteries.

But old mysteries provided no answers to the thoughts that troubled him now. And the one thing no book had been able to tell him was the nature of the force that was calling to him out of the depths of the night.

Tarod stared down at the books, and came to a decision. Tonight, he was sure, the dream would seek him out again . . . and he would be ready for it. Tonight he wouldn't sleep, but instead would keep watch on the astral plane. He needed little preparation beyond a quiet mind, and with an hour or more to go before the Castle's inhabitants began to retire for the night there was time enough.

He bolted the outer door to his rooms, then lit a brazier that stood near his bed. When the charcoal was glowing like a small, feral eye in the curtained gloom he sprinkled a few grains of a faintly narcotic incense on to its red heart, and lay down without bothering to undress. Whatever unknown denizen came to haunt him tonight, he would be ready.

The brief Summer darkness had finally fallen, and the first of the two Moons had risen to cast a sickly glow through the window when Tarod sensed that he wasn't alone in his room. For almost three hours he had lain motionless watching the faint glare of the brazier, but suddenly, although there was no sound and no movement, he felt an uninvited presence. His pulse quickened; like most Adepts he took basic precautions to ensure that no stray influences from other planes could invade his territory, and yet this— whatever it was—had breached the defenses with disturbing ease.

And then the murmuring began.

Come back . . . Back . . .

It seemed to emanate from some dark corridor of his own mind, and he sent a silent message in reply.

Back? Back to what?

Remember . . . Back . . .

Tarod concentrated his will, and shifted his consciousness onto the astral. His surroundings appeared as before, but now all the contours of the room glimmered with a faint, unstable aura. That alarmed him, for it suggested a similar instability in his own control. Each of the seven known astral planes—of which only five, according to Circle doctrine, were accessible to any mortal—had its own distinctive characteristics; this fluctuation told Tarod that he was not established on any one, but hovering in an unnerving limbo.

Trying to rally his concentration he looked down at his own body on the bed. The disturbing call was throbbing in his consciousness now, as if by throwing off the shackles of the physical plane he had made himself more vulnerable to the source of the message. Tarod had never been averse to playing with fire and had always come through unscathed—but on all such previous occasions he had been in sole control. Now the position had twisted a little; other powers were pulling him and it seemed his will wasn't strong enough to counteract them. Nor—yet—could he even begin to speculate as to what they might want of him . . .

For a time—it might have been minutes or hours, he had no way of knowing—Tarod kept watch. Then, at last, a knocking sounded at the door.

His instant reaction was that the knocking had emanated from the physical plane; that someone had unwittingly come to disturb him. Angry, he tried to return to his physical body—but something held him back. It dragged him away from his goal, pulled his mind into a black vortex that closed round him. The room disintegrated into chaos then just as swiftly righted itself again. But now its aura had stabilized, pulsing with light and power.

He was on a far higher plane; perhaps the fourth or even the fifth. *But he hadn't willed it to happen . . .*

Without warning the knocking at the door sounded again, and at once Tarod knew that his first assumption had been wrong. The outer door to his rooms was bolted, and yet the visitor—whoever or whatever it was—was at the inner door, immediately before him.

Aware that the atmosphere was too silent, too cold, Tarod moved to the side of the room, as far from the door as was possible, before allowing his mind to form a single, stern word.

Open . . .

Almost before the command took shape the door smashed back on its hinges, and framed in the gaping doorway Tarod saw his own double!

He recoiled in shock. The face was unmistakable, and the hair—but this motionless image was swathed in a black shroud. And even now he couldn't trust his first impressions, for the figure was altering.

The so-familiar face remained, but the hair became gold

and the eyes were constantly changing color . . . and he could no longer see the apparition's body, for it was suddenly wreathed in light that shifted through the range of the spectrum like an approaching Warp.

Who are you? Tarod tried to keep an edge of fear from coloring the silent question. For answer the vision smiled, and it was a smile of exquisite pride and disdain. Tarod felt himself drawn helplessly towards the being, and as their minds approached an overwhelming sensation of power struck him and swamped him. Here was the knowledge he had been craving—

And he shuddered violently as an invisible barrier sprang up between himself and the brilliant vision. Stubbornly, desperately he attacked it, but his efforts were useless; and the moment came when he realized the being had gone, leaving the room lifeless and empty.

The intangible forces no longer held him. Conscious of a sense of failure, Tarod returned to his body and opened his eyes. He was shivering convulsively, and so cold that his limbs were numb. Unsteadily he rose and stumbled to the hearth, where a fire had been laid but not lit. But his hands shook and the tinder refused to catch properly; after five minutes he gave up the attempt and returned to his bed, leaving the fire sullenly smoldering.

Despite the fur pelts that covered him Tarod was still shivering. Part of his mind wanted to think about the implications of his bizarre experience; but another, stronger part reacted violently against the idea. What he really needed now, he told himself as he closed his eyes, was sleep—and sleep without dreams.

Sleep came to Tarod that night, but it was racked with nightmares that clamored at him out of the darkness. There were shrill, strident voices, gargoyle faces that leered and gibbered wherever he looked, and, presiding over all, the golden-haired apparition with its knowing and disdainful smile. Tarod twisted and turned in his sleep, striving to escape the sights of his inner eye, but the images only became wilder and madder. Now and then the smiling specter would take on his own aspect, so that the color-flooded eyes flashed green and the hair became black, tangling with the grinning, elemental faces below.

Tarod was awakened at last by the sound of his own voice screaming wordlessly, and sat up to find a cold dawn filtering through the curtain. The brazier had burnt out and traces of stale smoke from the incense still hung in the room, smelling sour and acrid now. The sense of failure weighed heavily on him and it took some effort of will to rise and cross to the window to look out at the day.

The courtyard below was quiet. Only a few servants moved efficiently about their early morning duties, and every sound they made seemed magnified against the still background. Mist obscured the upper reaches of the four spires, and faintly in the distance he could hear the sea. The peaceful scene did nothing to soothe him; rather it emphasized his own unrest.

As he watched, someone emerged from a minor doorway and began to cross the courtyard in the direction of the dining hall. Doll-like from this distance, Themila Gan Lin walked slowly as though lost in thought; beside her, the woman in the white robes of a Sister of Aeoris was speaking, gesturing gracefully with one hand.

Lady Kael Amion . . . and suddenly Tarod recalled the conversation he had had with Themila last night. She had recommended him to Kael, and though he felt that his experiences might now have gone beyond the province of a dream-interpreter, he surely had nothing to lose by seeking the old Sister's counsel? His spirits lifting a little, Tarod turned from the window, hurriedly smoothed down the crumpled clothes he'd slept in, and left his rooms to intercept the two women.

A fire had been lit in the dining hall to combat the cold which pervaded even midsummer mornings in this Northern latitude, and Themila and Kael were warming their hands before the blaze when Tarod found them.

Themila looked up at the sound of his footsteps. "Tarod— you're an early riser today."

He smiled. "Not the earliest, it seems. Lady Kael— good morning to you."

The old seer acknowledged his bow with a small, grave nod, and Themila said, "It *is* a good morning—but not for you, I suspect, Tarod. You look worn; as though you have had no rest."

He was surprised and a little chagrined by her bluntness in Kael Amion's presence, but Themila, forestalling him, added, "I took the liberty of speaking to Kael about our discussion." She smiled obliquely at the seer. "I hope you'll both forgive my presumption."

Tarod looked quickly from one to the other. "On the contrary; I'm grateful to you! That is—if the Lady would consent . . . ?"

He thought that the gaze Kael Amion returned had an odd slant to it, but she spoke equally enough. "Certainly, Tarod. If you're troubled, and I can aid you, then that's the task for which I was trained."

Again, did he detect a note of reluctance? Themila seemed unaware of it, for she said, "I've apprised Lady Kael of all that you told me, Tarod; although it may not be enough for her to draw a full interpretation. If—"

"There's more," Tarod said.

"More? Oh . . . then last night—"

"Last night, yes." He stared at the stone of his ring, which was winking malevolently in the firelight.

Themila pursed her lips, and gathered her skirts about her. "Then I'll waste no more time, but leave you to discuss this matter between you," she said firmly. "No—" as Tarod was about to invite her to stay, "It's not my province, and I wouldn't presume to interfere. Kael—when you've done, perhaps you'll give me the pleasure of breakfasting with me?" And before they could argue she was walking briskly towards the hall doors.

Kael Amion lowered herself stiffly onto one of the benches that flanked the long table. Her faded but candid eyes regarded Tarod for a long moment before she said, "Well, now. If there's more to this than Themila has already told me, I believe I should know it, if I'm to help you."

Tarod sat on the edge of the table, one finger idly tracing an old groove in the wood. It wasn't easy to speak, to catalogue aloud the monstrous nightmares, the visitation, the sense of helpless horror he had felt at the encounter, be it dream or reality, with his own ghastly mirror image. But once the halting flow of words had begun, the floodgates opened of their own accord, and he found himself telling Kael of his experiences, his fears, as easily as if she had been Themila. The seer listened without reaction or comment, and when Tarod finally finished his story there was a long silence. The old woman seemed to be lost in thought, and at last Tarod's anxiety got the better of him.

"Lady . . . can you help me?"

She looked up as though she had forgotten his presence, and her pale blue eyes were narrow in the lined face.

"I . . . don't know."

The distance in her voice disquieted him, but he pushed the feeling away. Before he could speak, she folded her hands in front of her and, gazing at them, continued, "What you have told me is . . . not within my normal province, Tarod. I make no claims to omniscience, and I'll admit that such—experiences—as yours are rare, if not unprecedented. Which is, perhaps, as well." A faint smile caught at her mouth, but it was obviously an effort. "I need a little time—time to meditate on what you've told me, and to consult some of the older records." Now she looked up again. "You've been patient thus far—I merely ask that you be patient a little longer."

Frustration roiled in him, but there was no help for it; her request was reasonable enough, and at least she had given him hope. He rose.

"Lady Kael, I thank you. I'll do as you ask. And I'll pray to Aeoris that your meditations bear fruit."

Kael made the White God's sign before her breast—hastily, it seemed.

"Yes," she said. "Pray to Aeoris . . ."

She waited until Tarod's tall figure had vanished through the hall doors, then, taking a grip on the table edge, pulled herself with difficulty to her feet. Her hands weren't steady, and it took a great effort of will to stop her legs from shaking too. Her heart was racing, making breathing difficult, and she fervently hoped that her disquiet had not communicated itself to the young Initiate. For what she had seen as he told his story had spoken to her as loudly as a physical voice. *Evil.*

Unbidden, memory took her suddenly back to the night, years ago, when she and her escort had found the child Tarod in the mountain pass. He had saved their lives then—but he had also demonstrated unconscious control of a power that appalled her. She had feared such power might grow without the discipline of Initiation to contain it; and now it seemed that her fears had been well founded. The force that called to Tarod through his dreams was no sending of the white gods.

Slowly, Lady Kael began to make her way towards the doors. She would see Themila later, and apologize for missing their breakfast appointment; at present, her stomach rebelled at the idea of food.

On the threshold of the hall she paused and looked back. Then, suppressing a shiver, she moved stiffly away in the direction of the Castle's guest rooms.

The day was well advanced when Tarod sought out Themila. Again, he found her in the dining hall; but at this hour the room was a hive of activity. Servants were making preparations for the evening meal, and a few hungry early-comers had already taken seats at the long tables and were passing the time over a flagon of wine.

Themila started when Tarod's voice interrupted her reverie. She had been sitting by the fire, seemingly idly watching the flames, but when she turned her eyes were deeply troubled.

"I'm sorry," Tarod said, "I'd no intention of startling you. But I thought you might know of Lady Kael's whereabouts."

"Oh, Gods . . ." Themila stared into the fire again. "I was afraid of this . . ."

He frowned, apprehensive. "What do you mean?"

Themila half rose, then thought better of it and subsided again. "Tarod . . . Kael has gone. She left this morning."

"Gone?"

Themila nodded. "I tried to persuade her, but—she wouldn't stay. She gave me a message for you, Tarod, but I—I've been putting off the moment when I must tell you."

"Then in the name of the gods, Themila, tell me now!" He spoke more sharply than he had intended, but disquiet was rapidly giving way to fully-fledged alarm.

She glanced at him, then away again. "I've never seen her react in such a way before. She said to tell you that— that she can't help you. That there is nothing she can do."

Tarod swallowed. "You're telling me that she *refused*?"

". . . Yes."

The familiar, companionable bustle of the dining hall suddenly seemed a world away. For a seer to refuse counsel to anyone in need was unheard-of . . . and a seer of Kael Amion's reputation . . . he felt numbed by her rejection, and found his voice only with an effort.

"What—reason did she have for refusing?"

"She would give none. But—" Themila blinked suddenly, and there was a darkness behind her eyes. "I think she was very much afraid . . ."

Chapter 5

Five days after the Quarter-Day celebration, Tarod was seriously beginning to wonder if he was still entirely sane.

The dreams had recurred, as he had known they would; each night was worse than the last, and though he had brought all the resources of his formidable will to bear in an effort to control them, nothing made the smallest difference. Finally, realizing that the power of his own mind couldn't keep the nightmares at bay, he had resorted in desperation to the orthodox practices of the Circle. Perhaps he lacked faith in the elaborate exorcism he performed, perhaps not; either way, the effort was a failure and the smiling face of his supernatural tormentor had presided over the wild, skirling denizens of nightmare all through the dark hours.

On the sixth day, halfway through the morning, he staggered from his bed hollow-eyed and exhausted, and as he dressed—trying to ignore the fact that his hands were unsteady—he inadvertently glimpsed his own reflection in a mirror.

He barely recognized himself. His green eyes had lost their luster and were glazed with a half-crazed stare, his hair was ragged and unkempt, and he seemed to have aged ten years.

"Oh, *Gods!*" Tarod swung away from the mirror and smashed a fist down on the table, oblivious to the pain that drummed through his arm. The strain on his mind was nearing the point where it must snap, and he was no closer to a solution than he had ever been. Why the dreams and the entity who seemed to direct them had come to him, what they wanted of him, he couldn't even begin to guess, but unless he could either find the answers to those questions or gain some respite from the torment of his nightmares, he knew that he could lose his reason.

As he had done on three previous mornings he reached for a flagon that stood on the table by his bed. Wine was no shield against the dreams, but it helped him to see the days through, and he poured a generous cup for himself, splashing a good deal on the floor as he did so. He was about to raise the cup to his lips when someone hammered on his outer door. For an instant Tarod's mind flashed back to his astral experience of a few nights ago—but then a familiar voice called out from the corridor.

"Tarod? It's Keridil—are you there?"

Tarod reluctantly set the cup down. His recent mood had driven him to shun company unless absolutely necessary, but he knew he had to face the world sometime if he was to avoid drawing attention to himself and his state of mind. Slowly he moved to the door and drew back the bolt.

"Tarod?" Keridil stepped into the room and scanned his friend's face uneasily. "I've been looking for you this past hour; I didn't expect to find you here at this time of day."

Tarod made a gesture that was half dismissal and half apology. "I'm sorry, Keridil. I've been . . . preoccupied."

"And not a healthy preoccupation, by the looks of it. Tarod, what in the name of Aeoris is wrong with you?"

Tarod would have turned away, but Keridil gripped his arm. "Don't evade the question! For days now you've barely shown your face, and when you have you've been morose and troubled. If there's anything—"

Tarod cut him off. "There's nothing anyone can do, Keridil. I appreciate your concern, but this is a matter that involves me and no one else!"

"I'll dispute that! And I speak out of more than friendship." Briefly, anger flashed in Keridil's tawny eyes; whatever the cause, he didn't take kindly to Tarod's cavalier dismissal of his offer of help. "Like my father, I have a duty to your well-being as an Initiate aside of any other considerations. Constantly absenting yourself from Circle matters does no good to yourself or anyone else!"

Tarod disengaged his arm with a savage movement. "Involving myself would be of little benefit to anyone at the moment, believe me!"

Keridil bit back an angry retort as he realized that, contrary to his first impression, this was no simple transitory mood. Tarod was unpredictable at the best of times, but this. . . . He recalled a conversation with Themila, in which she had told him that his friend had been troubled by dreams. *Dreams*? It surely took more than a nightmare to bring about such a change.

Tarod was standing by the window, staring out over the courtyard, and Keridil decided that discretion would stand him in better stead now than any attempt to probe further. He said:

"Whatever you may feel about your value to the Circle at present, Tarod, the fact is that you're needed now." He too moved to the window. "Haven't you felt the change?"

"Change?" Tarod had only half concentrated on the question.

Keridil shivered. "The tension in the air. It's been building all morning. No one thought anything of it, until the sentinel in the north spire reported that the Spectre Lights have begun playing.''

He was relieved when his last words finally caught Tarod's full attention. "The Spectre Lights? And they're visible at this time of day?"

"Clearly. I climbed the spire to see for myself." Keridil grimaced at the memory of the exertion demanded by those seemingly endless spiral stairs. "It can only mean one thing—there's a Warp coming, and it's a big one; perhaps the biggest we've seen in years. That's why I've been trying to find you. Father has ordered every Adept of fifth rank or above to gather at the Marble Hall. We're to perform a Higher Rite, and try to pick up on the Warp and learn something of its nature." Keridil grinned suddenly. "I'd have thought you of all people would be eager to take part—or doesn't your memory go back that far?"

An old recollection of his last day in Wishet Province . . . that hadn't happened to Tarod, but to a nameless, clanless child who didn't understand his own latent power. That child was dead—long dead.

Briefly but warmly, Tarod smiled. "Keridil, you're no diplomat, but you've succeeded in reminding me that I have obligations. Go on ahead—I'll join you as quickly as I can."

Crossing the deserted courtyard five minutes later, Tarod silently chastised himself for having failed to notice the change in the atmosphere. As Keridil had said, a tension was building up; the very flagstones beneath his feet seemed charged with it and the air felt cloying and unnaturally still. Glancing at the sky he saw the first tell-tale signs; the Summer blueness was soured by a faint tinge of a shade that defied description and the first faint play of light was beginning in the distance. He was half tempted to climb the colossal spire and see for himself the Spectre Lights, the strange aurorae that shimmered sometimes on the Northern horizon and which were normally only visible in the dead of night; but the urgency of Keridil's summons drew him. And if, just for a while, the work ahead enabled him to forget his own preoccupations, it would be a much needed relief.

The oppressive atmosphere was intensifying rapidly, and as Tarod reached the colonnades he paused, looking back across the courtyard. Almost every window had been shuttered; there was no sign of life anywhere and only the fountain, still playing, gave any movement to the scene. Even as he watched the quality of the light was changing; suddenly the cascading water lost its sparkling brilliance and became colorless and dead, and an eerie shadow without a source seemed to fall on the courtyard. Listening carefully, Tarod could just make out the first, faint singing of the approaching storm, an echo almost beyond the threshold of human awareness. He shivered with what might have been a sense of premonition—or memory—then turned and began to move quickly along the pillared walk.

Even in the maze of passages that wound down into the Castle's foundations, the inexorable approach of the Warp could still be felt. The slight twist of time and space that held the Castle aloof from the outside world also served as a barrier against the ravages of these storms—although, as with so many of the Castle's properties, no one knew quite how or why—but the presence of a Warp nonetheless had a disturbing effect on the inhabitants. Old fears and superstitions died hard even among the Circle, and all those not answerable to the High Initiate's summons had shuttered their windows and bolted their doors until the fury was past.

Tarod's own attitude to the Warps was an odd blend of unease and fascination. His fear of the storms had ended on the day he had faced one and survived, yet their sheer titanic power still inspired him with awe. He would have given a great deal to know more about the nature of these deadly phenomena, but felt instinctively that the Circle's attempts to penetrate the veil of the mystery were doomed to failure. This was the third time in little more than a year that Jehrek had summoned the higher Adepts with the intention of trying to tap into the power behind the Warps. So far their efforts had yielded nothing, and Tarod was privately convinced that this occasion would be no different.

If the legacy left behind by the Old Ones had been anything more than legend and fragment, then the Circle might well have understood the true nature of these supernatural storms and possibly even have learned how to harness their power. But in the days after the final fall of the ancient race virtually all that unimaginable knowledge had been lost, as the Castle's new masters systematically erased every possible trace of their vanquished enemies.

According to what meager historical records did remain, the Old Ones had been servants of the powers of Chaos—and thus they stood for everything that was anathema to the worshippers of Aeoris. It was impossible to imagine what this world must have been like in the days when the dark gods of Chaos held sway; an unholy miasma of wildness, madness, dementia; a reign of terror that was only brought to an end by the direct intervention of the Lords of Order themselves.

But whatever the extent of their evil, no one could deny that the Old Ones' command of sorcery had been phenomenal—the Castle itself, created by Chaos's servants with Chaos's power, stood testimony to that. Beside them the Initiates of the Circle were pale shadows, striving but failing to understand matters which, to the ancient race, had been simple. In destroying the legacy the Circle had destroyed so much that could, if cleansed of its taint, have been invaluable, and again Tarod felt frustration welling up within him. *So much knowledge lost, that could never be regained. . . .*

The passage ended abruptly at a heavy door, breaking his chain of thought. By this time he could feel the intensity of the approaching Warp as an almost physical sensation; the very walls seemed to pulse with a strange energy and he sensed that the storm would indeed be abnormally powerful. *This time, if they could only break the barrier . . .*

The door opened on to a dimly lit, pillared vault, deep underground beneath the main hall, where the Castle's library was housed. There were two sections to the library; one the province of the scholars and historians, the other closed to all but Initiates and holding the sum total of the

Circle's occult knowledge, gleaned over countless generations since the destruction of the Castle's original masters.
Tarod had spent more hours than he cared to recollect
searching among the books and scrolls for some answer to
his personal dilemma; now though, he didn't pause but
crossed the deserted, shadowy room to where a small and
insignificant-looking door at the far side stood open. Beyond
it yet another passage sloped steeply downwards and Tarod
made his way quickly along it. A faint, nacreous light
filtered from the far end, growing stronger until another
door came into view—and the door itself was the source of
the light. It was made of some silver-colored metal that the
Circle could neither identify nor analyze, and it shone with
its own peculiar phosphorescence. This was the entrance to
the Marble Hall, at the very core of the Castle's foundations.

The Marble Hall was the Castle's greatest conundrum.
Scholars believed that it contained within its walls the
ultimate secret of the Old Ones' power, but, as with so
many aspects of the Castle, they had been unable to fathom
the mystery. Buried in the solid granite of the cliffs, it
defied all known spatial laws, and seemed to act as a focus
and magnifier for any occult activity—and fragmented
records hinted that it also held a vital clue to the nature of
time itself. Only one door to the Marble Hall existed, and
the key was kept in the close possession of the High
Initiate, who alone could authorize its use. Tarod had
entered the Hall four times in his life—twice with his
fellow Adepts on a mission such as this, twice with Jehrek
and the higher Council members to face his initiation trial
for the sixth and seventh ranks—and each time he had
been filled with a fascination that bordered on the obsessive. Now, as he eased the silver door open, the anticipation of seeing that awesome chamber again made every
nerve in his body tingle.

The higher Adepts were there, waiting for him—some
twenty men and women utterly dwarfed by their incredible
surroundings. The Marble Hall stretched impossibly away
in every direction, its walls—if it truly had walls—obscured
by a pale haze that pulsed with light in a disturbing blend
of pastel colors. Here and there slender pillars reared up

from the floor to vanish in the mist overhead, and the mosaic tiles on which Tarod walked seemed to shift and change subtly beneath his feet.

Keridil, at one side of the group, acknowledged Tarod's arrival with a grin, and the High Initiate nodded gravely in his direction. "Tarod—I think our numbers are now complete. If you will all follow me . . ."

He moved across the floor to a place where the pattern of the mosaic had been abruptly broken by a large circle of dense black. This, it was surmised, marked the Marble Hall's exact center, and therefore, as far as the Circle could judge, the heart of its power. As the Initiates took their prescribed places around it, with Jehrek at the Southernmost station, Tarod's eyes were drawn—as they had been before—to another part of the Hall, all but lost in the faintly shifting haze. He could just make out the dim shapes of seven colossal statues, looming nightmarishly out of the gloom. Though crudely carved, they clearly represented human forms . . . but the face of each one had been thoroughly and determinedly hacked away, leaving the heads jagged and mutilated. And, as before, he felt an irrational shudder as he looked at those ruined figures. They were, so legend had it, statues of Aeoris and his six brothers—once even the Old Ones had been followers of the Lords of Order and had erected these colossi in their honor; but after they turned to the ways of Chaos they had defaced the figures in deference to their new masters.

But if the statues were no more than that, Tarod wondered, why did they draw his mind in a way no other representations of the gods had ever done . . . ?

He was brought abruptly out of his reverie by a fellow Adept some way distant from him, who spoke in a carrying whisper to his neighbor:

"*. . . more important matters on his mind, no doubt, than mere Circle business . . .*"

Tarod looked up and met the hostile stare of Rhiman Han, a fifth-rank Adept some ten years his senior. As his own prowess in sorcery had become more and more noticeable, Tarod had realized that his skills provoked one of two reactions among his peers. Some admired his talents and gave credit where it was due; others envied them, and resented the fact that so young a man had reached the ultimate rank with such consummate ease. Rhiman had earned more honors with his sword in Festival-Day tournaments than he was ever likely to earn as an Adept, and though he occupied a minor seat on the Council he nonetheless missed no opportunity to broadcast the fact that he thought Tarod an upstart.

Tarod raked the red-haired man with one of his most contemptuous glances. "I'm indebted to you for reminding me of my duty, Rhiman," he said coolly, without bothering to lower his voice. "Perhaps if you'd care to focus your own mind on higher matters we need delay the High Initiate no longer?"

Rhiman flushed angrily, and Jehrek gave both men in turn a sharp look. From the corner of his eye Tarod saw Keridil hide a smile, then the High Initiate said with faint acerbity, "If we may begin . . . ?"

The Adepts as one bowed their heads and Jehrek started to intone the Prayer and Exhortation that opened every Higher Rite. Tarod did his best to concentrate as the too-familiar words flowed past him to be lost in the Hall's immensity, but it was difficult. Something kept tugging at his mind, calling him away from what should have been a sharp focus on the ceremony; and he had to admit to himself that he was bored. So much gravity and ritual; so much unnecessary preparation before anything could be done. . . . Aware that he should be attuning his senses to join with the others, he concentrated on the black circle around which they were gathered, trying to use it as a focal point. But still some nagging, insidious distraction was pulling him away from what should have been his goal. Jehrek's voice was hypnotic now, as the High Initiate moved towards the semi-trance state that signalled the moment for the ritual proper to begin. All around him his peers murmured the responses to the Exhortation, but though his lips moved in unison with theirs no sound came from Tarod's throat. Suddenly he caught sight of his ring, and the stone seemed to have taken on a ferocious life of its own, reflecting impossible colors back at him like a dazzling, unhuman eye. He could feel power beginning to emanate from the circle of Adepts as minds linked and locked, but his own mind was strangely apart, an observer . . . and the black circle on the floor seemed to be growing, spreading out, a dark flower . . .

Come back . . .

The words entered his head so unexpectedly that he had to bite his tongue to stop himself from gasping aloud in shock.

Come back . . . Remember . . . Time . . .

Time . . . the Marble Hall held the key to Time, it was said . . . Tarod shut his eyes, trying to blot out the unwanted interference that crept into his mind and concentrate on the task at hand—but it was impossible. *Time.* The clue, the key . . .

His immediate neighbor felt the shudder that passed through him and gave him a swift, anxious look. Tarod's face was frozen in a rigid mask as he fought the influence in his head, but it was growing stronger, overwhelming him. For an instant he had the terrible feeling that the seven defaced statues were converging on him, that the walls and roof of the Hall were caving in—he snapped his eyes open in an effort to clear the disorientation, and saw the black circle on the floor. But it wasn't a simple mosaic pattern any more; it was a vortex, a shaft that had opened up in the floor, plunging away into infinity and trying to drag him with it. The singing of the Warp, far overhead, seemed to be in his brain and carrying him on its screaming, howling way; he swayed, his balance was going—

It was something to do with the Warp, something to do with this Hall—the dream, the entity—

"Tarod!" Dimly he heard a voice calling urgently to him. He thought it was Keridil, but the inflection was twisted somehow. "Father, stop! We must stop! He's—"

Tarod didn't hear what Keridil might have said. At that moment a wall of darkness rushed out of nowhere towards him and hit him full on. As it struck, he had a momentary image of a star that flared into seven points of blinding light before he keeled unconscious to the floor.

* * *

"You're picking at your food." Themila Gan Lin spoke as she might have done to a recalcitrant child. "Eat, now. You heard what Grevard said."

Tarod glanced up at her and smiled wryly. " 'Lack of vitality in the blood, caused by neglect of the sustenance needed to maintain good health, both mental and physical. And too much overindulgence in wine.' " His mimicry of the physician's acid tones made her smile. "Yes, Themila, I heard what Grevard said."

She refused to be intimidated. "Then eat. Or I'll force the food down you myself, and don't believe I wouldn't!"

He turned his attention to the well-stocked plate she had set before him. He didn't want food, but would make himself eat it to please her. And doubtless Grevard had a point; he had neglected his own needs these past few days, and by all logical standards the diagnosis could well explain the incident in the Marble Hall.

But Tarod was none too sure that logic could be applied here. And when he looked across the table at Keridil, he knew that his friend was thinking along much the same lines.

"Keridil?" Tarod spoke softly, but something in his voice alerted the other man. He decided to be blunt. "From the look on your face, I'd say you no more agree with Grevard's diagnosis than I do."

Keridil stared at him. "No. I don't. But you've got the advantage of me, Tarod—I'm not privy to your innermost thoughts . . . or your recent experiences."

Themila looked from one to the other. "If you're suggesting, Keridil, that Tarod is—"

Keridil raised a hand, silencing her before she could say any more. "Themila, I appreciate your mothering instincts— I've been on the receiving end of them myself, often enough!—but you know as well as I do that there's more to this than Grevard's simple explanation! And with all due respect, you weren't in the Marble Hall today—you didn't see his face . . ."

Tarod wished that they were anywhere but the over-crowded dining hall. There was too much noise, chatter and laughter, too many interruptions. He had spent the past hour suffering Grevard's examination and the lecture which followed, and had only submitted to the physician's orders because to argue would have put him in even worse straits with the High Initiate. Jehrek, anxious both for the well-being of his Adepts and for the success of any Circle rite, had been furious to learn of Tarod's self-neglect— Keridil had recounted that after he was carried hastily out of the Hall the remaining Adepts had attempted to continue the Higher Rite, but the impetus was gone and they achieved nothing. Now though, Tarod felt that he had done his duty, and he wanted to escape.

But between them, Keridil and Themila wouldn't let him escape. Themila already knew about the dreams, if not in detail; Keridil's suspicions were sufficiently aroused to make him probe further. And it wouldn't be long before they put two and two together.

He hadn't wanted to confide in anyone. Since Lady Kael Amion's shocking rejection of his plea for help he had deliberately held his tongue, too unsure of himself to risk a second rebuff. But Keridil and Themila were his closest, dearest friends. If he couldn't trust them, he could trust no one. And perhaps, after all, it would help to ease his mind . . . ?

They were waiting for him to speak. He said, quietly, "You're right, Keridil. There is something . . . but this isn't the place to recount it. Come with me to my rooms, and I'll tell you as much as I can."

Tarod was surprised at the relief he felt when, finally, he finished telling his story. His two companions had listened without interruption as he recounted the dreams that plagued him each night, and described the disastrous attempt he had made to keep watch on the astral plane. When at last he stopped speaking, Themila nodded slowly.

"I see now why you were so anxious to secure Kael Amion's services," she said gravely.

"Lady Kael?" Keridil looked at Themila in surprise. "Was she involved?"

"She was not. She—" Themila glanced at Tarod for permission, and he acquiesced with a slight gesture. "She . . . declined to give her advice."

"Gods! That's all but unheard of!"

"Yes, Keridil, it is." Themila's expression told him that he was being tactless. "Nonetheless, it's a right any seer may reserve if they choose . . . and Kael chose to reserve it. What concerns us is Tarod's own view of the matter."

Tarod shrugged helplessly. "I have no view—or none that's formed enough to be worth airing. But I'd greatly value yours—both of you."

Even if Keridil didn't catch the faint, desperate inflection in his voice, it wasn't lost on Themila and her eyes filled with sympathy. "Tarod, I have no clear answers. This is something that's beyond my province; I'm a historian, not a seer. But I would like to ask you one question . . ."

"Ask it." Tarod was perplexed by her hesitation.

"Very well. It's simply this: since you first came to the Castle, all those years ago, and began your training with us . . . has the Circle been a disappointment to you?"

She saw the answer mirrored in Tarod's green eyes before he could hide it and, without giving him the chance to invent a careful denial, pressed on.

"I came to know you better than you think, during your early days here. I saw a child who longed to be a part of something that he thought great and splendid and arcane. And I have seen you grow into a man who still has that longing, yet who has found his heroes to be nothing more than fellow men, as uncertain as he himself is uncertain. Do I do you an injustice, my son?"

Keridil's indrawn breath was a strangled protest against such brutal frankness, but Tarod's eyes smoldered.

"No, Themila. You are very perceptive."

"Then answer my question truthfully."

Keridil couldn't stand by any longer. "Themila, this has nothing to do with the matter at hand!" he argued. "The dreams, the incident today—"

Themila interrupted him severely. "Yes, Keridil, the dreams. It's my belief—and I think Tarod agrees with me—that the dreams are trying to tell us all something that we should have acknowledged long ago. Answer me this— how many Initiates ever achieve seventh rank? How many achieve it within ten years of beginning their training in the Circle? How many have the skill to rise to even greater status, if such status existed?''

Keridil stared at her, then at Tarod as though seeing him clearly for the first time. Slowly, he ran his tongue over lips that were suddenly dry. ''Yes . . . yes, I begin to understand you.''

''I don't claim to know what lies behind Tarod's . . . shall we say . . . unusual talent,'' Themila went on, reckless now that her first premise had been accepted. ''But one thing is certain—he will know no peace of mind until he has explored it to wherever it wishes to lead him. And in that, it's our duty to help him in any way that we can!''

''Yes . . .'' Keridil frowned, still not entirely sure of himself. ''And yet . . .''

''Yet?'' Themila's question was a challenge.

''I don't know . . . an instinct, maybe, but—I feel there's more to this. Far more.'' He looked across the darkening room at Tarod and knew from his friend's expression that he'd found the mark. ''Of course I'll do all I can to help, but . . . I don't know if it'll be of any use.''

Tarod moved restlessly in the gloom. ''Useful or not, I'm grateful to you . . . to you both.''

''Well . . . three minds are better than one.'' Nonetheless Keridil wished he could banish the unease that lurked in a corner of his mind. ''I'll think on it, Tarod. There must be an answer; either a solution to the mystery or a way of preventing it from plaguing you any further.''

Silence hung in the room for a moment or two; an oppressive silence. Finally, Tarod broke it.

''Yes,'' he said. ''There must be an answer, somewhere . . .''

When Keridil and Themila had gone, Tarod sat in his room while the last of the evening light failed. Down in the courtyard a supply caravan was arriving from Chaun Province, but the noise of wagons being unloaded and drovers escorted away to the dining hall for victualling hardly impinged on his consciousness.

Themila had struck home with her question about the

Circle being a disappointment, though it wasn't something that Tarod had directly acknowledged to anyone before. Yet at the same time, she was wrong—or so he believed—in her assumption that his frustration was a cause of the dreams. Keridil, if anyone, had been closer when he intimated that there was far more afoot than any of them could guess as yet. But Tarod was convinced that their best efforts—and they would give of their best, he was sure of that—wouldn't even begin to break the conundrum. And while they deliberated, the specter of nightmare still hung over him like a sword poised to strike and he was as powerless against it as ever. And after what had happened today, in the Marble Hall, he believed that the strength of the unknown forces would be redoubled. . . .

The now familiar wine flagon stood on the table beside his bed, untouched. Reflexively he reached out to take some, then withdrew his hand. Wine had offered no relief thus far; no reason why circumstances should change now. He was tired—the food Grevard and Themila between them had insisted he should eat had fortified him, but the endlessly troubled nights were taking their toll. *If he could sleep without dreaming* . . . but that was impossible. All he could do—all he could hope to do—was face the night with whatever courage he could muster.

The courtyard had quieted as the last of the supplies were borne away to the Castle's storehouse. Tarod lay back on his bed, and tried not to think about the dark hours ahead as his green eyes closed.

Chapter 6

Fin Tivan Bruall, the Castle's horsemaster, stifled a yawn as he made his way down the long lines of stalls in the sickly pre-dawn light. His unexpected visitor followed a pace behind, assessing each animal in turn, once or twice shaking his dark head when Fin turned to indicate a possible choice.

Although he was disgruntled at being hauled from his bed at such an uncivilized hour Fin would no more have shown it than attempted to fly from the Castle stack. Like most of the non-Initiated who served here, he respected the Circle, even if their demands were often unexpected or inconvenient. And though he couldn't remember his visitor's name, the fact that the man was a seventh-rank Adept was enough to make him mind his manners.

Nearing the end of the line, he stopped before a stall where a taller than average chestnut mare moved restlessly and eyed him with a dangerous look. "If you want a fast, strong animal, master, you'll do no better than this mare here. Only fault is she's troublesome. Throw you soon as look at you, and an unforgiving temper . . ." He shrugged. "Depends whether the good outweighs the bad, if you take my meaning."

Tarod stared at the mare. She was well bred—southern stock to give her height and speed, but enough of the northern blood to add stamina to the mixture . . . and temper. Ignoring Fin's hasty warning he moved into the stall and laid a hand on the animal's neck. She showed her teeth threateningly, but he spoke to her quickly and quietly, and—to the horsemaster's bafflement—the mare quieted.

Fin made the best of it. "Well, master, she's taken a liking to you and I've never known her do that before!"

Tarod smiled thinly. "I'll take her. Have her saddled and ready for me in the courtyard half an hour from now."

He said nothing more, but left the horsemaster to carry out his orders while he went quickly back to his rooms. The Sun was just beginning to rise, but it was unlikely that any of the Circle would be stirring before he left, and that was how he wanted it. If Keridil or Themila had got wind of his planned excursion there would be questions, arguments, alternative suggestions, and Tarod had run through all the possibilities in his mind until he was sick of it. This was the only way left to him.

As he gathered together a few minor needs for two or three days' journeying he carefully avoided catching sight of his own reflection in the mirror. Fin Tivan Bruall's eyes had told him all he needed to know about his state of mind and body following the ravages of the last four nights, when the dreams had come screaming out of the dark to torture him, leaving him wasted and broken when morning finally dawned. Since the unhappy episode in the Marble Hall the dreams had, as he'd suspected, redoubled their intensity, until on the previous morning he had woken with the solution coldly and cruelly clear in his mind.

He couldn't fight the dreams. Not in any orthodox way, at least. The support of his friends was comforting, but it wasn't enough—far more drastic measures would have to be taken, or the only other option would soon be yawning like an abyss before him. And that other option was suicide.

A day's research in the library vault had told him all he needed to make his plans. Tarod had never studied the arts of herbalism closely, but he knew enough to guide himself through the library's vast tomes on the subject and find what he wanted. A small cliff plant that grew sparsely on the northwest coast; one of the most powerful narcotics known which could, in the hands of a skilled herbalist, combat any night-borne horrors, no matter what their origin. It could also be used to open the mind's psychic channels, and Tarod hoped that it might break down the barriers that had thus far prevented him from discovering the origins of the visitations.

It was a dangerous drug, and could kill unless certain

procedures were strictly followed, but Tarod was past
caring about the risks. No supplies of the Spindrift Root,
as it was colloquially known, were held at the Castle; even
if they were he doubted if he would have consulted Grevard
about them. He had a location, he had chosen a horse—
he'd ride out and find the plant for himself.

And so, carrying only a few food supplies, some water
and his knife, Tarod mounted the skittish chestnut mare
while Fin Tivan Bruall looked on anxiously.

"Watch her, master," the horseman advised as the mare
side-stepped under Tarod's light but firm guidance. "First
chance she gets, she'll tip you and run if I'm any judge!"

Tarod drew in the reins, felt the animal quiet under a
subtle exertion of will, and smiled. "I'll remember. And
I'll bring her back safe and sound in three days or so."

The gates ahead of him stood open, a dazzle of early
sunlight reflecting from the world beyond. He touched his
heels to the mare's flanks and she sprang eagerly forward,
leaving the Castle behind.

Dawn was breaking two days later when Tarod finally
guided the tired and sweating mare on to the towering
cliffs of West High Land Province. Some perverse instinct
had prompted him to take the shorter but harder route
directly through the mountains, avoiding towns and villages and—perhaps especially—the large Sisterhood Cot
on the main drove road, where Kael Amion was Senior.
The mountain way was notorious as a haunt of every
conceivable bane of travellers, from the huge Northern
wild cats to bands of ever-hungry brigands; but nothing
had threatened Tarod. He had stopped to rest only during
the short summer nights, driven by a fear of sleeping and
by the desperate need to reach his goal. And now, with the
first bloody rays of the sun breaking in the east, he emerged
on to a dizzily sloping sward of turf that rolled away to the
West High Land cliffs.

The mare snorted thankfully as Tarod at last released his
hold on her and slid from the saddle to stand gazing out
across the magnificent vista of sea and sky. Horse and
rider had reached a rapport during the long and arduous

ride, and before lowering her head to graze the untouched grass the mare nudged affectionately at Tarod's hand while he stroked her soft nose.

Tarod sank down onto the turf, glad to rest his aching muscles. A Westerly wind blew the tangle of black hair back from his face and for a while he simply watched the sky lightening as dawn gave way to full day. The sea, far below him, glittered like liquid glass and the black humps of a myriad tiny islets were emerging as the early mist began to clear. The air smelled of salt, clean and invigorating; in the distance the sails of a small fishing-fleet, tacking landwards, glinted as the sun cleared the cliff tops. For the first time in many days Tarod felt peace stealing up on him and he grasped and held the feeling gratefully. The urgency of his mission still goaded him—but for a while, a short while, he could be free of the dark influences that had haunted him for so long.

He made a pillow of his cloak and lay back, welcoming the sun's warmth on his face. Lulled by the drone of waking insects, the murmur of the sea, the comfortable sounds of his horse cropping grass a few paces away, he slept.

The mare woke him with a sharp, challenging whinny and he sat up, momentarily disoriented. Then memory came back, and he turned his head.

The sun was almost at meridian, although this far North meridian was still low in the sky. Light flooded the cliff tops, and against its dazzle he saw the silhouette of a horseman approaching slowly along the inland track. The chestnut mare whinnied again and he sent out a sharp mental command to quiet her. But the other horse was answering with a long-drawn noise that ended in a cough, and Tarod sighed. The solitude of this lonely place was a balm to his mind; he wanted no interruptions, but it seemed he had no choice.

The newcomer saw him at that moment and reined in with a husky-voiced order. He realized suddenly, from the voice and from the slightness of the figure that dismounted, that his first assumption had been wrong—the intruder was a woman.

She came towards him a little hesitantly, and as she moved against the Sun he saw her clearly. Whatever else she might be, she wasn't beautiful. Young—perhaps three or four years younger than he was—but not beautiful. Hair so fair that it was almost white hung over her shoulders, and the odd, amber eyes that regarded him through startlingly dark lashes were far too big for her pinched face with its over-generous yet solemn mouth. Her frame was small, almost boyish . . . and there was something else about her, something only an Adept would see; something he filed away in a corner of his mind. . . .

She didn't smile, but addressed him with the same solemnity contained in her expression. "I'm sorry—I didn't realize there would be anyone here. I hope I don't disturb you."

Inbred courtesy made Tarod rise and bow slightly to her. "Not at all." He could hardly say otherwise . . . the cliffs belonged to no man.

The girl nodded, then sat down on the grass a few paces away from him. "It's more than a year since I've been here . . . I wanted to see it again." She hesitated, then the ghost of a smile lit her plain features. "You're not from the fishing villages?"

Unshaven and unkempt though he was, his manner had given away that much . . . Tarod almost laughed without quite knowing why. "No—I'm not. And from what you say, neither are you."

The girl looked obliquely at him, as though suspecting some ulterior motive behind the question. She was a strange creature, he thought; dressed in trousers and shirt more fitting to a man, with a stained cape thrown carelessly over her shoulders despite the day's warmth. Her pony—a shaggy, surly, Northern breed—was harnessed with a simple bridle and a rough blanket, suggesting that she had been all but born to horseback, and his curiosity was aroused. He held out a hand. "My name is Tarod."

She clasped his fingers briefly, as if unaccustomed to such formality. "I am Cyllan."

"And your clan . . . ?" He reflected a moment later that

he, of all people, should be the last to care for someone's clan name.

The girl smiled quirkishly. "Anassan, for what it's worth . . . it's a long time since anyone took the trouble to inquire."

The clan name was unfamiliar, and Tarod was about to ask its origin when she added, almost as though reading his thoughts, "We are from the Great Eastern Flatlands. My parents were drowned at sea four years ago . . . now I'm apprenticed as a drover to my uncle."

A girl, apprenticed as a drover? The concept seemed bizarre.

"We've been trading livestock and hides up from Southern Chaun, on the coast road," she continued. "The men are sleeping off the effects of some successful dealing at an inn a short way from here, so I thought . . ." She lowered her head as though embarrassed at her own foolishness. "I thought to see the sea."

"Then I'm the one who's intruding." Tarod spoke gently, wanting to put her at ease.

"No—no, not at all. I don't doubt you have business here that's more important than my fancies."

He shook his dark head. "Nothing that can't wait a while."

Briefly she flashed him a look that mingled gratitude with uncertainty. "You have the advantage of me. I don't know what your . . . oh!"

He followed the direction of her gaze and saw, pinned to the cloak on which he'd been resting, the gold insignia of a Circle Initiate.

"I'm sorry," the girl said indistinctly, "I didn't realize—I wouldn't have dreamed of troubling you—"

Tarod stared at his insignia with something approaching distaste. "Oh, that . . ." he said carelessly. "It's unimportant. My purpose here has nothing to do with Circle business."

"Nonetheless, I shouldn't have presumed . . . I'll go now." She was in awe of him—as he himself would have been in awe of an Initiate, before he had learned better— and that angered him, for it created an artificial barrier between them. As she started to rise he said suddenly, "No—stay, please. Perhaps you can help me."

"Help you?"

"Yes. You know this coast, while I'm a stranger. I came here to find a plant that grows only in this region. A rare plant, called the Spindrift Root."

Cyllan's amber eyes narrowed quickly. "Spindrift?"

"You know what it is?"

"I know what it *does*." She looked hard at him, and in that moment Tarod's first instinct about her was confirmed. Then she said, "The help you need isn't of any order I could give."

Thinly, he smiled. "You do yourself an injustice, Cyllan. I believe that, rather than travelling the roads as a drover, you should have been at a Sisterhood Cot these past few years!"

Cyllan's cheeks flushed. She hadn't expected him to see beyond the barriers she had created. But then the chances were she had never met an Initiate before. . . .

"My talents are hardly worthy of anyone's attention," she said, then added with a hint of mischief that belied her solemn expression, "Especially that of a high-ranking Adept."

Tarod bowed, acknowledging the observation. "Nonetheless, the Sisterhood has need of anyone with a natural psychic skill."

"Perhaps. But they don't look favorably on orphan peasant girls with little status and fewer means."

She spoke carelessly enough, but her words told Tarod all he needed to know. Despite its theoretical acceptance of any girl who showed aptitude and promise, in practice the Sisterhood of Aeoris was founded on hard-headed pragmatism. And this odd, pale-haired girl would not fit into the close world of a Sisterhood Cot . . .

"Are you a seer?" he asked her. "Or a dream-interpreter?"

She looked uneasily at him, as though afraid that he was about to either laugh at her or censure her for her presumption. He smiled reassuringly, and she said at last, "I—read stones and sand. Sometimes I see a person's future in the patterns they make, sometimes events . . . I can't always predict.''

Tarod was intrigued. "I'm not familiar with the method."

"In the East, it's an old technique. But there aren't many left now who have the skill, and those who have are—not looked on kindly."

Again, her tone implied more than her words. Tarod had never visited the Great Eastern Flatlands, but he had met a few of its native traders at the Castle. They were a dour, humorless breed, superstitious and rigidly conventional; not the kind to welcome any psychic talent in their midst with open arms. He could well imagine that Cyllan's lot among her own kind wouldn't be altogether happy.

Fleetingly, he wondered if she might be persuaded to read her stones for him, whatever that might entail—then quashed the idea quickly. There was nothing a peasant girl could tell him that he didn't already know, and even if she saw his future she would probably be unable to interpret what her instinct told her. What had she said—"the help you need is not of any order I could give"? She was more perceptive, perhaps, than she realized.

Possibly Cyllan had been entertaining similar thoughts, for she rose suddenly to her feet. "You want to find the Spindrift Root," she said, a little abruptly. "I can show you where it grows, but we'll need to climb to reach it."

She was looking out to sea with an oddly blind stare, waiting for him to join her. He stood. "Very well. If you'll lead the way."

The chestnut mare whinnied enquiringly after him as he followed the girl down the sloping turf towards the cliff edge. From here, the view demanded calm nerves and a strong stomach; unremitting tides had hammered the coastline into a ragged jigsaw of soaring buttresses and sharp inlets where the ground fell sickeningly away into hundreds of feet of nothing. Tarod felt the wind snatch mischievously at him, saw it lifting Cyllan's hair away from her face in a pale cloud as she turned to call back, pointing to a spot at the edge of a near-vertical drop: "There's a way down here. The longshore fishermen use it."

He looked at the sea surging far, far below. "I'll go alone. No reason for you to take risks."

She shook her head. "I've climbed it before—it's safe." And before he could stop her she had slid her feet over the edge of the drop and was out of sight.

Tarod swore under his breath. The girl had no cause to endanger herself on his behalf; if her recklessness ended in tragedy it would be rightly on his conscience for as long as he lived. But by the time he reached the cliff edge she was already a good way down, moving with a quick, practiced agility. There was nothing he could do but follow.

The descent was easier than it had looked from above; crude hand- and footholds had been carved into the harsh granite, and although worn by the wind and by generations of climbers they were secure enough. He caught up with Cyllan as she reached a narrow ledge some two hundred feet above the bay, and they paused to catch breath and rest their muscles for a few moments. She didn't speak as he joined her but crouched staring at the sea, as though waiting for something. The wind was stronger here, slapping and gusting between the cliff walls, and suddenly Cyllan raised a hand.

"Listen! They're here—I thought they'd gone, but they're still here! And they're singing . . ."

Even as she spoke he heard the sound. Faint and far away, it was a chillingly sweet series of musical notes, carried in on the wind from somewhere out to sea. The notes formed an eerie, haunting harmony, rising and falling in a pattern that made Tarod's spine tingle. And he felt the quietly curious presence of other minds, unhuman minds, reaching out to him.

"The *fanaani* . . ." Cyllan said, and her voice was almost breaking.

Then Tarod saw them. From this distance they were little more than dark silhouettes rising on the crest of an incoming wave in the moments before it shattered on the rocks. They were moving slowly inshore, and he counted seven before he glanced at Cyllan and saw the tears that glittered on her dark lashes, the look of mesmerized wonder on her face.

He himself was moved by the sight of the strange, rare sea creatures that haunted the wilder coastlines of the world; from the Star Peninsula it was sometimes possible to glimpse them or to hear a distant echo of their bitter-sweet song, but never before had he seen them from such close quarters as this. The fanaani were warm-blooded animals, man-sized and almost catlike in appearance but with long, sleek bodies, foreshortened legs and webbed paws adapted for an aquatic life. And, like terrestrial cats, they were telepathic—though theirs was an intelligence of a vastly higher, if alien, order. Tarod felt privileged to have such rare contact with them.

The fanaani had now drifted almost to the narrow crescent of beach revealed by the ebbing tide, so that Tarod and Cyllan had to lean perilously out to see them. Once Cyllan almost lost her balance, so intent was she on the creatures far below, and Tarod reached out a hand to hold and steady her. The brief contact broke the spell, and even as they looked again the fanaani were turning, heading back seawards and already almost lost to view against the swell.

Cyllan sighed and surreptitiously wiped her eyes. "A good omen for you," she said softly.

"Perhaps." Tarod found himself irrationally wanting to believe her, and with that thought came a memory that he would have preferred to keep at bay in this peaceful place. It goaded him, and he added, "I think we should continue on."

"Yes . . ." Reluctantly she rose, and they left the ledge to resume the path down the cliff.

They found the Spindrift Root growing from a near-invisible crevice in the cliff wall, just out of reach of the worst Winter tides. It was an unremarkable, fleshy plant with greyish-green leaves, and only yielded reluctantly to Tarod's knife. But at last root and stem lay in his hand and he looked at it. There was little of it, but it should be enough for his purpose.

Cyllan was watching him, her amber eyes uneasy. As he slipped the root into his belt-pouch she said in a whisper, "Please . . . be careful."

Her words brought back the memory again. The idyll was over, he realized; and though while it lasted it had been pleasant, it was still an illusion. Grim reality beckoned, and grim reality told him he couldn't afford to delay what was necessary for much longer. Without further words they began the long climb back to the clifftop where their horses waited. The mare greeted her master with a good deal of snorting and head-nudging, while Cyllan's pony stood sullenly unmoving.

Tarod gathered up his cloak and dropped it over his shoulders, noticing the way Cyllan's gaze flicked quickly to the gold insignia as if by donning it he had recreated the barrier. The Sun was starting to wester and he wanted to reach the mountains by nightfall, ride through the night, anything rather than risk sleep during the dark hours.

"Thank you, Cyllan," he said quietly. "I'm in your debt—I hope we'll meet again."

She nodded. "I hope so, too. Good fortune go with you, Tarod."

Protocol held that he should leave her with the blessing of Aeoris, an Initiate's traditional and formal duty towards a layman. But he couldn't. The words would have sounded hollow and artificial, and widened the gulf between them. Instead, he said simply, "And with you. Goodbye, Cyllan."

Cyllan watched until the chestnut mare was out of sight. She had managed to stop herself from praying that Tarod would look back, but when he didn't the disappointment still hurt. Not that there was any reason why he should, she told herself; he was a Circle Adept, high-ranking; she was a peasant drover with nothing in her mind or body to interest him beyond the demands of courtesy. Their paths had crossed only briefly; they wouldn't meet again. And she was a fool if she entertained, even for a moment, any hopeless fancies about what might have been, or could have been; that was a lesson she had learned long ago, and relearned on each rare occasion when she looked in a mirror.

But all the same, the image of the tall, black-haired stranger with his feline green eyes and troubled soul would remain with her for a long time to come. Despite their differences he had treated her as an equal, almost a kindred spirit, and for a brief, illogical and glorious moment she had hoped that there could be more. The hope had died—as part of her had known it inevitably must—when he rode away without looking back. But she wouldn't forget him.

She swung herself onto her pony's broad back. As she turned the animal's head westwards, her eyes were stinging with tears that she told herself were nothing more than the effect of the sun's angry glare.

Chapter 7

Tarod arrived back at the Castle as a harsh dawn was breaking. He had ridden relentlessly through two nights and the day between them, driving himself and the chestnut mare almost to breaking point, stopping only when to press on would have killed one or both of them. The mare had shown her mettle and her breeding on the long ride but as they finally clattered through the Castle gateway her head was hanging with exhaustion.

Tarod felt little better than the animal. Such a journey was taxing on the most skilled horseman; his limbs ached fierily from the hours in the saddle, and his head was light and his mind dazed from lack of sleep. As the great black walls rose around him he felt the old sense of oppression returning, and thought wistfully of the vast skies and sunlit cliffs of West High Land, where for a short while he had been able to forget his torment. Images of the brief interlude haunted him; the scent of the unsullied turf, the eerily beautiful song of the fanaani, the girl Cyllan with her solemn eyes who had given him help and good company while asking nothing in return. . . . Wearily he slid from the saddle and led the mare towards the stables. A yawning lad was roused from his straw pallet to take care of the animal, and Tarod made his way slowly, reluctantly, to his rooms in the still silent Castle.

Alone in the confines of his apartments, he drew out the small, precious Spindrift Root and laid it on his worktable. Already it was beginning to wither—he would have to work quickly before its potency was lost, and the process of extracting and distilling its essence would take some time.

Tarod's hands were not quite steady as he began his painstaking work. Now and again a haze clouded his vision and his consciousness threatened to swim into a half-dream. Hours passed while he worked on behind the bolted door, oblivious to the everyday activity beyond his window as the Castle stirred into life. No one came to disturb him—for all anyone, even Keridil, knew, he hadn't yet returned—and at last, as the day faded and the Sun began to flare into a grim crimson ball of fire beyond the black walls, he was ready.

The distilled essence was a dark, reddish-purple, cloudy liquid that barely filled a phial. The disgusting stench it gave off pervaded the room, but Tarod was past caring —numb with exhaustion and depression, he had gone beyond aesthetic considerations. As he looked at the results of his efforts—which seemed, somehow, unclean and malignant—he tried to remember each stage of the operation, and ask himself whether he had taken all the necessary precautions. The herb could be a deadly brew in even the most experienced hands . . . but that hardly seemed to matter now. A tired fatalism had taken hold of him and made him reckless—whatever might or might not happen, his future was in the hands of the gods.

He waited until the long shadows had reached out across the courtyard to envelop his room in semi-darkness, then measured out a little of the Spindrift concoction into a cup, diluting it with wine. The smell of the brew and a last glimmering remnant of caution forestalled him, but only for a moment: he tilted his head back and swallowed the contents of the cup in one draught.

Even good wine couldn't disguise the herb's evil flavor,

and it nearly choked him. For a few moments he leaned against the window-ledge, coughing violently; then the spasm subsided and he made his way unsteadily through to his second chamber where he stretched out stiffly on the bed.

The taste of the Spindrift stuck in his throat as he lay watching the last light fade from the window. At times he felt as though he were choking, then abruptly breathing would grow easier and he relaxed. But when the first major effect of the drug struck him he was unaware of its cause, knowing only that his mind was dulling into a throbbing semi-existence that echoed the weariness of his limbs. His legs felt like leaden weights, there was a weight on his chest and shoulders, pressing him down into sleep . . . thankfully, Tarod closed his eyes.

But the pressure began to increase. Each breath was now a physical fight against pain, his lungs refusing to fill with air, his muscles refusing to respond. His mind couldn't rally to banish it; he was starting to asphyxiate. . . .

With a hoarse shout Tarod flung himself from the bed and fell heavily on the floor. He dragged his body painfully upright again, gripping the bedpost for support, and found he was barely able to stand. His numbed mind forced the realization that something had gone drastically wrong—he had made a mistake, and the narcotic had taken hold of his entire system, its poison spreading so rapidly that he couldn't fight it.

Help. The word crawled into his consciousness. He must seek help, or he would shrivel and die here in his own rooms, where no one could unbolt the door and find him in time. *Unbolt the door* . . . it looked a thousand miles away, but he launched himself desperately towards it and his hands groped and clawed at the latch. He had no more strength than a child, but somehow the bolt shifted at last and he all but fell out into the corridor. A torch burned steadily at the far end, but the passage was deserted. Tarod staggered in the direction of the stairs, unable to breathe, unable to drag enough air into his body to utter a sound, certain that he couldn't survive another moment of this ordeal. Yet he was still alive when he reached the courtyard and still alive when, finding no one to aid him, he stumbled along the pillared walk to the door that led down into the library vault. Instinct was drawing him towards the Marble Hall, and though he didn't understand it he still retained enough of a savage self-preservation to force himself on until at last, hardly able to stand upright, he entered the library itself.

The room was lit, suggesting that someone had recently been there and intended to return. But nothing moved among the dusty shadows. Tarod collapsed against a shelf, bringing a shower of books down around him, and with pain-glazed eyes saw the vault ebbing and flowing, harsh light pulsing from the torches on the walls as its outlines twisted and warped. *Why had he come here? There was nothing for him here.* . . . His clouded vision roamed the room—until he fancied he saw something move by the door that led to the Marble Hall.

With a tremendous effort he got to his feet and moved towards the door. It should have been locked, but it wasn't—instead as he leaned his weight against it it opened, so that he fell to his knees, staring half blinded at the passage beyond.

A sound like a gale rushed past his ears and he glimpsed a mad, gibbering face that seemed to hurtle towards him along the corridor before vanishing. Then another, and a third—all twisted, leering, mocking his delirium. The nightmare was beginning again. . . .

Remember . . . Come back . . .

Tarod gasped, trying to turn away as the sibilant whisper echoed from the distant silver door at the end of the passage. But his body refused to respond.

Remember . . .

Something was coming along the corridor, moving inexorably towards him. It neither walked nor ran, but seemed to shift without motive power of its own, dreamlike, drifting. The face—his own face—smiled, but the smile was an illusion, a human mask hiding something far more terrible. The long, narrow eyes changed color constantly and the gold hair flowed in a rising current of air as the apparition raised its arms, holding out gaunt, long-fingered hands towards him. The ground beneath Tarod vibrated and a high, thin singing note emanated from the grim figure, making him want to block his ears. But he couldn't move, his muscles were locked, rigid—

The being's lips parted and mouthed a single word. A moment later, Tarod heard his own name whispered in his mind—and as the echoes died away something within him snapped, shattering the hideous spell. Terror restored the strength taken by the drug and he twisted around, stumbling through the door and pulling on it with all his power, to slam it shut in the face of the approaching vision.

"I will have no more nightmares!" he yelled, his voice cracking insanely, echoing through the vault. "Get back whence you came—I'll have no more of it!"

The two people who were at that moment making their way down the vault stairs towards the library stopped in their tracks at the sound of the demented voice from below.

Themila Gan Lin blanched visibly. "What in the name of—" she began, then hesitated. There had been something familiar in the voice, barely recognizable though it was, and a terrible intuition took hold of her.

Keridil touched her arm, gesturing for her to stay back. "Wait here," he said quietly. "I'll investigate."

An almighty crash sounded in the library as he started down the last few stairs, and Themila saw his hand go reflexively to the short-bladed sword that hung from his belt. It was a badge of rank rather than a usable weapon, and she wondered fleetingly if she should fetch more help. If there was real trouble in the vault, Keridil was as good as unarmed. . . .

But it was too late to worry about Keridil's safety. He had reached the door, was pushing it open. She saw him flinch, then—

"Tarod!"

"Oh, Gods . . ." Themila's worst fears were confirmed, and she flew down the stairs.

As she entered the library, a second crash heralded the fall of an entire shelf of books, and a cloud of dust erupted as they hit the floor. Through it they saw Tarod backed against the wall, head turning violently from side to side as though he struggled to shake off some monstrous assailant only he could see. His teeth were clenched with the effort of trying to breathe, and he was soaked with sweat. Not stopping to think, Themila would have run to him, but Keridil held her forcibly back.

"Don't touch him!" he hissed.

"But he's—"

"I said, *don't touch him!*"

Their voices broke through the daze of agony and distortion in Tarod's brain, and he saw them for the first time. Cautiously Keridil began to move towards him, and something triggered in Tarod's warped mind. *Fair hair . . . fair hair . . . gold hair . . . he was responsible, this demon, this amorphous, deadly nightmare . . . he was the enemy . . . kill him . . . destroy him . . .*

One hand clawed to the knife at his hip, and the cold touch of the hilt awoke a bizarre synthesis of confidence and bloodlust within him. He started forward—but neither Keridil nor Themila was aware of the threat. They were both staring, transfixed, at the double-image of Tarod's own form which had suddenly and shockingly materialized behind him. It was a negative phantasm of the living man—dark and light, gold and black—and Themila felt a sensation as though a fist had slammed violently into her stomach as a chilly wind of power hurtled malevolently through the vault. The blow was a warning, and with a tremendous effort she came out of her near-trance in time to see Tarod stalking, the crazed glitter in his eyes, the knife—

"Keridil, look out!" she shrieked, and at the same moment Tarod sprang.

Pure reflex saved Keridil as the knife sheared up. He twisted aside, raising one arm to protect his face, and the blade slashed across his forearm in a shallow slice that he barely felt. Unbalanced by his own impetus Tarod stumbled, then swung round and dropped into a crouch; but his knife hand was shaking violently. As he launched himself forward a second time Keridil struck out, once.

It was like fighting a child. The knife fell from Tarod's grip, and for a moment a glimmer of sanity returned to the green eyes. Then he seemed to crumple, and collapsed to the floor.

Themila's heart was pounding painfully as she knelt at Tarod's side while Keridil turned his senseless body over. Neither was willing to be the first to speak of what they had both seen, but Themila felt an acute—and cowardly, she admitted to herself—desire to get away from the vault as quickly as she could. She climbed awkwardly to her feet, forcing herself not to look into the gloomy, shadowed corners.

"I'll fetch help," she said. "We'll need at least one more man to move him."

Keridil was trying to take Tarod's pulse, but aware of his own inadequacy. "Yes—and send someone for Grevard."

At the door she hesitated briefly, looking back and half expecting to see again the grim apparition which had appeared so briefly at the moment of crisis. All she saw was Keridil, eyes closed, making the familiar sign of Aeoris as he murmured what she suspected was a prayer over Tarod's still figure.

By the time Keridil and two more men brought Tarod on a makeshift stretcher back to his rooms, a crowd had gathered in the corridor outside. News—especially bad news—travelled fast in the Castle, but the onlookers had to be content with a few terse words from Keridil about an "accident."

The moment they entered the outer room, the men were struck by the lingering stench of the brew Tarod had prepared. One turned back towards the door with an oath of protest, and Keridil, gagging, signalled frantically for the windows to be opened. Themila arrived as Tarod was being lowered on to his bed and made as comfortable as possible, and reported that Grevard was not in his chambers, but was being sought urgently.

"But that smell—" she crumpled a corner of her shawl and put it over her mouth, coughing. "What in the name of Aeoris is it?"

"I don't know . . . something about it's familiar, but I can't place it."

"That phial—" Themila's sharp gaze alighted on the table by the window. "There's something in it. . . ."

Keridil picked the phial up and cautiously sniffed it. His stomach heaved as the full stench assaulted his nostrils, and he put the tiny glass container aside hastily. "Whatever it is, it's deadly . . . Gods, where is that damned physician?"

As though invoked by Keridil's frustration Grevard's voice sounded from the outer room, cutting authoritatively through the speculative babble of voices.

"Keridil?" The physician was rumpled and his clothes awry, and under happier circumstances Themila might have been amused. Grevard had never taken a wife, but he still enjoyed his pleasures when there was a woman available and willing to oblige. Now though, his professional manner was back in full force. Keridil explained in as few words as possible, and Grevard examined the cup. One sniff, and his expression darkened.

"Spindrift! Where in the name of the Gods did he get that? It's the most dangerous narcotic known!" He stared for a moment at the still figure on the bed. Then: "I want every superfluous person out of these rooms. Keridil and Themila, you may stay if you wish; but everyone else must go."

They filed out, and Grevard locked the door firmly behind them. When he returned he began to examine Tarod, and Themila was the first to break the silence. "Grevard, what can you do for him?"

The physician continued his work without answering for a few moments. Then at last he straightened, sighed and said, "Nothing."

"*Nothing?*" Keridil swung round from the window, his voice rising harshly in protest. "But—"

"It's a simple matter, like it or not," Grevard interrupted him sharply. "The Spindrift Root, as it's known, is a valuable drug when used correctly. Used incorrectly, it's deadly—and there's no antidote to it." He turned back to the bed and pulled back one of Tarod's eyelids, grimacing at what he saw. "What escapes me is the reason why Tarod should have wanted to meddle—poison himself, damn it—with such a drug."

"You think it was by his own hand?" Keridil sounded incredulous, and Grevard snorted.

"Don't be a fool, Keridil—of course it was! How could anyone, let alone Tarod, be persuaded or tricked into drinking a concoction like that? Besides, we don't have any would-be murderers in our midst."

Keridil shook his head helplessly. "Tarod, suicidal? I can't credit that, Grevard!"

"Then you'd better start thinking of a better explanation. He could have made a mistake in the preparations; that would be my guess, at any rate. But it doesn't take genius to get the brew right, and I find it very hard to believe that a seventh-rank sorcerer would make such relatively simple mistakes."

This time, when Keridil looked at Themila she refused to meet his eyes, and only said softly, "Perhaps there are circumstances where anyone would make an error. . . ."

Grevard gave her a very hard glance. "Perhaps. But for the time being that's neither here nor there. I'm only concerned with his physical condition. We can worry about his mental state later—if he survives."

The words shocked both of them, and Themila cried, "He must! Grevard, you don't think—" she couldn't finish.

Seeing her face, the physician's manner unbent. "I'm sorry, Themila; sometimes I tend to be too blunt for my own good. But the truth is, I don't know. Tarod has a peculiar constitution—you or I would probably have been dead within minutes of swallowing that concoction. But the fact that he has survived this far is proof of his strength. If it's within the capacity of mortal man to fight this level of poisoning, then yes, I think he'll live." He began to gather his belongings together. "Will you inform Jehrek of this, or shall I? There'll have to be a full investigation."

"I'll speak to my father." Keridil didn't relish the interview, for he could predict what Jehrek would have to say. The High Initiate had never lost his original forebodings about Tarod, and although he was always scrupulously fair in his dealings with the black-haired sorcerer he nonetheless felt strongly that Keridil's own judgment was prejudiced by friendship. Keridil anticipated a thorough tongue-lashing for allowing matters to come to such a pass without taking action.

"You'll keep me informed of anything you discover?" Grevard asked.

"Yes—yes, of course."

"Good. Now—I'll visit regularly, but I want someone here with Tarod at all times. If there is any change whatever, I must be summoned instantly."

Keridil nodded, and the physician laid a hand on his shoulder. "I'm only sorry there's nothing more I can do for him."

"You're doing all that's humanly possible."

Keridil persuaded Themila to leave with Grevard, and when they had gone he sat down on the edge of the bed and looked at his friend. Tarod's face was bleached white but for the dark, hollow circles around his eyes; his breathing was stertorous and halted. He looked as if he could die at any moment. For a while Keridil watched his immobile face, trying not to think about the torments which had brought him to such a desperate and perhaps fatal pass. The signs had been clear for anyone wise enough to see them; and though he had seen, he hadn't acted in time.

But there was more—far more—to this than was thus far apparent to anyone, Keridil thought, and shivered suddenly as though with a premonition. He had been wrong in not informing Jehrek at an earlier stage . . . now, the wrong had to be righted.

If it wasn't too late . . .

Tarod didn't regain consciousness during the night, nor for many days and nights after that. Those who kept vigil reported no change in the motionless figure, and anxious enquiries—especially from Keridil and Themila—to Grevard always met with the same response: "No development—I can do nothing more."

Yet within the damaged world of his own mind, Tarod was, after a fashion, awake and aware. To him it seemed that he hung timeless and ageless in a twilight of dreams and delirium. Endless processions of events marched past his inner vision; he relived his own past, though the memories were so distorted that they only served to create a monstrous confusion.

Then as coma deepened the faces began to appear. At first they were sly and subtle, but as the nightmares gathered momentum they grew bolder, so that wherever he turned he found himself confronted by wall after wall of screaming, gibbering elementals. The bloated, idiot features, the insane sounds they made, recalled another time and another life, when he had been able to deal carelessly with such minor spirits and control them. Now he was helpless against their onslaughts and could only twist and turn as if bound by invisible ropes, while the sea of faces tossed around him and their shrieking beat against his senses like a tide. And finally the last shreds of his resistance broke down, so that the dark chaos of nightmare became the only reality.

But at last there was a change. At first Tarod's battered mind was hardly aware of it, but eventually he realized that the endless horrors were fading, giving way to a peculiar, tense hiatus. There was something familiar about the haze of pale and ghostly colors that suffused the air around him; something familiar about the dimly visible pillars that soared towards an invisible roof . . . suddenly memory came back, and Tarod realized that he was in the Marble Hall.

He couldn't think clearly enough to wonder how he had been brought here; and anyway, it seemed that his presence was purely astral. But the relief of finding surroundings that were known to him, and to which he could anchor his consciousness, was indescribable. He turned—drifted—in search of the most familiar landmark of all: the seven defaced colossi that had always fascinated him.

They were there, menacingly indistinct in the shimmering mist. He projected himself towards them, his mind reaching out—

One of the statues moved. Tarod felt a shock strike through him and stopped, staring harder. Again, unmistakable now; a shudder as though the ancient stone were struggling against centuries of immobility, coming to a ghastly semblance of life. And as he watched, the outlines of the colossus seemed to waver and disintegrate, metamorphosing into a fully human figure, man-sized, which stepped lightly down from the granite plinth.

The face—so like his own—smiled, the eyes constantly changing color in their frame of gold hair. This was no mortal man—the chiselled features, beautiful yet cruel mouth, tall, graceful frame, were too perfect to have any true humanity. This was some denizen of a world beyond imagination . . . and as the entity extended a long-fingered hand in greeting, Tarod felt a terrible thrill of recognition, a sensation that delighted and yet repelled him at the same moment. *This was the figure which had haunted his dreams—the architect of his nightmares!*

"Tarod . . ." The being spoke, his voice ringing clear and musical in Tarod's mind. He fought against the constriction that held him, and finally managed to form words.

"You—who are you?"

"Do you not know me, Tarod? Do you not remember Yandros?"

Remember . . .

Elements of the dreams came back to him, and he shuddered, he felt, to the core of his soul. He *knew* the name, knew it as well as he knew his own, and yet understanding eluded him. And the memory was so deep that no will in the world could call it out of the nether darkness. . . .

"Why?" Tarod croaked at last. "Why are you haunting me?"

Yandros ignored the question, instead fixing him with a stare under which he felt himself blanching. "You are dying, Tarod," he said at last. "The poison you took is in your blood, and perhaps an end to your mortal life is what you desire. But it is not what we desire for you."

"We . . . ?"

Yandros made a dismissive gesture, again ignoring the

question. "Your will, of course, is your own; your life too, to dispose of as you please. But I don't believe you truly wish to die."

Did he? Confusion raged in Tarod, and he tried to break it down and remember more clearly. He had cared nothing for his own existence when he distilled and drank the Spindrift; but now, faced with the reality of death, his perspectives were changing. And Yandros's will seemed to be influencing his own in ways that he couldn't hope to combat. . . .

He said, harshly, "You tell me I'm dying. Surely my desires are therefore irrelevant?"

"No." The entity shook his head, and the mist of colors shivered and re-formed. "It is within my power to save you, if you ask it. But there will be a price."

A little of the old dark, cynical humor returned to Tarod's answering smile. "You already hold my life in your hands—I have nothing better than that to offer you, Yandros."

"On the contrary. There is a task—a destiny, you might call it—which must be fulfilled. That is the price, my friend."

"Destinies?" Tarod was derisive. "I'm no hero!"

"Nonetheless, you are the only inhabitant of this world who can fulfill it. And it must be done." Venom tinged Yandros's voice momentarily. "It is inescapable, Tarod. And one day you will understand, and be glad."

The dreams . . . suddenly, Tarod knew that here lay the source of the nightmares which had led him to this moment; the power which had been calling him for so long—the reason why he was different. And he knew Yandros told the truth when he said such a power was inescapable. If he turned his back now, it would continue to haunt him and there would be no second chance. This—or death—was the only path he could take.

He said quietly, "What is it you want of me?"

Yandros smiled, triumphant. "As yet, nothing. Bide your time, and you will learn all you need to know when the moment is right."

He had no choice. . . . "Then I accept," he said.

The being—whatever he was—nodded. For a moment there was a flicker of mischief in the many-colored eyes. "You bind yourself on an oath you cannot break. Do you accept that?"

"I accept it."

"Then no more need be said. Except . . ." Yandros hesitated, and the mischief flowered suddenly into malevolent amusement. "The tides of life and death cannot be overmanipulated once they are set in motion. You will not die, Tarod—but another life will be forfeited in your stead."

"Another life . . . ? No! I won't allow that!" Tarod protested.

"You cannot stop it." Yandros's smile broadened. "You have given your oath."

"Then I gave it on a false assumption!" Tarod felt a mingling of fury and panic. "If you had told me—"

"But I did not tell you. I was remiss, perhaps; but it's too late for second thoughts."

Yandros had trapped him, he realized with a sick sensation. And because of this being's machinations, some innocent soul would die in his place . . .

"We will meet again before long," Yandros said. "And then it will be clear to you why I do what I must. Much depends on you, old friend. Never forget that." He reached out, and touched Tarod's left hand lightly, his fingers brushing across the silver ring. "Time. That is the key, Tarod. You will understand."

Even as the being spoke, Tarod felt a new sensation somewhere in the darkest pit of his consciousness. A slow, regular pulsing like a monstrous heartbeat . . . its pitch was almost beyond the threshold of awareness but nonetheless it seemed to take hold of him and suffuse through and beyond him, until its awesome rhythm filled the entire Marble Hall. A terrible half-memory snatched at Tarod's mind; he looked wildly around him through the Hall's quivering, shuddering mists, but before he could begin to form an answer the memory evaded him and vanished.

Abruptly the outlines of Yandros's figure began to waver and dim, and Tarod cried out, "Wait!" There was so much more he had to ask, needed to know. But Yandros merely smiled.

"Yandros, *wait!*"

His voice echoed into a sudden, shocking emptiness and silence.

. . . "Yandros!"

The young first-rank Initiate who had been dozing in a chair beside Tarod's bed sprang up as though flailed, and the heavy book which he was supposed to be studying thumped to the floor. Heart pounding with shock, the boy looked at the sick man—and almost cried out in alarm. Tarod's body was jerking in violent spasms beneath the blanket that covered him and his eyes were open, staring madly, blindly at nothing as he seemed to struggle to speak or shout.

"Gods!" The boy backed away, frightened, then rushed for the door to find Grevard.

"Simik Jair Sangen requested an interview with me this morning," Jehrek Banamen Toln said.

"Inista's father?" Keridil was instantly wary, though he hid it well as he reached forward to pick up his wine-cup from the table and take a sip. "Did you oblige him?"

"I could hardly refuse. He owns some of the best arable land in Chaun Province, and we need his goodwill if we're to continue receiving our yearly tithes without a lot of haggling."

Keridil's heart sank. "Then I suppose I needn't ask what he wanted . . ."

"He made a formal dowry offer, Keridil. He believes that you and Inista would make an excellent match . . . and his arguments were very persuasive."

Keridil rose and began to pace the room restlessly, hiding his expression from his father. He knew that a man destined to take on one of the highest ranks in the world should have the stability of a wife of good breeding, and was aware of Jehrek's concern that he had not, thus far, shown an inclination to marry anyone. Many matches in the higher echelons were made for reasons of status or convenience, and most of them worked well enough; if his father were to put forward a candidate with whom he could get along on a passable level Keridil would have done his duty and agreed. But not Inista Jair . . .

At last he turned to face the older man again. "Is that your feeling, Father? That the arguments are persuasive?"

Jehrek sighed, looking at his only son with a mixture of affection and wistfulness. He normally enjoyed these occasional quiet evenings, when there was time to discuss Circle and Council matters at leisure and perhaps progress a little further with the grooming that was so necessary if Keridil were to one day succeed him as High Initiate. But sometimes he could sense the personal war in his son; the conflict between the demands of duty and the desire to be free and unrestricted that was only natural in a young man. Sometimes the war spilled over and led to clashes between the two of them, and that was something Jehrek deeply regretted—but his responsibilities were clear, and he believed that he was slowly winning the battle. The Circle needed a strong leader for the future; someone who could stand against the insidious tide of change and uncertainty that Jehrek felt in his bones had been creeping up on the world and on the Castle in particular. It was a formless fear still, despite years of increasing concern, and Jehrek felt that he was now too old and too jaded to have any hope of resolving it.

If Malanda had lived, perhaps his task would have been easier. From the day he married Malanda Banamen, as she was then, she had been not only his anchor, but also his talisman and a fount of sound, earthy wisdom. To die in childbirth, giving life to their only offspring . . . it was an irony that Jehrek had been hard-pressed not to fight against, and only his deep-rooted belief in the unshakeable, if sometimes incomprehensible, justice of the gods had sustained him then. But Keridil, growing up without a mother—Themila Gan Lin, widowed and childless herself, had done all in her power for him but she was nonetheless a surrogate—hadn't had that same anchor through his formative years. And now, perhaps, they were both paying the price.

He attempted to answer his son's question at last, but

found the specter of his long-dead wife standing between him and what he wanted to say. He couldn't wish for a more suitable daughter-elect than Inista Jair . . . yet his own marriage had been such a love match . . .

"Yes," he said at length. "The arguments are persuasive. But before I even consider a final decision, I'd like to know your feelings on the matter."

Keridil bit his lip. "And do you want me to be honest?"

"Of course."

Keridil opened his mouth to speak—but at that moment something beyond the uncurtained window distracted him. Some commotion in the courtyard . . .

"Pardon me, Father . . ." He reached the window in three strides and peered through the glass. Then he swore—or so Jehrek thought—under his breath.

"Keridil?" The old man stood up stiffly. "What's amiss?"

"I thought . . . yes! It's Koord, running as though his life depended on it—"

"Koord?" Jehrek was puzzled, and Keridil made an impatient gesture. "The boy, first-ranker—he was set to keep vigil with Tarod—"

The High Initiate frowned. "Perhaps there's been some change. If so, it's long overdue!"

"Father, I must go and see what's to do!" Keridil was already halfway to the door, foreboding eclipsing all other considerations. But Jehrek protested.

"There's nothing you can do, boy! Leave it to Grevard, at least until we've—"

Keridil rarely interrupted his father, but he did so now. "No—I should go. Forgive me." He pulled the door open, and would have gone out into the corridor—but a sudden cry from Jehrek halted him in his tracks.

"*Keridil!*"

The old man was on his feet, but suddenly doubled over as if in terrible pain. One hand clawed blindly in Keridil's direction, a plea for help which Jehrek couldn't put into words.

"Father . . . ?" Keridil's eyes widened in horror. "Father, what is it, what's the matter?"

His only answer was a strangled gasp, and Jehrek swayed dangerously. Keridil ran forward—and was just in time to catch the High Initiate as he fell.

Slowly, Tarod became aware of an almost intolerable aching that throbbed throughout his body, and fancied he saw a dim room with a single shaft of cold light filtering through half-drawn curtains. Gradually his senses began to stir and he thought he felt another presence at his side—but this time it wasn't a return to the world of nightmare. Cautiously, not sure of his own physical and mental state, Tarod opened filmy eyes.

He had been right; there was a room and the light was the light of the twin moons beyond the Castle walls. And there was someone else present . . .

A hand, small and cool and firm, touched his forehead. He tried to reach up to take hold of the fingers, but the strength wasn't in him. Then the indistinct figure leaned closer, and he recognized Themila Gan Lin.

"Tarod? Can you hear me?"

Her words awoke a memory that took him back over the years to the moment when he had awoken from the delirium of injury and exposure, to find himself in the Castle for the first time. But this was no delusion; he was back in the world of reality.

He tried to answer Themila, but his throat was too dry. She held a cup to his lips; he tasted cold water and it was like the sweetest wine, easing the constriction until he could speak.

"Themila . . ." He was too weak to touch her, but at least he could smile.

Her voice shook as she whispered, "Don't try to move. Grevard will be here as soon as he can."

"Grev—? Oh. Yes." *He was alive*. The realization was almost impossible to believe. But he *was* alive.

"Is it night?" he asked, when he had voice enough.

"Deep night," Themila told him, and there was a peculiar catch in her voice that he didn't understand. "Oh, Tarod . . . we've feared so for your life! Grevard despaired of you time and again, and now . . ." Abruptly she stood up and went to the window, gazing out into the moon-tinged darkness. "Perhaps it's a good omen despite everything . . ."

Tarod was nonplussed. As yet his mind was still cloudy, and he could remember little of events that had led up to his delirium, still less of his experiences during the coma. But something was tugging at the recesses of his memory . . .

Themila opened the curtains a little wider, and for the first time he saw her clearly. She wore a long night-shift with a wrap over it—and over the wrap was a purple sash fastened at her left shoulder and right hip. Purple was the color of death . . . Themila was in mourning.

He tried to sit up, and cursed the weakness which put the effort beyond him. "Themila—the sash—"

She turned back towards the bed, but before she could answer the bedchamber door opened and Keridil entered. He was carrying a lantern which threw harsh light onto his face, and Tarod saw immediately the strain etched into his features. Keridil approached and stood looking down at him, but seemed incapable of speaking. And Tarod saw that his eyes were reddened and that he, too, wore a purple sash, identical to Themila's but for a single, simple design embroidered in gold thread just below the shoulder-knot.

A double circle, bisected by a lightning-flash. Only one such sash existed, and only one man in the world was ever privileged to wear it. It was the sash of a High Initiate in mourning for his predecessor.

And then the memory came back. *Yandros . . . a life for a life . . .*

With a strength that he shouldn't have possessed Tarod took hold of the nearest bedpost and pulled himself painfully upright. His eyes met Keridil's in a torment that the other man didn't comprehend, and he said, "When?"

"My father died two hours ago, at First Moonrise." Keridil sank onto the bed, head hanging, pushing his hands through his tawny hair as though desperately tired.

Tarod shut his eyes against the thoughts that tried to fill his mind. "Aeoris keep his soul . . . ." he whispered.

Chapter 8

The words on the page were dancing before Tarod's eyes, turning into spiderlike images that made no sense. He took a deep breath, pinching the bridge of his nose between thumb and forefinger, then shook his mane of dark hair and looked again.

It was no use. He had simply been trying for too long, and his brain was rebelling against the endless hours of reading. With a sigh he shut the book and crossed the library vault to return it to its place among the shelves. As he gave the spine one final, resentful flick to line it up with its fellows a footfall sounded beside him, and he looked down to see Themila, hands on hips, staring at him accusingly.

"Tarod. Will you never learn? You *know* what Grevard said—no mental exertion until he pronounces you fully recovered! And here I find you, barely seven days out of bed—"

Tarod silenced her by laying a finger lightly on her lips, then bent to kiss her forehead while she fumed. "I'd just finished." He could have added, *and failed*, but did not. Neither Themila nor Keridil knew just how much time he spent searching through these ancient files, nor the reason why he did so—and as yet Tarod wanted to keep his secret intact.

"You shouldn't have started!" Themila admonished him, "After all you've suffered—"

"Themila, please . . ." He took hold of her shoulders and shook her with gentle affection. "I appreciate your concern, believe me. But between you, you and Keridil would make me into an invalid if I let you! I'm well, Themila. Now, will you stop trying to mother me every hour of the day?"

She bit her lip in confusion, then her posture relaxed. "If I'd had a son half as troublesome as you, I'd have been grey before my time! Very well, then; you're as fit as can be; I accept it. In which case, why are you not catching up on some sleep, in readiness for tomorrow?"

He had forgotten tomorrow . . .

"Firstly," Themila continued, "you've promised to escort me at the procession. And I'm sensible of the honor—it isn't often that a mere third-ranker has the chance to appear at important ceremonies with a high Adept. Secondly, your name is down on the list for the arena."

"What?"

"It is. Look at the list posted in the dining hall, if you don't believe me. "You volunteered three nights ago, at Keridil's urging."

"I must have been drunk."

"You were—both of you; and a disgraceful exhibition you made of yourselves!" Themila laughed at the memory, knowing the while that both Tarod and Keridil had been trying to expunge some emotion in the wake of Jehrek's death that could not be exorcised by normal means. "But that doesn't change the fact that you're listed to meet Rhiman Han in the first horsemanship trials, and to show our honored guests that Initiates are more than pale, withered ascetics!"

"Gods . . ." Tarod sounded disgusted, but in reality Themila's small magic was beginning to work. No one, high or low, could escape the demands of the seven-day-long celebration that would begin with the next sunrise— and maybe such a diversion was what he needed now, far more than either Grevard's pills and potions or the dark machinations of his own mind . . .

He held up both hands in a gesture of defeat. "Very well, Themila, I give you best! I'll retire to my bed, and think no more of reading or study until the festivities are over!"

He kissed her again, on the cheek this time, only just avoiding her lips, and with a mingling of love and concern she watched him leave the library.

There was still something desperately wrong with Tarod.

Themila knew it as certainly as if he were her own flesh and blood, but was no nearer than she had ever been to understanding the truth. Tarod skillfully diverted all her attempts to probe, and—especially since Grevard had pronounced him fit enough to leave his rooms—he had been outwardly so much more content than she could ever remember him that she often wondered whether her misgivings were imaginary. But intuition was an old friend to Themila, and intuition told her that the outward appearance was a mask. Beneath the surface something moved Tarod that she couldn't even begin to comprehend, and in her weaker moments she had to admit that it frightened her. She would gladly have striven to overcome that fear to help him, but until he was ready to speak more openly her hands were tied.

With an effort she recalled her original purpose in coming to the library; a scroll—one of the older historical records that she needed to reread in order to prepare a children's tutorial. Locating it, she tucked it under her arm and walked to the door of the now quiet vault. On the threshold she looked over her shoulder, and memory came back of the night she and Keridil had found Tarod in the grip of insanity in this room. That image—it had been so fleeting as to be almost unreal; but it had happened. And its ramifications were yet, she believed, to be fully faced or understood by anyone. . . .

Shivering, and telling herself it was no more than the chill of approaching autumn, Themila hastened away up the stairs.

Tarod was no longer afraid of sleep, but nonetheless tonight the rest that he knew he needed eluded him. Summer was having a final, defiant fling as it faded, and the air was unusually oppressive. One moon had risen and its light, green and sickly, filtered through the window as he lay in bed—yet he knew that neither the closeness nor the moonlight was responsible for his restlessness.

Tomorrow, the inaugural celebrations for the new High Initiate of the Circle would begin. Seven days that combined complex formal ceremony with an abandoned rejoicing, drawing vast crowds from every part of the land; aristocratic Margraves, religiouses from every Sisterhood Cot, nobles, merchants, traders, peasants . . . every man, woman or child capable of climbing onto a cart or riding a horse would be made welcome, their numbers spilling across the Star Peninsula when the Castle precincts proved insufficient to accommodate them all. The official period of mourning for Jehrek Banamen Toln was over; his son Keridil had faced the final tests and passed them to take his father's place, and everyone now looked to the future.

But Tarod alone knew the truth of how and why Jehrek had died. Grevard had pronounced that the High Initiate's heart had proved unequal to the demands of his calling: Tarod knew better. And while he lay all but helpless in his rooms for nearly two months, chafing against the weakness that hampered him as he slowly recovered, he had had a good deal of time to think back to the vision that had come to him while he was still in the grip of delirium.

Yandros. Still the origins of that name eluded him. He knew it, and yet it came from no known source. But the figure which had confronted him in the dreamlike dimensions of the Marble Hall had been real, tangible; no figment of a twisted imagination but an entity whose existence was in no more doubt than his own.

But what manner of entity? Tarod shifted uneasily, staring towards the square of his window as though looking for inspiration in the cold moonlight. One thing he knew with unshakeable conviction; Yandros was not, and had never been, human.

Yet he had spoken as though a kinship bound them . . .

Tarod forcibly crushed the small inner voice, unwilling to follow such a dangerous speculation. All he could be certain of was that Yandros—whoever, whatever he might be—had kept his word, and with a vengeance. A life for a life . . . and the golden-haired being had wielded a power that took the life of the High Initiate in exchange for Tarod's own.

He hadn't confided his experience to Keridil, and nothing would induce him to do so; the guilt and confusion were still far too strong. He felt that he alone was responsible for Jehrek's death; the conviction tormented him ceaselessly—and yet Yandros had insisted that there was a vital reason why Tarod should live in another man's stead. A destiny, he had called it.

But what manner of destiny? Tarod shuddered with an unnameable trepidation. Yandros wielded a power far beyond the experience of the Circle's highest Adepts—but did that power come from the gods, or from another, darker source?

It was an unanswerable question, and didn't make for pleasant speculation. Tarod thought of the Old Ones, who had ruled the world for countless centuries before their own degeneration had led to their final fall, and of the black gods whom they had worshipped . . . but no. Chaos was gone, banished from existence along with its human marionettes, and no power in the universe could bring them back to this world.

And, whatever the truth about Yandros might be—emissary of Aeoris or otherwise—there was no escaping the fact that he owed the strange being his life. He had pledged himself on oath; and an oath was something that Tarod never broke. Time, Yandros had said, was the key, and in time he would understand. Those words had disturbed an old, old memory which had eluded Tarod even as he grasped for it and since then had obdurately refused to return. Now he felt that he had no choice but to wait until the task which he had been charged to accomplish was revealed to him—but until then he knew that he was sentenced to exist in a kind of semi-limbo. Thoughts of what he might or might not be called upon to do obsessed him, yet every attempt he made to delve deeper into the mystery was thwarted. He had found no clue among the library's shelves, despite the fact that almost every historical and mythological treatise in existence could be found there. And his efforts to penetrate the veil by magical means had also failed—in fact it seemed to him that, though his physical strength had recovered in full measure since his illness, his occult strength was another matter entirely. Doors that had previously been open were suddenly closed to him, and the power that once he had held easily—and often literally—at his fingertips could no longer be summoned in the old way. Night after night he had sat alone in his rooms, striving to invoke the forces which so recently had been child's play to him. Always he failed . . . and always his failure was echoed by a chillingly distant resurgence of that dark, pulsing heartbeat which had come to him in the Marble Hall, and which he associated irrevocably with the influence of Yandros. And if Yandros could hold sway over life or death, it would surely be a small matter for him to manipulate a mere mortal to his desires. . . .

Tarod had never allowed himself to be manipulated in his life—except by Themila, but that was another matter altogether—and his instincts reacted violently to the thought. But he was philosophical enough to realize that as yet he could do nothing to alter the situation; he must simply bide his time.

And meanwhile he might be well advised to take Themila's advice and concentrate on the more mundane matter of the celebrations that lay ahead. He owed another and more personal debt to Keridil, although Keridil didn't know it, and had seen the degree of change which had taken place in his friend since succeeding Jehrek. Keridil felt his responsibilities very acutely whilst still grieving for his father, and the resultant strain was already telling on him. If he could support the new High Initiate in his task, Tarod felt that it was his duty to do so.

He turned over, away from the window, suddenly tired and glad of it. The next seven days might provide the catalyst that the entire Circle needed, and when they were over there would be a period of calm while the Castle community settled into its new pattern. And with that calm might come some of the answers he had been seeking for so long. . . .

The first day of the inaugural celebrations dawned bright and promising, the Sun rising into a clean-washed sky and only a brisk breeze to mark the onset of Autumn. For two days a small army of men—servants, some Initiates and as many of the Castle's children as could escape their lessons—had been working to prepare for the great event, and the grim building was transformed by pennants and streamers that flew from every available window and hung in swathes over the black walls. Official guests from every province had been arriving since dawn, anxious to reach the Castle early and ensure a good view of the proceedings. Following the suggestion of an elderly Council member who remembered his father's inauguration, Keridil had sent out a detachment of armed men to escort the visitors through the mountain pass, and the colorful caravan of wagons and closed carriages had come thundering through the gigantic gateway with seven mounted and caprisoned Initiates at its head.

Every Provincial Margrave in the entire land was present today, each with a retinue of family and servants. Senior Province Councillors had braved the long journey northward, overawed by what was, for the majority, their first sight of the Star Peninsula, and wealthy landowners and merchants had come from as far afield as Prospect Province and the Great Eastern Flatlands. Even the Margrave of Empty Province, the barren north-eastern fastness whose only value was as a breeding ground for milk- and meat-providing herdbeasts and the tough little northern horses, had arrived with his small family, all dressed with the sobriety that befitted their lifestyle.

Only two notables, in fact, were missing from the guest list—the two individuals who, with the High Initiate, made up the ultimate ruling triumvirate of the land. The Lady Matriarch Ilyaya Kimi, absolute head of the Sisterhood of Aeoris, had written in a flowery but unsteady hand from her Cot in Southern Chaun, expressing her deep regrets that arthritis made it impossible for her to undertake the journey and heaping the blessings of the gods upon the new High Initiate. Keridil had never met the elderly Matriarch—who must be at least eighty by now—but knew her by repute as a warm-hearted if faintly eccentric woman who had held her post for some twenty years. And if the Lady Matriarch could not attend in person, she had nonetheless ensured that her Sisterhood would be well represented, to judge from the number of white-robed figures who were making their way towards the Castle.

The third and theoretically most influential member of the triumvirate had also sent a message to Keridil—a stiffly formal and slightly gauche letter that awkwardly expressed all that protocol demanded. Fenar Alacar, the High Margrave, was just seventeen years old, and struggling to become worthy of the hereditary title to which he had succeeded a bare month earlier, when his youthful and vigorous father was killed in a hunting accident. He alone had not been expected to attend the inauguration— the High Margrave, as first ruler of the world, traditionally did not leave his home on the Summer Isle in the far south except in dire emergency; and when the festivities were ended one of Keridil's first duties would be to present himself at the Summer Isle court for final ratification. Until then, Fenar Alacar was and would remain simply a name to which no one had yet put a face.

But although all attention was centered on the nobler guests who arrived at the Castle, the higher ranks were vastly outnumbered by the flood of common folk converging on the Peninsula. Traders had seen an unheard-of opportunity to profit from such a great gathering, and itinerant bands from every part of the country set up makeshift camps on the Peninsula in the hope of selling the goods they had on offer. Along with them came countless numbers of farmers, fishermen, herders, craftsmen, until the entire stack on which the Castle stood was alive with milling humanity.

Among the throng as the first day of the celebrations dawned were several parties of drovers, and one party, led by a burly, middle-aged man with grizzled hair, had settled themselves on the main Peninsula to see what was to be seen. One of their number, a girl dressed in rough men's clothes, slipped away from the group as soon as she prudently could and made her way to the twin cairns that marked the giddying causeway. A young Initiate in formal clothes, with a short cloak thrown over his shoulders against the early morning chill, leaned against one of the stone piles, idly watching the newest arrivals, and he smiled at her as she approached. She nodded shyly back then stopped, lacking the courage to go any further.

To Cyllan, the scene was like something out of a dream. It was one thing to hear stories of the Star Peninsula, but another to actually be here, to see the Initiates' stronghold with its towering cliffs and breathtaking grandeur with her own eyes. From this aspect the Castle itself was invisible, but Cyllan knew from hearsay of the strange barrier that kept it aloof from casual scrutiny. If she could summon the courage to approach the cairns, walk past the sentinel and cross the granite bridge, then she could see the Castle; a privilege that would be something to hold to for as long as she lived. . . .

She admitted to herself, though reluctantly, that she had another motive beyond the simple desire to view the Castle's splendors with her own eyes. A memory that she kept in a secret corner of her mind, of a brief meeting with the tall, black-haired sorcerer whose eyes had hidden so much pain. They had spent such a short time together, but she had not forgotten one moment of the interlude. He had been the first man in her life who had treated her as an equal and a friend, rather than looking upon her either as a potential whore or a nonentity unworthy of notice. She wished that she could see him again . . . and although she nursed no illusions about the possible consequences of a second encounter, at least if she could find her way into the Castle precincts she might catch a glimpse of him. . . .

She was still hovering indecisively in the vicinity of the cairns, and started when, unexpectedly, the young Initiate spoke to her.

"You may cross if you wish to," he said.

Cyllan stared at him, and he added, "The causeway's not that frightening once you've set foot on it."

He had mistaken the reason for her reluctance, and she shook her head. "No—I'm not afraid of the bridge. But I thought . . ." Involuntarily her eyes were drawn to a party of gorgeously dressed women riding by at that moment, and the young man understood.

"There are no barriers today," he told her with a kindly smile. "Anyone may come and go as they please."

"I see. Th-thank you."

His smile broadened. "When you reach the far side, take care to walk through the darker patch in the grass. That's the gateway of the Maze—without it, the Castle's hard to find!"

"I'll remember." She gave him a grateful look which lit her face, making him think that she wasn't as plain as first impressions suggested, then moved between the cairns. As she was about to step on to the causeway a female voice shouted, "You there! Out of the way!"

Four tall and beautifully groomed horses shouldered past, almost knocking her down. The leading pair were ridden by Sisters of Aeoris in white robes and headbands, while two younger girls, both richly dressed but wearing the gauzy white veils that marked them as Novices, followed. One of the girls glanced down at Cyllan and she had a momentary impression of a soft coil of copper-brown hair framing an exquisitely beautiful face whose expression held confidence and arrogance in equal measure. Then the horses were ahead of her, their riders sitting straight-backed and graceful as they trotted across the causeway. Cyllan's mouth twitched once in wry envy, and she started out across the dizzying bridge in the horses' wake.

Although she had never before visited the Star Peninsula, Sashka Veyyil had all the cool composure of good breeding that enabled her to hide the awe she felt at her first sight of the Castle. She loftily ignored the gasps of the other Novice at her side as they passed through the Maze and the vast, ancient structure began to materialize, and kept her eyes sharply focused on the main gateway that lay ahead beyond the milling crowds. They were later arriving than she would have liked, and Sashka silently cursed the elderly Seniors who had accompanied them from the Cot in West High Land and whose dithering had held up the journey. Her parents would be here already, and would no doubt have established for themselves a better view of the inauguration ceremony than she could hope to find, and she regretted her decision to attend as a Novice-Sister rather than a Veyyil of Han Province.

Sashka had entered the Sisterhood less than a year ago, but already her personality was beginning to make its mark. Her father—a Saravin—and her mother—a Veyyil, from whom she took her own name—represented the two most influential clans in their district, and from the day of her birth their only daughter had been destined to raise the family's status to even greater heights. Her entry into the Sisterhood had added another star to their horizon; no longer merely noble, she had become overnight both noble and deeply respected. And the fact that she studied at the West High Land Cot, where Kael Amion was head Senior, added extra weight to her standing.

But for the course of the next seven days Sashka's mind would be on other matters than those normally expected of a Novice Sister. She was nearly twenty years old, and in her home province that was a good age for a girl to be married. The Sisterhood provided no barriers to wedlock— she could easily divide her time between the Cot and a matrimonial home of her own without jeopardizing her studies—but Sashka had set her sights high. And these celebrations in honor of the new High Initiate might provide the ideal opportunity to make the acquaintance of clans who could provide more eligible candidates than had thus far come her way.

They were approaching the gates now, clattering under the cavernous black arch, and Sashka felt a sudden thrill that was half excitement and half unease course through her. Even her carefully nurtured insouciance wasn't proof against her first sight of the vast courtyard, the myriad glittering windows, the titanic spires that soared sickeningly into the brightening sky, remote and aloof, and she swallowed hard against an involuntary gasp. Servants came forward to help her and the other women dismount, and two men bearing the gold badges of Initiates greeted them formally before escorting them towards a corner where a large group of Sisters were already gathered. As Sashka followed them she heard a voice calling her name, and turned to see her father hailing her from a short distance away.

"Sashka! My dearest child!" He embraced her exuberantly. "I set Forvan to keep watch for your arrival. Where are you to be seated?"

Sashka kissed him on both cheeks then indicated the direction in which her companions were being led.

He snorted. "You'll be lost among the rabble over there! Come; your mother and I have a fine vantage point, and you'll be able to see everything perfectly." He clasped her about the waist, hugging her fondly. "And others will be able to see you, which is perhaps more to the point, eh?"

He always understood . . . "Thank you, Father," she said warmly and, without a second glance towards her friends, let him lead her away.

As the sun climbed towards meridian, filling the vast sky with a blood-crimson light, the procession that marked the inauguration of the new High Initiate of the Circle emerged into the courtyard. At its head walked three ranks of dignitaries in tightly formed lines; first, the official representatives of the High Margrave, in full court attire, each holding a gilded staff of office like a sword in front of his face; second, the higher ranking members of the Council of Adepts; third, a file of senior Sisters of Aeoris, all wearing the yellow sash that identified them as direct emissaries of the Matriarch herself. Following these heralds, and feeling more alone than at any moment before in his life, was Keridil, a gold-embroidered cloak on his shoulders and a circlet bearing the High Initiate's insignia on his brow. As he reached the courtyard his gaze flicked briefly across the crowd and he licked his lips nervously; then with an effort he regained his composure and stared steadily ahead. And making up the bulk of the procession came Adepts, Councillors, Margraves and Province Elders, each carefully placed according to rank, moving with slow dignity into the courtyard amid an impressive and almost eerie silence.

The procession slowed to a halt in the great square of the courtyard where the Inaugural Rite would be conducted. The official emissaries turned about, and Keridil stepped

forward to stand facing them, the focus of all attention.
The procedure was simple enough, despite its solemnity.
First, the High Margrave's officers would make a speech
pronouncing the ruler's ratification of the new High Initiate; then the Matriarch's chief representative would give
her blessing, and finally all those who owed allegiance to
the Circle would file past and pledge loyalty and fidelity to
the High Initiate's seal. When all was done, the procession
would move on beyond the Castle so that the throng who
had been unable to squeeze themselves into the embrace of
the black walls could see Keridil for themselves, and
Keridil would lead the entire gathering in a Prayer and
Exhortation to Aeoris.

Themila stood beside Tarod, acutely conscious that being
escorted by a seventh-ranker placed her much further forward in the processional hierarchy than she could otherwise have expected. The trailing hem of her Councillor's
robe—brought out of a trunk and dusted off for this rare
occasion—had almost tripped her twice, and her arm—
which rested in a formal posture on Tarod's arm—already
ached from the strain caused by the differences in their
height. As they negotiated the steps from the main entrance she glanced obliquely at her partner. He was dressed
austerely by comparison to most of his peers and made a
more striking figure because of it—but he looked preoccupied; there was a disquiet in his eyes, a restlessness in his
manner. She let her hand, overlying his, contract a little;
he felt the light touch and looked at her.

Themila smiled. In a whisper perfected during long
sessions in the Council chamber she said, "I think Keridil
will be glad when this part of the celebration is over."

Tarod watched Keridil's broad back for a moment. Already the burdens of responsibility were telling, and he
and Themila were by no means the only ones to have
noticed the change. "Thank the gods it's but a short
ceremony," he murmured. "Once it's done with our new
High Initiate might be allowed to enjoy his position at
last."

"Indeed. But don't you *dare* get him drunk tonight!"

Tarod raised his dark eyebrows in mock chagrin, then

abruptly his expression sobered. "I suspect I'll be too concerned with getting myself drunk to worry about Keridil."

"What?" Themila hadn't heard him clearly.

He smiled at her. "Nothing. Let's concentrate on the ceremony."

The formalities were over. The long speeches had been made, the presentations completed, and the Circle and their guests could at last drop the stiff masks of ritual and begin to relax in preparation for the livelier festivities that lay ahead.

Tonight there would be a banquet in the great hall, followed by music and dancing, and as he moved through the crowd towards the Castle's main door Keridil hoped that the older guests would be willing to take their cue from him and not insist on turning the evening into a stultifying exercise in manners. He needed the chance to unwind a little, forget the rigors of the inauguration. Duty was one thing, but there were limits to the amount of ritual a man could endure and Keridil felt tired and in need of relaxation.

People stopped him at every turn to offer congratulations, and it was some while before he finally reached the main door. When he did he found Tarod leaning against the carved stonework of the entrance, waiting for him.

Keridil clasped his friend's shoulder in a brief gesture of greeting. "Well, the worst part's over." He lifted the circlet to wipe sweat from his forehead. "There'll no doubt be any number of new faces to meet and be polite to tonight, but I should cope with that passably enough, once I've had a cup of wine to fortify me!"

"You've coped magnificently so far, Keridil," Tarod observed. "I was very impressed by your speech outside the gates. Your confidence did you credit."

"From you, that's high praise indeed!" Keridil said malevolently, then laughed. "Seriously though, the confidence was a sham. You can't imagine what it's like standing out there before that vast sea of faces, knowing that every eye is focused on you . . . it's like a public trial."

Yet even as he spoke he remembered how moved he had
been by the experience; the throng of people stretching
almost as far as the eye could see, all eager, all listening,
all wishing him well . . . "I almost forgot the words of the
Exhortation," he admitted in an undertone. "That would
have been a stylish beginning, wouldn't it?"

"But you didn't."

"No. I didn't." Keridil paused for some while, then
sighed. "Tarod, I believe I envy you."

"Envy me? Why?"

"Oh . . . don't mistake me; I'm having no real doubts.
But I'm no longer my own man. From today forward—
until I die—everything that I do must be done for the good
of the Circle, and my own wishes come a very poor
second. It's inevitable, of course, and I accept it; I'm very
proud of the honor. But that doesn't mean I don't—won't—
regret it from time to time."

Not having been privy to Keridil's last conversation
with Jehrek before the old man's death, Tarod didn't
understand the full significance of the remark. Nonetheless, he could sympathize.

"It's not something any man could face with equanimity," he said, staring down at his own hand which played
restlessly on the hilt of his knife, "If I were in your
place—" He shrugged.

"Be thankful you're not!" Then Keridil shook his head.
"No; I'm being unfair. It's just the demands of the day
. . . I'll feel differently about things by morning." Suddenly he smiled. "But that still won't stop me wishing you
were meeting me and not Rhiman Han in the horsemanship
trials tomorrow!"

"You'd win," Tarod said sourly. "You always do."

"Did," Keridil corrected him. "It's beneath the dignity
of the High Initiate to cavort in the arena, so from now on
I'll have to resign myself to being a mere spectator. If
I'd—damn!"

Alerted by the sudden venom in Keridil's voice Tarod
looked over his shoulder. Cleaving determinedly through
the crowd towards them was a thin middle-aged man,

followed by a plump, red-haired girl whom Tarod recognized.

"Inista Jair and her father . . ." Keridil said through clenched teeth. "The two people in this world whom I feel least inclined to meet at the moment . . . forgive me; I'll be on my way before they reach us."

He disappeared hurriedly through the doorway, and Tarod turned and began to move at leisure down the steps. Inista and her father passed close by him; he nodded coolly to the girl and received an uneasy scowl in return.

Towards the gateway the press of people eased a little, although there was still a good deal of two-way traffic through the huge arch. Tarod followed a group of farmers who were leaving the Castle, agog with all they had seen, and emerged onto the smooth grass of the surrounding sward. Here the wind was brisk and refreshing, and the sun, near setting, cast a quiet red glow over the Peninsula and the sea beyond. Booths, tents and stalls were set up in a random jumble, and traders were doing brisk business among those who were staying on to see the festivities. One or two shouted to Tarod as he passed, trying to interest him in wine or food or some trinket or other; he merely shook his head and walked on.

He didn't see the girl at first, and was unaware that she had been watching him for some while. Cyllan's sorcerous talents were small, but when she saw the tall, dark figure emerge from the Castle gate she had used all her will power to make herself merge into the general background, suddenly struck by a wave of fear that, if he did see her, he wouldn't remember her.

Backing away as he drew nearer she collided with the owner of a wine stall, who first swore roundly at her then began exhorting her to try a cup of whatever ungodly brew he was selling. Opening her mouth to refuse, Cyllan suddenly thought better of it and dug into her belt-pouch. She had a few coins from the grudging pittance her uncle paid her to buy food, and nothing better to spend them on. Besides, the wine might boost her courage a little. So she argued the price with the stallholder, beat him down to

what she considered a fair level, and took the brimming
and none too clean cup.

The wine was vilely acrid, but strong. She had forced
herself to take three or four mouthfuls of it when she
sensed someone beside her, and looked up into Tarod's
eyes.

Tarod had been idly investigating the next door booth,
ignoring the holder's persuasions, when he saw the girl in
workmanlike clothes with the strikingly pale hair. Memory
stirred but he couldn't put a name to her, and curiosity
prompted him to move closer. Now she looked into his
eyes, blinked once, and said, "Tarod . . ."

He remembered the slightly husky voice—and an image
of a girl recklessly climbing the sheer cliffs of West High
Land came to his mind. That, and the eerie song of the
fanaani . . . and other things, best forgotten . . .

"Cyllan . . ." Slowly his face broke into a smile, and
the fact that he even recalled her name astounded her. She
returned the smile threefold, and he said, "I didn't think to
see you here."

"Even my irascible uncle wouldn't miss such an opportunity to do business. And I—nothing in the world would
have kept me away from such a great occasion."

He looked faintly surprised, then asked, "What's that
brew you're drinking?"

"Oh . . . I'm not sure. Something the stallholder offered me . . . I wouldn't recommend it."

"May I?" he took the cup, tasted its contents, then spat
and upended the rest onto the grass. "That isn't fit for an
animal!" Turning, he snapped his fingers at the stall-
owner, who was staring at them both with open curiosity.
"You—you're here to sell wine, not poison! Find two
cups of something that merits the name!"

The Initiate's badge on his shoulder was clearly visible,
and the stallholder blanched. Mumbling apologies he produced a jug from under his table and filled two fresh cups,
all the while wondering what in the name of all the gods
an Adept was doing in the company of a drover-girl. He
couldn't summon the courage to ask payment for the wine,

but retired resentfully to the back of his stall as Tarod led Cyllan away.

Discomfited by the display of authority, she didn't speak for a minute or two—until she saw that Tarod was trying not to laugh.

"I'm sorry," he said. "But there are times when a small display of ill-temper raises the spirits . . . besides, I've no patience with dishonesty."

She nodded gravely over the rim of her cup. "Thank you."

"It's nothing. So; how are the drove-roads these days?"

"Little changed. The summer has been kinder than usual; though when winter comes we'll likely move South." Her voice tailed off as she realized that he could hardly be interested in such trivialities. "And what of you?" she asked. "The Spindrift—did it serve your purpose?"

Cyllan didn't quite know what had goaded her to ask such a bold question and was shocked at herself. The wine, on an empty stomach, was making her careless. But Tarod didn't seem offended. Instead, he replied quietly, "Oh, yes. It served. But not quite as I'd intended."

She didn't like to enquire further, but couldn't stop herself from saying, "After that day at West High Land, I—thought about it a great deal. I wondered if—if you might come to harm."

"Harm? Well . . ." Tarod's green eyes flickered with an odd emotion, then his lips twitched ironically. "Not harm, no. Not in any usual sense."

Cyllan had the terrible feeling that either she was making a complete fool of herself, or there was far more behind Tarod's expression than she could ever guess at. Either way she was wading in waters that were too deep for her, and following that thought came a surge of embarrassed misery. Frantically she looked about her, trying to find something in the colorful scene that would provide a welcome change of subject—and saw a thin, ratlike little man with a straggling moustache muscling through the gathering in her direction. He had already seen her, and hastily she drained her cup.

"I must go," she said, glancing apprehensively at the

thin man again. "One of our men is approaching—my uncle must be looking for me . . ."

Tarod assessed and dismissed the drover with a single glance. "Will you be staying for the celebrations?" he asked.

Briefly her amber eyes met his. "I—think so. For a while, at least."

"Then perhaps we'll meet again."

"I hope so . . ." She didn't wait for him to answer, but turned and began to walk quickly away.

"Where have you been?" the scrawny drover's voice barked at her the moment he was in earshot.

Cyllan looked over her shoulder and saw Tarod heading back towards the Castle. "Just looking at the stalls," she said.

"Oh, I see. Lady of leisure now, are you?" His hand snaked out in a cuff that Cyllan, with an old expertise, dodged. "Get back to the tents! There's food to be cooked, and if you think anyone else is doing a woman's work, you can think again!" Suddenly he leered at her as he realized that she was still gazing after the tall, retreating figure of the Initiate. "And you'd better set your sights lower than that, girl," he added scathingly. "They've better whores than you to choose from at the Castle!"

Cyllan flushed and bit back a furious retort. With one final backward glance she turned and followed the drover towards the causeway.

Someone else was watching Tarod with speculative interest as he re-entered the Castle courtyard and walked towards the main door. Thanks to her father's influence Sashka had had a perfect view of the day's proceedings; she had noticed the black-haired man among the procession, and her interest was aroused. When the ceremonies were over she had seen him with the High Initiate, and it was clear that the two men were the best of friends. A few discreet enquiries had revealed his name and the fact that he was a seventh-rank Adept, and Sashka was intrigued. Not only did she find his aura of cool arrogance attractive, but it also seemed that he was influential in the Castle hierarchy.

She would like to meet him, and at the banquet tonight she believed that an introduction would not be difficult to arrange. Furthermore, he might even provide the means to an encounter with the High Initiate himself. . . .

She turned to her father and her slim fingers played fondly on his arm. "Father . . ."

He smiled indulgently, proudly at her. "What is it, my love?"

"Father, will you do something for me? As a great favor? Tonight, at the feast . . . ?"

Chapter 9

"And so my friends, fellow Adepts, good sisters and sirs—" Keridil paused to allow his gaze to roam across the assembly, and smiled with faintly diffident hesitation. "It only remains for me to thank you, in all humility, for the kindness and good wishes that have been showered on me today. My gratitude for the honor that you do me is something I cannot express in words, but I solemnly pledge that I will do all within my power to justify your faith in me. I hope and pray that I will prove worthy of you. Thank you, my friends—and may Aeoris bless you one and all."

The applause as the High Initiate concluded his speech was as properly sober as the occasion demanded, yet the warmth of his reception was unmistakable. With youth and an ingenuous charm on his side, reinforced by Jehrek's rigorous schooling, Keridil was finding—much to his own surprise—that his popularity was assured from the beginning. He had misgivings still, but the day's events had done much to boost his flagging confidence.

As he moved from his seat at the high table in the Castle's dining hall and the applause died away, a group of musicians positioned in the gallery at the far end of the hall struck up the first notes of a formal set dance. Keridil looked about him for a moment, then held out a hand to Themila Gan Lin and led her onto the floor. They moved with stately grace between the twin ranks of watchers, then when they had completed one circuit of the room others began gradually to join in, until the hall was filled with a motley of dancing couples, gowns swirling, jewels glinting in the light of the great banks of candles and torches.

From his own place at the high table Tarod watched the dancing, a slight smile on his face. It had been his suggestion that the High Initiate should choose Themila as his partner for the all-important first set; a diplomatic move designed to ensure that no noble family with an eye to the future could claim their own eligible daughter had been slighted in favor of another. He had also thus far succeeded in fending off the advances of Simik Jair Sangen, Inista's father, contenting the landowner with the assurance that there would be time in plenty to speak with the High Initiate at a later stage. And there had been others, anxious to secure an audience and viewing Tarod, who was known to be Keridil's close companion, as their surest potential ally.

Tarod found the flattery, machination and occasional outright bribery intensely irritating. So far he had kept his quick temper under control, aware that he would do nothing to help Keridil by losing it, but his patience was running out. Not for the first time he gave silent thanks that he had resisted the temptation ever to embroil himself in the politics of the Circle; whatever status a high office might have brought him, the sacrifices would have been more than he could stand.

Suddenly he became aware of a presence at his side. He turned reluctantly, steeling himself for yet another encounter with an importuning father—and was surprised to find himself looking into the candid brown eyes of a woman younger than himself.

She smiled, and tossed back the fine, translucent veil

she wore so that he could see her face clearly. A Novice-Sister—and she was beautiful. Despite his tendency to asceticism Tarod was as susceptible as any man to feminine beauty, and this girl appealed to him in a way that could never be matched by the lovely but somehow insipid females with whom he had had passing—and usually very brief—affairs. There was something challenging in her expression, a pleasingly willful tilt to her chin; she carried her tall, graceful frame with a confidence that suggested she was accustomed to commanding and seeing her wishes carried out. He smiled back, and inclined his head courteously.

"May I be of service to you?"

At close quarters, Sashka thought, he was more formidable than he had seemed from a distance; the easy grace made faintly intimidating by his unusual height and by the unremitting steadiness of his green eyes. Nonetheless, something about him—an aura, her Sister-Tutor would have termed it—quickened her pulse in a way that intrigued and excited her. He was very attractive; and there were depths to his nature, she surmised, that would warrant exploration by a woman who had the necessary courage. Sashka believed that courage was a quality which she was far from lacking, and her initial goal of persuading Tarod to grant her an introduction to the High Initiate began to seem less urgent.

She decided to match Tarod's cool confidence rather than pretend to demureness, and indicated the solemnly dancing couples. "I saw that you had no dancing partner, my lord. I, too, find myself in the same predicament, and so I wondered if you might do me the honor of escorting me."

Her voice was a warm contralto, and Tarod found himself disarmed by her bluntness. Her invitation—in itself a flagrant breach of protocol—was so charmingly and unashamedly put that he could only hold out his arm for her to take.

"A great pleasure, lady."

They moved onto the floor, and the formation parted fractionally to allow them to take their place. The girl was an accomplished dancer, reinforcing Tarod's initial impression that her clan could afford to indulge the social graces, and although normally he had little interest in such forms of leisure he was surprised to find after a few minutes that he was enjoying the dance.

Keridil, still partnering Themila, passed them twice and on both occasions caught Tarod's eye with an enquiring look which Tarod returned impassively. At last the music ended, the dancers politely applauded, and Tarod and Sashka crossed to an empty table at one side of the hall, under a tall window. Huge torches had been lit in the courtyard outside and the light, diffused by the half-opaque glass, cast a glow over the girl's hair and added a soft sheen to her skin as she took the chair he pulled out for her.

"Thank you, my lord," she said, still using the formal mode of address but giving him a challenging, promising look as she did so. "I was beginning to fear that I'd spend the evening as a neglected stranger at my father's side!"

He smiled, amused. "This is your first visit to the Castle?"

"Yes . . . I've heard a great deal of it, of course. But nothing that could compare with the reality." She glanced about her at the lights, the colors, the movement, then cast her eyes down self-deprecatingly. "I'll confess I feel more than a little out of my depth."

Tarod signalled to a passing servant and took a flagon and two cups. "I've always found wine to be a good remedy for uncertainty. May I?"

"Thank you." She waited while he poured, then they raised their cups and touched the rims lightly together. The girl sipped, and nodded with approval. "A good vintage. Southern Chaun—is it the last but one season?"

"It is. I congratulate you on your knowledge."

She laughed, showing perfectly even teeth. "Oh, it's something instilled in me since childhood! My father owns a number of vineyards in Han Province, and we have always envied the climate and land conditions of Southern Chaun."

"But you've shown no wish to follow your father's

inclination?'' He reached out, and one finger lightly brushed the veil she wore.

She smiled. ''It's hardly a woman's place—not in Han, anyway. My clan deemed it more fitting that I should join the Sisterhood.''

He found it hard to imagine this girl bending the knee to the wishes of anyone, unless they coincided with her own. . . . ''And you?'' he asked.

''Oh, I'm more than content with that. To be a Sister is a highly-prized accomplishment—especially at the West High Land Cot.''

''West High Land? Then you're under the tutelage of Kael Amion—''

Sashka was surprised and impressed to hear her companion speaking so casually of the woman who was, to the Novices under her wing, only one stage removed from a deity. ''I don't know the Lady personally, of course; not to speak to—but yes, she is our highest Senior.'' Suddenly anxious not to allow herself to look small in his eyes, she straightened her back. ''I am Sister-Novice Sashka Veyyil, daughter of Frayn Veyyil Saravin.''

Tarod raised an eyebrow. He was aware of the influence of the clan Saravin—little wonder that a Saravin daughter had gained a place with Kael Amion. Yet although Lady Kael's standards were known to be high, he could detect little if any of the latent talent of a Sister in Sashka; and with faint irony remembered the almost painful feyness of the drover-girl, Cyllan, whose lowly background had effectively barred her from putting her natural talents to any good use. . . .

The train of thought was interrupted by Sashka's well-modulated voice. ''Well, sir, now you have the advantage of me. You know my name, but I don't know yours.''

He met her eyes. ''I am Tarod.'' And when she waited for him to say more, he added, ''seventh-rank Initiate of the Circle.''

''Just 'Tarod'? What of your clan name?''

Tarod smiled thinly. ''I have no clan name.''

A highest echelon Adept, who chose not to reveal his clan . . . Sashka was doubly intrigued, her imagination stirred by all manner of pleasant speculations. She was about to ask a carefully formulated question that might persuade him to reveal more about his background when they were interrupted.

"Sashka—so there you are; I've been searching for you." Frayn Veyyil Saravin took his daughter's arm and looked speculatively and not approvingly at Tarod, recognizing the Initiate's badge but uncertain of the tall man's rank. "Good evening to you, sir."

Sashka, freeing herself, made frantic surreptitious gestures designed to drive her father away, but he ignored them. Tarod regarded the portly man until the eyes under their beetling brows looked aside uncertainly, then replied coolly, "Sir."

Frayn cleared his throat noisily and spoke up to make himself heard above the music that was just beginning again. "You weren't dancing earlier, Sashka—thought you might like to partner me—"

"I was dancing, Father," Sashka said, trying to keep her voice even through furiously clenched teeth. "The Initiate saw that I had no partner, and kindly offered to escort me."

"Hm, yes. Considerate of him. Considerate of you, sir; I thank you. But now, Sashka, you'll indulge an old man. . . ."

She had to acquiesce if she was to avoid an embarrassing scene. Composing her face she turned to Tarod once more and bowed in the manner of the Sisters. "Thank you, Tarod. I hope I may see you again before the evening is out."

She was determined to have the last word despite her father's obvious chagrin, and Tarod met her gaze with an answering flash of amused approval. He took her hand briefly. "I have no doubt of it."

Frayn Veyyil Saravin led his daughter onto the floor with almost undignified haste, and as they took their position in the dance formation he hissed apoplectically, "Not dancing indeed! I've never seen such cavalier disregard for common decorum in all my life! I'm ashamed of you!"

"Ohh, Father . . ."

"Don't 'Oh Father' me, girl! To walk boldly up to a stranger without introduction, to accept his invitation without so much as a by-your-leave, and then to sit indulging in an idle flirtation in full view of the entire assembly—"

"He is the High Initiate's closest friend!" Sashka retorted in a harsh whisper. "And if you hadn't been so tardy in keeping your promise to introduce me to him—"

"Aeoris preserve us, d'you think I'm a miracle-worker? These things take time, Sashka! Besides—" Frayn fumbled for the right words; he had no wish to upset his daughter, but what he had observed had sounded warning bells in his mind. "Besides, I thought it was Keridil Toln himself you wished to meet?"

She glanced obliquely at him, and smiled sweetly. He had seen that look before, and knew all too well what it meant. "The High Initiate has many other would-be claimants, Father," she said softly. "I'm not sure that I like the thought of jostling for position in a long queue. It's undignified."

So that was where the land lay . . . he had feared as much. "If that's your feeling, then you could take your pick from a thousand or more, Sashka! But not that one—he has a dangerous look that I don't like."

"He is also a seventh-rank Adept." She waited for the information to take effect and was gratified to see her father's stern disapproval waver. "Seventh . . . ?"

"Yes. And he's only a few years older than I am—which means he has a great future before him. The clan could fare a good deal worse."

"Gods, girl, you're not thinking—"

"I'm thinking nothing, Father, not yet. But I would like to meet with him again."

Frayn knew he was defeated. Since she was a tiny child Sashka had been able to manipulate him as though he were clay in her hands; if she wanted to investigate the possibilities of an alliance with the tall, black-haired Adept then he would be powerless to stop her. And if the man was seventh rank, he had to admit that there could be potential in the liaison. . . .

"Come, Father." She squeezed his hands, smiling brilliantly and utterly disarming him. "This is a celebration. Don't frown at me—let's enjoy the dance, and let the future take care of itself for a while!"

". . . It's a growing problem, High Initiate, and I don't mind admitting that our resources are sorely stretched in trying to stem the tide." The Margrave of Prospect Province grimaced and shook his greying head, staring down at his own silver-buckled shoes. "During the last two moonphases our towns and villages have suffered no less than five brigand raids—and that's not counting any incidents which may not have reached my ears. It's almost as if all the diverse bands have formed themselves into some kind of organization . . . or that some outside force is motivating them."

Keridil saw Tarod's quick frown and, glancing at him, nodded almost imperceptibly. The old Margrave's words had rung a disquieting bell in the intuitive depths of his mind, and Tarod's like feeling came as no surprise. He had already heard reports from two other provinces of the sudden and inexplicable increase in the activities of brigand groups. Trading caravans plundered; farmers' and herders' livestock decimated; small, remote villages raided and crops burned in the fields . . . it threatened to assume the proportions of an epidemic. And there seemed to be no rhyme or reason behind it; no emergence of a leader under whom the bands were uniting. The widely scattered outlaw bands had apparently increased their activities independently of each other, yet with a timing that suggested they were acting in concert. It had to be more than coincidence.

"We protect the province folk as best we can, of course," the Margrave went on, sounding tired. "But we have only a limited number of volunteers at our disposal at any one time, and fewer still skilled men-at-arms to train them." His dark eyes met Keridil's briefly, and Keridil recognized the appeal in them—he had already encountered it twice tonight. "If it were possible for a small number of Initiates, no more than two or three, to be amongst our numbers . . . the ability of the Castle's swordsmen is legendary . . ."

Keridil sighed, wishing that he could do more than

merely repeat the answer he had already given to the Margraves of Empty Province and the Great Eastern Flatlands. "Their abilities, sir, are unfortunately confined only to combat in the arena. Maybe if we were to look back through the records we'd find a time when Initiates had a role to play as enforcers of law as well as its champions, but," he smiled wryly, "our lands have been at peace for so long now that the role couldn't apply even should we wish it."

"Nonetheless, the mere presence of men of the Circle—"

"Would do a good deal less to frighten a band of determined brigands than either you or I might wish," Keridil said. He felt frustrated by his inability to offer the man anything beyond advice and comfort; words would not remove Prospect's troubles, but they were all he had. After a moment or two he added, "I will, however, bring the matter personally to the attention of the High Margrave when we meet."

"Of course . . . you'll be journeying to the Summer Isle when the celebrations are over . . ." The old man nodded, trying to make the best of it. "Well, High Initiate, I thank you for listening to me. I hadn't wanted to sour the festivities with our provincial problems, but—"

"You've done no such thing—I'm indebted to you for drawing my attention to it."

The Margrave turned to go, but Tarod suddenly spoke up. "The brigands, Margrave—are they the sole source of trouble in Prospect?"

The Margrave paused. "I'm sorry, I don't quite take your meaning . . ."

"I wondered, sir, if you had experienced an equally sudden increase in other forms of mischief." He glanced at Keridil. "Something came to my ears earlier this evening, and our own experience bears it out . . . Margrave, has the incidence of Warps been increasing?"

The old man licked his lips. "Now that you mention it . . . these past months—since the death of the old High Initiate, in fact, if you'll pardon me, sir—yes; there have been several Warps." He shivered abruptly. "They are something which one prefers to put out of one's mind as quickly as possible, and so I didn't think. . . . but surely there can be no possible connection between the two?''

"No direct connection, no," Tarod agreed. "But I wonder if the sudden increase in both could be an indication of something which we're as yet unaware of."

He was conscious of Keridil's keen stare, but the Margrave's expression was unhappily blank.

"If there is a connection, sir, then Aeoris help us all!" he said feelingly. "But I confess the idea of it is beyond me!"

As soon as the old man had taken his leave, Keridil turned on Tarod.

"You've told me nothing of these suspicions of yours."

"How could I? I hadn't heard the tales of the brigands before tonight. But now that I have, if I add them to our own recent experiences here at the Castle then I have a recipe which I don't like, Keridil. There's something afoot, and the smell of it sticks in the nostrils."

"Logic surely dictates that there can be no conceivable connection between the Warps and brigand attacks, Tarod."

"Damn logic!" Tarod said sharply, then lowered his voice, aware that people in the immediate vicinity were listening. "Logic is for the likes of the Margrave of Prospect—and that's well and good; no one expects him to explore beyond the bounds of what he can touch and hear and see. But we're supposed to transcend such restrictions—or are we beginning to forget our true purpose?"

"That's nonsensical—"

"Is it, Keridil?" Tarod's green eyes glittered dangerously. "Or are we all deluding ourselves, here in our stronghold, with none to question us or judge us or find us wanting? Three Margraves have asked the circle's aid tonight, and what have we been able to offer them? Nothing! We're impotent! Gods, perhaps the old man was right—perhaps we'd serve this land better as a force of mercenaries than we do as a community of sorcerers!"

Though he tried not to show it Keridil was stung by the condemnation, not least because it echoed his own frustrations. The frequency of the Warp storms was something that had deeply troubled Jehrek—and since his death the incidences had increased sharply. Yet the Circle's best efforts had brought them no nearer to understanding the reasons for the sudden change that seemed to be infecting the world, let alone its source. Tarod, however, was the first to voice the unease that had been growing in the marrow of Keridil's bones.

"I know as well as you do what our sorcery has—or perhaps rather has not—achieved lately," he said quietly, meeting Tarod's gaze with candid eyes. "Do you have a better answer?"

Tarod sighed. "Before one can form an answer, one first has to know the nature of the question."

"Exactly. The gods alone know there's something afoot, something wrong. We've both heard the evidence of it tonight, if we needed confirmation. It's been hanging over us like a storm on the horizon, and since my father died—"

"I know." Tarod forced down the thought that had occurred to him too many times of late. Like Keridil he was sceptical about coincidence, and the fact that these disturbing events had gathered strength and intensity since the old High Initiate's passing was far from reassuring. Though he told himself time and again that there could surely be no link, he could not forget that bizarre, delirium-haunted encounter with the being called Yandros. . . .

He started as Keridil suddenly clapped him on the shoulder. "Tarod, this is neither the time nor the place to speculate. When the next seven days are over, I'm due to travel to the Summer Isle to pay my respects in person to the High Margrave. If I can impress on him the gravity of the problems in the provinces, we may at least make some move towards solving the situation on an exoteric level."

"The High Margrave's little more than a child."

"Nonetheless he still embodies temporal power. And I've heard that he has a reputation for intelligence, if not experience. It's the best I can do for the Margravates at present."

"And the Warps?" Tarod asked softly.

"Ah, the Warps . . . that's another matter, isn't it? I may be High Initiate, Tarod, but I'm realist enough to acknowledge that as a sorcerer I'm a babe in arms by comparison to you. And if you have no answers, then the Circle is as impotent as you say.''

Tarod looked away, but before he did Keridil saw something in his friend's eyes that he could only interpret as pain. In an undertone, he added, ''Don't distress yourself. Greater minds than ours have wrestled with the nature of the Warps for generation upon generation, and failed. There's no ignominy in that. And the frustration's something we've all learned to live with.'' From an anteroom a burst of laughter broke out, followed by the sounds of musical instruments being tuned. ''Listen—'' Keridil said. ''There are some who are determined to see the night through in more entertainment. Aeoris knows I've all but lost sight of the fact that today is intended as a celebration; but it's not too late to remedy that. Let's join the guests, Tarod. If we can forget for a while, the picture may seem less bleak by morning.''

Tarod regarded him briefly, then shook his dark head. ''Keridil, I'm sorry. You're right; we are here to celebrate, and I'm at fault for letting other things take too strong a hold.'' He smiled as from the adjacent room someone began to play a manzon, the long-necked, seven-stringed instrument that demanded a high degree of musical ability. The player was skilled, and moments later a woman's voice joined in with an old, haunting song that Tarod knew well. Without a further word he clapped Keridil on the shoulder and the two men moved towards the room.

As they entered the dimly lit chamber, Tarod wished profoundly that he could rid his mind of the doubts and fears that plagued him, and which had been at the root of his unease tonight. He hadn't intended to burden Keridil with his suspicions today of all days, but somehow the words had been out before he could stop them. And over and beyond the evidence which he had heard tonight from the Margraves there was an inner conviction of something savagely, terribly wrong which refused to be shaken. Try as he might he couldn't defy the feeling; nor could he counter the certainty that recent events were inextricably linked with Yandros's strange prediction concerning the quest which he would be called upon to fulfill.

Frustration welled in him and he clenched both hands, feeling the contours of his ring dig sharply into his left palm. He sensed and suspected so much, yet knew nothing—and the long days of waiting for some sign, some move from whatever power Yandros wielded was becoming almost more than he could bear.

Abruptly he pinched the bridge of his nose between finger and thumb. He was tired, and the gesture was an attempt to banish weariness as well as the unpleasant trains of thought. He hadn't been attending to the music or his surroundings, but as the song ended he was surprised by the strength of the applause that followed, and realized that the room was quite crowded. Keridil was clapping enthusiastically, lending his voice to the chorus that called for more, and for the first time Tarod looked towards the small space in the center of the room where the impromptu performers sat. The manzon-player was hunched over his instrument making fine adjustments to the tuning, and the low candlelight, catching and winking on a single small gold spear that hung from one ear, marked him as Ranil Trynan, son of one of the Castle stewards. How he had inveigled his way into such a company was a mystery, but his skills as a musician opened doors that would otherwise be barred to him, and when he finally looked up the smile on his thin, sly face showed that he considered himself in his natural element.

Yet despite Ranil's obvious satisfaction it was the singer at his side who drew the more attention. For a few moments Tarod didn't recognize the tall young woman with the soft contralto voice, for she had changed her gown and cast off the Sister-Novice's veil. Then she looked up, and Sashka's dark brown eyes met his gaze with a challenge that he remembered from their earlier encounter.

Tarod's lips curved in a cool smile, and he was gratified to see her blush in response. Then she made an imperious gesture to Ranil and the young musician played the opening chords of a song that was currently popular in West High Land; a complex melody demanding the utmost from player and vocalist alike. Sashka began to sing, and one or two of the more knowledgeable among the listeners immediately applauded her courage at attempting such a difficult piece. Tarod felt the music soothing his ruffled emotions; half closing his green eyes he allowed it to take a hold of his mind, carrying him along with the rest of the audience, until Keridil's voice in his ear broke the reverie.

"She sings sweeter than anyone I've heard in many a long month . . . is she a bard, I wonder?"

Without thinking, Tarod shook his head. "No. She's a Novice, from the West High Land Cot."

"Oh, yes . . ." Keridil grinned. "Now I've placed her—she's the one you were dancing with after the banquet ended. I compliment you on your good taste, Tarod. What is her name?"

Aware that Keridil was good-naturedly trying to embarrass him, Tarod returned the grin with an utterly impassive stare. "Sashka Veyyil."

"Not the Veyyil Saravins?" The High Initiate raised his eyebrows. "Then she's a catch, right enough!" He paused. "And beautiful, too . . . there's a rare look about her; as if she could present a challenge to any man." His tone was wry as he added, "She's a far cry from the Inista Jairs of this world."

"Yes," said Tarod non-committally.

Keridil was silent for a while as they both listened to the music. Then, in a slightly different undertone, he said, "It would be unwise to cross her clan. They're very influential."

Tarod frowned, glancing at him. There had been something in Keridil's voice that hinted at jealousy, and that was unlike him.

"I've no intention of crossing them," he said. "Gods, I only encountered the girl for the first time this evening!"

"Nonetheless, she's singing this song for you and you alone—I can see it in her eyes," Keridil countered. "I suspect that any light affair with that one could lead to trouble."

A cold anger rose in Tarod, and his eyes glittered as he looked at the other man. Keridil's uncharacteristic sour envy rankled, and he took even less kindly to the implication that his own ethics were under scrutiny.

"I imagine the lady's of age and can decide her own preferences," he said icily. "Although, of course, if you feel that my reputation's dubious it's obviously your solemn duty to warn her against me. That is, if you think that she'll be deterred by it."

Before Keridil could answer, he had brushed past and was making his way through the crowded room towards the window, from where he would have a better vantage point. Sashka's gaze followed him, and when she thought she had caught his eye she allowed her expression to break into a sweet, hesitant smile.

"Sashka." Tarod took the girl's hand and bowed over it. "Thank you for your singing. You've changed what would otherwise have been a dull and dreary occasion into something that I'll cherish."

Even as he spoke he was surprised to find the compliment coming so easily and so genuinely. He had always been capable of playing the courtier but rarely chose to do so; when he did, a cynical part of his mind was well aware that the words were a glib means to a purely self-indulgent end. Yet somehow, faced by this girl with her patrician face and candid eyes, he could do nothing other than speak the truth. In the space of two brief meetings she had had a profound effect on him, and the resulting sense of vulnerability was something Tarod was unused to.

Sashka lowered her gaze, allowing only a small part of her delight to show in her expression. "Thank you. But I fear I'm badly out of practice—my studies don't allow a great deal of time for other pleasures."

"You underestimate your talent." He was still holding her hand, and from the corner of his eye caught a glimpse of Keridil watching them from across the room. The night's entertainment was finally over and the revellers drifting away to their beds, though a few diehards still sat drinking and talking quietly near the banked-down fire. Sashka's father was not in evidence, nor any senior Sisters, and Sashka herself showed no wish to leave.

"I had hoped," she said softly, "that I might have danced with you again tonight. But it seemed you were too busy to rescue me a second time."

He smiled thinly. "In the face of your father's disapproval? I wouldn't incur the wrath of a Veyyil Saravin!"

"Oh, that . . ." Sashka had the good grace to flush slightly. "You mustn't mind his manner—he was simply annoyed with me because he had planned to introduce me to your High Initiate and I was nowhere to be found."

Involuntarily, Tarod glanced at the place where Keridil had been standing, but the other man had moved away. A flicker of the old anger returned and he replied coolly, "If that was what you wished, you need only have asked."

"I didn't say it was what I wished." Now Sashka's eyes issued an unmistakable challenge. "And I think I'm of an age to make my own decisions in such matters."

The anger faded and vanished, and Tarod laughed gently. "Lady, I wouldn't dream of doubting it!"

"Then perhaps we might resume what was so abruptly curtailed earlier?"

Tarod was aware that this girl was using her charm and skill to maneuver him, but her wiles hardly seemed to matter. He had a powerful desire to touch her, push his hands through the heavy masses of copper-brown hair, taste her, explore her, find out what true manner of woman hid beneath the beauty and the guile. It was a heady sensation, new to him, and he wasn't sure how best to react to it.

Sashka, however, had no doubts. Her second meeting with the tall, dark Adept had more than confirmed the first impressions she had formed, and now that she had another opportunity to express her interest without family interference she was determined to make the most of it. Seeing Tarod hesitate at her blunt question, she added, pitching her voice very low, "My father and mother are long abed, but I couldn't sleep if I tried. I am too . . . stimulated."

The words were ambiguous to say the least, and Tarod smiled, taking her hand once again. "So how may I entertain you?"

She made a small shrug that somehow conveyed far

more than was obvious on the surface. "I should like to walk for a while," she said. "It's such a fine night . . . I've heard that there are many hundreds of people camped beyond the Castle walls. Their fires must be a spectacular sight."

The tiredness that Tarod had felt earlier was suddenly as far from his mind and body as it could have been. He gestured towards the door, through which the last of the guests were gradually departing. "Then if I may escort you . . . ?"

She smiled mischievously. "With or without my father's permission?"

"Your permission is all that matters to me."

"Then you have it." Aware of a swiftly growing inner excitement, Sashka allowed him to lead her out into the low-lit corridor.

Chapter 10

Under the eerie double-zenith of the two moons, Tarod and Sashka stood together on the high Castle rampart, gazing out at the scene that lay spread before them. Keridil had ordered the Maze to be opened for the remainder of the festivities, suspending the supernatural barrier between the stack and the world beyond, and the distant contours of the stark coastline were dimly visible under a pewter-dark sky.

Far below them, so far that they looked as unreal as a child's toys, the tents of those who had made camp on the Peninsula were scattered in clusters, illuminated by the sparking light of more than a hundred small fires. The patterns of firelight stretched away on the far side of the causeway, and very faintly, on a rare inland breeze, came snatches of sound which suggested that in some quarters revels still continued.

Sashka stared down for a long time without speaking. She was thrilled by the sense of glorious supremacy that standing on this tremendous height gave her; but for the Castle's four titanic and brooding spires, which dwarfed even the ramparts and which she preferred not to look at, she might have been poised on the very roof of the world. Carefully, not wanting to break the spell of the night, she stole a glance at the man beside her. The moonlight hardened the angles of his profile, putting her in mind of a bird of prey; the wind lifted his hair back from his face and his eyes were unquiet. Sashka moved a step closer to him, allowing her sleeve to brush against his hand as he did so.

He looked at her—somehow she had the feeling that he'd forgotten her existence—then the illusion fled as he smiled.

"Does the sight fulfill your expectations?" he asked.

"Threefold . . ." She drew a deep, satisfied breath. "It's so peaceful—I'd dearly love to live in this place, and have such a view at my disposal whenever the mood took me."

He nodded towards the black bulk of the south spire, a bare few steps from where they stood. "The vista's better still from the very top. Would you like to see?"

"No—" The refusal was hasty, and accompanied by an involuntary shiver. "No, I—I think not. I'm content where I am." She moved again, this time standing a little in front of him and presenting a shoulder half bared by the low-cut neck of her gown. Moments later a hand came lightly to rest on her skin and she closed her eyes momentarily with the satisfaction of another small triumph, another step in the direction she wanted to take. Tarod's hand was thin but immensely powerful, she noticed; the ring on his index finger caught the nacreous light and magnified it, making her want to reach out and touch the stone. She forced herself to stay passive, only tilting her head back a little in unspoken invitation.

Tarod gazed down at her slim figure, aware of emotions stirring within himself that he'd never known before. In spite of her guile, which she made little effort to hide, Sashka had affected him deeply and he felt more and more helpless against the tide of his own feelings. A still, small inner voice urged him to caution, but he was fast approaching a point where he knew he would throw caution to the winds for her sake. He was captivated . . . and as he leaned towards her, his lips experimentally touching her hair, he knew that in all his life he had never wanted anything as much as he wanted this beautiful, mercurial girl.

How long they stayed there under the night sky, what they said, what either thought, Tarod couldn't later remember. An eternity seemed to pass until the moment when he found himself leading her slowly back towards the steep steps that wound down into the courtyard. As they passed under the spire its gigantic finger blotted out the moons and cast the way into dense shadow. Sashka stumbled against him and his hands closed about her waist; she turned in his grasp, her face an indistinct oval, and then he was kissing her with an intensity that shocked him. For a moment only she stood very still, as if frozen—then she returned the intensity with a passion of her own, hands clawing and clasping at his shoulders with an almost animal desire.

Suddenly she broke away. Her eyes, wide with emotion, met his and she stepped back, gently freeing herself altogether.

"I—must go . . ." she said incoherently. "It's late, Tarod—I must go!"

"Sashka—"

She didn't wait. Already she had turned, and was half-running towards the stairs. It was a few moments before Tarod's confusion allowed him to follow, and when he reached the top of the flight she was halfway down, hurrying recklessly towards the torchlit courtyard. Near the foot of the steps she paused, looked back—and he thought that she raised a hand either to wave or to blow him a kiss. Then she was gone.

Even the most determined celebrants had finally given up their singing and dancing, stumbling away to the shelter of their tents or simply sleeping where they happened to fall, and at long last the Star Peninsula was utterly silent save for the faint murmur of the sea hundreds of feet below the granite cliffs.

Cyllan woke suddenly and unexpectedly, to find herself wrapped in the folds of her one blanket, her head pillowed on a tussock of grass. For a moment, as the last vestiges of what must have been a dream fled from her mind, she couldn't remember where she was—and then recollection returned.

From this angle she could see the Castle and the lights that still glowed within. It must be deep night; the two moons were moving towards the horizon now, the smaller seeming to balance upon its greater twin, and a single gaunt shadow reached out from the distant structure.

Cyllan sat up, rubbing chilled arms. Something was tugging at a part of her mind; something disturbing and unhappy, and she looked quickly around her but found nothing untoward. She had elected to sleep outside tonight rather than share the noisome tent with her uncle and his drunken drovers, and by now they would be dead to the world—nothing to fear there. What, then?

She thought back over the night's events. Earlier she had managed to slip away a second time and had returned to stand outside the Castle walls, listening to the distant strains of music as the noble company continued their festivities. She had wondered if she might see Tarod again, but not even a servant had emerged through the gate, and finally she had given up her vigil and returned to the camp where she made herself as comfortable as she could and fell asleep through sheer exhaustion while the carousing continued all around her.

But sleep was a world away now. She had dreamed, that much she knew, and in the dream had been a warning. Cyllan had long ago learned to trust auguries of all kinds, and the fact that this one now refused to reveal its nature disturbed her. *Something* was wrong—and she couldn't rest until she knew what it was.

Moving with slow caution she sat up, pushing off the blanket and pausing a moment or two to make sure that there was no sign of life from the drovers' tent. When she was satisfied, she felt in a small leather pouch which she wore at her waist, concealed under her stained jerkin, and drew out a handful of small, blue-grey stones worn to an almost gemlike smoothness by the sea. She had gathered them on the grim beaches of the Great Eastern Flatlands and they never left her possession; they were a focus for the small power which she had learned to wield in her most secret moments, and if anything could solve this conundrum, the stones might provide the answer she sought.

Stealthily, Cyllan crept towards the cliff edge where no tents were pitched. She had no sand, but the soil here was thin and gravelly and might do almost as well. Finding a patch where no grass grew, she crouched facing north-ward and smoothed the earth as best she could into a rough circle, before grasping the stones tightly in her clenched fists and willing her mind to free itself from the confines of the mundane and enter a different world; a world where all things were possible. For a few minutes she feared that the old skill would fail her . . . then a tingling sensation at the nape of her neck told her that her consciousness was slowly, subtly beginning to change.

Odd colors swirled beyond Cyllan's closed lids; she felt a presence before her that she knew was illusory but to which she nonetheless held fast. The stones in her hands shifted as though alive and, judging her moment, she cast them onto the bare ground.

They fell into a pattern that was unfamiliar to her—she sensed it even before she opened her eyes and saw with her physical senses. One—the largest—lay alone at the very center, while the others scattered outward in a rough, eccentric seven-armed spiral. As she stared at the stones Cyllan felt a sudden and violent resurgence of the fear generated by her dream, but still the source of it eluded her, and try as she might she couldn't recapture even the bones of the nightmare. There was only one other course she might take, and she closed her eyes once more, letting her hands move slowly until they were spread, palms down, over the pattern of fallen stones. Her own shallow breathing reverberated in her head; then through her splayed fingers she began to sense a faint, measured pulse. It was as if she were making contact with the very heartbeat of the land, drawing on its power to add to her own, to feel her way towards the goal she sought.

Gradually then an image began to take form in her inner vision. At first it was too indistinct to make sense, but as the pulse in the depths of her consciousness strengthened, so the image strengthened with it. The real world was fading, all awareness of the cold and the wind and the hard ground gone, so that Cyllan felt as though she hung suspended in a strange and unpredictable limbo.

With startling abruptness the astral image before her suddenly focused. She seemed to be looking through a dimly defined window, into a room lit only by a torch that burned sluggishly low in a bracket on the wall. Two people stood in the room, close together; a woman with long, rich auburn hair, and a man, much taller, dark, somehow familiar . . .

Cyllan's stomach lurched with a sick hopelessness as she recognized Tarod's lean frame. If this was a true vision—and she had no reason to believe otherwise—then it had turned her own fantasies to ashes.

Yet reason, struggling to break through the sharp sliver of pain, reminded her that the ominous sensation that had woken her tonight had nothing to do with her own half-formed desires—it had been a portent, and one which rendered any personal feelings insignificant and meaningless. Biting her lip, Cyllan forced herself to concentrate on the tableau before her inner eye, willing understanding to come, trying to banish the useless jealousy that flared in her. She saw the tall, black-haired man move, his head turn as if he could sense her astral presence—and she almost bit through her tongue in shock as in that moment his form changed, and in his place a face that was terrifyingly alien yet terrifyingly familiar smiled malevolently back at her.

He was so like Tarod that they might have been twins—but his hair was gold, and a deep instinct told Cyllan that he was not, and could never be, human. His smile widened and she saw his eyes changing color—he seemed to be speaking but she couldn't hear the words; instead she

suddenly felt suffocated by a rising, cloying fog of something deadly, something evil—

"*No*—" Her own voice, breaking out in an involuntary
protest, snapped the fragile web of the spell and she
rocked back on her heels, almost falling, as the physical
world twisted back into place around her like a cold slap.
Shivering with the shock of such a violent return to consciousness Cyllan started to get to her feet—then froze.
Someone was standing on the far side of the Peninsula,
beyond the scattered hummocks of tents and stalls and
wagons. A tall, gaunt figure in a long cloak or shroud that
hid his body from view was watching her. A peculiar aura
like the deceptive Flatland marshlights shimmered around
him, and through it his hair gleamed gold.

Cyllan's heart started to pound painfully as the dream-
inspired fear flooded back. She jammed the heels of her
hands against her eyes, shaking her head violently, then
looked again.

There was no one to be seen.

"*Aeoris* . . ." She hissed the word as a protective
charm through clenched teeth, at the same time involuntarily making a superstitious sign against evil. Even if her
eyes had deceived her, her mind had not—real or illusion,
that eerie figure was significant. But the nature of its
significance . . . ah, that was another matter, and it would
take a greater mind and a greater power than she possessed
to resolve that mystery.

Shivering, she hastily gathered up her stones and ran
back towards the drovers' camp. Glancing towards the
distant Castle the thought flitted through her mind that she
might go there again, seek out the black-haired Adept, tell
him of her forebodings; but she savagely dismissed it. She
had no evidence—and too many confused motives. . . .

The fear was like a small spark inside her that refused to
be extinguished as she lay down once more, pulling the
blanket tight around her thin frame. The moons were
setting, bringing true darkness . . . a short way off a pony
stamped and snorted, making her jump. She took a mental
grip on herself and huddled down further in the blanket's

folds, shutting her eyes and willing sleep to come and drive away the night.

Cyllan's wasn't the only sleepless soul that night. Back in the sanctuary of his rooms Tarod sat as he had done for near on two hours, staring out over the Castle courtyard. Torches still burned there, warming the cold black of the stonework and casting a peaceful, kindly glow over the scene; by the gates a lone watchman yawned and paced slowly about to stretch stiff legs; a cat slunk through the colonnades on some private business.

Tarod would have given much to be able to sleep, but knew it was impossible. How many wakeful nights had he spent at this window, chafing against the long hours of darkness, afraid even to try to rest? There was no fear this time, but a different emotional turmoil; and an image of a pale oval of a face in the darkness, a sweet, pliant body, a soft voice . . . She had left him so quickly that there had been no time to catch hold of the confusion of feelings between them; now though, he would have given half his life to be with her again. And if this confusion of agony and joy was love, then it had taken hold of him with a vengeance.

Again and again he tormented himself with questions. Had he moved too fast and too far for her? Had he given offense? Was she merely indulging in some idle flirtation to pass her time at the Castle? Vulnerability was something that rarely troubled Tarod—but he felt desperately vulnerable now, even though a part of him railed against his own weakness. He wondered if, despite her outwardly bold manner, Sashka too was unsure of herself—if that was true, then he had overstepped the bounds of propriety, and the chances were that she wouldn't dare to face him again. . . .

Abruptly he stood up, pacing across the room. He felt like an animal caged against its will—so many unanswered questions, and nothing he could do would bring him any nearer to a solution. Sashka possessed the key to the cage; she alone could give or withhold it as she chose, and the knowledge of that hurt.

Realizing that this restless pacing was only making matters worse, Tarod turned back to the window and was about to sit down again when he heard—or thought he heard—a sound at the outer door. For a moment an irrational hope flared in him and he quelled it, telling himself it was nothing more than self-delusion.

Then he heard it again. Not quite a knocking, not quite a scratching, as though someone were trying to attract his attention without drawing attention from elsewhere.

Tarod's pulse was abnormally and uncomfortably rapid as he crossed the room and drew back the bolt. The door swung open—and Sashka, in a thin night shift with only a shawl around her shoulders, gazed steadily at him from the darkened passage.

"I couldn't sleep . . ." She slipped into the room as, too stunned to speak, Tarod stepped back. The door closed with no more than a light tap which nonetheless made every nerve in his body tingle. Sashka stared silently about the room, her eyes wide and drinking in every detail, and at last he found his voice.

"Sashka . . ." Reason fought back through the emotion. "Your parents—if they find you gone—"

She shook her head, her hair rippling. "They're asleep, Tarod. They'll not wake till morning." She said nothing of the lecture she had received from her father on returning to their suite—to her fury, he had waited up for her—nor of the pinch of a strong herbal powder she had slipped into his glass of hot mulled wine when he finally, grumblingly, agreed to go to bed. The skills she was learning at the Sisterhood Cot were already proving their worth.

For a long time after her father fell asleep she had stood before the long glass in her own bedchamber, allowing her hands to move with slow languor over the contours of her body while she debated with herself what she should do. Could she have misjudged the look she had seen in the black-haired man's eyes tonight? She thought not—but there was always the possibility that he was merely toying with her; and she would be a fool if she assumed herself shrewder and more worldly wise than a Seventh-Rank Adept. Yet an unerring feminine instinct told her that she had done right to leave him when she did, however much her own nature might have urged otherwise. Above all, she didn't want to seem too forward; didn't want to cheapen Tarod's opinion of her. Other men—and she had known a few, experimenting like so many girls of her age and station—might be manipulated with ease; this sorcerer was another matter. She wanted him, but knew he could not be won on simple terms.

Now though, the question that had haunted her since she had taken such precipitate leave of him earlier was answered. As his hand reached out, longing to touch her yet half afraid, she moved closer to him so that his fingers brushed her shoulder.

"Why did you go so suddenly?" His voice was hoarse.

"I—had to." She bowed her head. "I think I was afraid of you."

"And now?"

"No. Not now."

His hands closed on her arms, drawing her towards him. She gasped, involuntarily but softly, as his lips touched her neck, then leaned into the embrace as he held her more tightly. For a moment they stood motionless, then, unexpectedly, he released her and stepped back.

Sashka understood, and the realization that he was unsure of himself gave her a heady sense of power. She smiled, suddenly confident and wanting to reassure him, and he saw the answer to his hopes reflected in her face. He took her hand, and as he began to move towards the inner room she followed him compliantly, knowing she had won.

The bedchamber was almost dark, lit only by the warm crimson glow from a dying fire in the grate. Tarod seemed no more than a shadow in the dimness, but the body that pressed close against hers was real enough . . . Sashka closed her eyes, and the soft sound of the door closing had a finality that thrilled her in a way she had never known before . . .

"*Wed* her?" Keridil stared across the room at Tarod, and though surprise was foremost in his expression there were also other, less easily decipherable feelings lurking beneath the surface.

Tarod gazed back, his eyes slightly narrowed. "Is the idea so very disconcerting?"

"No—no, of course not. Just . . . surprising." Keridil hunched his shoulders. "You, of all people . . . I find it hard to imagine you willing to compromise your independence."

It wasn't the reaction that Tarod had hoped for, and resentment flared along with the disappointment. He had decided to follow the Circle tradition of formally asking the High Initiate's blessing for his marriage—but Keridil's response had soured what should have been an occasion for congratulation.

Very softly, but with an edge of venom, he said, "And harder still, perhaps, to imagine my inveigling my way into a liaison with a Veyyil Saravin?"

Keridil's cheeks went scarlet. "I implied no such thing!" He half turned away, then stopped and made a sharp, angry gesture. "I'm sorry, Tarod—maybe I was ungracious; I didn't intend to be." A faint smile caught his mouth. "Even you must surely admit that the news was unexpected."

Mollified to a degree Tarod nodded, and Keridil added, "Nor would I have anticipated your being such a stickler for protocol. I'd have thought a precipitous flight with the girl one dark night would be more your line!"

The atmosphere eased as Tarod laughed, and the High Initiate crossed to a small, locked cabinet. They were in what he ironically referred to as his headache room—Jehrek's old study—where he conducted most of the formal business that now made up the major part of each day, and he opened the cabinet and drew out a black glass bottle and two small silver cups.

"For special occasions and desperate measures only," Keridil said. He pulled the cork, and splashed a finger's measure of a brilliantly sapphire-colored liquid into each cup before holding one out to Tarod. "It's distilled in Empty Province from the flowers of a bush that blooms once in fifteen years, and its name's unpronounceable. But I'll vouch that a whole clan of drovers could be drunk insensible on a quarter of a bottle!"

Tarod smiled thinly. "Special occasions and desperate measures—which is this?"

"The former, I assure you! Now that I've had a minute or two to adjust to the notion . . . But no; seriously, Tarod, I offer my solemn congratulations." Keridil raised his cup and made the sign of Aeoris's blessing. "You've chosen well—and so has she. I drink to you, and to your bride."

Formally they sipped the spirit, then Keridil slumped into a chair and swung his feet up on the table, the too-casual movements an attempt to mask his sudden embarrassment. "So . . . how does Fyran Veyyil Saravin react to you as a prospective son-elect?"

"Ah . . . that I've yet to learn."

"You haven't bespoken him?"

"No." Only this morning—the last day of the High Initiate's inaugural festivities—Tarod had suggested to Sashka that he should request an interview with Frayn without further delay. She had smiled up into his face, her eyes mischievous as her arms twined around his neck.

"There's no urgency, my love. And besides, Father will present no obstacle."

He kissed her. "You seem very confident . . ."

"I *am* very confident! My father is an ambitious man, Tarod—when he knows I'm to wed a seventh-rank Adept of the Circle, he'll be beside himself with delight! Oh, don't look at me that way—I know how you feel about rank and privilege, and I share your contempt. But what harm is there in making the most of his fond illusions?"

And so he had capitulated—as, during these last, half-crazed six days, he had indulged her in everything. Frayn Veyyil Saravin could wait—to Tarod, nothing mattered beyond the barely believable fact that, after only five wild days and nights, Sashka had agreed to become his wife. . . .

His attention returned to the present as Keridil said, "Well, I wouldn't delay overlong, if I were you. There'll be plenty of rivals for a girl such as Sashka Veyyil . . . safer to take the marriage oath as soon as you can!"

Was there still a rankling element in Keridil's easy words? Tarod recalled the sharp exchange between them on the first night of the celebrations, when Keridil had cast—or seemed to cast—aspersions on his motives; then he dismissed the thought as unworthy. They had, surely, been friends for too long to allow jealousy to cloud the issue.

"That's what I'd wish myself," he said. "In fact I thought that possibly when you return from the Summer Isle—"

"Gods, don't remind me!" Keridil grimaced. "I'm due to leave as soon as the sun rises tomorrow, and I don't relish the prospect of a fifteen-day ride, panoply or no."

"There are a great many more people anxious to see their new High Initiate with their own eyes. And besides, once you reach the High Margrave's court you'll be able to think of us poor Initiates shivering in the grip of winter whilst you enjoy the southern sun!"

"And enjoy waking nightmares about what those old fools on the Council will do without me to restrain them," Keridil countered sourly. "Most of the senior members should have been retired into graceful oblivion long ago. It was only Father's sense of obligation that prevented him from making overdue changes."

"Nonetheless, when you return—"

"Oh, yes, when I return . . . I want to reform this community of ours, Tarod, and I blame you for the feeling. Do you recall what you said to me on the first night of the celebrations, when we'd listened to the Margraves' grievances? You were right—we are stagnating, and in danger of becoming little more than a worthless anachronism. The Warps, the brigand activity—it all adds up to a condition that threatens to get out of control, while we sit idly by and do nothing." Keridil got to his feet again, fired by his own thoughts and pacing the room restlessly. "You did me a service that night, and I won't forget it. And I'll need Adepts such as you—further-seeing, less hidebound—to help me."

"You only need ask. I've no intention of leaving the Castle; I mean to bring Sashka here to live with me."

"Yes . . . yes, of course." Keridil frowned, as though he'd forgotten the matter of Tarod's impending marriage. "Then on my return, there'll be a great deal to set in motion." He looked at the other man. "I know I can rely on you." Suddenly he seemed to shrug off the chain of thought, and picked up his cup again. "In the meantime—good health to you again, my friend. You're a luckier man than I think you know!"

When Tarod had gone, Keridil sank back into the ornately carved chair that tradition obliged him to occupy during meetings in this room. He knew he should go to bed if he was to be fit to travel in the morning; but knew too that he wouldn't sleep.

He had behaved less than honorably tonight. He should have been glad for his old friend's happiness, willing to rejoice wholeheartedly with him; but instead the worm of discontented envy had poisoned the interview.

He had no right to be jealous. Sashka Veyyil had chosen of her own free will, and—as he had said—chosen well. But while Tarod's future now seemed to follow a path of assured happiness, Keridil felt that his own was clouded by uncertainty, and by obligations that he would have given anything not to have to fulfill. It wasn't the matter of the freedoms that had been so acutely curtailed when Jehrek died; from childhood Keridil had been schooled for that eventuality, and was resilient enough to cope. Part of him—albeit a small part—even quite enjoyed the pomp and circumstance attached to his new role. No; it was the other obligations, the more personal ones, that hurt.

His father, so he believed, had intended that he should marry soon, and at their last meeting—which had ended in such tragedy—he had intimated clearly that he wished his son to wed Inista Jair. An eminently suitable match. Inista would make a perfect complement to the High Initiate's station; her breeding was impeccable, her qualifications couldn't be faulted. Jehrek had wanted to do the very best by his only heir. And Keridil, like any loving and dutiful son, could not bring himself to go against what had been, in effect, his father's dying wish.

And Tarod was to marry Sashka Veyyil . . .

It was ridiculous; he had exchanged barely a dozen words with the auburn-haired Novice-Sister. But even that had been enough to tell Keridil that, compared with her, the Inista Jairs of the world were as dull granite to a jewel. Oh, he might do what was expected of him, wed Inista, father a son to succeed him when he went to Aeoris in his turn. But while Tarod and his bride lived among them, could he ever be content?

Recklessly, Keridil reached for the black glass bottle and filled his cup to the brim. Better to wake tomorrow with hammers in his head than stay wakeful all night with the envy eating at him like a disease.

Was she lying with Tarod tonight? Rumor spread like a forest fire in the castle, and enough people had heard about Tarod's locked door and the girl missing from the suite of rooms allocated to the Novices for the tale to be likely true. And a mere few minutes ago Keridil had given his blessing to their union, forcing himself to keep the painful jealousy out of his mind. When he returned from the Summer Isle, the formalities would be completed and Sashka Veyyil would be tied to another man.

It wasn't that he was in love with her, Keridil told himself bleakly. He couldn't even claim a proper acquaintance, and there was far more to love than the pangs of infatuation from a distance. But that situation could change with such dangerous ease, and if his only consolation lay in the charms of Inista Jair, then it was cold consolation indeed. . . .

He drained his cup, and the floor under his feet seemed to sway as he got up to lock the bottle away again. The spirit had worked with a vengeance, but it still wasn't potent enough to blot out the frustration. Perhaps, he told himself, his sojourn in the south would help to set matters in a healthier perspective; by the time he returned the whole issue might seem like a storm over nothing. But deep in his heart, he doubted it.

Someone knocked softly, hesitantly on the door, and old Gyneth Linto, Jehrek's steward who had now transferred his allegiance to Jehrek's son, looked in.

"Oh—pardon me, sir; I thought you'd retired. I was about to extinguish the lights." He made to withdraw, but Keridil beckoned him back.

"It's all right, Gyneth—I'm just away to bed. You shouldn't have waited up."

"No trouble, sir." Gyneth smiled his vague, gentle smile and shuffled across the room. Methodically, he began to snuff out the candles one by one. "The torches in the courtyard have been doused, sir, now the celebrations are over. Most of the folk out on the Peninsula have gone, too; though a few are waiting to wish you good speed tomorrow."

"Yes. Yes, thank you."

"And I've completed the packing and the loading myself, sir, so all's ready for an early start." The old man paused, looking up at Keridil from his stooped position over a smoking candle. "Is anything amiss, sir? You're not feeling unwell?"

Old Gyneth was far too shrewd for comfort . . . Keridil forced himself to smile, and shook his head. "No, Gyneth, I'm fine. Simply tired, that's all. I'll bid you good night."

"Thank you, sir. Good night."

He was snuffing the last of the lights as Keridil opened the door. The High Initiate glanced back once, his spirits feeling as dark and as cold as the room now looked. Then he walked quietly out into the passage and away towards his private rooms.

Chapter 11

"I don't want you to leave. You know that, don't you?"

Sashka closed her eyes and let her head droop forward on Tarod's chest. "I know. But it's for such a short while . . . and I don't want to risk putting myself in the Lady's bad favor; not now of all times."

He sighed and, though he couldn't argue with her reasoning, released her only with great reluctance. An irrational part of his mind feared that out of sight could become out of mind—once reinstalled at the Sisterhood Cot, might Sashka find that as time went by it became easier and easier not to return to the Castle?

She gleaned something of his thoughts, and added cajolingly, "It will also give me time to visit my parents, and tell them the news. They'll want to begin preparations immediately—and they'll be so happy for us."

Tarod looked gravely at her, his eyes unquiet. "Will they?" he asked. "You've seemed almost reluctant to tell them . . . as though they might not approve. Or—do you have doubts, Sashka?"

"No, my love!" The denial was so vehement that he wished he'd held his tongue. Her fingers traced a line lightly from his throat across to his left shoulder and arm. "Tarod, trust me. I'd give anything not to be parted from you, but I must go. It will be only a short while, and then we'll be together again . . . forever."

Not entirely contented, but knowing her answer must suffice, he nodded. "So be it, love. Though how I'll occupy myself enough to stay sane while you're gone I daren't speculate."

Sashka returned his smile warmly. Strange, she thought, how such a vulnerable and emotional soul had proved to lie beneath this man's cool exterior. When their courtship began she had been a little afraid of him—though never outwardly admitting it. Now, knowing him better, she believed she understood the powerful inner feelings that moved him, and she was no longer afraid.

She reached up again, standing on tiptoe to kiss him. "If I don't go down to the courtyard, the party will leave without me . . ."

"You should have allowed me to take you to West High Land, instead of insisting on riding out with a regular party."

"The two of us, alone?" She laughed, but gently and with an underlying sensuous pleasure. "Would we ever have reached the Cot, love? Or would you have spirited me away to some secret place where no one would ever hear of us again?"

"Would you have minded if I did?"

"You know I would not . . . but we must be patient just for a little longer. And then . . ." Sashka left the sentence unfinished, qualifying it only with another smile that expressed more than words.

On a sudden impulse Tarod reached to his own shoulder, where the gold Initiate's badge glinted dully in the light from the window. Unpinning it, he pressed it into Sashka's hands.

"Hold fast to it." His voice wasn't entirely steady. "It will bring you back to me."

"Oh, Tarod . . ." Sashka clutched the brooch so tightly that the bright metal dug into her palm. A talisman—and a token, to prove Tarod's intentions in the face of any scepticism. When her father saw a seventh-rank Adept's badge in her possession, he wouldn't dare to chastise her for pledging herself without his permission! And as for her fellow Novices . . .

She slipped the brooch carefully into the pouch at her waist, and her heart was light as they walked down the main Castle stairs and out into the courtyard. The rest of the party—a few Initiates attending an assize in West High Land, and three stewards sent to buy horses at Chaun—were waiting, already soaked by the fine drizzle that had been falling since dawn, and Sashka was gratified to see that her own horse had been blanketed to keep the saddle dry. She pulled up the hood of her expensive hide coat so that it covered her hair, and turned to Tarod.

"I'll return as soon as I can, my love. And I'll send you a message by the first courier from the Cot, to tell you what my father and the Lady have said."

Not caring that the impatient riders—and probably a good many others besides—were watching, Tarod pulled Sashka towards him and kissed her. "I'll be waiting."

From a vantage point at the massive Castle gates he watched until the party was dwarfed in the distance, Sashka's face no more than a faint blur as she looked back. Then he walked slowly back across the courtyard, oblivious to the increasing activity around him, and returned to his rooms.

He felt as if a vital part of his own being had left the

Castle with Sashka. During the early part of their courtship
he had fought against the emotional pull that threatened to
make him dependent on her and therefore vulnerable; now
he could no longer sustain the mental battle, and had
capitulated. And the experience was more exquisite, more
inspiring, more painful than he had imagined possible. The
time without her stretched ahead dismally—in the eight
days since the inaugural celebrations ended and Keridil
had left for the South Tarod had lived only for Sashka.
Now, he must try to take up his old place in the Circle,
which he had utterly neglected since the night the girl had
walked into his life.

His bedchamber, lit only by the thin grey daylight,
looked shadowed and dreary. On the window-ledge a pile
of books was gathering dust, and one pillow in the disor-
dered bed still bore the imprint of where Sashka's head
had lain. Tarod sighed. He would have to shake himself
out of this mood, or his life until she returned would be
intolerable. If he could—

A sound, like a sharp, derisive laugh, came from behind
him. He whirled—but the room was empty. Tarod's pulse
quickened, and an instinct he had all but forgotten in the
last heady days surfaced. The timbre of that laugh had
betrayed the truth—a faintly unreal echo that told him it
had not originated in any human dimension—and with the
realization came a memory that, since meeting Sashka, had
lost its meaning and potency. The dreams, the fever, the
bizarre meeting with Yandros on another plane . . . and
the promise he had made. All set aside since more earthly
considerations had taken precedence. . . .

He had still told no one—least of all Sashka—of the
visitation by the enigmatic entity. And lately he had duped
himself into thinking that perhaps Yandros and all he
implied were nothing more than the aftermath of a bad
dream; that the pact he had made—or believed he had
made—would come to nothing. His need to delve into the
mystery had faded, and even the waning of his one-time
occult power had hardly seemed to matter any more.

But now he saw that he had presumed far too much,
walking into a trap of false assumption and complacency.

Yandros, whoever or whatever he might be, was not about to let go his hold on Tarod—he was simply biding his time, waiting, as he had said, until the moment was right.

A blackness of spirit washed over Tarod. That laughter had been such a small sign, but no sorcerer worthy of the name could have mistaken it. Sooner or later, he would be called; and no power in the world could resist that call when it came. And if whatever Yandros had in store for him were to endanger or alienate Sashka, it would be a price he couldn't pay.

He moved towards the window, and his right hand absently fingered the silver ring. The stone felt unusually warm to the touch, almost as if a small, independent life pulsed within it. Yandros, he remembered, had touched that stone as though it carried some significance that was beyond his understanding. And that was the trouble—there was too much that Tarod didn't understand.

He had to find out. Now that he had been forced to face up to the truth instead of hiding from it, it was more vital than ever before that he should learn what Yandros planned for him. Otherwise, his future with Sashka would be in jeopardy.

Slowly, almost reluctantly, he took the top book from the pile, brushed the worst of the dust from its cover, and sat down to begin reading.

It was peculiarly unnerving feeling to look back after reaching the safe ground on the far side of the causeway and see the Peninsula stack rising gaunt and grey out of the sea, with not the smallest trace of the Castle visible. Sashka suppressed a shudder, then turned her face forward once more in preparation for the long ride.

One of the younger Initiates in the party turned to look back at her and smile encouragement. "It's hard to credit, lady, but we'll find being in the mountains a blessing in weather like this. The crags keep the worst of the rain off, and provided we watch out for the cataracts that come down off the rocks we'll stay drier than we would anywhere else."

Sashka nodded acknowledgment without speaking. She

had no particular wish to engage in small talk with her travelling companions—as a Veyyil Saravin and wife-to-be of a high Adept she didn't intend to encourage presumption from mere third and fourth rank Initiates. And so, to pass the time, she began to indulge in pleasant speculation about the reactions of her family and the Sisters to her betrothal. Even if her father hadn't taken an immediate liking to Tarod during their one brief meeting, he would be delighted. As far as Sashka knew, no clanswoman on either the Veyyil or the Saravin side had ever married into the hierarchy of the Star Peninsula; certainly none had ever wed an Initiate of Tarod's rank. Although whether she would want to stay at the Castle after their marriage was another matter—the place was impressive, certainly, but to one accustomed to the hedonism of West High Land's upper echelons life in the Castle could pall after a while. Still, she reflected, it should be easy enough to persuade Tarod around to her way of thinking. They could, perhaps, divide their time between the Peninsula and her own homeland; and there would be any number of opportunities for further social advancement. To a seventh-rank Adept and his wife very few doors indeed would ever be closed, and Tarod would surely agree with her that there was more to life than the closeted existence he had known in the Circle.

She had already decided that she would complete her training and remain in the Sisterhood. There were no strictures against marriage for Novices and full Sisters alike, and although it would mean devoting time to her qualifying studies to no real purpose, the status would nonetheless stand her in good stead in her future role.

All in all, Sashka was well contented with life. Strange how fate held its secrets until the least-expected moment—she had gone to the inaugural celebrations with interest but no serious intent; she had left as the betrothed of a highly placed member of the most feared and respected community in the land. Letting her horse pick its own way for a few moments she felt in her pouch and closed her hand round the gold Initiate's badge, as if half-convinced it might somehow have been spirited away. Then she smiled at her own foolishness, and concentrated on the road ahead.

* * *

"That's the last for today . . ." Themila Gan Lin closed the register of depositions and yawned behind her hand. "And thankful I'll be when Keridil returns to take charge again! No Council member—least of all a junior one like me—can have any true idea of the responsibility that poor young man has to carry!"

The three men who had been assisting her in the tedious task of reading the bundle of letters, pleas, complaints and tithe-lists brought in that morning by a courier from Prospect Province rose to leave. One—an elderly, senior Councillor—made a great fuss of tidying his share of the documents before handing them over. He resented the fact that the new High Initiate had placed so much in the hands of junior and less experienced Initiates; some even—and his gaze rested briefly but sourly on Tarod, who was rereading one of the depositions—not even Council members in their own right.

"The High Initiate should be with us again within seven days or so," he pointed out. "If the weather permits. Until then, it is our duty to do our utmost to lighten the burden." Nodding cursorily to each in turn, he went out.

Rhiman Han scowled after the old man's departing back. "Aeoris help Keridil when he does return," he said with rancor. "If he has to continue contending with pedants and procrastinators he'll be grey before his time!"

"The man's old, Rhiman," Themila chided gently. "Give him the courtesy due his age and long service to the Council."

Rhiman sighed, exasperated. "It's bad enough having to deal with such an unprecedented number of complaints!" he said, slapping one of the papers with the back of his hand. "Will the Circle put this right, can the Circle intervene here, what does the Circle mean to do about that—what are the Provincial Margraves doing with their time?"

Tarod folded the deposition he had been reading and handed it back to Themila. "The Margraves of most provinces have their hands too full to cope, Rhiman. The number of brigand attacks has been increasing still further, and now there are other troubles. Floods in the Great Eastern Flatlands, freak storms in Prospect, Warps—''

Rhiman sneered. "I'm obliged to you for telling me something the Council has known since the summer ended! And as far as Prospect is concerned, my own clan—''

"Rhiman, sit down and stop overreacting," Themila told the red-haired man sharply. "We know you're as aware as anyone of the troubles in the provinces. The question is, what's to be done about it?"

Rhiman snorted and snatched up to the top paper from the pile on the table. "Listen to this—three merchant caravans ambushed in the past month, with the loss of seventeen lives; one a tithe-train bound for the Castle! And we sit closed in our stronghold, doing nothing—''

Tarod was reminded uncomfortably of his own words to Keridil on the night of the banquet. "What would you suggest?" he asked.

"Damn it, there are enough men among us with highly developed fighting skills to put down this plague before it gets completely out of hand!"

"That's not the answer. We're not law-enforcers, Rhiman; not in such a mundane sense. I agree we should aid the Margravates, but there must be other, better methods."

"The idea of fighting beneath the dignity of a seventh-ranker, is it, Tarod?" Rhiman taunted. "Or are you afraid of showing up your own inadequacies?"

Tarod's face whitened angrily, then he said, "I don't recall having too much trouble with you in the lists recently."

Rhiman flushed a furious scarlet, and Themila realized that it would be a long time—if ever—before he forgave Tarod for the defeat he had suffered during the celebrations. Rhiman took his swordsmanship very seriously, and the fact that a combination of speed, guile and luck had given Tarod the victory was, to him, a barely tolerable insult. Now, the red-haired man stood up, almost knocking his chair over.

"I've got better things to do than argue with fools and cowards," he snapped. "If you need me, Themila, you know where to find me." And he stalked out, the door slamming behind him.

Themila sighed. "Rhiman Han makes a dangerous enemy, Tarod. You shouldn't have reminded him of that defeat."

"He'd make a more dangerous friend . . ." Tarod's dislike of the other man had been increasing lately; especially since he had traced the source of some spiteful remarks concerning his betrothal to Sashka. Rhiman was not the only one who would be glad when Keridil returned.

Themila rose and began to put the papers away, deciding it was prudent to change the subject. "Speaking of Keridil as we were earlier, have you read the letter he despatched from Shu-Nhadek?"

"Yes. I'm relieved to hear his view of the new High Margrave. The boy sounds as though he has a good head on his shoulders."

"So speaks the Circle Elder!" She laughed. "Have a care, Tarod, or we'll make a Councillor of you yet!"

"Thank you, but I'm content to stay as I am."

"Are you? Just lately, I've begun to wonder."

He looked up quickly. "What do you mean?"

Themila sat down once more. "Tarod, are you happy? I've seen your joy in Sashka and I've rejoiced for you, but . . . are you happy in yourself?" She hesitated, then decided to risk speaking her mind. "In honesty, something about your whole aura has started to remind me of your condition of some months ago . . . before Jehrek died."

Tarod said nothing, only continued to look at her, and, encouraged, she continued. "After your . . . fever, you seemed recovered in spirit, but now it's as though you're slipping back to that old time. Tarod, is it the dreams again?"

"Ah, Themila . . . you told me you were no seer . . ."

"It doesn't take a seer to guess at what's obvious. Especially when I've known you since you were a child." She reached out, took his hand and held onto it when he tried gently to pull away. "It wouldn't do, would it, to begin your new life with Sashka while a cloud still hangs over you?"

She echoed his own thoughts so closely that he felt a stab of pain. In her last letter—delivered by one of her father's servants who had ridden from Han for the purpose—

Sashka had explained that she must stay a little longer with her family but urged him to join her, so that, in her words, her parents might "see for themselves why it is that I love you with all my heart." But although he ached to go, to be with her, awareness of the risk he might be running held him back. He couldn't embroil Sashka in this—he had to be free of it, before he could fulfill his pledges with a clear heart and mind.

But how could he stand against Yandros when all he knew of the strange being's nature and intent were the confused memories of a fever-dream?

And Themila was shrewd enough to have guessed that he had been dreaming again of late: not the monstrous nightmares of the past, but strange, half-astral experiences that were dominated by a deep, heavy pulse, as though some titanic pendulum were eternally marking out the passing of time just beyond the fringes of consciousness. He didn't understand the dreams' meaning, but knew that they were significant. The hour Yandros had spoken of was drawing closer . . .

He looked at Themila once more, then made the decision over which his mind had been hovering for some days. He couldn't challenge Yandros alone—but with help, help that he could trust, there might be a chance. . . .

"Themila," he said, "I don't want to explain it all, not yet. But when Keridil returns, I will have something to ask of you both."

The sorceress's eyes were sympathetic. "You know I'll help you in any way I can. But can you not tell me now?"

He shook his head. "No. Forgive me, but this is something that must wait on Keridil. I need his consent as High Initiate, as well as his aid, for what I want to do."

"Very well, Tarod; I'll not press you. But in my turn, I'll make a request of you."

"Anything." He echoed her own words with a smile. "You know that."

She nodded, her face unhappy. "Don't delay longer than you need to. I have a feeling—just a feeling, mind—that it might be very unwise . . . ."

* * *

"Keridil, I envy you so!" Themila smiled broadly at the High Initiate as they touched their wine-cups together. "A toast—to your success, and to your obvious good health! And thanks be to Aeoris for your safe return to us."

They both made the traditional sign, then Keridil leaned back in his chair with a sigh of satisfaction. He was glad of this opportunity to spend his first evening back at the Castle in the quiet and peaceful company of only his closest friends. Tomorrow the cloak of responsibility would settle on him again—but tonight he wanted to savor a brief respite from ceremony.

"My brown skin is due more to the west wind than any sun," he said wryly. "Gods, I didn't think Shu and Southern Chaun could be so bitterly cold even at this season!"

"But the Summer Isle . . . ?" Themila prompted.

"Ah, that was another matter entirely. It's beautiful, Themila—such rich gardens, superb hunting land, and the High Margrave's court is . . ." He shook his head, unable to find the words to describe what he had seen. "I didn't know this world boasted such craftsmanship! The stone, you know, is a form of quartz, and at dawn and dusk the entire palace sparkles like one vast jewel as the crystal facets catch the angled light . . . And although it's but a small island, you might think it was a great continent, there's such variety contained in it." He smiled, remembering. "When you stand on the eastern beaches and look out across the sea, and think that beyond the horizon lies nothing and still nothing, right to the end of the world . . ."

She laughed. "But we have such a sight right here at the Castle!"

"I know . . . but there's a great difference. Northward, the prospect is chilling, bleak—but there, the world seems full of hope and life." Keridil glanced up, embarrassed. "I'm sorry—I'm beginning to sound like a third-rate ballad-maker."

"Nonsense." Themila leaned forward. "And what of the White Isle? Did you see that, too?"

The High Initiate's expression sobered, and she saw a glint of reverence in his eyes. "Oh, yes . . . From a

distance only, of course; no one but the appointed guardians are permitted to set foot there unless a Conclave has
been called. But we sailed as close by as we could before
putting in to port at Shu-Nhadek. There was a heavy
sea-mist, but I was able to glimpse the summit of the
Shrine.''

Themila drew in her breath. It was the ambition of all
Initiates to see for themselves the most sacred place in the
entire land—a small island lying off the far southern
coast. There, legend ran, Aeoris himself had taken human
form, and had summoned his six brothers to enter the last
battle against the powers of Chaos. And there, deep in the
heart of an ancient volcano, lay the Casket which had
never been—and, she prayed fervently, never would be—
opened. Only in the event of terrible catastrophe could a
High Initiate, in the presence of the High Margrave and
the Sisterhood Matriarch, open that sacred relic and call
back the Lords of Order to the land.

''So,'' Themila said at last, still awed by the thought of
Keridil's experience, ''your journey was a great success.
I'm so glad, Keridil . . .''

He smiled warmly at her. ''Nonetheless, Themila, I'm
thankful to be back home. Despite our northern climate
the Castle still calls me, and I can't stay away from it for
long.''

They lapsed for a few minutes into a companionable
silence, then Keridil said, ''Where's Tarod? I thought he
was to join us this evening.''

''He is.'' Themila suddenly seemed intent on a small
scar on her hand. ''I asked him to allow me some time
with you first. When he arrives, I've persuaded Gyneth to
have a meal served to us in private, here.''

Something in her voice gave her away. Keridil leaned
forward. ''Themila, is there anything wrong?''

''Wrong . . . well . . . yes, I believe so.''

Unbidden, a thought slipped immediately into Keridil's
mind. *Something between Tarod and Sashka*—and he was
shocked at the small flicker of hope that followed. Guilt
made his flesh crawl; he shook the idea off, tried to
pretend that it had never occurred.

"What's happened?"

Themila chose her words with care. "Nothing has *happened* as such, Keridil. But eight days ago, Tarod asked for our help. He put it very obliquely—you know the way he is—but the message was clear enough. And I believe it has something to do with the dreams that brought such disaster before."

Keridil hissed softly between clenched teeth. "I thought that was all past and done with . . ."

"So did I. He's been so different since his recovery, and particularly so now that he has Sashka. But I can see it, Keridil. The old darkness is back."

"What of Sashka?" the High Initiate asked, having to force the words out. "Is she still at the Castle?"

"No, thanks be. She returned to West High Land some time ago, and now she is with her family, making the marriage preparations. I believe . . ." Themila hesitated, wondering if she was betraying a confidence, then decided not. "I believe she has been writing to Tarod, trying to persuade him to go to her. He will not—and nor will he bring her back to the Castle."

"If your suspicions are right, that's wise of him. So, what does he—" and Keridil stopped as someone knocked on the door.

Themila looked relieved. "Let's hope we're about to find out," she said.

Tarod signed his name at the foot of the page, sprinkled sand over the wet ink and shook it dry. He'd wanted so much to explain the truth to Sashka, but at the last had thought better of it and compromised. In the letter, he had said only that vital Circle business still compelled him to stay at the Castle—which, in effect, was true enough—but that he would leave the Peninsula and meet her at the West High Land Cot within a few days. Then they could speak with Kael Amion together, and make the final arrangements for their marriage. As he wrote, he prayed silently that he would be able to fulfill that promise. What he and Keridil and Themila planned to do could prove very hazardous—but it was the only way to resolve the questions that must be answered before he dared take any further steps to secure his own happiness. Either way, he would know soon enough if they had succeeded.

He had been desperately relieved—though not showing it—when Keridil had agreed to his request for access to the Marble Hall. As the focal point for the Castle's peculiar powers it was, Tarod believed, the one place where the magical working he planned to attempt stood any hope of succeeding. Yandros had appeared to him there once before . . . there was a good chance he might do so, or be compelled to do so, again. And with three minds instead of his one, the power they raised would be greatly enhanced. On one matter, however, Tarod had stood firm in the face of Keridil's objections.

"No," he had said in answer to the High Initiate's suggestion as to the nature of the ritual. "I want no accepted ceremonial structure, Keridil. No Prayer and Exhortation, no circle, no triangle."

"That's impossible! Even if we could raise the power without the right preparations, to do so could be suicidal! You're flying in the face of every tradition we've ever known!"

"Then grant me permission to enter the Marble Hall, and I'll work alone. I don't want to involve you or Themila in anything against your wills," Tarod said stubbornly.

"Don't be ridiculous—neither Themila nor I would let you face something like this without our help. Besides," Keridil admitted, "I'm as anxious as you to get to the truth, Tarod. If Yandros is threatening you then he's threatening the Circle, and—all considerations of friendship aside—that makes it very much my concern. Very well, then; if you feel so strongly we'll conduct the evocation as you wish it." He paused. "It won't be a popular move if news of it gets out."

"There's no reason why it should."

"No . . . all the same, I'd like to take the precaution of working at night. I may be High Initiate, Tarod, but I'm bound on oath not to go against the majority will of the Circle." He clasped his hands together, staring at them. "I think tonight at second moonset might be an appropriate time to begin.''

Tarod sealed the letter, then doused the candles and made his way down to the deserted hall. A courier would be departing in the morning, riding through Han on his way to Wishet, and he left the letter at a collection place before crossing the hall to where the huge courtyard doors stood partly open. As he stepped out into the night a small figure detached itself from the deeper shadows.

"Tarod . . ." Themila took his arm. "Keridil will meet us in the library."

He nodded, looking down at her. "There's still time to change your mind. I wouldn't think the worse of you for it."

She didn't even answer him, just squeezed his arm and led him down the steps and towards the colonnaded walk. The courtyard was utterly deserted and silent; both Moons had set, and when he looked up Tarod could make out the towering Castle walls only as denser areas of blackness against a cloud-laden sky. They walked quickly but quietly, Themila shivering in the cold while Tarod contemplated the work ahead. He believed he had been right to tell his friends the truth about Yandros and the pledge he had made in exchange for his life—though he had still been unable to bring himself to speak of the link with Jehrek's death. That, he felt, was a matter best left quiescent, whatever his conscience might say.

They had almost reached the pillared walkway, showing ahead as a faint pattern of barred shadow, when a stirring of an old instinct made Tarod look at the sky again. For a moment he saw nothing untoward; then suddenly he pulled the sorceress back.

"Themila—"

She looked, frowned, and her voice was a whisper. "What is it?"

Tarod didn't reply immediately. His senses were attuned to something that seemed to be emanating from the ground under their feet—something threatening, distant still but coming closer; a vibration that echoed in every nerve.

"The clouds . . ." he said at last. "They're breaking up—look. There's light behind them . . ."

Themila followed his direction and drew in her breath sharply as she, too, recognized the weird amalgam of color that was beginning to tinge the sky beyond the rapidly disintegrating cloud-bank. The clouds themselves were being ripped apart like rags, and now Themila also felt the distant, underground vibration, heard the first faraway scream of the deadly voice out of the north.

"A Warp . . ." Her fingers tightened convulsively on Tarod's arm.

He continued to stare at the sky, unwilling to acknowledge the irrational excitement conjured by that terrifying sound. "Do you believe in omens, Themila?"

She looked quickly at him, her skin tinged now by a sickly reflection from the lights in the sky. "Let's join Keridil . . ." was all she said.

The library was unlit, but Tarod and Themila could see Keridil silhouetted against the dim, nacreous glow from the passage that led to the Marble Hall. He greeted them with a nod, and Themila said, before Tarod could speak, "Keridil, there's a Warp coming. And I feel—somehow I feel in my bones that there's something not right about it . . ."

Even if Themila didn't see the abrupt flash of alarm and suspicion in the High Initiate's eyes, his reaction didn't escape Tarod. Easily—too carelessly, Tarod thought— Keridil smiled. "I'd expected something to occur, Themila. It may be no bad portent. Shall we go on?" He gestured for them to precede him, and they entered the narrow corridor.

Tarod experienced a strong and unpleasant flashback to the last time he had set foot physically in the Marble Hall, when he had unwittingly wrecked a Circle rite, and the feeling sapped his confidence. Since recovering from the poisoning his powers had been at an unprecedented low ebb. Tonight, when he needed them as never before, would they be found wanting . . . ?

There was no time for speculation—they had reached

the end of the corridor and Keridil was unlocking the silver door while his companions averted their eyes from the almost intolerable brilliance that radiated from the metal.

A click, and the door swung noiselessly open. They moved slowly across the mosaic floor, the peculiar, pulsing haze of light folding round them like a sea-mist. Tarod saw Themila's eyes widen in awe, and realized that the sorceress, as a third-rank Initiate, had seen the Marble Hall no more than once or twice in her life, if at all. He said nothing, only moved across the floor, guided by an instinct that he didn't question.

Keridil stopped by the black circle and looked up enquiringly, but Tarod shook his head, walking on. Some subconscious empathy was at work between the three now, putting them under a mutual pact of silence until the moment when Tarod began the evocation.

Following the tall, black-haired figure through the deceptive mists of the Hall, Keridil forced down the qualms that threatened to upset his concentration. He would be the first to admit complete faith in his friend's prowess in sorcery, but at the same time a part of him wondered just what Tarod might be unleashing tonight. And beneath the calm which his will imposed, Keridil was afraid. . . .

Tarod stopped suddenly, and looked up. Following suit, Keridil almost swore aloud in shock as he saw the seven colossal shapes of the ruined statues looming through the haze. He'd rarely stood in such proximity to them; had forgotten their sheer immensity at close quarters. Why, in the name of all the gods, had Tarod chosen this spot over all others for the work to be done?

His question had to remain unanswered, for now Tarod had moved to stand before the statues, his back turned to them. Silently Keridil and Themila took up stations on either side of him, and as the echoes of their last footsteps faded an intense silence descended. They waited, minds calming and attuning to each other and to the atmosphere. Then, after what seemed a very long time. Tarod spoke.

"*Yandros.*"

His tone was so alien to anything Keridil had ever heard

that he felt his heart constrict with unease. *The voice had sounded barely human. . . .*

"Yandros."

It was a summoning, an evocation that chilled Keridil to the core. Remembering his promise he struggled to link his consciousness with Tarod's, but there was a barrier, a wall which he couldn't penetrate. The Hall felt stiflingly oppressive now, as though something lurked just beyond its borders, and Keridil had to force himself not to look uneasily back over his shoulder.

"Yandros."

It was like listening to an elemental voice, something prehistoric, pre-human . . .

"Yandros."

He had to keep a hold, Keridil thought. For Tarod's sake, for all their sakes, he had to try. He closed his eyes, summoning all the will he could muster, trying to break through. . . .

Tarod was unaware of his two companions. He seemed to be suspended between two levels of consciousness, neither fully on one plane nor the other. The voice that repeated Yandros's name over and over again wasn't his own; it came out of a time far, far in the past; another world, another life; and the ease with which his mind had slipped into that nothing-place had shocked the small vestige of self-awareness that he still retained. Somehow, he had known what he must do. No ceremony, no elaborate evocation—simply a name, spoken again and again, cutting through the bounds of dimensions both temporal and spatial. . . .

And yet he was afraid to cross the final barrier.

He could sense it, like a wall, before him. A pulsing band of indescribable darkness that called to some deep, awakening memory. *So old . . . so very old . . . back through Time itself . . .*

He couldn't do it. He was too human not to fear the chasm that lay between him and his goal. One slip, and he would be nothing—he couldn't do it. . . .

His hands had clenched unconsciously at his sides until

the nails drew blood from the palms. The silver ring cut into his finger, almost startling him out of the trance-state. His right hand moved involuntarily, closing over the clear stone; and a shock like a bolt of pure energy shot through his hands and arms, filled his body until he felt his bones would shatter with the sheer force of it. He was on fire—body, mind and soul—the pressure was building, building; he couldn't fight it—

"*YANDROS!*"

Tarod shrieked the name like a creature possessed, and as he did so a curtain of blackness smashed down on the Hall. A single, titanic crack, so deafening that it went beyond the threshold of hearing, hammered out of nowhere and the blast of it hurled the three off balance and threw them with bone-jarring force to the floor. As the incredible noise roiled away Tarod tried to get to his feet, his head spinning and the trance shattered. He felt sick, his limbs wouldn't obey him—a few paces away Keridil was shaking his head violently as he too tried to rise, and Themila, fragile-looking as a doll, was only just stirring. Tarod tried to speak, but knew the effort was useless. Neither would be able to hear him—they would be deaf to all sound until the effects of that colossal concussion had worn off.

Keridil called out something, his mouth seeming to move silently, and Tarod made a negative gesture to indicate that he couldn't hear. The High Initiate started to move painfully towards him—then stopped, his eyes widening in disbelief as a voice from behind them spoke a single word that they all heard with terrible clarity.

"*Tarod . . .*"

The tone was like molten silver . . . Keridil turned, almost falling again, and Themila sat up.

He was dwarfed by the vast black statues that stood motionless behind him—and yet something about him made them seem nothing by comparison. Gold hair flowed over his shoulders, and the narrow eyes, which constantly changed color in the stark face, flicked with amused disdain from one to another of the three humans before finally resting and lingering on Tarod. The expression changed then to one of affection, and the malevolent mouth smiled.

"Greetings, my brother," said Yandros. "It gladdens me to be reunited with you at last."

Chapter 12

He understood.

In the moment when Yandros spoke his name he had finally known the truth, and the knowledge was like a disease eating at his soul. He had walked into the trap set for him—opened the door that should have remained locked forever, turned the key, and damned himself. He had used the power he possessed without once questioning its source. And all along, the ring had been the focus. . . .

Tarod was aware of Keridil and Themila moving slowly forward to stand at his side, and he bitterly regretted his decision to involve them in what should have been a confrontation between himself and Yandros alone. He would have given anything to turn back time, change the now horribly inevitable pattern of events, but it was far too late.

Keridil was the first to speak. With a confidence which confirmed Tarod's belief that the High Initiate did not yet know what manner of entity he was dealing with, he demanded, "What are you?"

Yandros laughed. "You ask impertinent questions, my mortal friend. Perhaps you should look to Tarod for your answers."

Keridil glanced quickly at the black-haired man beside him. Tarod's face was dead-white; he didn't speak, and Keridil faced Yandros once more, adopting an almost ritualistic stance and regarding the entity with a cold, steady stare. It was an effective enough approach during Circle ceremony, but Tarod knew it would cut no ice with Yandros.

"We are not in the habit of summoning such as you in order to answer questions for ourselves," Keridil said sternly. Despite his outward composure he felt on unsafe ground—Tarod's insistence that they abandon the strict procedures of evocation meant that he couldn't entirely trust the entity to obey his commands and strictures. And his doubts were growing with every moment . . .

Yandros smiled and raised his perfect eyebrows in amusement. "Such as me? But there's the rub, High Initiate. What am I? You do not recognize me . . . but Tarod does, now." Again affection showed in the many-colored eyes as he looked at Tarod, and he added quietly, "It has been a very long time."

"Damn you!" Tarod turned away, fists clenched. "Leave me in peace!"

"Peace, my brother? You've known little enough peace lately. You knew little enough before I offered you your life as part of our pact."

A hand closed over Tarod's fingers and he felt Themila close beside him.

"And who has been the architect of Tarod's torment?" she demanded. "But for you, he'd not have suffered at all!"

Yandros bowed slightly to her. "You make a fair point, lady, but I must correct you. Were it not for us, Tarod would have died in Wishet Province on the day he unwittingly killed his cousin." He smiled. "Such a soul in the body and mind of a child, Tarod. That early life must have been hard for you."

Keridil's eyes narrowed. "You? You were the instrument of his arrival at the Castle?"

"We were." Yandros turned his back. With an easy carelessness he walked to the first of the defaced statues and laid a hand almost lovingly on the black stone. "Not perfect likenesses, but acceptable to us in their time. A pity that so much dedicated effort had to be despoiled by ignorance . . . do you remember them when they were whole, Tarod? Do you remember how we guided the artisans, how we inspired their dreams?" He laughed, and the sound made Keridil's courage shrivel. Desperate, he looked to Tarod for help. Unutterable questions and hideous, half-formed fears and suspicions were clamoring in his mind, fuelled by Yandros's cryptic references, but Tarod refused to meet his gaze.

"Look at the statues, High Initiate," Yandros commanded, and Keridil was impelled, willing or not, to obey. "What do you see?"

Keridil swallowed. "Nothing but defaced figures of granite."

"Do you know what they represent?"

". . . No."

"Then look again." The entity extended a graceful hand, and both Keridil and Themila gasped as for a single, fleeting moment the stone colossi took on another aspect. In that instant they were whole, as they had been centuries before—and with a terrible, sick feeling Keridil recognized two of the proud yet frighteningly maleficent carved faces.

"Tarod—" he turned again in desperation to his old friend. "Tarod, you must help us! If you know what this means, what it portends—"

"He knows, mortal," Yandros interrupted. "How long is it, Tarod, since you and I made our bargain? How long since I took the old High Initiate's life in payment for yours?"

Themila gave a small, involuntary cry of distress, and Keridil went rigid. *"What—?"*

Tarod had known it must come. Yandros wouldn't miss such an opportunity, and he felt the sick bleakness of despair in the pit of his stomach. Keridil's face was grey with shock, and when Tarod looked for understanding in his friend's eyes he found only revulsion and a slowly dawning hostility. Bitterly, he turned on Yandros. "That was no true bargain! You duped me—you exacted my oath before you named the price of your pact!"

"Nonetheless, the bargain was made." Yandros's eyes hardened. "And you know why. Now, you understand why I did what I needed to do—whatever the price!"

Very slowly, Keridil raised a hand, pointing at Tarod like an accuser unsure of the crime. His whole body was shaking as though with a palsy, and Tarod hardly recognized his voice when he finally managed to speak.

"Are you saying—damn you, are you saying that this—this demon killed my father?"

Any attempt to deny the cold fact would be futile, and Keridil was appalled by Tarod's calmness as he raised his eyes and said, "Yes, Keridil; he killed Jehrek Banamen Toln."

"And you—you knew—"

"I knew."

"*Gods!* And now you stand there and admit to it, as though you were telling me the time of day—in the name of Aeoris, Tarod, if you knew what this monstrosity was doing, why didn't you try to stop it?" Keridil couldn't believe the enormity of the betrayal; all his loyalties and assumptions had been turned about and smashed, and he was suddenly bereft.

Tarod, however, only said quietly, "If you knew Yandros's true nature, you'd not ask that question."

"Then tell me what his true nature is!" The High Initiate took hold of Tarod's shoulders and shook him so violently that for a moment Tarod was too surprised to react. "In the name of all that's sacred, *tell me!*"

Tarod shook him off with a sharp, angry movement that left the two facing each other like adversaries. Keridil's demand must inevitably lead, Tarod knew, to the final and most appalling revelation of all . . . but he couldn't evade it. If he didn't speak, Yandros would.

Controlling his voice with a great effort, he said, "He is Chaos."

"Chaos . . ." Keridil made the sign of Aeoris; it was a reflex and he couldn't stop himself. "No—that's insanity! Chaos is dead—its rulers were destroyed—our legends—" He stepped back.

"Banished," Yandros corrected him with a malign smile. "Not destroyed. You cannot destroy what is fundamental to the Universe, Keridil Toln—you can only remove it from the field of conflict for a while. But a time must inevitably arise when it will return again, and challenge the wisdom of those who were responsible for its demise." Amusement lit the many-colored eyes. "The circle comes full turn, one might say. We have waited—now we are strong again. And your good friend Tarod is about to play his part in our renaissance.''

"No!" Before Keridil could react, Tarod had stepped forward to confront the golden-haired entity. ''I'll not listen to any more of this, Yandros!'' He was fighting against a rising tide of fear, knowing that the Chaos Lord was succeeding in alienating Keridil from him and desperate to avert the increasingly threatening consequences. ''The pact we made was no pact at all—I was deceived, and I reject any obligation you claim of me!''

Yandros sighed. The aura of color that surrounded him rippled slightly as he shrugged his shoulders. ''Tarod, truly I'd expected better of you. You're thinking and speaking like a mortal!''

''I *am* mortal! As mortal as Keridil and Themila who stand here beside me—I was born of a mortal woman, as they were, and I'll die a mortal death, as they will!'' Tarod countered savagely.

Yandros's eyes narrowed, and he smiled again in a way that made Keridil and Themila shudder. ''Will you?'' he asked, so softly that the cold, silver voice was barely audible. ''Or will you allow your true nature to shine at last through the miasma of humanity? You know what you are . . . you know your power and your destiny, my brother. Can you renounce that, in exchange for the pitiful few years of increasing age and decay that human life has to offer you? Can you live as a slave of Order, when you know you were once a master of Chaos?''

''Keridil, stop him!'' Themila couldn't keep silent any longer. ''If anyone has the strength to end this nightmare, it must be you!'' She had taken hold of Tarod's hand again and, like a mother bird protecting her young against a marauding cat, placed herself between Tarod and Yandros. She addressed the Chaos Lord, though she was unable to look directly at him. ''You claim kinship with a man who is no less than a son to me—you say he is something other than human. I call you a liar, Yandros of Chaos!''

''And I, madam, call you a fool!'' Yandros took a pace forward and Themila reflexively shrank back, pressing against Tarod. He put an arm about her waist, feeling the overrapid pulsing of her blood. She was terrified, and he felt humbled by her courage in the face of such opposition.

"Lady." Yandros stared hard at Themila, who blanched. "I can only admire your loyalty to my brother, but it is misplaced. For what manner of mortal is it who carries his soul in the stone of a ring?"

There was a terrible silence. Themila looked up at Tarod, her eyes silently pleading for a denial, while Keridil could only stare, stunned, at the black-haired man. Tarod struggled to find words that would reassure them both, but they refused to come. His left hand burned as though he had thrust it into a fire, and he could feel his ring—the contours of the silver base, the weight of the strange, colorless stone—like another living entity on his finger. He knew the truth, as he had known it from the moment when Yandros had called him "brother," when he had felt the old, old power flooding back into his veins and had understood the full nature of his own origins. Fragments of memory that reached across an unimaginable gulf of time had fused together into completion—he couldn't look Keridil or Themila in the face and deny Yandros's words.

Softly, like an insinuating dream, Yandros's voice served the knot of confusion. "Tarod was born of a mortal woman," he said. "But his soul is the soul of a Chaos Lord. And he knows, as we know, that Aeoris has ruled long enough in this world. It is time for that rule to be challenged, and he is the instrument through which the challenge shall be issued!"

The affinities . . . the hideous, aeon-old bonds that tore at him . . . Hardly knowing what he was doing, Tarod pushed Themila away so violently that she stumbled and almost fell.

"I'm human!" His voice grated, barely recognizable. "And I serve Aeoris, not Chaos! This is proof enough!" With a violent gesture he jerked a fist against his own shoulder, where the Initiate's badge of rank should have been.

There was nothing there but the smooth fabric of his clothing. And then he remembered that he had given the badge to Sashka, as a token and an amulet to keep safe until they should meet again. . . .

Tarod laughed, but there was no trace of mirth in the sound. It was a bitter and ugly irony that had snatched away the one vital symbol, however small, of his loyalty to the Circle and the powers the Circle served. And though the explanation for it was simple and innocent enough, the coincidence couldn't be ignored.

"The joke appears to be against me . . ." He looked at his own clenched hand, still against his shoulder. The ring on his index finger winked in the light of Yandros's aura and Tarod added, "I could take it off, Yandros. I could throw it from the northernmost point of the Peninsula and let the sea make what it pleases of the offering . . ."

"Could you?"

Tarod's hand flexed convulsively, and he knew the answer to the sly question. No matter what the cost, he couldn't abandon his own soul. . . .

"My brother, you cannot deny the destiny you carry with you." Yandros spoke quietly, yet with a power and conviction that made Themila block her ears with shaking hands. "Whatever you might say to the contrary, in your heart you know that you owe your very existence to Chaos, for you are a part of Chaos. And in spite of the human flesh in which you're clothed, our realm is your only true home, and we your only true kin. You *must* fulfill your quest, Tarod—you must bring Chaos back to this world!"

"*No!* I serve Order!"

"You cannot serve Order, for you *are* Chaos!"

"Wait!" Keridil spoke up suddenly and the sound of his voice shocked Tarod, who had been so intent on the confrontation with Yandros that he had almost forgotten the High Initiate was present. Keridil had placed one hand on the short ceremonial sword that hung from his belt. He was watching Tarod, hawklike, and seemed unsure of what he wanted to say.

"Tarod . . . this creature, this—this demon—he has made many claims about you—claims that frighten me. Is he speaking the truth?"

Tarod couldn't lie, but he couldn't bring himself to

answer the question with complete honesty. In a barely audible voice, he said, "I serve Order, Keridil. I always have—and I always will."

"And if Chaos should wish it otherwise?"

"Then I'll fight them. I took the oath to Aeoris when I became an Adept, and my loyalties are steadfast."

"Your loyalties, brother, are misguided."

Tarod and Keridil both turned on Yandros, and Keridil was the first to speak.

"What does Chaos know of loyalty?" he challenged. "Your watchwords are deception and malevolence—we know your ways, Yandros of Chaos! Our records tell—"

Yandros interrupted him with a laugh that made the mists of the Marble Hall shiver. "Your records tell!" he mimicked with mocking contempt. "Then if you are a historian as well as a leader, Keridil Toln, you'll know that your cherished ways are crumbling back into the arid dust out of which they were born! Order has reigned unchecked for so long that it has stagnated, and you—" he pointed a long finger at Keridil, "have become an anachronism!"

"You dare to—" Keridil began furiously.

Yandros made a gesture, and the High Initiate found himself silenced. "Yes, mortal, I dare! Your revered Aeoris is nothing to me, for he too has become as anachronistic as his servants!" His voice dropped in pitch, suddenly unhumanly persuasive. "Order has become so ingrained in this sad little world that its servants no longer have a reason to exist. Oh, your Circle continues, and you pass on to your new Adepts the sum total of your centuries of knowledge. But with no adversary to stand against you, all your knowledge is worthless. With nothing to combat, no wrongs to right, you have no value. What are you, Keridil Toln? What is the justification for your existence in a world where Aeoris reigns unchallenged? To do his will, uphold his laws? His will is done and his laws upheld without the need for your intervention—you have no good reason to exist!"

There was a horrible echo of the thoughts that had lately been plaguing Keridil's darker dreams in what the entity said, and he was appalled to find himself half-swayed by the insidious argument. And then he remembered who, with apparent innocence, had engendered the doubts and fears in his mind to begin with . . .

Fighting off uncertainty, he countered, "No good reason, demon? And what of the troubles that plague our land now? What of the Warps, the brigands, the—"

"Oh, yes. The Warps. Since you usurped the stronghold of our old servants you have singularly failed to understand their nature, haven't you? The Warps, my friend, are a manifestation of those ways of ours which you claim to know so well—as is this very Castle in which you live, and in particular this very Hall in which we all now stand." The thin, perfect lips twitched faintly. "We like to pride ourselves that we haven't been entirely forgotten in this world."

Abruptly the concept made a terrible sense to Keridil as he recalled the efforts of generations of Circle Adepts to fathom the mysteries that the Old Ones had left behind when they were finally consigned to whatever hell Yandros and his kin designed for their followers. He no longer doubted that the pale-haired entity was what he claimed to be—but the idea that a Lord of Chaos could manifest in a world ruled entirely by Order horrified him. It went against all the doctrines and beliefs he had learned since childhood; the doctrines that stated Chaos was gone and could never return. But the anomalies of the Warps, the Castle itself, had defeated the Circle's greatest minds throughout their history . . . Yandros's claim rang all too true.

"So, Keridil Toln," Yandros continued gently, "do you not agree that Chaos has its place in your world? That without Chaos, there can be no true Order?"

The being's argument was dangerously seductive, and Keridil felt his will weakening. Surely, a small voice inside him said, the forces of Order would be better for having a true adversary to fight against, a real challenger to oppose instead of merely the contrived battles of the arena—

Abruptly he pulled himself out of the train of thought, and his skin crawled as he realized how close he had come to falling under Yandros's deadly spell. To think that he could argue against a Lord of Chaos—Keridil shook off the shudder that went through him at the very idea, and knew that there was only one thing he could do. Yandros was too dangerous—he must be bound and banished, before his influence pervaded beyond the point of no return.

He forced himself to look away from the golden-haired being, although it took a tremendous effort of will. Then he drew the ceremonial sword from its decorated scabbard and held it upright before his face. He was sweating profusely, and some deep, subterranean force seemed to be trying to hold him back, but he made himself speak.

"Aeoris, Lord of Light, Keeper of Souls and Master of Destiny—"

He heard someone—he thought it must be Tarod—draw in a harsh, involuntary breath, but he summoned all the self-control he could muster, and continued.

"Thou who took mortal form upon the White Isle, hear this thy servant in his hour of need— Hear thy servant and spokesman, Aeoris, who bids and binds these powers of dark corruption—"

"Keridil, as you love life, don't do it!"

Keridil stopped in mid-sentence, the semi-trance state into which he had already fallen shattered. Feeling suddenly violently sick, he stared at Tarod, who had broken the ceremonial words.

"What—" Keridil couldn't formulate the question.

Tarod was shaking. He had instantly recognized the opening words of the Circle's most powerful rite, and one which could only be invoked by the High Initiate in person in a case of extreme emergency. The Seventh Exhortation and Banishment was a sacred tract for the sole purpose of disciplining an astral entity that wouldn't respond to any lesser—and safer—method. It was one of the most extreme measures known to the high Adepts; but Tarod was all too well aware of what its effect on Yandros could be.

"Keridil," he repeated urgently, "don't use it—don't try to challenge him!"

Keridil stared at Tarod with a mixture of mistrust and

uncertainty in his expression, while Yandros watched both men, seemingly amused.

"Damn you, Tarod, what are you trying to do?" Keridil hissed. "This is the only way!"

"It's no way at all! Don't you realize, Keridil—the Circle's rites are nothing to Yandros! He's not some astral demon—he is *Chaos*! And if he chose, he could destroy you like that!" He snapped his fingers in front of the High Initiate's face.

Keridil couldn't deny the truth of it—but there was no other option open to him, and anger against Tarod surged.

"Then what would you have me do?" he demanded. "Welcome him among us? Stand aside and allow him free rein? Or do you think you have the power to stop this nightmare?"

Tarod glanced speculatively at Yandros and felt the silver ring pulse on his finger. He licked his lips, which were suddenly very dry. "Yes, I have the power . . ."

Yandros's expression darkened. "You'd not dare—you are bound by our pact! And if you try—"

"No, Yandros, you won't destroy me—you can't destroy me, not now." The momentary flicker of uncertainty in the being's look had confirmed what Tarod suspected. With the realization of his own true nature—and the nature of the ring he carried—the old power which had lain dormant within him had come surging through in full measure. And that full measure was far greater than his wildest imaginings could have conjured—the forces he had summoned from within himself years ago to kill first Coran and then the brigand leader were a child's trick compared with what he was capable of now. The power of Chaos itself . . . no; even Yandros couldn't destroy him. And though he might loathe the nature of that power, he would use it if he had to . . .

Keridil, too, had seen the implications of Tarod's answer to his question—and it had brought them both, he knew, to the brink of the final and most crucial test. So much was at stake—he had to find out where Tarod's true loyalties lay.

"Tarod." He spoke urgently, his voice shaking. "If

you have that power, you must use it now. You can't serve two masters—are you loyal to Order, or to Chaos?"

Tarod's eyes were tormented. "I serve Order!" he replied with harsh vehemence.

"Then, as your High Initiate, I order you to banish Yandros from this world!"

The ancient links were calling him, tearing at him anew—to obey Keridil would be to betray a part of himself . . . but in all his years at the Castle Tarod had learned to loathe and revile Chaos and all it stood for. And to allow those affinities to take hold of him now would be a far greater betrayal; a betrayal of the land and the people he looked on as his own.

Yandros knew Tarod's intentions even before he turned to face the golden-haired being, and his face twisted.

"Don't be a fool! You are bound—"

Tarod felt the pull increasing; wild, beautiful images assailed his mind. He gathered all his strength to fight them, and declared, "I am bound by nothing! I reject you, Yandros—I am of the Circle now!"

"Then you betray yourself for the sake of an illusion! Tarod, brother—"

Before he could say more, Tarod raised his left hand. The stone of his ring flared into brilliant life and he felt the power surging through him, swamping him, as the jewel reflected the Chaos Lord's aura back on itself.

"*Go!*" Tarod commanded thunderously. "Return whence you came, Yandros of Chaos—I reject you, and I banish you! *Aroint!*"

Yandros tried to speak, but no sound came from his lips. His form twisted, warped—for an instant Tarod's own face was superimposed over his, then, with a sound like glass splintering, his shimmering figure seemed to erupt in a column of white fire, and he vanished.

Tarod stood rigid, breathing heavily and having to exert all his self-control to prevent his legs from buckling under him as the power-surge drained away. The Marble Hall was deathly silent, and he was conscious of Keridil and Themila flanking him. What they had seen, what they had felt as Yandros was banished, he didn't know—but he sensed their fear like a tangible presence. And suddenly he had to get away from them. He couldn't face their confusion and uncertainty, and he was horribly afraid of their condemnation.

He turned and headed for the door, so quickly that by the time the others realized it he was all but lost in the Hall's shifting mist.

"Tarod!" Themila called, her voice echoing. "Wait!"

"No—" Keridil pulled her back as she seemed about to run after him. "Let him go, Themila. I think it's better—we all need a chance to recover our senses." He guided her at a slower pace until they too reached the silver door, and as they stepped through into the passage Keridil locked the door carefully behind them. Neither spoke as they walked back to the library and climbed the vault stairs, and when at last they emerged into the night, the sky overhead was quiet and still. The Warp that had been rolling in from the north as they began their work had gone.

Themila quickly scanned the courtyard for some sign of Tarod, but nothing moved and no lights shone from any of the Castle windows.

"If you're not too tired, I can offer you some wine in my rooms," Keridil said. "And the fire will still be alight—old Gyneth staunchly refuses to bank it down until he knows I'm in bed and asleep."

He was trying to counter the shock by pulling them both back to a semblance of normality, and Themila smiled gratefully. "Gyneth's a good man . . . your father held him in the highest regard. Yes, I'll join you—thank you." She glanced up at at the High Initiate's strained face. "And I think, too, it would do us good to talk this over before we try to rest."

Back in Keridil's rooms they made themselves comfortable before the fire while Gyneth, who had been waiting like a faithful shadow for his master's return, served mulled wine and biscuits, hovering solicitously until Keridil ordered him to bed. Themila sipped her wine, grateful for its warming effect, then said, "Well, Keridil, what's to be done now?"

He looked at her, his eyes filled with uncertainty. It was

daunting to force his mind back to the night's events, which were already taking on the quality of an ugly and half-forgotten dream. "Answer me one thing first," he said. "Do you believe that—Yandros—was what he claimed to be?"

"Yes. I don't doubt it for a moment." She shivered.

"And—Tarod?"

Themila didn't answer, and Keridil sighed. Her silence was enough in itself—she knew the truth as well as he did. Oh, Tarod had protested his loyalty to the Circle, and hadn't balked when Keridil had demanded that he prove that loyalty. But he had not once denied the kinship that Yandros claimed with him. And the fact that he and he alone had had the power to banish the entity was surely proof in itself.

A man, to all appearances mortal, but who carried his soul in the stone of a ring . . . the soul of a Lord of Chaos—it was an obscenity! But Tarod hadn't denied it—and he had known, and had hidden the knowledge, that Yandros was directly responsible for the death of Keridil's father. A life taken in exchange for Tarod's own life saved . . . not even Themila's tenacious loyalty could condone *that*.

Keridil knew that he could no longer cope with the unanswered questions alone. He needed the support and wisdom of his peers to help him reach a decision on what was to be done in the face of tonight's revelations. And besides, he couldn't now afford to keep the matter secret. If word were to get out—and it would eventually, he was sure—then his own position would be very precarious indeed.

He put down the biscuit he was holding, unable to eat it. "I'll have to convene a full meeting of the Council," he said.

"Oh, Keridil . . . is that necessary?"

"Themila, I appreciate your motives in wishing to protect Tarod, but it has to be done! I can't hide this—and I can't carry it all on my own shoulders. Tonight a Lord of Chaos has appeared in our midst, and Tarod summoned him! It's possibly the most portentous event that we've had to cope with for generations—and you ask me if a Council meeting is necessary?''

She laid a hand on his arm. ''I'm sorry, Keridil. I spoke without thinking; but you're right. It must be done. Though the Gods alone know how Tarod will feel about it . . .''

No matter what the circumstances, Keridil thought with an acid sense of jealousy, Themila always considered Tarod's point of view first. She had taken him under her wing on the day he first arrived at the Castle, and her concern had never wavered since. Suddenly he felt very isolated and more than a little resentful, and it was on the tip of his tongue to remind Themila that Tarod had been, at least indirectly, responsible for Jehrek's death. He controlled the impulse, aware that it was unfair as well as serving no real purpose, and instead said, ''He'll have his chance to speak, of course. But if the weight of opinion should go against him . . .''

''What do you mean?''

''Themila, Tarod has friends, but he also has enemies. Take Rhiman Han and his petty envies.'' Keridil ignored the small inner voice which accused him of being more than a little hypocritical. ''And there are many older Council members who view anything that smacks of Chaos with an almost obsessive superstition. They'll want to take every precaution possible.''

Themila didn't like the direction in which Keridil's argument was leading, and she said, ''But Keridil, what does this mean? You say, if the weight of opinion should go against Tarod—but what would happen in that case?''

There was a long pause before Keridil replied, ''Truly, Themila, I don't know. It's not up to me any longer; it can't be. I have no right to make decisions on behalf of the Council of Adepts.''

''You're the High Initiate!''

''Yes, Aeoris help me, I am! But when I was inaugurated, I took a vow that I would govern our Circle according to the will of its members. I may in theory have the authority to override the Council; but in practice I daren't use it. Whatever the majority of the Council should decide, I must abide by that decision. If I don't, then I'm not fit for the rank I hold!''

Despite her overwhelming concern for Tarod, Themila understood Keridil's predicament. She was free to champion whom she chose, at the dictates of her heart and conscience—Keridil was not, and it was clear that the opposing pulls of friendship and duty were tearing him in two.

Or at least . . . no. Themila dismissed as absurd the notion that had suddenly occurred to her. There had always been a friendly and humorous rivalry between Keridil and Tarod, but it went no deeper than that. After all, Keridil was High Initiate—what had he to be jealous of?

She stood up. "Keridil, forgive me. I am tired, despite my preoccupations—and so, I suspect, are you. You're right—a full Council meeting must be called, and quickly. And whatever the outcome, let's both hope and pray that it will be soon settled."

Keridil also rose, and came across to kiss her cheek fondly. "I count on your support, Themila. Sometimes I think yours is the only sane voice in a mad world."

"Good night, my dear son . . ." She turned and left the room.

When Themila had gone, Keridil sat at the grooved and battered table occupied by so many High Initiates before him, and covered his face with his hands. His father, he knew, would in his place have knelt before the votive lamp and prayed to Aeoris for guidance, but Keridil didn't have Jehrek's quiet conviction of spirit. And there were too many warring thoughts in his head to make clear contemplation possible.

Tarod . . . a creature of Chaos . . . The concept still seemed insane, but the evidence couldn't be refuted. And so many factors fitted the appalling picture—the manner of Tarod's arrival at the Castle, his extraordinarily rapid rise through the ranks of Initiates, the rebellious streak that had never fitted in with the ways of the Circle . . . Tarod was, and had always been, different. And now they knew what that difference truly was.

Tonight Tarod had protested his loyalty to Order and to the Circle of which he was a part. But Keridil had seen the

inner struggle that took place in his old friend even as he
made that protestation, and he was frightened by it. For
the foreseeable future, perhaps, Tarod would hold fast to
those loyalties, and Keridil didn't doubt for a moment that
he was sincere. But might there come a time in the future
when the other forces, the old forces, would start to call to
him again? Already they had made their mark on him, and
tragedy had resulted from that. If it were to happen again—
and it could, whether Tarod willed it or no—how much
worse might the consequences be?

Keridil just managed to quell a sudden, violent impulse
to pick up his wine-cup and hurl it into the fireplace with
sheer frustration. His head ached and clear thought was
impossible—perhaps he should follow Themila's example
and go to bed . . .

He was halfway to the door when he remembered Sashka
Veyyil.

Tarod's marriage was due to take place as soon as the
final arrangements could be made . . . he himself was to
officiate, give the girl into an indissoluble bond with a
man who . . .

Who isn't fully human, said a tiny voice within Keridil.
A man whose soul owes its existence to Chaos . . .

Abruptly Keridil sat down again. Was it possible that
Sashka knew the nature of the man to whom she was
betrothed? No—even Tarod himself hadn't known it until
tonight, or at least not consciously. And if she did know,
what would she think, what would she do? If she abandoned Tarod now, when he needed her perhaps more than
ever before, it could break him. Keridil knew the strength
of his friend's feelings for the girl. And yet . . . was it just
to allow her to enter into a marriage contract with her eyes
unopened to the truth?

A worm of discomfort moved in Keridil, condemning
his own motives. Was he really trying to be fair and
altruistic, or was the old jealousy behind the thoughts?
Was it Sashka's well-being he cared about—or his own
infatuation with a woman who might, if the facts about
Tarod were revealed to her, suddenly move within his own
reach?

He slammed a fist down on the table, biting his lip as pain jarred through his arm. He was High Initiate—as everyone seemed so fond of reminding him. He had a duty to uphold the truth, conceal nothing, and that duty made personal considerations irrelevant. And if he couldn't reconcile his own conscience where Sashka was concerned, at least he could—*should*, he told himself—inform Kael Amion, her Senior. Beyond that the matter would be out of his hands, and he could live with himself.

He pulled open a drawer set into the table, and took out several sheets of parchment. Spreading one out before him, he dipped a pen into the inkpot at his side and slowly, carefully, began to compose a letter. He worked steadily for some time, and when he finally finished, he shook sand across the resulting three sheets and slid them into a small, oiled leather pouch that bore the High Initiate's personal insignia.

Should he send the message? His conscience attacked him afresh and his hand hovered over the pouch, on the verge of pulling the parchments out and consigning them to the fire. But a mental image of Sashka's face held him back. Surely, he was doing no more than his duty in informing the Lady Kael of this development? His father would have done no less. . . .

Keridil was still hesitating when the door opened, and the surprised and concerned face of Gyneth appeared.

"Sir . . . I thought you were abed." A faint avuncular accusation tinged the old man's words, and Keridil shook his head.

"There's much to do, Gyneth. Tonight, we—oh, never mind. You'll learn about it soon enough, I imagine." He looked again at the pouch. "Gyneth . . ."

"Sir?"

He had to decide, now . . . Keridil stood up. "I have a message here for the Lady Kael Amion, at West High Land Sisterhood Cot. It's of the utmost urgency—"

"I'll have a rider woken immediately, sir. If he sets out within the hour, he'll be there in less than two days." Gyneth came forward and took the pouch from Keridil's

hand, and as he did so Keridil felt a weight lift from
his spirit.

"Yes . . ." he said, turning to stare into the fire. "Yes.
I think that would be as well."

Chapter 13

Sitting in a chair in his rooms and forcing his muscles to
relax, Tarod found it impossible not to think about the
hours that lay ahead. Waiting was the worst part of all—
the Council meeting had been convened for sunset, and
since noon he had felt the inner tension building up, until
it reached the point where he felt he couldn't take any
more pressure. Time and again he had risen and paced
restlessly to the window, peering out at the sun which still
stayed obstinately in the sky and willing it—fruitlessly—to
set. And time and again he had gone over in his mind what
he planned to say when he stood before the Council of
Adepts for judgment.

There was no doubt in his mind that judgment was
what he would face tonight, no matter the terms in which
it was officially couched. Even Keridil had admitted as
much when, early that morning, he had sought Tarod in
his rooms to inform him of the meeting. And there had
been something amiss in his old friend's manner—he'd
sensed it the moment he saw Keridil's face, and it was
what he had feared. A gulf had opened between them,
separating them—and in the gulf was the specter of Yandros.

By now, Tarod had grown used to the mingling of
revulsion and confusion that crept up on him whenever he
thought of the golden-haired entity. He was honest enough
not to deny that he owed Yandros a debt, however immor-
ally it had been incurred; but as an Adept of the Circle that

was sworn to serve Aeoris, all that Yandros represented was anathema to him.

And yet, try as he might, he couldn't deny the power that resided in him, drawn from the Chaos-soul that lay within the stone of the silver ring—and no more could he deny the truth of Yandros's revelations about his nature. The knowledge that his own soul was a soul of Chaos had been. at first like a living nightmare. Late last night, alone, he had reached his nadir, a crisis of heart in which the full implications of what he had learned had brought about such misery and despair that he had ended up on his knees beside the bed, silently praying to Aeoris that he might die and be released. But Aeoris hadn't responded, he had lacked the courage to take his own life, and the crisis had passed with the coming of dawn, leaving him with a faint but sure glimmering of hope. Whatever his origins, he was human enough to have loyalties and emotions and conscience, and last night in the Marble Hall he had realized that control of the soul-stone's Chaotic powers rested in his hands alone. He had defied Yandros, freed himself from the Chaos Lord's influence—and, too, from the pact that Yandros had tried to enforce. If he chose to turn his back on those old affinities, pledge his existence to Aeoris, then no power in the world could prevent him.

But would the Circle see matters in the same light? Easy enough for Tarod to reiterate his loyalties; there would be factions who wouldn't be convinced. Yet he must convince them—and not merely for his own sake. In his heart he knew that Yandros would not accept defeat; he had been banished once, but he would return, and in a direct conflict Tarod feared for the ability of the Circle to stand against him. In one respect Yandros was right; the followers of Aeoris had lost many of their one-time skills, but those skills would be needed as never before if Chaos planned to try to return to its old place in the world. And if the Initiates couldn't regain them in time, Yandros might well have no need of Tarod's help in furthering his malignant aims.

Tarod stared down at his ring, thinking that it was at one and the same time his greatest enemy and his greatest ally.

Without it, he would be freed completely from the ancient links that had tried to bind him to the powers of darkness. Yet with it, he controlled a weapon which might in the final event prove to be the sole force strong enough to combat Chaos. Oh, as a man and a sorcerer in his own right he had power. But with the soul-stone that power was magnified immeasurably. He dared not give it up. And with the aid of the other Adepts, he believed that he could ward off its pervasive, evil influence and stay true to himself and the Circle.

He had to convince the Council that he was right. He had to overcome the suspicion and prejudice he knew he would encounter tonight—and he believed he could do it. With the support of Keridil and Themila—and there were none better qualified to speak up for him, for they alone had come face to face with Yandros in person—the Council could be swayed, whatever the effort. . . .

Someone knocked on his door then, and he looked up, surprised. A quick glance at the window showed that the sky was turning a dull, angry red as the sun began to set, and Tarod's pulse quickened. "Come in . . ."

Two young second-rankers, dressed in the livery of Council stewardship and both carrying torches, entered the room, and one bowed to him. "We've been sent as escort, sir. The Council of Adepts is convening."

Tarod rose, surprised and a little disconcerted to realize the Keridil had paid strict attention to formality. Normally the more elaborate protocols weren't invoked unless the matter at hand was very grave indeed, and the thought that Keridil considered it necessary worried Tarod. But if he wanted to win the Council's confidence, he'd be well advised to comply . . .

He fetched his ceremonial cloak and cast it round his shoulders, then ran his hands through the unchecked mass of his hair to smooth it. "Very well," he said. "I'm ready."

There were few people, barring servants, about in the Castle as the two young Initiates, walking in step, escorted Tarod towards the Council chamber which adjoined the

High Initiate's rooms in the central wing. As they approached the chamber along a rapidly darkening passage, Tarod was further surprised to see a full ceremonial guard of seven men, swords drawn, mounted outside the double doors. He waited with growing apprehension as the formalities of challenge, identification and admission were completed, then at last the doors swung open and they were allowed to pass through.

On the threshold, Tarod stopped dead. The Council chamber was one of the largest rooms in the Castle—and it was packed to overflowing. On a high dais at the far end Keridil sat, flanked by the senior Councillors. He wore the gold cloak and circlet of his rank, and the regalia made him look remote and a little unreal. On a lower platform before the dais were the other Council members; among them Tarod recognized an unhappy-looking Themila, and two places from her the conspicuous red hair of Rhiman Han.

And filling the remainder of the hall, in the places traditionally granted to non-Councillors who wished to attend meetings, were other Initiates. Tarod surmised that almost the entire Circle must be present, sitting or standing as space permitted and leaving only a narrow aisle between the door and the Councillors' platform. Every face was turned towards him, every pair of eyes regarding him with curious interest, and he suppressed a shiver.

At the far end of the hall Keridil rose. "Will Tarod, seventh-rank Adept of the Circle, come forward."

The whole spectacle was beginning to take on the aspect of an unpleasant dream . . . or a trial. Tarod walked between the staring ranks of Initiates, until he reached the single chair that had been placed in the aisle before the dais. He looked up at Keridil and saw unease in his friend's eyes; Keridil tried to smile reassuringly but the attempt was a failure. He cleared his throat.

"I call to order this meeting of Adepts in full Council." He nodded, and at the signal the guards closed the doors with an echoing slam. As the noise died away someone shuffled papers with a good deal of unnecessary fuss, and Keridil glanced down at the documents that had been set before him.

"As many of you know, this meeting has been called so that Council and Circle alike can be acquainted with the full facts surrounding an event which took place last night, in the Marble Hall," he said.

So the Council had already been told . . . that could well explain the insistence on formality. Tarod felt discomfited, but his expression remained enigmatic.

"Our task," Keridil continued, "is to assess the implications and possible consequences of this event, and to decide in full Council what action, if any, should be taken. I therefore propose to begin these proceedings with a detailed account of last night's occurrence, so that you may all be fully informed of the facts." He looked up once more, and nodded to Tarod. "Will you please sit."

He obeyed mechanically, knowing with a terrible sense of fatalism that his hopes of swaying the Council to his way of thinking were all but gone. They had already been told enough to bias them; looking at the ranks of faces he could almost read their minds behind the carefully controlled expressions—were he the world's finest orator, he would balk at the idea of winning them over now.

And so Tarod listened silently while the full story of the encounter with Yandros was told. Keridil was scrupulously thorough and accurate in his account, leaving out not one detail of the entire story from its very beginning, but as he spoke Tarod saw the faces of the Councillors closing, hardening. Often they would make the sign of Aeoris before their own faces, as though to ward off some evil presence, and it was all Tarod could do not to get to his feet and walk out of the chamber. He controlled the impulse, knowing that any ill-tempered behavior now would damn his cause.

At last Keridil finished, and for what seemed a very long time the hall was silent. Then, gradually at first but with increasing intensity, the questions began.

"A Lord of Chaos—and we have heard that you consciously and deliberately summoned this being! Is that true?"

Tarod stared at the old Councillor who had snapped out the question. "I did. But I didn't know at the time who—what—I was evoking."

"But now you have no doubts?"

"I have no doubts." A dangerous admission, but he had to convince them that Yandros's threat was real.

"How can you be so certain?" The speaker pounced quickly on Tarod's reply. "There have been documented cases of even the highest ranking Adepts being deceived by astral entities, yet you seem utterly sure of your ground . . ."

Answering these questions was like trying to walk on broken glass. Tarod said carefully, "I believe, sir, that you have already heard the High Initiate's personal view about the—authenticity of the manifestation. Neither he nor I nor Themila Gan Lin doubted Yandros's nature for a moment—and with respect, had you been present, neither would you!"

The questioner pursed his mouth and muttered something to his neighbor, and another man spoke up.

"And yet, knowing the nature of this entity as you say, when the High Initiate began the Seventh Exhortation and Banishment, you prevented him from completing the rite. Why?"

"Because I wasn't about to stand by and see him killed!" Tarod retorted angrily. "Yandros could have destroyed him without even thinking about it, and he would have done if—"

"Ah, so you have a privileged insight into the mind of a Lord of Chaos, Tarod?" a new and familiar voice interjected. From the lower platform Rhiman Han was staring with hostility at his old rival, and when Tarod didn't answer immediately, the red-haired man continued, "I think, my friends, that we are now approaching the heart of this matter. Tarod claims inner knowledge of Yandros's ways— and Yandros, as we have heard, claims kinship—literal kinship—with Tarod. If that's true, there is simply one question to be answered, and that is, what manner of serpent have we been harboring in our midst all these years?"

Tarod's face whitened with fury, and Themila rounded on Rhiman. "How dare you say such a thing! If you've no more constructive comment to make, Rhiman, then hold your tongue!"

"My dear Themila, I am being more constructive than all our respected colleagues put together!" Rhiman retorted. "And I repeat—if Tarod is kin to the demon Yandros, then he is no true mortal man!" He rose, and Tarod realized that everyone in the hall was listening intently. He half expected Keridil to put a stop to Rhiman's outburst, but Keridil still sat motionless, his expression tight and uneasy.

"What man," Rhiman went on, "carries his soul in a piece of jewelry? What man is visited in dreams by monstrosities which haven't walked this world since the days of the Old Ones, and consorts with them as easily as two old friends in idle conversation?" He pointed accusingly at Tarod, who had also risen to his feet. "*We* have never known where our seventh-ranking friend came from. He was a foundling, a stray, with no clan name and no kin to claim him. No *human* kin! Well, my friends, it seems that now we have solved the conundrum. Tarod is no man—he's a demon!"

There was sudden pandemonium as every Councillor seemed to be trying to speak out at once. Many were standing, gesturing angrily for attention, and a good few onlookers added their voices to the confusion. Over it all Keridil shouted, striving to make himself heard, but only when he snatched up his staff of office and smashed it down like a club on the table did the uproar finally subside.

"I will not tolerate such disorder!" Keridil's voice was controlled but everyone heard the fury underlying it. "This is a meeting of Adepts, not a tavern brawl! Rhiman—I don't for a moment challenge your right to speak, but you must keep yourself under better control! This is not an emotive issue, and I'll have no personal prejudices brought into it."

"Rhiman Han does not understand you, Keridil," Tarod interjected, his voice carrying clearly. "In my experience, he knows of no other standard by which to judge anything!"

Keridil turned and stared at him. Tarod was standing, left hand resting on the hilt of his knife as if at the smallest provocation he would draw it and attack. The stone of his ring glared in the light of the torches, and his face was

venomous. Never had Keridil seen him look more dangerous, and he was suddenly and unwillingly reminded of the
brief glimpse Yandros had shown him of the seven colossal
statues in the Marble Hall, their faces restored and all too
recognizable.

"Sit down," he said savagely.

Tarod's green eyes challenged him, and Keridil repeated,
"I said, *sit down!*"

He had the gathering under control again, but only just.
And he knew now that what he had expected and dreaded
was true—almost to a man the Council was ranged against
Tarod. Rhiman's words had struck home, and even Keridil
found himself asking whether the red-haired man could be
right in his implication that Tarod was, by his very nature,
untrustworthy. That ring . . . he could have destroyed it,
abandoned it—but he hadn't. And if he had the power to
banish Yandros, then it followed that he also had the
power to summon him back, if he should ever wish to.

But Tarod didn't wish to. He had pledged his loyalty to
the Circle, and in spite of his errant nature Keridil couldn't
deny that he had always been scrupulously honorable. He
was in fact shocked by his own doubts—they had been
close friends since childhood, and to begin to mistrust a
close friend was tantamount to full-blooded betrayal.

But Tarod wasn't truly human . . . Nothing could wipe
that fact from the slate. And Keridil's first duty must
always be to the Circle. . . .

He realized suddenly that the crowd was waiting for
him, and hastily shook off the confusion of unhappy
thoughts. Tarod had seated himself again, as had Rhiman,
and Keridil looked tiredly around the room.

"Has anyone a further question or comment?"

"Yes, High Initiate." Themila stood up, a tiny but
determined figure.

"Speak, Themila."

"I have heard Rhiman condemn Tarod out of hand, and
I wish to reply to his accusation. I think perhaps no one
here tonight knows the full truth about Tarod and the
kinship claimed by Yandros. We have no direct experience
of Chaos, for we've been free of its taint since the Old

Ones were destroyed. But we do know Tarod, and have done since he was barely thirteen years old. Can even his enemies," and she looked sternly at Rhiman as she spoke, "deny that he is a man of honor? Can they deny that he has never once failed to stand steadfast in his loyalty to Aeoris and to the Circle?"

Rhiman, realizing that his advantage was being eroded by Themila, intervened quickly.

"I cast no aspersions on honor, Themila. My argument is plain—Tarod is not one of us. And whatever he claims to the contrary, we can't trust him—for the sake of the entire Circle, we *daren't* trust him!"

A murmur of agreement rippled through the hall, and Tarod felt his skin break out in a cold sweat. Themila's efforts were failing; the vast majority of the crowd were in agreement with Rhiman, and Rhiman knew it. Themila, however, was not about to give up.

"You can't conveniently set aside the evidence of so many years!" she protested. "Tarod may have power that we can't match, but—"

"And if some day he chooses to use it against us, and call back his infernal brethren to rule this world? What then, Themila Gan Lin? Will you welcome him with open arms? Will you embrace your precious adopted son while Chaos tears your land apart?"

"That's ridiculous!" Themila was almost in tears. "Tarod would no more bring harm on our community than—"

"*Can he prove that*?" Rhiman roared.

"He doesn't need to prove it! If your jealousy has blinded you to the truth—"

"No, Themila! You are the one who's blinded! That creature—" and Rhiman pointed again at Tarod, his hand shaking with rage and emotion, "is a demon, incarnate among us! You've seen for yourself what he's capable of—are you willing to risk allowing him to remain in this Castle?"

"No!" The word came from many throats together, both on the Council dais and in the crowd of spectators.

Keridil stood up once more. He looked exhausted, but this time didn't have to shout to make himself heard.

"Rhiman, you run too far and too fast!" he said. "Tarod is not on trial here."

Rhiman's confidence had grown to new heights with the weight of opinion so firmly behind him. "Then perhaps, High Initiate, he should be!" he countered.

"He hasn't even had a chance to speak ten words, let alone defend himself against your accusations!" Themila protested.

"Very well." Rhiman held up both hands. "I've no wish to be unjust—Tarod must be allowed to say whatever he believes will exonerate him. But before we proceed, High Initiate, I—and I think the majority of those here— would be grateful for your ruling on the nature of the decision to be made."

It was the one question Keridil had dreaded most, and he saw that Rhiman had maneuvered him skillfully into a corner. He couldn't evade the issue—as High Initiate and head of the Council he dared not—but to speak it aloud, while Tarod watched him . . .

Playing for time, he said, "I hardly think that's necessary at this stage, Rhiman."

"But I—*we*—" Rhiman indicated the other Councillors at the tables, most of whom nodded emphatically, "think that it is."

He was trapped . . . Keridil licked his lips. "Very well. The decision to be made by this Council is whether Tarod should remain as an Adept of the Circle, or be formally expelled, and asked to leave the Star Peninsula."

He couldn't look at Tarod, but he felt the stunned intensity of his stare. Rhiman smiled coldly. "And what of the third option, High Initiate?"

"Third option . . . ?"

The red-haired man walked slowly out from behind the table. He had the full attention of the entire gathering once more. "Unpleasant though it is to contemplate, there have been precedents—and none, I submit, as grave as this! If this meeting should find against the Adept, Tarod, I formally request that the option of execution should be considered."

"Execution?" Keridil echoed, barely able to believe

what he had heard. "You can't be serious—that's insanity, and by the Gods I'll not tolerate it!"

"You may have little option, Keridil." Rhiman dropped the formal mode of address to emphasize his point. "We're all aware of your long-standing friendship with Tarod, and understand that you are unwilling to consider such drastic measures against him. But your position is such that you can't stand against a majority verdict. Nor, I believe, would you wish to for one moment." He bowed slightly as though paying a compliment, and Keridil knew he was defeated. Rhiman smiled, and added his final barb. "As High Initiate, we look to you for guidance on the matter."

The threat was all too clear. They had contrived this turn of events, Keridil realized, out of a combination of fear and envy—and though Rhiman was clearly the prime mover with the most personal motive, he had gathered enough support from the superstitious Councillors to gain the victory that he wanted.

When the High Initiate didn't speak, Rhiman said gently, "Perhaps you would agree to put the question to a vote, before we proceed any further?"

At last, Keridil forced himself to look in the direction of the solitary chair in the aisle. Tarod was deadly pale, motionless, only the green eyes showing any animation. And Keridil had never seen such a cold rage in anyone before.

He couldn't veto Rhiman's request. Though—as he had said last night to Themila—he had the theoretical power to overturn any decision made even in full Council, to do so now would be tantamount to self-destruction. By allying himself openly with Tarod in the face of so much opposition he would be admitting to a partiality which, as High Initiate, he dared not show if he wanted to keep the respect and confidence of the Circle. Whatever the moral obligations of friendship, the vote had to be allowed—and Keridil must live with his conscience as best he could.

He stood, his fingers closing round the staff of office as though to draw strength and comfort from it. "Councillor Rhiman Han requests that a vote be taken on the issue of whether execution is to be considered. The request is

granted—I ask all Councillors to make their views known
in the formal way.''

A steward who had been standing behind Keridil's chair
moved forward, took the staff from him and carried it
carefully around the table. He stopped before the first
Councillor, who glanced quickly at Keridil and then laid
his hand on the staff.

"Aye for Councillor Rhiman."

People began to whisper, the sounds rising, sussurating.
The steward moved on.

"Aye for Councillor Rhiman."

"Aye for Councillor Rhiman."

"Aye for Councillor Rhiman."

One after another, and each answer was the same. Tarod
couldn't move, couldn't think; he could only continue to
stare at Keridil in disbelief. In the short space of time since
the meeting began his most trusted friend had stepped
back, cast aside the bonds of friendship and put on the
mask of a High Initiate with, it seemed to Tarod, no
attempt to compromise. Even the formality of the meeting
was a safe barrier behind which Keridil could shield himself. The will of the majority . . . Keridil alone had the
right to stand against that will, override it, and speak out
for reason. And he had done nothing.

The vote ended at last, With only three exceptions
including Themila, every member of the Council of Adepts had sided with Rhiman Han. And Rhiman was relishing his triumph. He turned as the staff of office was
returned to Keridil, and said, "I am indebted to you, High
Initiate. Perhaps now you would like to continue with the
proceedings of this meeting."

"No." Keridil stood up abruptly. His head ached fiercely,
and the stir of murmurings around the hall reverberated in
his brain. He had to have time to think—Rhiman had
forced his hand thus far, and he was not prepared to be
pushed any further.

"I intend to recall this meeting tomorrow at noon," he
said, raising his voice to ensure that all present heard him.
"This entire situation has sprung up too quickly for us to
be able to assess it clearly in the space of one night—

especially when emotions are running high. Thank you all for attending—this session is now ended.''

Rhiman, nonplussed, seemed about to argue, but the look on Keridil's face changed his mind. Instead, he remained in his chair, frustratedly tearing at sheets of paper, while the surprised and disappointed crowd began to drift out of the hall. At last, only a handful of people were left—Keridil, three of the older Councillors, Rhiman, Themila—and Tarod.

Tarod had moved to the Councillors' dais, away from the others, and was scoring grooves in the old wood with the point of his knife. He had to speak to Keridil—but with Rhiman present, he couldn't trust himself even to turn round. He heard low, urgent snatches of talk, dominated by Rhiman's voice, but paid little attention until Keridil suddenly said, "Rhiman, I am tired! We'll reconvene tomorrow—until then, be satisfied that you've made your point!''

"Making the point isn't enough, Keridil!'' Rhiman persisted angrily. "By all that's sacred, we *know* the truth about Tarod now—he's no more human than his cursed friend Yandros! Are you telling me that you're prepared to stand by a demon of Chaos? The same evil travesty that murdered your father?''

Something black and uncontrollable went through Tarod like fire, fuelling the hatred and the sense of betrayal until he couldn't contain it. He turned, and Rhiman swung round, alarmed, as Tarod's voice cut savagely across his own.

"Rhiman Han!''

Rhiman tried to look unconcerned, but his insouciance wasn't quite proof against the murderous expression on Tarod's face. Tarod raised his left hand, so that the stone of his ring glittered, half blinding the other man.

"I once took an oath, Rhiman Han, that I would remain true and loyal to our Circle.'' Tarod spoke softly but with a terrible menace. "I do not break my oaths, for I don't make them lightly. Remember that, for I make another oath now. If ever I should call upon the powers that I control, you will be the first to understand what it is to be the plaything of Chaos!''

Abruptly the rage that had taken hold of him loosed its grip, and he realized what he had said. With a single sentence he had condemned himself; but the words had been out before he could stop them. The others were staring at him, appalled. Themila made as if to move towards him, but Keridil pulled her back.

"Tarod . . . you must retract that!"

Tarod took a deep breath. He couldn't save the situation now. "Would anyone here believe my word if I did?" he replied harshly.

"Of course they would! But by this behavior you add fuel to the accusations—I can't stand by and allow it to go on!"

"Then do what you know is right, Keridil!" Rhiman took a pace towards Tarod, his confidence returning. "You've seen for yourself now what he is! You heard what he said! Is this creature to be allowed to go on living, so that he can unleash his filthy kind on our world when the mood takes him? The Circle can't tolerate a devil in its midst—and by Aeoris, if you won't have him killed, I'll do it myself and be damned!" He had half drawn his sword, and as he came forward again like an enraged bull, Tarod whipped the knife out of its scabbard in a single, rapid movement.

"Tarod, don't!" Themila pleaded. She broke away from Keridil and ran towards Tarod's side, intercepting Rhiman's path. "Don't let him provoke you, don't give him justification!"

Tarod turned as she approached. Whether Themila had intended to block Rhiman from his quarry or not he never knew; everything happened too quickly. Rhiman couldn't stop his own headlong rush, Themila was too intent on Tarod, who couldn't reach her in time to snatch her aside. Themila and Rhiman collided, and Rhiman's drawn sword pierced her, ramming to the hilt in her back before he could prevent it.

"Themila!" With a bellow of disbelief and horror Rhiman attempted to catch the small woman as she fell, but he was too clumsy and she hit the floor with a sickening thud. Scrabbling on his knees, Rhiman tried to gather her into his arms. "Themila! Oh Gods, no, no! Themila!"

He was still repeating her name when a hand took hold of his shoulder and pulled him violently away. Rhiman struggled and the hand twisted deftly and with incredible strength, almost breaking his collar bone. Tarod flung Rhiman across the floor as though he were a child's rag doll, and dropped to his knees at Themila's side.

"Themila . . ."

She was conscious and raised her head, gazing at him with unfocused eyes. "That was a stupid thing to do . . . I'm sorry, Tarod . . ." She managed to smile wanly.

He held her, silently thanking Aeoris for the fact that she was alive. "Don't try to speak, Themila—and don't argue with me. We'll get you to Grevard . . ."

"I'm—all right. Truly. I'm all right." Themila coughed, and blood bubbled between her lips, trickling down her chin.

"Keridil!" Tarod yelled. "Get the physician!"

Keridil and two of the older Councillors were already forming a makeshift hammock from their cloaks, in which Themila could be carried without disturbing the blade in her back. Tarod wouldn't let them touch her, but lifted her small body into the folds of the hammock and held her hand tightly as she was maneuvered towards the door. Rhiman meanwhile had picked himself up and stood brokenly alone at the far side of the hall. At the doorway, Tarod looked back.

"If she dies—" he began.

"Tarod, don't." Keridil laid a hand half fearfully on his arm. "It was an accident—you saw Rhiman's grief!" He paused. "Themila won't want you to jeopardize yourself for her."

Tarod stared at him with eyes that glittered cruelly. "Am I not already jeopardized, High Initiate?" His tone was bitter. "Perhaps it would be better for all concerned if I put paid to any lingering doubts by showing you all what I'm really capable of!"

"Tarod!"

Keridil's plea fell on deaf ears. Tarod had already turned and was stalking down the corridor behind the two hurrying Councillors and their burden.

Throughout the long night, Tarod sat in the empty corridor outside Grevard's rooms, waiting. To his relief the physician had wasted no time with questions, but in his usual abrupt manner had had Themila laid on a couch and called for his two senior assistants to be woken immediately. His cat—a descendant of the original—sat on the window-ledge, watching the proceedings with interest, and Tarod wanted to stay too, but the physician was adamant.

"Out. I've enough to do without unqualified hands getting in the way." He saw Tarod's face, and smiled thinly. "Believe me, I share your concern, Tarod. We all love Themila. Wait outside if you can't sleep; I'll inform you as soon as there's any news of her progress. And I'll do everything in my power."

Tarod nodded painfully. "I know you will . . . thank you."

With only the poor light of a slowly failing torch in its bracket on the wall for company, the vigil was long and bleak. Through a high window at the far end of the passage the first chill grey of dawn was beginning to creep in when at last the physician's door opened.

Grevard himself came out. He looked haggard, and Tarod knew what he was going to say before he spoke. He rose unsteadily.

"The Gods know I tried . . ." Grevard shook his head in distress. "I did everything, Tarod, but it wasn't enough—youth wasn't on her side, and she hadn't the strength to rally. She died ten minutes ago."

Tarod was silent. Grevard looked at him, wondering privately if he should insist that Tarod take a sedative. Then he decided that he wouldn't dare ask.

"Would you like to see her?" he suggested gently.

"No." Tarod shook his head, covered his left hand with his right and stroked the silver ring—an odd gesture, Grevard thought. He seemed to be lost in some dark contemplation, which the physician was thankful he didn't share.

"We'll all mourn her loss," he said uncomfortably.

"She died needlessly, Grevard."

"I did all I could."

"I know. Thank you for trying to save her." And he turned and walked away.

Tarod kept walking, in a daze, until he reached his own rooms. The outer door slammed behind him and he stood, hands pressed to the table, while his body shook with uncontrollable spasms. A blindness had come over him, a red mist that swam before his eyes as the numbness of grief was eclipsed by a terrible, ravening fury. It built up until he felt his head must burst, and through it came an insatiable lust for revenge.

Today, he would be condemned. He knew it as surely as he knew the sun would rise. Keridil had betrayed him; Themila was dead—he stood alone against the Circle.

And so, he told himself, the fury glowing white-hot within him, if the Circle believed him to be evil, he could show them what true evil was. For Themila's sake. She would have understood.

Tarod moved as softly as a cat back to his door. The lock clicked once as he turned the key, and he walked with the slow and careful deliberation of one who knew himself to be not quite sane through to his bedchamber to close the curtains.

Chapter 14

"Gods, Keridil, you know it was an accident!" Rhiman rocked forward in his chair in the High Initiate's study, covering his face with one hand whilst reaching out for the cup at his side with the other. "May Aeoris strike me dead if Themila isn't the dearest, kindest—"

"Rhiman, try to get a grip on yourself." Keridil carefully slid the black bottle of Empty Province spirit out of the red-haired man's reach and put it safely away in his

cupboard. He had proffered it as a dire necessity, but
Rhiman was too dangerously close to hysteria to be allowed any more. "We all know what happened, and you
can't be held to blame. Themila acted without thinking—no
one could have foreseen the consequences!"

"But if she dies—"

"Grevard is doing everything possible! We must wait,
and hope." He added, with more conviction in his voice
than he felt, "She'll live, Rhiman. I'm sure of it. Now,
listen to me—you need sleep; it's the best known cure for
shock.'"

"I couldn't sleep if my life depended on it!"

Keridil stared down at Rhiman's bowed head. All his
arrogant self-confidence had vanished in the aftermath of
this tragedy, leaving him drained and broken. Although he
had good reason not to like the man—and felt privately
that but for his hot-headedness the accident would never
have happened in the first place—Keridil was moved by
his genuine grief and remorse, and pitied him.

"Nonetheless," he said firmly, "you should try. Grevard
would advise it."

"Grevard has more urgent matters on his mind now
. . ." Rhiman grimaced. "Perhaps I should go to his
rooms—there might be news of her—"

"'No, Rhiman." Keridil interrupted him quickly. "I
think it would be best to wait."

Something in his tone alerted the other man, and he
frowned through his confusion. "Why?" he demanded.
"Surely there can be nothing more to lose by asking!"

"It would be best to wait," Keridil repeated, then,
realizing that Rhiman wouldn't be satisfied with such an
evasive answer, sighed. "Rhiman, Tarod is there. He's
keeping a vigil until there's news of Themila."

Rhiman's face twisted. "That filthy, devilish—"

"Rhiman!" In spite of his sympathy Keridil felt a resurgence of the anger he'd experienced in the Council Hall.
Controlling his voice, he said, "There's been enough damage done tonight without adding more fuel to the fire.
Your quarrel with Tarod has no place in this!"

"Hasn't it?" Rhiman retorted bitterly. "If it hadn't

been for that piece of offal, Themila would have been safe!''

''Don't be ridiculous!'' Keridil felt suddenly that he couldn't hold back from censuring the other man—remorse was one thing, but he wouldn't sanction any attempts by Rhiman to evade responsibility for his own actions. ''Whatever your personal feelings may be, you can't turn your back on the facts. And you can't hold Tarod to blame when—''

He didn't finish the sentence. With no warning the study door had been flung open, smashing back against the wall, and a blast of cold air from outside set all the lights in the room dancing and flaring. Keridil spun round—and came face to face with Tarod.

The High Initiate's breath stuck in his throat as he stared at his old friend. Tarod was almost unrecognizable—every trace of the familiar, fallible man had been eclipsed by something alien and terrible; a black, arctic aura that made Keridil's flesh crawl. The light in his green eyes was unhuman, and the ring on his left hand blazed like a glaring and malevolent star. With a shock that struck to the pit of his stomach Keridil saw in him the incarnate image of Yandros. . . .

''Tarod—'' He spoke the name only to break the appalling silence, already knowing that he couldn't hope to reason with the creature that confronted him.

Tarod stared at him and through him, then said softly, ''Themila is dead.''

Behind Keridil, Rhiman made a choking, inarticulate noise, and Tarod's gaze snapped past the High Initiate. ''*You*—'' The word was like a death sentence. Keridil heard a cup crash and rattle to the floor as Rhiman stumbled back, and he made one desperate attempt to avert what every instinct told him was about to happen.

''Tarod, no!'' He stepped into Tarod's path and clasped his shoulder, then recoiled at the ice-coldness of the skin he touched. Knowing he was all but helpless, he pleaded, ''As you value our friendship, I beg you, don't harm him!''

Very slowly Tarod turned his head. ''Friendship?'' he

echoed, as if he had never heard the word before. "What is the price of your friendship, Keridil Toln?"

"There's no price! For the sake of Aeoris, stop this!"

Tarod's lips twitched slightly, contemptuously. He made a brief gesture, and a force like a hammer-blow hurled Keridil across the room. He crashed against a cabinet which fell with a tremendous racket, catching his skull and half stunning him, and before he could recover his wits Tarod had raised his left hand.

Keridil could see what was coming, but was powerless to stop it—and Rhiman didn't stand a chance. The High Initiate's last image of him was as a hunched, cowering figure caught in a grisly tableau, hands raised as though to protect himself, before a titanic flash of blood-red light blasted against his eyes. Rhiman jerked spasmodically, then seemed to leap into the air like a puppet out of control. A single shriek cut Keridil's nerves like a knife-blade, and Rhiman was dead before the remains of his body hit the floor.

The sudden quiet and calm that followed in the aftermath of what Tarod had done was so shocking that for a few moments Keridil thought he was going to be sick. He managed to quell the spasm as his head began to clear after the blow, and very slowly and unsteadily got to his feet.

Tarod was standing in the middle of the room. The aura that had made Keridil recoil was gone, the madness with it—he was wholly human again, and his eyes as he stared at Rhiman's corpse were blank.

Keridil forced himself to look at the thing on the floor and his stomach rebelled. Only traces of red hair made Rhiman recognizable; the rest—he looked away again quickly.

"Keridil . . ." Tarod spoke in such a low whisper that at first the High Initiate thought he'd imagined the sound. "Keridil, that—that was—" He swayed and just managed to snatch reflexively at a chair-back, half falling onto the seat. "I didn't—"

Keridil crossed the room and ripped down one of the curtains from the window. He flung it over the corpse, averting his face as he did so, and Tarod spoke again, this time more coherently.

"Did I kill him . . . ?"

Keridil spun on his heel, incredulous. "You don't *know*?" The condemnation in his voice made Tarod's blood run cold. Somewhere in a dark recess of his mind was a half-memory of a fury he hadn't been able to control, further fired by grief and an unhuman vindictiveness against the man who now lay under the curtain; but nothing was clear or concrete. His left hand ached and he could barely flex the fingers; he tried to find words that would explain.

"I—can't remember. Only a rage, Keridil, and . . . the power . . ."

Keridil took a deep breath, torn between conflicting pulls of revulsion, pity and fear. "You killed him," he said softly. "He didn't stand a chance. You burst in, and I couldn't reason with you." He turned away. "I pray I never have to witness anything like that again."

Gradually fragments of memory were beginning to piece themselves together in Tarod's mind, and with them came the stirrings of blind panic. The Chaotic force had taken a grip on him and he'd been powerless to prevent it—he'd been carried on a tide of hatred and had revelled in the annihilation of Rhiman. There could be no justification for what he had done—and if it had happened once, how could any living soul predict that it wouldn't happen again? He couldn't fight it alone—he'd thought himself strong enough, but he was wrong. Yandros had used him, was using him still, to further his aims. Somewhere, he thought, the Chaos Lord must be laughing. . . .

"Keridil—" He had one chance, he knew, to appeal to the High Initiate, and there was far more at stake than their old friendship. "Keridil, please—for the sake of the Circle, you must help me!"

"Help you . . . ?" Keridil's face was tightly immobile.

"To fight this!" Tarod forced his still unwilling left hand into a clenched fist, displaying the ring which now glowed sullenly. "I'm not strong enough to combat it, not without aid; but if I fail then it isn't only my future at risk! You know what Yandros wants—he means to use me as a vehicle to bring Chaos back to the world to challenge the rule of Order. I'll pit all the strength I have against him, but without the Circle to stand with me it's not enough. And if he wins, the gates that have kept Chaos at bay all these centuries will stand wide open!''

Keridil still continued to watch Tarod without expression. At last he said, ''You could renounce that ring, Tarod. You said as much to Yandros—you could throw it into the sea . . .''

''Oh, yes, I said it. But what would that achieve? If I reject the ring, I lose the power that it can give me; and the Gods know it's a burden I loathe. But while I possess it, we have a chance to defeat Chaos's ambitions. I can *use* the stone's power, Keridil, and with our Adepts I believe I can control it—it's the only chance!''

Keridil had stepped back a pace as though mistrusting and fearing Tarod's vehement plea. Tarod drew breath, then said very quietly, ''Besides . . . I'd be rejecting something that isn't merely a source of power . . . it's my own soul, Keridil.'' He looked up, his eyes tortured. ''Yandros didn't lie—I know it, I can *feel* it, like something eating at me. But how can I separate myself from it? Even if you reviled your own soul, could you destroy it? What would I become once it was gone?''

Keridil was silent, struggling inwardly with Tarod's desperate reasoning. What *did* a man become without his soul? He didn't know, and wouldn't care to find out. A husk, perhaps—a living human shell without depth or motive. No, he thought; nothing could induce him to take such a step were his own future at stake. And yet he was at this moment probably more afraid than he had ever been in his life. Tarod's soul was no ordinary mortal spirit—it had been born of Chaos, and the power in that ring was too great and too deadly—too evil—for the Circle to risk allowing it to rise again. Tarod argued that it could be turned, used against its creators—but could such a promise be trusted? Tonight the power had taken hold, resulting in the gruesome death of a foolish and hotheaded but fundamentally innocent man. If Tarod chose—or was driven—to use it again, what chance would the Circle stand?

Playing for time, he asked, "What do you want me to do?"

The words were like a lifeline to Tarod. "I need the Circle's help, to control the influence of Chaos and use it against Yandros," he said pleadingly. "You know I'm loyal to our gods—and whatever anyone may think or fear, I'm human!" Savagely he chopped the edge of one hand against his arm. "I feel pain, as any man does! I love and hope and dream in the same way—if you were to take a knife now and stab me through the heart, I'd bleed and I'd die! I'm no demon!"

Keridil had to make a decision. It wasn't easy to cast aside the habits of a long-standing friendship, and there were stirrings of pity for Tarod within him. But as High Initiate he had a duty first and foremost to the Circle . . . and in the face of what he had seen tonight the gulf between himself and Tarod had widened beyond repair.

And, too, the old resentment was rearing its head again. . . .

Trying to keep any censure or emotion out of his voice, he said, "Tarod—does Sashka know anything of this?"

"Sashka?" Tarod's face tightened with a swift look of pain. "No. How could she? I didn't learn the truth myself until she was safe at her father's house."

"Of course . . . but will you tell her?"

Tarod covered his face with his hands. Keridil had asked the one question he had been subconsciously avoiding—it had been easy enough not to think of Sashka amid the chaos of recent events, but now he felt as though the one blunt query had stripped him to the bone.

"Gods," he whispered, "I don't know what to do . . . I can't hide it from her . . . and yet . . ."

"You don't trust her?" Keridil hadn't intended the comment to sound barbed, but it did.

"Yes, I trust her! But when she knows the truth, will she trust *me*? How can I convince her that she has nothing to fear, Keridil?"

"*Has* she nothing to fear?" Keridil demanded.

Tarod's face whitened angrily. "Nothing from me!"

They stared at each other. Slowly, inexorably, Keridil's

mind was propelling him towards a choice—and it was, he told himself, the only choice. There was simply no other path open to him . . .

He made an abrupt gesture that might have contained a hint of contrition. "I'm sorry. Perhaps that's a subject best left alone." He hesitated. "I'll aid you, Tarod—if I can."

Tarod stared at him and for an alarming moment the High Initiate wondered if he might be looking beyond the surface to the thoughts that lay beneath. But the doubt was dispelled as the black-haired man nodded.

"I can't express my gratitude . . . by standing with me you could be jeopardizing so much."

Tarod's gratitude was the last thing Keridil wanted at that moment, and he dismissed the thanks with an awkward wave of one hand. "Never mind that. We must think about what's to be done from here." He glanced, briefly, at the curtain and what it concealed. "I'll need time to talk to the Council and persuade them to a different point of view than they hold now . . . and as for Rhiman—"

"What happened can't be hidden," Tarod said unhappily. "And I couldn't deny the truth . . . I couldn't lie . . ."

"I know that, and I share your feeling. But with a little time, I believe I can plead mitigating circumstances and make the Council see reason." He rose. "Tarod; you must go now. Go back to your rooms, try to sleep for a while, and above all don't be seen about the Castle until I've had a chance to reconvene the meeting and explain." Doubt filled Tarod's eyes and Keridil added, "Trust me."

"I do. But . . ." His gaze shifted to the curtain.

"I'll enlist Gyneth's help to move Rhiman. Gyneth's the one man I can rely on to do my bidding without asking questions or spreading rumors. Please—go, now."

For a moment he thought that Tarod was going to argue; but instead he bowed his head, acquiescent. He stood, and clasped Keridil's shoulders briefly, unable to express what he felt in words. Keridil managed to quell an overwhelming urge to shudder and pull away at the touch, and closed the door quickly behind Tarod as he left the study. Then he took two deep breaths to regain his composure, picked up a small handbell that stood on his table, and rang for Gyneth. When the old servant appeared Keridil was standing in front of the fireplace, hands braced on the mantel as he stared into the ashes.

"Sir?" Gyneth half bowed as the High Initiate turned his head, then saw the draped and unidentifiable bulk on the floor and frowned. "What—"

Keridil cut the question off before Gyneth could formulate it. "Gyneth, this is an emergency. I want you to go discreetly to all the elder members of the Council of Adepts in turn, and ask them to wait on me here immediately. That—" he pointed with a suddenly unsteady hand at the curtain, "conceals the remains of a Council member who was murdered in my presence only minutes ago."

Gyneth's eyes widened, but before he could speak Keridil continued, "You understand now why I stress the urgency of this matter. Remember—each Council Elder, and no one else."

The old man nodded, valiantly controlling his incredulity. In a careful tone he said, "Very good, sir. Should I—explain the nature of the emergency to the respected Elders?"

Keridil bit his lip. This was the final turning point—his decision now would map out the future path once and for all, and once committed he couldn't turn back. An image of Tarod as he had looked when he burst into the study seared his inner vision and the fear came back like a cold, clutching hand. Fear, and disgust, and—almost—a kind of hatred . . .

"No, Gyneth," he said. "Rumor spreads too easily and too fast in the Castle for that to be wise. You may just tell them . . ." He clasped his hands together. "Tell them that I need the Council's sanction to order an execution."

Trust me, Keridil had said. *I do*, he had replied. But now, sitting behind the closed curtains of his window, Tarod was haunted by a doubt that refused to give way to reasoning. Even the twin torments of his grief for Themila and memory of the horrific retribution he had taken couldn't eclipse it; it ate away at his consciousness, nagging, immovable, an instinct that gave him no rest.

Keridil had promised the Circle's aid; and throughout all
the years of their friendship—even from childhood—Tarod
had never known him to break his word. But yesterday in
the Council Hall there had been a chasm between them; and
it was only now that Tarod realized that chasm had appeared and been slowly growing since Keridil's inauguration
as High Initiate. Events of the past few days had caused it
to widen immeasurably, until it had seemed to him last
night that he was facing judgment by a stranger . . . and
a stranger who bore him no goodwill.

He could hardly hold Keridil to blame if their old friendship had perished in the light of all that had happened. To
support one whom most right-minded men would look on
as a demon—for Rhiman's accusation had left its mark—
and who had been indirectly responsible for the death of
his own father, was more than Tarod had the right to ask
of him. Nonetheless, Keridil had pledged his support and
his help . . . and yet something in his manner, in his
voice, had stirred an unpleasant intuition.

Tarod couldn't believe that the High Initiate would betray him. It wasn't Keridil's way; he might have condemned outright, but to resort to deception and subterfuge
was unthinkable, unless Tarod had gravely misjudged him.

He rose and moved to the window, drawing back the
curtain to look down into the courtyard. Guilt, remorse
and a terrible fear for the future lodged like a lead weight
in him. If Keridil had spoken the truth then he believed he
could, with the Circle to give strength to his endeavors,
fight the influence of the soul stone and the corruption of
Yandros, and have something to hope for. But without that
help, he was lost.

His attention was caught suddenly by a figure in the
courtyard, a man moving as fast as his advanced age
would allow and drawing considerable surprise from onlookers. He had emerged from a direction of the High
Initiate's chambers, and Tarod tensed as he recognized
Gyneth Linto. The old man was in a great hurry and even
from this distance his agitation was obvious. An urgent
errand for his master . . .

Abruptly the agonizing doubts crystallized into a cold

certainty. Tarod felt the old, dark anger rising again and
had to exert all his self-control to crush it. He told himself
that he couldn't be sure—one small incident wasn't proof
in itself.

But if his suspicions were right, a small inner voice
warned. . . .

He let the curtain drop, shivering as he turned back into
the gloomy room. He had to find out—instinct told him
that, if he valued his life, he couldn't give Keridil the
benefit of the doubt now. He was shaking as he lowered
himself into a chair, unable to believe that the High Initiate
was perfidious, but no longer daring to trust that belief.
Slowly, he raised his left hand.

He hated the stone of the ring as it glowed back at him,
yet knew that he depended on it, needed it. Its aura
seemed to increase, flowing out into a sudden starburst of
light as Tarod focused his powerful mind on the High
Initiate's rooms. . . .

"We're agreed, sirs." Keridil stood, indicating that the
discussion was at an end. His face was devoid of color or
expression, and he wouldn't meet the gaze of any of the
ten Elders also present in the study. "Thank you for your
time and attention—I believe we've come to the only
conclusion possible."

The eldest of the Councillors nodded gravely. "I must
confess to a certain relief, High Initiate. This has been the
hardest decision any of us has ever had to make—and we
realize that your own long-standing friendship with Tarod
has put you in an unenviable position. But I believe I speak
for all here when I say that we commend your wisdom,
and give our fullest approval to the decision."

A murmur of agreement went round the table, but Keridil
knew that Tarod hadn't been the only one on trial at this
meeting. His own credibility as head of both Circle and
Council had been at stake, and any attempt to plead on
Tarod's behalf would have been disastrous. He had known
it an hour ago during the terrible moment when he had
been too frightened to refuse Tarod's plea for help, and it
was doubly confirmed now. He had made the only right

decision; could have done nothing more. And, with the memory of Rhiman's grisly death still sharp in his mind, he knew also that he had wanted it no other way.

"Thank you for your faith in me, gentlemen," he said. "I hope that above all else I know my duty to the Circle— and that duty extends far beyond the calls of any friendship." He hesitated. "But I'll also confess that pure duty wasn't my only motive. Like you, I'm frightened of what Tarod could do—and unlike you, I've been an unwilling witness to those powers at first hand. I fully concur that we can't take the risk of allowing him to live among us."

Another general assent followed, then someone said: "There is, of course, still the question of the—ah—means, High Initiate. Although we are, strictly speaking, morally bound to follow the proper procedures, it occurs to me that under the circumstances a full trial might not be advisable."

"Yes . . ." another agreed. "After all, no man goes to his death willingly. And once Tarod learned of the Council's decision, he'd become a deadly adversary. From what we've learned in this room, it's clear he could destroy any or all of us as easily as we might swat an insect."

Several Councillors glanced involuntarily towards the floor. Rhiman's body had been removed, still wrapped in the curtain, but before it was taken they had all seen for themselves the results of Tarod's power. Someone coughed nervously.

Keridil stared down at the table, where his own hands were spread palms down, the knuckles white. "We have good swordsmen," he said quietly. "If two were to arrive at Tarod's door with no forewarning . . . it would be over before anything could be done to stop it. And a merciful end."

The Councillors looked at each other silently. At last the youngest cleared his throat. "There'll be willing volunteers in plenty, Keridil. After yesterday's revelation . . ."

Keridil shut his eyes momentarily, as if taking a grip on himself. Then he nodded and said sharply, almost angrily, "Very well—then send for them. Give them their instructions, and tell them to act before Tarod has a chance to retaliate."

"Now sir?"

"Yes, now! You've reminded me that we can't afford to waste time, and you're right." Suddenly, the knowledge that he was betraying friendship, betraying principles, didn't seem to matter any more. Chaos in the Circle's midst was a greater betrayal still, and with the sanction of the Council to support him Keridil's conscience felt just a little clearer. "Send for them," he said. "Let's get this ugly business over and done with!"

Thanks to some careful manipulation on Keridil's part, the Castle corridor that led towards Tarod's rooms was deserted as the two fourth-rank Initiates made their way along it from the direction of the main staircase. They walked quickly and quietly, neither speaking, both with a hand resting uneasily on the hilts of the short-bladed but businesslike swords at their belts.

It had come as no surprise to Keridil to find that there were indeed willing volunteers for the unpleasant task at hand. No one relished the prospect, but feeling among the Adepts was running high in the wake of the previous night's two deaths. Rhiman's, they all agreed, was indisputable cold-blooded murder; and, although he hadn't personally harmed her, Tarod had been entirely to blame for the events that led to Themila's stabbing. With him alive and free in their midst none could feel safe. Without him, the Circle would be rid of an evil and fast-spreading plague.

The two fourth-rankers had been selected for this mission on the combined merits of their skill with weapons and their vehement sympathy with the Council's decision. Both had been students of Themila's in childhood and had felt a special affection for her; one was related, through a married sister, to Rhiman's clan. Before leaving Keridil's chambers they had knelt with the High Initiate in a prayer to Aeoris for the triumph of justice and, awed, had been allowed to partake of the Wine of the White Isle—the flask containing an age-old recipe used only in the gravest sacraments. The ceremony had fortified their determination, but both had to admit privately to a growing sense of apprehension as they neared Tarod's door.

The door was closed, and no light glimmered beneath it. The younger of the Initiates reached out to grasp the latch, but the other forestalled him, shaking his head.

"The High Initiate said not to arouse his suspicions in any way," he said in a hoarse whisper. "Knock."

His companion nodded. His lips were tightly compressed as he rapped with a bunched fist on the door, and both listened to the silence that followed.

"He's not there," the younger whispered. "Either that, or—"

"Wait! Listen . . ."

Neither could tell whether the faint sounds they now heard beyond the door were footsteps or imagination—but seconds later came the unmistakable grate of a bolt being drawn. At a rapid nod from the elder, both men drew their swords, keeping them hidden under the folds of their short cloaks.

The latch clicked, the door creaked open . . . and the Initiates found themselves staring into an unlit and apparently empty room.

They stood on the threshold, taken by surprise as their confidence waned. The elder pushed tentatively at the door, which swung fully back against the wall, allowing no room for anyone to conceal himself behind it. It had unlocked and opened with no hand to touch it, and the younger man felt the bile of sick fear rise into his throat.

"He knows . . ." he hissed.

"Quiet! There may be another explanation . . . don't lose your nerve now!" His companion took a deep breath, then moved carefully, soundlessly, into the room. Now that his eyes were becoming accustomed to the gloom he could make out the hunched shadows of furniture and saw that the curtains at the window in the inner chamber were drawn . . . yet still the lack of light seemed unnatural. Reminding himself that Tarod couldn't possibly know anything of the Council's intentions he took another step forward, and the other, encouraged, followed. Something loomed to his right; he started violently then chided himself as he realized that it was nothing more than a tall cupboard which, by a trick of the uneven glow from the torchlit corridor, had momentarily taken on an illusion of life. He half turned towards the inner chamber, signalling his companion to stay close—

And the door at their backs slammed with a noise that jarred them both to the bone.

The two men spun round even as the light from outside was cut off, and the younger swore aloud with shock, making the sign of Aeoris before his own face.

Tarod stood between them and the door. Even in the darkness they could see him clearly; a peculiar, colorless light emanating from the ring on his left hand highlighted his sharp-etched features, the tangle of black hair, the unhumanly green eyes. He smiled with neither humor nor rancor.

"You were looking for me, gentlemen?"

The younger Initiate tried to form the words which they had carefully memorized, intended to dupe him into believing that he was summoned to an urgent meeting of the Council. They had planned to win his confidence—or at least dispel most of his doubts—and then strike with a swift and effective blade from behind, despatching him before he could retaliate. Now, it seemed a ludicrously futile exercise. "The High Initiate . . ." he began, then his tongue dried in his mouth and the words with it.

Tarod looked from one to the other and his smile widened, suddenly predatory. "The High Initiate . . . ?" he prompted with a mildness that didn't deceive his listeners. When neither answered he took a step towards them and they, in unison, backed away.

"The High Initiate," Tarod continued, in a voice now soft with malevolence, "sends his compliments and his regrets. The High Initiate decrees that I am no longer fit to live as an Adept of the Circle—indeed, that I am no longer fit to live at all. The High Initiate is afraid of me, and therefore sends you to do his work for him, stealthily, like brigands slitting throats in the night. Or do I misjudge the High Initiate?"

He knew the answer without needing to look at their

stricken faces. Slowly he closed his right hand over his left, touching his ring lightly, almost contemplatively.

"So Keridil has made his choice at last." He looked up again, and the Initiates blanched. "He believes I am a liar, and he believes I am evil. Perhaps now he'll discover what true evil is . . ."

The younger of the would-be assassins panicked. Goaded by Tarod's words, blind terror overcame all reason and with no warning he leaped at the black-haired sorcerer, sword swinging up and striking to kill. For an instant Tarod was startled; then, so fast that neither man saw it coming until too late, he whipped his knife from its sheath and swept it up to deflect the blow. Metal clashed discordantly, sparks spat as the two blades met, and Tarod's knife sheared through his adversary's chest and shoulder, biting to the bone.

The Initiate swayed, dropping his sword and staggering back against the wall. His face had turned grey with shock and pain, and blood pumped brilliantly from the long, crescent-shaped gash in his torso. As he sagged to his knees, Tarod turned his attention to his companion.

The elder Initiate had assumed a half-aggressive, half-defensive posture, sword held poised in both hands. Tarod stared at him briefly—then with his left hand made a careless gesture. The ring flared into momentary life, and the man reeled back with a yell as a colossal force struck him full on and agony seared across his eyes. Blinded, he fell and Tarod stood over him. His voice when he spoke was barely under control.

"Tell your treacherous High Initiate that if he wants a reckoning with me, he'd be well advised to do the deed himself, instead of sending children in his place!"

The blinded Initiate was too frightened and in too much pain to answer him. He opened his mouth, but no words would come, and his hand, groping, found nothing. He felt the air around him agitate as though someone or something moved; and the last sound he heard before he slid into oblivion was the savage slam of the outer door.

*   *   *

If the Seven Gods and all their legions had stood against him and barred his way at that moment, Tarod would have blasted them aside without a second thought. He strode towards the main stairs and took them three at a time, emerging into the main hall and crossing it, careless of the bloodied knife now back in his belt and staining his clothes and his left hand. Every sense was numb; all he felt was a towering, choking bitterness at the magnitude of Keridil's betrayal. To pretend to friendship—to play on the bond they had shared since childhood—only to resort to a cold and cynical assassination attempt . . . he couldn't yet believe it. But the two men with their drawn swords had been no figment of his imagination.

Seemingly from a vast distance someone called his name; he ignored the summons, brushed a servant out of his path and heard a surprised exclamation. As yet few of the Castle's inhabitants beyond Keridil and the more senior Council members had heard the details of Rhiman's and Themila's deaths; Keridil wanted the facts suppressed until Tarod was dead, and so no one made any attempt to stop him as he stormed to the hall's double doors and out into the courtyard.

Bright sunlight dazzled his eyes and he stopped, confused. The only desire in his mind had been a savage, animal need to find Keridil and kill him, but reason was fighting its way back through the miasma in his brain. He might exact revenge, but he would still have the entire Circle to contend with—and even he couldn't stand against their combined strength. He didn't want to die . . . his vengeance on Keridil must wait.

Abruptly he turned and headed in the direction of the stables. It hadn't occurred to him to wonder where, in all the world, he might go; all that mattered was to get away from the Castle and the taint of misery and betrayal.

His arrival at the stables caused the horses to stamp and kick in their stalls. Fin Tivan Bruall, who had been enjoying what he considered a well-earned doze among a heap of straw bales, woke with a start and began to swear roundly at the intruder who had upset him and his charges. One look at Tarod's face killed the curses on his tongue.

"The chestnut mare," Tarod said icily. "Is she here?"

"That bad-tempered beast? She's here, master, but—"

"Saddle her." Tarod rounded on the horsemaster as he began to protest again. "Don't argue with me, man, if you value your neck! Saddle her!"

Fin's face lost its florid color and he scrambled to obey. The mare recognized her one-time rider and had caught something of his state of mind. She fought Fin as he struggled to fit saddle and bridle, snapping at him and rolling her eyes in agitation. By the time the horsemaster had manhandled her out into the courtyard she was sweating profusely and on the verge of panic.

"Master, no man could ride her in this condition!" Fin pleaded breathlessly. "It'd be suicide!"

Tarod strode forward and took hold of the mare's bridle. "Damn your flusterings!" He wrenched the mare's head round and, as she side-stepped in protest, pulled himself up into the saddle. The mare bucked and Tarod lashed her across the flank with the looped ends of the reins. At this moment he felt that he loathed every living thing in the entire world, and he wasn't about to be bested by an animal.

Fin Tivan Bruall jumped aside as the mare plunged forward. Tarod was well aware that they were attracting attention from people in the courtyard, but if they wanted to stop him they had left it too late. He held the creature back by sheer force until they were almost at the Castle gates; then he gave her her head.

The raucous echo of hooves on stone was almost deafening as the mare flung herself through the great arch and out on to the sward beyond. They headed at breakneck speed through the Maze, and the contours of the vast, brooding northern coast seemed to spring out of nowhere with giddying suddenness as the animal galloped onto the treacherous path of the causeway.

Tarod wouldn't have cared if the mare's headlong flight had hurled them over the edge of the narrow granite bridge and down to the wild sea so far below. He was yelling at her now, lying flat along her neck and urging her harder, faster; almost goading her to kill them both. But she gained the far side safely, racing on across the Peninsula, and as they left the Castle behind, the blind, raging madness that had taken hold of Tarod at last began to fade and to be replaced by an emotion that wrenched him to the core.

He had left behind everything he had ever known, severed the links which had bound him since childhood. They had spurned his loyalty, cursed him, condemned him . . . he was no longer a part of their world, but an outcast. Friendship had turned overnight to bitter enmity; his dearest mentor and only champion was dead . . . the Circle held nothing for him but pain.

Where could he go? The Circle had been his life; he had no kin, no friends beyond its confines. All he had was one single belief, and one single hope.

Sashka. By now she must have left her father's house to return to the Cot at West High Land and await him. He had no illusions that, once news was abroad, the Lady Kael Amion would join in the condemnation as vehemently as any Circle Initiate; but Lady Kael was neither Sashka's parent nor her guardian. And his beautiful, faithful, headstrong lover would pay no heed to the warnings or strictures of her elders, but would follow her own heart.

He needed her now, as never before. Once they were together again they could make plans and decide what was to be done—their future would be very different now, but whatever happened they would never need to part again. . . .

The mare had slowed, her wildness expended. More gently than before, but with if anything a greater determination, Tarod gathered up the reins and urged her forward, towards the narrow and dangerous road that led deep into the heart of the mountains.

Chapter 15

Even with full winter approaching, and the few trees that grew this far north already stripped of their leaves, the garden of the West High Land Sisterhood Cot was a pleasant place to spend an hour or two. Sashka had come out from the recreation hall, where she and the other Novices were expected to pass their free time amusing themselves with pastimes suited to girls of their elevated station, and was thankful to have escaped from what she considered the inanities of her peers. During her visit to her parents she had almost forgotten how tedious life in the Cot could be. Whichever way she turned she came face to face with authority in one form or another; and for a girl used to having her own way in all things the strictures of the Sisterhood could be very irritating indeed.

She smiled to herself as she walked slowly down one of the paved paths of the garden, stopping to pick a late flower from one of the well-tended shrubs. In truth, she had to admit to herself that there were other factors involved in her rapidly changing attitude towards the Sisterhood. Tarod had opened her eyes to horizons that stretched far beyond anything she had previously imagined; now the Sisterhood—once the peak of her ambitions—seemed like a pale substitute compared to her taste of the Circle and its ways.

She slipped a hand into her waist-pouch and for the five hundredth time fingered the Initiate's gold badge hidden there. She remembered her father's reaction to the love-token with satisfaction; it had been her final triumph over any lingering disapproval or doubt, and since proudly displaying it she had heard nothing but praise for the high-ranking Adept who was about to honor their clan with his name, and urgent pleas that she should bid him welcome to their house at the earliest possible opportunity.

The one small discontent that nagged at her was the fact that as yet Tarod had not fulfilled his promise to come and claim her. That had been partly behind her sudden decision to return to West High Land; her parents' entreaties were becoming tiresome and she had longed for the comparative solitude of the Cot in its isolated valley. She still had no doubts that he would come as soon as he could, but it would do him no harm to arrive at her father's house and find her gone. A promise, Sashka reflected, was a promise; if Circle business had kept him at the Star Peninsula longer than he'd anticipated, then he would have to learn that her needs took precedence over anything the Castle might demand of him.

However, she had quickly realized that she was as restless at the Cot as she had ever been in her parents' household. And her state of mind wasn't helped by the eager curiosity of her fellow Novices, who were agog with banal questions about the Adept to whom she had pledged herself, or by the tacit but unmistakable disapproval of the Senior Sister, the Lady Kael Amion.

Sashka remembered her interview in Lady Kael's study with some discomfort. The Lady had proffered congratulations, obviously feeling that she had no option in the matter, but her manner had been distant, almost cold. Sashka had been bold enough to ask her outright if she disapproved of the alliance, and Lady Kael had come close to losing her temper—something rare in such a normally stoical character.

"The advisability or otherwise of your marriage is the concern of your clan, Sashka," she had rejoined tartly. "All I can say is that, as a Novice of this Sisterhood, you should by now have learned a wisdom and a judgment that is denied to less fortunate women. I hope that you'll use it to your own best advantage."

Sashka had pondered the old Senior's words for some days before deciding that her admonition stemmed from nothing more than jealousy. Lady Kael had never married, and the younger girls were fond of speculating on the manner of disappointments she must have suffered in her youth. It amused Sashka to reflect that, were Kael fifty years younger, she would probably have made a play for Tarod herself.

"Sashka!" A breathless voice hailed her from some distance away, and Sashka stopped, turning. Vetke Ansillyn, her closest friend and study-companion at the Cot, was puffing along the path towards her, hampered by her skirts and an excess of weight. Her face was bright scarlet, and she looked agitated.

Mercilessly, Sashka made no attempt to ease Vetke's distress by going to meet her. She merely stood where she was, idly pulling the petals from the flower she had picked, until the plump girl panted to a halt beside her.

"Sashka, the Novices have been looking everywhere for you! The Lady wants to see you in her study, at once!"

"The Lady . . . ?" Sashka frowned. Whatever could the Lady Kael want with her . . . ?

"Oh Sashka, I hope it's not bad news!" Vetke was agog with curiosity. Uneasily, Sashka brushed her aside.

"Good or bad, you'll know soon enough, the way gossip travels in this place . . ." She started off along the path, Vetke in pursuit. Sashka's long stride soon outdistanced the other girl, and in the empty main corridor of the Cot she broke into a run until she arrived outside the Senior's door. Her knock produced an instant response, and she entered to find Kael Amion seated at her desk, her face pale. In her hand she held an unfolded letter, and before she laid it down Sashka thought she glimpsed the High Initiate's seal on the outside.

"You sent for me, Madam?" Despite her avowed contempt of authority it was a reflex for Sashka to curtsey; few dared openly treat a Senior of the Sisterhood with anything less than the utmost respect.

"Sashka . . ." Kael Amion rose, and her voice was filled with a concern and sympathy that made the girl quake inwardly. "Sit down, please. I'm afraid I have news to tell you that is not at all happy."

Her father? Her mother? Not Tarod, please Aeoris, not Tarod . . . Sashka sank into the nearest chair, white-faced.

Lady Kael spoke slowly, her wrinkled face taut with an emotion Sashka couldn't interpret. "I have today received an urgent letter from the High Initiate in person, and its contents have disturbed me deeply. It's not my habit to allow Novices to be privy to correspondence of such a high order . . . but under the circumstances, I believe you have a right to know the letter's contents." With an abrupt gesture she thrust the parchment towards Sashka.

The girl took it with shaking hands. At first, absurdly, her only coherent thought was that Keridil Toln wrote in a neat and graceful hand, well suited to his position . . . then she shook her head to clear it, and forced herself to take in the words.

For a very long time there was silence in the Lady's study. A stray shaft of sunlight struck through the window onto Sashka's bowed head, making her hair glow like copper. Kael Amion watched the girl carefully and shrewdly. There was so much more she herself could add to the letter's contents; whether she spoke out or kept silent would depend on the girl's reaction. . . .

Eventually, Sashka looked up. Tears glittered in her eyes, and her mouth twisted into a grimace as she hissed under her breath. "*No!* I don't believe a word . . . Lady, I don't believe it!"

It was no worse than Kael had expected. After all, the girl had thought herself betrothed to this serpent in their midst—no one could expect her to accept the truth immediately when it had been thrown so unexpectedly at her feet.

"Sashka . . . my child, listen to me. I understand your feeling—but the High Initiate is a man of justice and honor." She licked her lips. "You must know that he has been a close friend to your—to the Adept Tarod since they were both children. It is as hard for him to make this statement as it is for you to accept it."

Chaos . . . The word seemed to burn into Sashka's brain. *Tarod, a denizen of Chaos, not truly human* . . . She tried to find the words of protest she wanted, but they refused to come; in sheer frustration she burst into a storm of tears, and was only dimly aware of Lady Kael moving stiffly round the desk to hold her and comfort her as though she were a small child.

At last the storm subsided and she gulped noisily into a handkerchief, finally dabbing angrily at her eyes, aware even through her unhappiness that blotched cheeks did nothing for her beauty.

"Better?" Kael Amion asked gently.

"Y-yes . . . thank you, Madam . . ."

"I know it must have come as a terrible shock to you, Sashka, but you must believe that the High Initiate is in earnest." Kael took the parchment from the girl, smoothed it, glanced over the last few paragraphs again. "He says there can be no possible doubt—that Tarod himself doesn't deny the truth of these allegations. And he asks me to convey to you his deepest sympathies. He particularly mentions you, Sashka—he clearly thinks a good deal of you."

The words broke through Sashka's confused misery and she remembered Keridil's phrasing. "*Please convey my warmest regards to the lady Sashka Veyyil, and my deepest sympathies in what must be for her a time of the gravest trial.*" A message from the High Initiate, to her in person . . . and she hadn't even known that he was aware of her existence. . . .

"My child." Kael Amion had retaken her seat behind the desk, but leaned forward to take hold of Sashka's hands. "You must see that this casts an entirely different light on your marriage plans. The Gods know it's a hard thing for me to say, but—"

Sashka interrupted her. "Lady, has—has my father been told of this?"

Kael blinked. "No—I only received the High Initiate's letter this very morning. But he will have to know, Sashka. You can't hope to keep such news from him."

A faint note of censure had crept into her voice, and Sashka swallowed. "I—I didn't mean . . ." She felt the tears starting again and forced them back.

Kael saw the seeds of rebellion, and decided that they must be stopped before they could germinate and take root. She had privately worried about her Novice's forthcoming marriage since the news had been imparted to her; and Keridil's letter served to confirm, albeit in a way she would never have dreamed possible, the fears and doubts she had long harbored about Tarod. She reflected bitterly that most of the blame for Tarod's rise to prominence in the Circle could be laid at her own door; had she not given succor to the waif lost in the northwestern mountains so many years ago, it was unlikely he would have survived to bring this havoc on them all. It was an unworthy thought, particularly as the child had saved her own life and several others; but Kael was essentially a pragmatist, and wished that her seeing powers had not failed her so badly on that fateful night.

She turned her attention to Sashka once more. The girl was staring at her, but Kael had the impression that her brain made no sense of what she saw. Shock—it was understandable, but the girl had to be brought out of it as quickly as possible and made to see reason. Otherwise, her headstrong nature might begin to assert itself and all manner of foolish, defiant notions could enter her head.

"Sashka," she said sternly, "one thing must be made clear from the very beginning. Your marriage cannot now possibly take place."

Sashka half rose from her chair in protest. "But—"

"No! I will have no argument. I know it's hard for you now, but in time you'll understand and be thankful. To marry this man would be to throw away your entire future; everything that both your father's and your mother's clans have worked for generations to achieve. The Circle won't tolerate such a creature among them, and even a high Adept isn't a law unto himself. At best this man is likely to be stripped of his rank and banished from the Circle. At worst . . ." she hesitated. "There has been no execution at the Castle in the memory of any living person, but the precedent isn't unknown."

Sashka was silent.

"It would be within the High Initiate's jurisdiction to order his death," Kael continued. "Keridil Toln is a just man, but this," she tapped the parchment for emphasis, "is something beyond crime. It is a sacrilege and a blas-

phemy against our lord Aeoris. Even if Tarod is allowed to
live, he will be an outcast, a pariah. Would you wish to
ally yourself with such a one, and incur the scorn of
Aeoris to become an outcast at his side?''

Still Sashka said nothing, and Lady Kael knew that her
words had gone home. The Veyyil Saravins were a proud
and ambitious family, and this girl had inherited her fair
share of their traits—the idea that standing by Tarod would
lose her honor, position and prospects would make its
mark once she had had time to consider its implications. If
she could add just a small flavor of fear to the recipe, Kael
thought, her duty would be done.

''My dear.'' She settled herself more comfortably. ''You
probably don't know this, but I myself have had direct
experience of the sorcery of which Tarod is capable and of
which the High Initiate writes so shockingly in his letter.''

Sashka looked up in surprise. ''You, Madam?''

''Yes. It was many years ago, and he was no more than
a scrap of a child—but even then his powers were appall-
ingly evident. Listen to me, and I'll tell you the story . . .''

The chestnut mare slithered to a halt on the wet and
slippery shale and hung her head, panting for breath.
Tarod felt the convulsive heaving of her sides under him
and wondered if her wind was broken. He hoped not—he
had long recovered from his bout of angry resentment
towards the animal; and besides, he might well need her
services again before too long.

From the high vantage point of a ridge that marked the
mountains' southeastern extremity, he looked down the
smooth sides of an ancient, glacial valley. Detail was half
obscured by the heavy rain which had been falling since
sunrise, colors dulled and smudged under the veil of falling water, but still the place looked like a haven after the
harsh terrain of the peaks. On the far side the mountains
rose again, black and menacing, their highest crags lost in
fast-moving tatters of cloud; but below were farmsteads
and crofts, herdbeasts standing with ponderous stoicism in
what shelter they could find. And in the distance, half
shrouded by a copse of trees and surrounded by neat,

well-tended fields, the white walls of the West High Land Sisterhood Cot.

Odd emotions welled up in Tarod as he looked at the tranquil building. He could be there long before dusk; and within those walls was Sashka, waiting for him . . . but he dared not move from this place until darkness fell. It was possible—just possible—that a message from Keridil might have reached the Cot; it was, after all, the one logical place in the world where the Circle would expect him to go, and he could take no risks.

Tarod had driven himself and the horse to the limit since his flight from the Castle. Now he was bone-weary, aching from cold and sleeplessness, and the rain had soaked him to the marrow—in his haste he had brought neither food nor a cloak, and the wind bit through his sodden shirt, numbing his skin until he could barely feel his own chafed hands on the reins. But he would have to suffer a while longer . . .

He slid from the saddle and almost fell as his legs threatened to give way. Supporting himself by hanging on to a stirrup, he maneuvered the mare back from the ridge's edge and into the lee of a steep cliff. He had noted a safe path down the side of the valley, negotiable even in darkness; until night came he'd take what shelter he could find under the cliff, and wait.

Tarod hoped that he might sleep for a while, but the wind changed direction, blowing the rain in heavier gusts that spattered against the cliff face where he crouched; and that coupled with the gnawing pangs of hunger kept him awake. Although it was already late afternoon, dusk seemed an interminable time coming; at last though the easterly sky began to darken from grey to pewter towards black: the valley sank into a deep gloom, and Tarod pulled himself to his feet.

It was all he could do to haul his body into the wet saddle, and he had to clutch at a handful of the mare's mane to steady himself. She seemed in better spirits, and set off willingly enough at a touch. In gathering darkness they made their slow way down the path, leaving the mountains behind. The wind dropped away as they neared the valley floor, then they were moving across rough pasture, dotted here and there with the indistinct silhouettes of bushes and brambles and the occasional slumbering herdbeast which lumbered to its feet and shambled away with an indignant bellow. Lights glowed faintly from two cottages nearby, but no one was aware of the stranger riding quietly past; and at last the walls of the Sisterhood Cot loomed palely ahead.

Tarod reined in and, dismounting, tethered the mare to the first of the surrounding trees. From the outside the Cot showed no lights; following tradition it had been built with a high surrounding wall, intended to deter would-be swains from mooning after the Novitiates. There would be a postern gate, locked but probably not watched; to open it should be a small matter . . . if he had the strength.

Tarod fingered his ring, feeling the stone cold but faintly pulsing to his touch. Again, he needed it—under normal circumstances his own basic skills would be sufficient, but exhaustion had taken too great a toll. He turned to stroke the mare's nose reassuringly and heard her snort uneasily as he slipped out of her sight into the darkness. The wall lay directly ahead: he skirted it silently until he found the gate. A grill, set high in the wood, showed a glimmer of light on the far side, but nothing moved. Tarod closed his eyes, willing his mind to focus and concentrate . . . and after a few moments he heard the scrape and thud of a heavy bolt moving back. He tried the postern, and it swung open on greased hinges, admitting him to the Cot garden.

Now the Sisterhood Cot resolved into a comfortable jumble of low, white buildings of one or two stories. Ahead, in the largest, lamplight glowed from a row of tall windows and he could glimpse long refectory tables within, a few white-robed women sitting near a well-made fire. Beyond that lay two lesser but still quite large houses which, he surmised, contained the quarters of the Seniors and full Sisters; beyond that again several cottagelike structures must house the Novices. . . .

Tarod moved quickly, keeping well clear of the lamplight, until he came to the first of the Novice cots. He was about to approach when a door opened and two girls with coats pulled over their hair emerged. Giggling and shrieking at the rain they ran no more than an arm's length past the deep shadows where Tarod stood motionless, and vanished in the direction of the refectory.

He waited until their voices had finally faded into silence, then moved towards the Cot. Intuition led him to the back of the building, where he found two windows framed by a creeping vine; one in darkness, the other showing a bar of light through half-drawn curtains.

He sensed her presence long before he reached the window and looked cautiously through, but when he saw her it still gave him an unexpected twist of emotion. She was sitting at a small desk, head bowed and haloed by the candlelight, and she seemed to be reading.

Tarod's hand had reached involuntarily towards the window as though to open it before he checked himself. He didn't want to alarm her—the Gods alone knew what she would think to see him stealing in on her like some brigand. He drew back, and returned to the door from which the chattering Novices had emerged. It wasn't locked, and, slipping noiselessly through, he found himself in a narrow, unlit hall.

Sashka's door lay to the left at the further end. His hand on the latch was silent; the door opened easily and for a moment he stood watching her as she sat still engrossed. Then he stepped into the room, closed the door as quietly as he had opened it, and said softly, "Sashka . . ."

She screamed, stifled it by instinct and spun round, the chair scraping on the floor. As she saw him her eyes widened and the color drained from her face; she stood, backed away a step, and whispered his name as if she couldn't believe what her senses told her.

Tarod crossed the room towards her. "I'm sorry—I didn't mean to frighten you, but I could think of no other way."

She knew. He saw it in her eyes—somehow news had travelled ahead of him, and Kael Amion had seen fit to pass on the message from the Castle. Suddenly hope and certainty crumbled away and he felt bereft—had they corrupted the one living soul whose faith he had thought he could count on?

Sashka, however, was rapidly regaining her composure. To see Tarod standing in her own room, not five paces away, when at that very moment she had been obsessed with thoughts of him was a shock; but now she took a grip on herself and swallowed to ease the pounding of her heart.

"*Tarod . . .* Gods, what are you doing here?"

"I came to find you."

"But—your clothes, your hair . . . you're soaked through, and you haven't got a cloak!"

"There wasn't time for any preparation. I—left the Castle in too much haste." He paused, then: "They've told you, haven't they?"

She looked at his face and her mouth trembled. "Told me . . . ?"

"Sashka, in the name of Aeoris don't pretend! Word's reached this Cot about me. You *know.*"

She started to cry; not a storm of tears but deep, gulping sobs that shook her whole frame. She looked so helpless, so vulnerable, that Tarod could only draw her to him and hold her despite his dishevelled state. For a moment he thought she would pull away, but then she relaxed against him as if drawing on the little strength he had left.

"Yesterday, the Lady Kael summoned me . . ." Her voice was muffled, halting. "She—she showed me a letter that had just arrived by messenger from the Castle—from the High Initiate in person . . ."

"What did he say?"

"He said . . . that something terrible happened, that you—had summoned a demon from Chaos. And . . . he said there was fear that you weren't loyal to Aeoris, but owed your allegiance to evil . . ."

No messenger could have reached the Cot faster than he himself had ridden, unless the man had wings . . . Keridil must have despatched his letter on the very night of the summoning in the Marble Hall. "Was there nothing more?" he asked.

"Only that . . . the High Initiate asked Lady Kael that I should be warned of the danger . . ."

"Yes," Tarod said speculatively, "I imagine he would have said that . . ."

Sashka's shoulders heaved and she sobbed out, "Tarod, the Lady told me that our marriage can't take place, that if I wed you we'll both lose everything we've ever known and be outcasts! Please—please tell me it isn't true!"

He couldn't lie to her. It would have been so easy, looking down at her pleading face, to assure her that all would be well, to leave with her now and take her into the exile he faced—but he couldn't. She above all others deserved the truth.

"Sashka, I must tell you the whole story." He released her gently and moved to a chair—he had to sit; his exhausted body wouldn't support him any longer. "I've ridden from the Peninsula without stopping, but before I rest I *must* tell you." He glanced towards the door. "Are we safe here?"

"As safe as anywhere . . . even the Novices' own rooms are sacrosanct."

"Then listen. Since that letter was written, much more has happened . . . on the night that followed, I killed a man."

"You . . . oh, no, I can't believe—"

"You *must* believe, because it's true!" He had deliberately couched the revelation in cold, harsh terms, knowing that any dissembling would do more harm than good. Now as she stared at him he recounted the entire sequence of events in painful detail, without emotion and without meeting her gaze. He felt as though he were baring himself to the bone before her, but it was the only way—to hide anything would be to do her a terrible injustice. He could only trust to his own belief that she would keep faith.

At last, the full story was laid before her. She was silent, and the silence was unbearable.

"And now," Tarod said, "there's a price on my head, Sashka. I'm far worse than an outcast—I'm a condemned man."

"Oh, Tarod . . ." Twisting her hands together in distress Sashka turned and paced across the floor to the window. Her voice shook as she asked, "What will you do?"

"I don't know . . . so much depends on you."

"Me . . . ?"

"Sashka, you're the only one I can trust not to betray me! You hold my life in your hands. I can live—I can go far to the south and start afresh; and the Gods alone know it's easy enough to create a new identity. That's a small skill to any Adept. But without you there's nothing to live *for*. Lady Kael was right—you'd lose everything you've ever known; clan, friends, station . . . but we'd be together. Isn't that what matters above all?"

She took a deep breath and thought for what seemed a very long while. Then, slowly, she said, "Yes . . . that's what matters, my love."

Tarod could have wept with sheer relief. He gazed at her where she stood still with her back to him—even looking at her hurt, though he accepted the pain gladly. He rose. "Then—"

"No." She turned and came towards him, placing her hands on his arms. "Then nothing, until you're rested. You say you rode without stopping—when did you last eat?"

It had been before Themila died . . . Tarod made a negative gesture. "That's unimportant."

"It is *not* unimportant! By the look of you you couldn't even sit astride a horse, let alone ride. You're to wait here, and I'll fetch food for you. After that, you sleep—and later we'll leave quickly and quietly before anyone suspects anything amiss." She nodded towards the window. "The rain has stopped—if the sky clears it'll be dangerous to go before second moonset anyway."

He hesitated. With freedom so close he was reluctant to put their flight off for any reason—but his own body was arguing on Sashka's side. He was bone-weary, too exhausted to think beyond the next moment; he needed sustenance if he was to be capable of anything. . . .

"Sashka . . ." His uncertainty showed in his voice and she bent to kiss him softly. Her lips lingered on his, awakening memories of their time together at the Castle.

"Don't be afraid, my love," she whispered. "All will
be well. Depend on me . . ."

He closed his eyes, nodding, suddenly too tired to answer her. Her hand smoothed his hair and she said, "Wait
here—I'll fetch food, and then you can sleep."

She stole to the door, opened it, peered out into the hall
and found it deserted. Looking back over her shoulder she
saw that Tarod's head was already drooping, and she
slipped outside. As soon as the door had closed behind her
she leaned against the wall, shut her eyes tightly and made
the sign of Aeoris over her own breast. Her heart was
hammering again, with a mixture of the shock brought on
by Tarod's revelation and relief at having escaped from the
room. She hadn't believed it—she had pretended compliance
to the Lady whilst secretly rebelling against the news, but
now her thoughts and feelings had been violently overturned.

Bitterness and disappointment filled her. She had had
such hopes, such dreams . . . and in one dismal night they
had all been snatched away. A condemned man . . . a
seventh-rank Adept, with a price on his head, accused of
consorting with Chaos . . . she didn't pretend to understand half the implications and was impatient with them;
but the consequences were clear enough. And tonight he
wanted her to go with him, run away and face a future that
held nothing. . . .

She'd been a fool. She should have realized from the
very beginning that there was no smoke without fire—and
instead of speculating and worrying and gnawing over the
injustice done to Tarod, she should have been more concerned with the injustice to herself. Now though, her path
was clear. And the tone of the High Initiate's letter, the
message he had imparted to her personally, gave her new
hope. . . .

Exhausted as he was, Tarod's sleep was punctuated by
dreams that allowed him no real rest. Several times he half
woke, aware of the strange room and disconcerted by it,
then he would fall into yet another fitful and unsatisfying
doze.

On the fourth such occasion, something more than the

dreams shook him out of his uneasy state. He could barely open his eyelids, and when he did the room seemed misty and blurred. And someone was moving towards him. . . .

Tarod blinked, trying to see more clearly. White-robed figures . . . several of them. And at their head was Sashka.

He tried to speak to her, but mistook dream-state for reality and uttered the words only in his mind. She stood over him; holding something; a stave he thought. . . .

Intuition roused him suddenly, but not in time. He had one glimpse of Sashka's furious, half-terrified, half-vengeful face before the wooden staff cracked across his skull and an unbelievable pain pitched his consciousness into oblivion.

Lady Kael Amion, leaning heavily on the arm of the plump-faced Mistress of Novices, pushed through the crowd of whispering, wide-eyed women in the doorway and stared down at the still figure of the man slumped in Sashka's chair. A livid crimson mark was already spreading across his forehead where the stave had struck him and, soaked, dishevelled and helpless as he was, he looked incapable of any atrocity. For a moment Kael saw him again as the thin and badly injured child of so many years ago; then she remembered the contents of Keridil's letter, together with her own fearful precognitions, and hardened her heart.

"You did well, child." She eased her arthritic body round so that she could regard Sashka. "It was a terrible decision for you to have to make; but it was the only right way."

"Thank you, Madam." Sashka didn't meet Kael's gaze: her face was flushed and her voice bristled with thinly disguised fury that hadn't abated since the moment she had burst dramatically into the refectory and announced that a dangerous man, sought by the Circle for consorting with Chaos, was in their midst. The reaction of the Sisters had been gratifyingly spectacular, and under the gaze of Kael Amion, who had hastened as best she could from her rooms which she rarely left these days, Sashka had told Tarod's full story to a stunned audience. Now as the girl glanced at him, still clutching the stave, Kael had the distinct feeling that she would be prepared to use it again

at the smallest provocation. Could all the love she had
professed have turned to hatred so suddenly and vehemently, Kael wondered? She had struck Tarod down almost
with relish, as though he were her lifelong enemy rather
than the man she had been on the brink of marrying . . .
the old seer shook her head, dismissing the speculation.
She couldn't pretend to understand a girl like Sashka
Veyyil—and whatever her motives, she had captured a
dangerous man, a murderer and worse. That was all that
mattered.

A breathless Sister approached along the corridor, running with skirts hitched up and no regard for dignity.

"The men from the farmstead have been sent for,
Madam—they're bringing scythes and hoes and anything
that'll serve as a weapon."

"Weapons won't be needed now, thanks be to Aeoris,"
Kael said. "But we'll need good men to serve as escort
back to the Star Peninsula. How much have they been
told?"

The Sister shook her head quickly. "Nothing, Lady,
save that a wanted criminal has been apprehended."

"Good. As well not to alarm them with any talk of
sorcery, or they'll vanish into the night like frightened
rabbits. Now—I want Sister Erminet Rowald brought to
me here. We'll need her herbalist's skills to keep this man
drugged until he's safe back at the Castle." Someone ran
to do her bidding and she looked again at Sashka. "My
child—are you *sure* Tarod made no attempt to deny the
High Initiate's accusations?"

Sashka's eyes glittered angrily. "Yes, Madam! He said
it was all true—and worse, far worse, as I've told you!"

"Very well, very well—no one's doubting your word;
we simply have to be certain." Kael paused. "If there's a
price on his head as you say, then it's likely the Circle will
have sent out men to hunt for him, and our Cot could be
one of their first destinations. With Aeoris's blessing on
our side, our party might meet them before we even reach
the moutains."

"Lady . . ." Sashka was still staring down at Tarod,
and the expression on her face was a peculiar mixture of

resentment, pride and guile. "Might I have your permission to ride to the Castle with the escort party?"

"Ride to the Castle? Child, whatever for?"

Sashka tossed her hair back. "I believe I can give the High Initiate the clearest account of all that's happened here tonight. And—I should like him to know that I was personally responsible for his enemy's capture."

Kael immediately saw the drift of the girl's thoughts, and didn't know whether to give her a scalding reprimand for her arrogance or laugh at her sheer presumption. Then she recalled the wording of Keridil Toln's letter, the concern he had shown for her, and wryly reminded herself that Sashka's hopes and plans had been cruelly dashed from her grasp tonight—however devious she might be, she at least deserved a second chance in recompense.

"Very well," she conceded. "You can be chaperoned by Sister Erminet, as her services will be required on the journey."

Sashka turned towards her, her face lit by a smile as sweet and innocent as a flower. "Thank you, Madam!"

The party left at dawn, and comprised four burly laborers from the valley farmsteads, mounted on their heavy, placid horses and acutely aware of their elevated responsibility. They carried pitchforks and staves, holding them upright like lances, and formed a guard before and behind the two women—Sashka and Sister Erminet—and the chestnut mare, found grazing beyond the Cot walls, onto which Tarod had been tied.

Sister Erminet's narcotics had ensured that Tarod stood no chance of regaining consciousness until the day was well advanced, and he was roped in the saddle with his hands bound beneath the mare's neck so that he lay with his face buried in her mane. After one brief, contemptuous glance at him Sashka didn't once trouble to look back as the small cavalcade wound its way up the valley sides towards the mountains rising grimly in the distance. She was still simmering with the anger of having been cheated, as she felt, but overtaking that was excitement at the prospect of meeting the High Initiate again, and under circumstances which held so much potential.

The horses gained the rim of the valley and started along the road. As they went, Sashka felt something hard digging into her side which irritated her. She felt in her pouch—the apparent source of the trouble—and brought out the gold Initiate's badge which Tarod had given her. It seemed so long ago now, and the token meant nothing. For a moment or two she stared at the gold circle with its bisecting lightning flash as it lay in the palm of her hand. Then, with a careless gesture, she flung it aside into the undergrowth. The metal winked brilliantly among the grasses and one of the farm horses snorted and side-stepped, alarmed by the glittering, alien thing. Then a cloud passed across the crimson face of the sun, and the small gold light went out as the party continued on its way.

Chapter 16

"We owe you a debt, Sister-Novice Sashka Veyyil." The elderly Councillor took Sashka's hand and bowed over it in a manner normally reserved only for high-ranking— and older—women. "You have done us a great service, and the Circle's gratitude is entirely yours."

Sashka suppressed her pride and pleasure under a mask of proper sobriety, and curtsied. "I believe that I did nothing more than my duty to Aeoris, sir. But I'm very honored by your kindness." As she spoke she glanced briefly and obliquely at the fair-haired man who stood a little apart from the others in the elegantly furnished room. He was the only one who hadn't yet spoken a word to her, and she was both disappointed and disquieted, wondering if she had upset or offended him in some way. After all, he had been a close friend to the man who now lay uncon-

scious in a heavily guarded room in another wing of the
Castle . . . but the letter, his letter, she reminded herself,
had seemed to hold so much promise. . . .

Keridil saw the girl glance at him and his pulse quickened uncomfortably. The look in her eyes had combined
appeal with challenge, but although he believed he had
interpreted her meaning he was still reluctant to speak.
Thus far he had allowed the Council elders to offer the
elaborate thanks and praises that were due to Sashka,
preferring to stay in the background until he was more sure
of himself.

He couldn't entirely banish the memory of the shock he
had felt when the party from West High Land arrived at
the Castle a scant hour ago. For a moment, confronted
with Tarod's immobile figure bound to the mare's back
without regard for respect or dignity, guilt had gnawed at
him like a hungry rat. Then he saw Sashka, and the guilt
was lost under an onslaught of other emotions.

Listening to her story, which she told with a quiet calm
that greatly impressed him, the old hopes began to stir
afresh in Keridil's mind. He no longer had cause to be
jealous—Sashka had broken all ties with Tarod of her own
volition, and was free again. If her change of heart was
genuine—and Keridil had no reason to believe otherwise—
then the frustratingly unreachable had suddenly become a
possibility.

He realized that he was staring at her like some callow
stable lad, and hurriedly averted his gaze. If he could just
find the opportunity to speak to her alone. . . .

Sashka, too, was harboring similar thoughts. Although
she revelled in the praise heaped on her by the Councillors, she nonetheless wished the old men would have done
with their speeches and go. She wanted the chance to look
more openly around this room, which she gathered was the
High Initiate's personal study; and she wanted a chance to
speak to the High Initiate without the encumbrance of so
many observers—and most of all without the encumbrance
of her chaperone.

Sashka made no secret of the fact that she loathed and
despised Sister Erminet Rowald. Skilled herbalist she might

be, but in Sashka's view she was also a withered, viper-tongued martinet whose suspicious mind and prying eyes missed no breach, however small, of her own exacting standards. She could be sure that Sister Erminet would report every detail of her encounter with the High Initiate back to Kael Amion, enriching the mixture with her own acerbic observations. And Sister Erminet would be unlikely in the extreme to allow her charge to leave her sight for a moment. . . .

Sashka jumped when the elderly Sister suddenly spoke, as though activated by her sour thoughts.

"Sirs, if you will permit me, I really think I should return to my patient." Throughout the journey she had primly referred to Tarod as a "patient." "Your physician is, of course, a fine man; but as I've attended to the necessities thus far . . ." She pursed her mouth in an eloquent dismissal of Grevard's capabilities and added, "I'd never forgive myself if anything were to go amiss now."

Before any of the Councillors could reply, Keridil stepped forward. "I'm sorry, Sister," he said, smiling an apology. "We've been selfish in detaining you—you've had a long and difficult journey. As soon as you've satisfied yourself that all's well, you must take time to rest. Gentlemen," he nodded to the Councillors, "we must take our leave of the good Sisters until later."

Sister Erminet was impervious to charm. Firmly, she repeated, "I must attend to my patient first, High Initiate. With respect. Perhaps if one of your womenfolk can take charge of Sashka—"

"Gladly. But—with your permission, of course—I'd appreciate the chance to speak with her alone for a few minutes." He drew the Sister a little aside so that they couldn't be overheard. "It's a necessity I regret, but she must be questioned more fully—there may be details that only she can tell us which have a bearing on this dismal affair. And I suspect she's less likely to feel intimidated if she isn't surrounded by inquisitors."

Sister Erminet inclined her head. "It's as you wish, High Initiate, naturally." Then she glanced up and her eyes were suddenly candid. "I don't pretend to understand the girl's motives in doing what she did, however dutiful. There's something unnatural in a betrayal of that nature."

Keridil felt himself coloring. "Nonetheless, we've very good reason to be grateful to her, Sister. So possibly the whys and wherefores are less . . . relevant than they otherwise might have been."

She cast her gaze down. "Quite so."

Sashka offered a silent prayer of thanks as she watched Sister Erminet leave the study with the Councillors following in her wake. The small miracle she had hardly dared hope for had happened: she was alone with Keridil.

For what seemed to her a very long time they stood facing each other, neither speaking. Finally, it was Keridil who broke the silence.

"I'm glad to have this chance to thank you personally," he said quietly.

Sashka stared down at her own clasped hands. "I appreciate your kindness, High Initiate. Under the circumstances, I wondered if—you might perhaps not feel—" She stopped, licking her lips uneasily.

Keridil sighed. "Tarod and I were friends since childhood," he said. "I won't deny that the decision I made has been one of the hardest of my life—but your decision must have been infinitely harder."

This, she knew, was the test. Keridil wanted—perhaps even *needed* —to know that the severance of her ties with Tarod was truly final. Her answer now could be crucial . . . and she hoped she hadn't misjudged his motives.

Turning towards the window, she said, "Tarod and I would have been married here in the Castle. He told me that you had agreed to officiate."

"Yes . . . Do you still wish it could be, Sashka?"

"No." Her answer was so immediate and so firm, that it surprised him. Then she added, still not looking at him, "You see—he told me. Far more than was in your letter. In fact, I don't believe he hid anything from me."

"Then you know about . . . Rhiman Han?"

"The man he killed? Yes. He told me that, too."

Keridil believed he was beginning to understand. Only a few days ago, in this very room, he had asked Tarod point-blank whether Sashka had anything to fear from him. Tarod had vehemently denied the possibility; but it seemed that Sashka felt differently—and fear, Keridil knew, was a soul-eating destroyer. Suddenly he pitied the girl; and with pity came a resurgence of the other feelings.

"Sashka . . ." He moved towards her and tentatively laid a hand on her shoulder. He'd intended the gesture to be—or at least seem—nothing more than kindly, but she half turned towards him, so that he could see the warmth and hope in her dark eyes.

"I'm sorry . . ." he said indistinctly. "You must have suffered so much . . ."

She gave a little shrug. "It hardly seems to matter now. It is as though this has all been a bad dream . . . and besides, my troubles are of no consequence to you, High Initiate."

"Keridil," he corrected her gently. "And you do yourself an injustice, Sashka—your troubles *are* of consequence." His hand still touched her shoulder, and she made no attempt to move away. So softly that her voice was hardly audible she asked, "What will happen to Tarod, now?"

Keridil hesitated. He was anxious not to upset her, and yet the question couldn't be avoided forever. She'd learn the truth before long, even if he tried to hide it from her now.

He said, "The Council of Adepts has condemned him, Sashka. There was no other choice."

"Then he'll die?"

"Yes . . ."

She nodded slowly, as though giving herself time to absorb the fact. Then she said, "How?"

"It might be better if you weren't to know." Keridil was thankful that at this moment she wasn't watching his face. "It'll be a Circle matter. I would have wished it otherwise, but . . . certain procedures must be followed."

Sashka turned to look up at him, her dark eyes narrowed. "In dealing with a demon?"

Keridil stared at her in consternation, and her look became almost challenging. "It's the truth, isn't it, Keridil? Please, don't try to spare my feelings! A man whose soul resides in the stone of a ring can't be truly human, can he?" She stepped away, back towards the window. "I've thought a great deal about it on the journey from the Cot, and I believe I'm strong enough to face cold facts. If I'd wed Tarod, I would have wed a demon." She looked at him again. "Isn't that true?"

True, yes, Keridil thought; *or close enough to the truth . . .* Aloud, he said, "You're very courageous, Sashka. Few women could face that thought with such equanimity."

She smiled bleakly. "What could I gain by deluding myself? I prefer to give thanks for my good fortune in finding out before it was too late."

"Yet there must be regret."

"Oh, regret; yes. Though maybe not quite the degree of regret that you might think, Keridil."

He felt his pulse quickening and wished that the room didn't seem so stifling. "No?"

Sashka shook her head. "Even before this, I'd wondered, asked myself, was I doing right in pledging myself to Tarod? And the answer troubled me a great deal."

"But you loved him," Keridil reminded her. Some perverse part of his mind had to challenge every statement, doubt every hope.

Sashka smiled. "I *admired* him; and I believed admiration and love were one and the same. I was wrong. And now, I think that we would have made each other very unhappy."

It was a statement that even in his wildest fantasies Keridil hadn't expected to hear from her lips. Somewhere at the back of his brain a small voice protested that her change of heart seemed too glib, or even callous; but it was overridden by the rising tide of infatuation with the beautiful girl and he pushed it aside.

"Perhaps," he said gently, "I can help to assuage just a little of your unhappiness?"

She lowered her gaze demurely. "You're very kind."

"Not kind—selfish." He took her hand. "If you'll do

me the honor of dining with me tonight . . . I can arrange
for a meal to be served to us here, alone.''

A flicker of amusement showed in Sashka's eyes. ''Sister Erminet will be outraged.''

''I'll tell Sister Erminet that I wish to spare you from the
ordeal of public attention. I'm not above using my rank to
get her agreement.''

Sashka giggled, stifling it with a hand over her mouth,
and the High Initiate grinned. ''There—I've made you
laugh in spite of your tribulations! That's a good beginning.''

''Yes,'' she agreed more soberly, but with an answering
warm smile. ''A very good beginning.''

''Sashka . . .''

Sister Erminet turned, startled by the unexpected voice,
and saw the man on the bed beginning to stir. She muttered an imprecation under her breath, and reached towards
the array of phials and pots on the table at her side.
By rights he should have remained unconscious at least
until evening; he must have the constitution of a northern-
bred horse to have shaken off her last dosage of narcotics
so quickly.

Rolling up her sleeves, she began to mix together pinches
of two different powders from her own supply and to blend
the result into a cup of wine. In her long experience she
had discovered that even the most recalcitrant of patients
could usually be persuaded to take wine. . . .

''Sashka . . .''

The voice came again, stronger this time though still
slurred with the effects of the drug. Sister Erminet abandoned her preparations and crossed to the bed, where she
stared down for a moment before expertly pulling up one
of Tarod's eyelids. The eye was glazed; he could see
nothing, and she doubted that he had any control over his
limbs as yet, which made him harmless enough. She was
about to move back to her table when a hand suddenly
reached up and, weakly but surely, gripped her arm.

''Please . . .''

''Aeoris!'' Erminet's heart lurched painfully in shock,
and Tarod's eyes opened.

He couldn't see her. His mind was fighting a losing battle against a fog of numbing confusion, he had no more strength than a small child—but he was aware of her presence, and an unerring instinct told him that he was back in the Castle. He couldn't reason why that thought should fill him with anger and dread, and part of him wanted to laugh at his own foolishness.

"Castle," he said.

Sister Erminet's mouth pursed. "Yes, we're in the Castle. Though the Gods alone know if you're capable of understanding what that means. You shouldn't be." She eyed her collection of drugs suspiciously.

"Sashka—had to tell Sashka." Gradually his mind was clearing a little, though any coherent memory of recent events still eluded him.

Sister Erminet didn't answer. She had already made up her mind to dose her charge with a further potion that would keep him physically helpless, while allowing him to maintain a reasonable degree of mental coherence. Too much tampering with the brain could be very dangerous, and her own ethics wouldn't permit her to risk damaging her patient in any way.

"Here," she said briskly, "drink this, if you can." She thanked good fortune that Tarod was still too confused to argue, and watched with relief as he swallowed the contents of the wine-cup that she held to his lips. A seventh-rank Adept wasn't a man to be trifled with at the best of times; and if half the tales she had heard about this one were true then she wouldn't wish to meet him face to face if he regained his full sensibilities. She took the cup away, returned it to the table—and when she turned back again she was shocked to see that the green eyes were fully open, intelligent, and fixed in an unwavering gaze on her face.

Tarod said harshly, "Who are you?"

The Sister-Senior took a deep breath to calm herself. "I am Sister Erminet Rowald. You've been put in my charge until further notice—no, please don't try to move. I'm afraid you'll find you're not capable."

Tarod had attempted to raise one arm, but found the

effort beyond him. For a moment he all but panicked; then he realized what was afoot.

"You're a herbalist." His mouth curled in a chilly, humorless smile, though it took a great effort. "You've drugged me."

"On the orders of the High Initiate and the Lady Kael Amion, yes." Sister Erminet paused, then suddenly returned the smile wryly. "I'm sorry."

"*Sorry?*" He almost spat the word, and she shrugged her narrow, sinewy shoulders.

"Spurn my sympathy if it pleases you, Adept, but you'll find it from few other quarters here."

Tarod was beginning to piece together the fragments of his twisted jigsaw of memory. He remembered the stave that had felled him . . . and the hand that had wielded it. A terrible sensation that he couldn't identify swelled suffocatingly within him, and he whispered, "*Where is Sashka . . . ?*"

Sister Erminet had learned enough of the background to Tarod's story to take an inspired guess at the remainder, and she frowned. "Take my advice, and don't trouble yourself about Sister-Novitiate Sashka."

"I said, *where is she?*"

The old woman sighed. "Very well, then; have it your own way. At this moment, I would imagine she is engrossed in private conversation with the High Initiate, in his study." She glanced slyly at him. "He seemed inordinately anxious to speak with her alone."

Keridil . . . The sheer magnitude of his deviousness and treachery hit Tarod like a knife in the gut, but he couldn't respond to the feeling; the narcotic kept all but the weakest, simplest responses out of his reach.

He stared at the hard-faced Sister and realized that, despite her brusqueness, the sympathy she had proffered was genuine enough. Trying to inject acidity into his voice, he said, "And you, Madam, clearly don't approve of such a liaison . . ."

Sister Erminet had rarely heard such bitterness. She regarded Tarod for a long moment, then replied, "That's nothing to me. We've all had such moments in our youth. But I don't approve of cold-blooded betrayal."

"Then she . . ."

"Betrayed you? Oh, yes. Betrayed, jilted, call it what you please; the little bitch knew exactly what she was doing." She smiled again, grimly this time. "A seventh-rank Adept's one matter; a man with a price on his head is quite another. She's a Veyyil Saravin, after all—I'm surprised you didn't have the common sense to realize where her path lay."

She seemed to be torn between relishing his predicament and pitying him, and Tarod didn't know whether to loathe her or be grateful. He shut his eyes against a surge of impotent misery, and Sister Erminet came back to stand over him.

"I'm sorry for you, Adept," she said more gently. "No matter what you've done, or what you are, no one deserves such treatment from the hand of one who professes to love him." She hesitated. "I shared your feelings, once; though I doubt that's any comfort to you. I was jilted by a youth whose clan thought me beneath them. I believed he'd defy them for my sake, and I was as naïve a fool as you. When I realized my mistake, I first tried to kill myself, then when that failed my family packed me off to the Sisterhood." She licked her lips, suddenly surprised at herself. In forty years she'd not spoken of that long-ago incident to a living soul . . . but then she reflected that it could do no harm to confess it to a man who would, before many more days were out, carry her secret into eternal damnation. . . .

Tarod was watching her. "Maybe," he said softly, "we're two of a kind, Sister Erminet."

She grunted contemptuously. "As like as chalk and cheese!" Reaching out, she took hold of his left wrist. The new drug had taken full effect now, and he could do nothing to stop her. She rubbed her thumb over the stone of his ring. "That's a pretty bauble. The Initiates have been trying to take it away from you, but it won't come free. They say you keep your soul in it, and that you're not really a man at all, but a thing from Chaos. Is it true?"

Tarod's eyes glittered. "You use the word lightly enough. Aren't you afraid of Chaos, Sister Erminet?"

"I'm not afraid of *you*. And, Chaos or no, you'll be done with before long, so where's the need for fear?"

This time, it wouldn't be a sword-blade in the back . . . Keridil would resort to the orthodox rites of the Circle—and Tarod was all too well aware of what lay in store for him before they finally extinguished his life. Purification, exorcism, damnation, fire . . . he knew the prescribed ways as well as any man, despite the fact that they hadn't been used in centuries, and they were barbarous. He might persuade Sister Erminet to administer some pain-killing brew before the death-ritual began, though he imagined she was as likely as not to refuse out of sheer perversity. Otherwise, he had only agony to look forward to before he finally went to Aeoris. . . .

Agony. The prospect of such physical pain meant nothing to Tarod; it seemed as remote and divorced from reality as he felt. He closed his eyes, suddenly crushed by a wave of exhausted despair. He hadn't even the strength to rail against his own destiny; it no longer mattered. The bitter taste of Sashka's betrayal had sapped his will, and oblivion would be a blessing. . . .

Sister Erminet's voice broke gratingly into his dismal reverie. "How do they intend to dispose of you?" she asked detachedly. "Do you know?"

He opened his eyes again and stared dully at her. "I've a good enough idea."

"And it won't be an easy death?"

" . . . No."

She grunted. "I'm no scholar outside my own field, but I've read enough of these things . . ." Her eyes, bright and beady as a bird's, fastened on his face and she added almost diffidently, "I could give you a narcotic. Not enough to numb you to all of it, or the Circle would suspect something amiss. But it would make matters . . . easier."

"You're very kind."

Erminet shrugged and turned her face away, disconcerted. She hadn't for a moment anticipated that she, of all people, could find herself moved to pity and even faint stirrings of affection for a condemned stranger; but the feelings were there, and she was honest enough not to deny them. Perhaps it was a natural empathy with one who had fallen victim to a traitorous lover, as she herself had once done; perhaps it stemmed from her deep-rooted dislike of Sashka and other girls like her, whom Erminet considered worthless dilettantes. Either way, she didn't like to see a strong life broken and wasted.

"I'm not kind," she told Tarod, with an edge to her voice. "I'm simply luckier than you are. You're destined to die, while I live on to try to instill some glimmering of herbal lore into empty-headed Novices. And if that's as Aeoris wills it, I'm not about to argue. Besides, if you are what they say you are, we're doubtless well rid of you."

Tarod laughed. It was a soft sound, but unmistakable, and the Sister turned to regard him curiously. "You're an odd one," she observed. "I've seen many die in my time, but none have ever laughed at the prospect."

"Oh, I don't laugh at the prospect of death, Sister," Tarod said. "Only at you."

"Me?" She bridled.

"Yes. Helpless as I am, thanks to your pretty potions, you say you're well rid of me." For a moment an odd fire glimmered in his eyes, then dulled. "I hope for all your sakes, Sister Erminet, that you're not mistaken!"

The sky above the Castle was the color of old, drying blood, tinging the vast flagstones in the courtyard with a gory reflection. From the window of his study Keridil could see the first of the higher-ranking Adepts gathering, making their way towards the door that led down to the library and thence to the Marble Hall. The angry sunset reflected, too, in their white robes, giving them a grim and faintly unhuman aura; they moved slowly as though already constrained by the demands of the ceremonies that lay ahead.

With an effort Keridil tore his gaze away from the window and concentrated on the task at hand. The room was bitterly cold—this particular rite demanded that no fire should be lit in the High Initiate's presence on the day chosen—and he was almost glad of the heavy ceremonial clothes, in spite of the fact that generations of disuse had given them a cloyingly musty smell. He wondered who the last High Initiate to wear these purple garments with their elaborate sapphire-thread embroidery had been, and the nature of the crime that had been expurgated on that occasion; and forced the thought away. Last night he had been plagued by the most monstrous nightmares he had ever known, in which Tarod, transformed beyond all semblance of humanity, had pursued him through a warped landscape of mountains that screamed his name like accusers, and winds that burned his flesh until, charred but somehow still living, Keridil had hurled himself face down onto the unyielding ground and prayed for death. He had woken sweating, yelling hoarsely, and only a cup of wine and the warm arms of the girl who shared his bed had banished the hellish memory.

That girl now sat silently on a chair at the far side of the room, wrapped in a heavy cloak to ward off the worst of the cold. Apart from the time she had spent soothing Keridil in the wake of his nightmare Sashka had slept as soundly as ever, and her face was calmly impassive as she watched him preparing for Tarod's execution. In the seven days since her arrival at the Castle she had spent almost all her time in Keridil's company, and it was now widely accepted that she was, in all but name, the High Initiate's consort. Her parents, summoned from Han Province, had arrived in a flurry of haste expecting to find their daughter shamed and bereft, and instead had been confronted by a girl radiant with a triumph that far outstripped her previous ambitions. They were so grateful for the unexpected change of fortune after the appalling news concerning Tarod that they turned a blind eye to the fact that Sashka disappeared to Keridil's private rooms after dinner each night and was not seen again until morning.

Sashka was already discovering that Keridil was far more malleable and easy to understand than Tarod had ever been. She had quickly learned to use all her skills to divert him from any qualms of conscience, and during the past two days, as final preparations for the Higher Rite that would send Tarod to his death were made, she had meekly submitted to a passive role. Once, she had hinted hopefully that she might be allowed to witness the rite, but had accepted Keridil's refusal. Nonetheless, she would have liked to be present . . . it would have set the final seal on her triumph.

She had made no attempt to see Tarod. Rumor had it that he still lay all but senseless in a locked and guarded room, subject to the ministrations of Sister Erminet; but Sister Erminet never spoke of him—in fact she seemed to be deliberately avoiding Sashka, which suited the girl well enough. Nonetheless she wondered occasionally how he fared, if he ever thought of her and if he knew that she had betrayed him to the Circle. She would have liked him to know . . . with a peculiar mixture of bitter resentment and the jealous vestiges of the desire she had once felt for him, Sashka hoped that he was aware enough of his impending fate, and suffering for it. . . .

Keridil was unaware of her train of thought as Gyneth, with studied and unnecessarily fussy deliberation, finally cast a heavy black cloak over his shoulders while he stood immobile. The clasp—solid gold, and bearing the High Initiate's insignia—clicked shut at his throat, and Keridil was ready. At a nod from the old steward, two white-robed sixth-rank Adepts moved from the doorway where they had been waiting, and took up positions at either side of the High Initiate. Keridil laid his right hand briefly on the massive ceremonial sword that hung from his hip, and its solidity helped settle his queasy stomach. His eyes met Sashka's and, anticipating him, she rose and crossed the room towards him. Her face was very grave as he cupped her cheeks with his hands.

"It'll be done by morning, love," he said softly.

Tarod would take all night to die . . . Sashka quelled the flicker of satisfaction within herself and only nodded. Gently Keridil leaned forward to kiss her. "Go to your mother and father, and keep them good company. With the dawn, we can all begin afresh."

His set expression, the somber garb, thrilled her with an excitement she dared not show. She returned the kiss then stepped back, watching as the three imposing figures left the room. Only when both they and Gyneth had gone did she allow herself to smile.

Keridil and the two Adepts walked the Castle corridors to the main door in a chill silence. Circle members whose ranks were beneath that demanded for this ritual had gathered to watch them on their way, and all inclined their heads respectfully as the party passed. The doors stood open; as they moved out on to the steps an icy north wind bit Keridil's face and hands. The last of the daylight was fading, the sunset's bloody glory over, and the courtyard before him looked bleak and malignant. On the far side the other Adepts waited, their ranks now swelled and all but complete. Ghosts, Keridil thought; in the uncertain twilight they might all have been ghosts from a long-dead past . . . he shivered.

No one spoke as the ranks of Adepts parted, forming two lines between which Keridil walked. Reaching the door that would lead them deep underground to the Marble Hall he turned, and they all waited.

The light that glimmered from the main Castle entrance flickered once, and went out. Then, in the windows of the dining hall, others followed suit. On the upper floors more torches dimmed and were extinguished, one after another, until not a single light remained in the entire Castle. The spectacle chilled Keridil to his bones as he wondered how long it was since this grim ritual had been observed. No light or fire would burn anywhere in the great black building tonight, until the moment when the High Initiate's own hand conjured the supernatural cleansing flame that would finally scourge and destroy Chaos.

The queasiness returned at the thought of what he must do tonight, but he forced it down. This thing had to be—Keridil had steeled himself to what was necessary, and the knowledge that he had right on his side suppressed his conscience. He only wished that it could have been cleaner, but since the failed attempt to kill Tarod before he fled the Castle he had thought long and hard, and realized that a simple death might not put an end to the evil. A demon wouldn't die as easily as a man—Tarod must be destroyed by occult means, if the taint were to be truly eradicated. And besides, a quick death wouldn't satisfy the Council, nor the Sisterhood, nor the countless numbers of ordinary folk who looked to the Circle as their spiritual mentors. News of the serpent in their midst was abroad and spreading now—only the full might of a death-ritual would restore their wavering confidence.

A rustle of movement among the Adepts alerted Keridil suddenly, and he looked up. Across the courtyard, barely discernible in the deepening darkness, a group of figures had emerged from the main door and was moving slowly towards them. Most were white-robed; one, in their midst, was dressed in black and almost incapable of walking; two of his guards supported him and he made no attempt to resist their rough handling. Heading the small procession came another Adept with a shallow hide drum strapped to his wrist, his gaze fixed on the ground before his feet.

Keridil had a sudden picture of the unseen watchers who must be thronging the Castle's darkened windows, witnessing this small spectacle which was all they would see of the night's rituals. And then the approaching figures halted—and for the first time since the night of Rhiman Han's death Keridil found himself face to face with Tarod.

Under the tangled mane of black hair it was hard to see his face. He swayed, fingers flexing but without coherence. Sister Erminet Rowald had done her work well . . . and Keridil was both surprised and relieved to find himself unmoved by the sight of his one-time friend in such a condition. He raised one hand, intending to signal for the procession to the Marble Hall to begin—but before he could move Tarod suddenly jerked his head back. He struggled to focus his eyes, then seemed to get a grip on his senses, and fixed Keridil with a drugged stare.

"High Initiate . . ." The voice was no more than a cracked whisper, but it was still venomous. "You must be very content with your triumph . . ."

Keridil didn't answer. The ritual forbade him from speaking until they were in the Marble Hall; even without that stricture he would have had nothing to say.

"Dead things . . ." said Tarod. "Damnation and anni-hilation. All of us, Keridil. All of us."

A sharp shake from one of his guards silenced him and Keridil turned abruptly away. Drugged beyond sense though he was, Tarod's rambling words evoked an uneasy feeling. He glanced over his shoulder at the ring, still shimmering nacreously on Tarod's left hand from which the Initiates had been unable to remove it, and suppressed a shudder. Without looking at the black-haired sorcerer again, he nodded to the group of Adepts.

The Initiate who bore the hide drum raised his free hand. With a deft flick and twist he struck the skin, and a dull, funereal sound echoed through the courtyard. Slowly the procession began to move towards the library door, their steps marked by the steady thudding of the drum, as regular and as somber as a dying man's heartbeat.

Chapter 17

It was the sound of the drum that first began to rouse Tarod's senses from the miasma imposed by Sister Erminet's drugs. He stumbled between his captors, feet dragging, limbs refusing to co-ordinate, and with only the haziest idea of where he was or what was happening. Dimly he recalled being forced to drink something that tasted bit-terly acrid, trying to resist but not having the strength; now, his clouded brain sensed danger but he felt too dulled and apathetic to care.

Until the drum started to impinge on his awareness . . .

At first he thought it was the muffled beating of his own heart, but then he realized that the sound was coming from beyond his body. It seemed to disturb the air around him, suffuse the floor under him; unconsciously he started to walk in rhythm with it, his movements gaining more coherence. Walls swam into the blurred limits of his vision; a narrow corridor, leading down . . . he sensed power that flowed upwards, hungrily, from roots unimaginably deep in the rock far below, and the drumbeat was its slow, inexorable pulse. Like a pendulum, swinging constantly, eternally, marking out the passing of time—

His frame jerked with a sudden spasm as a blinding pinpoint of light flickered across his vision. It lasted only an instant, but in that instant he was left with an indelible mental image of a seven-rayed star . . .

Someone shook him violently and he almost fell, regaining his balance only when he was forcibly pulled upright. Now there was another light; paler, filling the corridor, and the procession slowed to a halt as, with a final roll of the Adept's fingers, the drumbeat ceased.

But Tarod still heard it. It continued in his mind, throbbing, insistent, like a strange, sourceless call. He saw the silhouettes of men turning aside to shield their faces from the cold radiance as Keridil bent to unlock the door of the Marble Hall, but found that he was able to look directly at the pulsating brilliance without flinching. The door seemed unreal, as though he viewed it from a plane that was one step removed from reality. . . .

A hollow click, and the door swung open. Slowly the Adepts advanced into the coruscating mists of the Marble Hall. Tarod felt weightless, motivated by a force outside his control—he tried to turn his head to look into the shifting, shimmering columns of light, but couldn't. All he could do was move forward, towards the very center of the Hall. And there, he knew, something waited; a pent, eager power that froze his mind with a fear greater than anything he'd ever known. For a moment ice-clear reason returned, and he realized that he had only a few short hours to live.

He might have tried then, with one last effort, to fight back against the injustice and finality of his predicament, but his numbed brain and body hadn't the capacity to rally. Yet the moment of clarity had brought other memories— memories of the girl to whom he had pledged everything and who had carelessly abandoned him to his fate while she turned her fickle affections to another man who could offer her greater status. Keridil and Sashka would sleep easier in one bed without his existence to trouble their dreams, and somewhere deep within Tarod a cold rage began to take on shadowy form . . .

They reached the place where the tortuous patterns of the floor were broken by the impenetrable black design that was, so the Circle believed, the heart and focus of the Marble Hall's power. Now though, the mosaic was obscured by the bulk of a huge altar carved from black wood, waist-high and about the length and breadth of a tall man. It was roughened with age, gouged with marks that might have been made by fingernails or knife-blades, and slowly recognition dawned in Tarod's mind.

This was one of the oldest artifacts in the Circle's possession. For several generations now it had lain disused in one of the Castle's deep cellars, but over the centuries it had borne mute witness to some of the most powerful and devastating rites known to the highest Adepts. On its unyielding surface, long-forgotten perpetrators of evil had been magically bound, cursed and destroyed—and tonight, another name would be added to the toll.

It was the sight of that grim travesty of an altar that brought the shock of understanding to Tarod's numbed mind. He faced the realization that he was about to die—that his life would be bled and burned from him on that block—and for the first time he was afraid. Yet the fear of torment was eclipsed by the infinitely greater terror of what might follow in the wake of his destruction.

He *had* to live. No matter what the cost, he had to defeat Keridil. The knowledge came with ice-cold clarity, sweeping aside the last remnants of the drugs' effects on his brain. The Circle could kill him, but they couldn't wipe out the spirit contained within that stone. They might seal it away, bind it with the most powerful magic known to them, but Chaos wasn't so easily bested; Yandros would find a way to wield his dark influence through the gem again. And if the Circle tried to use the stone against its masters, they would unwittingly open the gate that had been shut since the fall of the Old Ones; the power locked in the stone would manipulate them like children, as it had manipulated Tarod himself. The Adepts were strong, and they had the wisdom of generations behind them—but they didn't understand Chaos. Only one who had once *been* Chaos—and he shuddered inwardly at the aeon-old memories that came crowding into his mind—could hope to use their own forces against them.

He had to thwart them. In the final extreme, only one power in the world could crush the soul-stone and banish it forever—Aeoris himself. And only one man could fight the stone's pervading influence for long enough to see such a task through to its conclusion. He *had* to live!

Once, he could have stopped this madness with the flick of an eyelid; but now, even though his mind was clearing rapidly, he didn't have the strength of will to summon the power he could have once wielded. If only—

"Hold him!"

The voice barked out, shattering Tarod's thoughts and echoing eerily through the Hall. Freed from the constraints of silence, Keridil had moved to the northward-facing head of the altar and now turned to face Tarod. He had some suspicion that the black-haired Adept might make some effort to fight, and was disconcerted when Tarod seemed incapable of offering resistance. His two guards forced him to his knees at the altar's foot so that he half sprawled with arms outstretched across its pitted surface. Their gazes met, and the High Initiate said, so softly that Tarod wondered if the voice might be a delusion, "The ring, Tarod." In the dark colors of his ceremonial garb Keridil looked unreal, a dream figure, and Tarod involuntarily clenched his left hand.

"You have a choice," Keridil continued when it became apparent that his adversary wasn't going to speak. "Surrender the ring to us of your own will, or we'll take it." His hand played lightly on the pommel of his ritual sword.

Tarod looked up into his face and saw that his one-time friend's eyes were stone cold, emotionless. A strange mixture of jealousy, hatred and fear seemed to lurk behind the coldness, and a momentary insight also betrayed the specter of Sashka in the High Initiate's look. To reason with

Keridil, to plead with him, would be a mockery . . . and, fed by the burgeoning but as yet unrealized rage, a spark of rebellion flared. Tarod still had pride—and this man, who had now betrayed him twice over, would never know the satisfaction of seeing him capitulate. With an effort he twisted his haggard face into a malevolent smile.

"Then take it, High Initiate," he managed to whisper ferociously. "Take it—if you can!"

He expected them to try to wrest the ring from his finger, and so was unprepared for Keridil's reaction to his challenge. Almost as he spat the last words, hands clamped down on his wrists, pinning them to the altar, and though he tried to twist away the Adepts were too strong for him. Keridil moved slowly, deliberately around the altar until he stood directly over Tarod. Then unclipped the sword from his belt and reversed it, so that as he hefted the scabbard the pommel formed a heavy club. He nodded briefly to the two men beside the altar, and they tightened their grip on Tarod's wrists as the High Initiate raised the sheathed sword.

There was nothing Tarod could do. Pride made him bite back any protest or plea. He tensed, jerked his head aside as Keridil swung with full force—then a scream of agony tore from his throat as the sword-hilt smashed his left hand, shattering fragile bones, breaking the silver ring so that the soul-stone fell free to leave only the buckled base on his ruined finger. For a moment, through a scarlet haze of shock and pain, he saw Keridil's face triumphant, his hand clasping the glittering prize. Then, as the Adepts released his arms, Tarod slid to the floor as a merciful oblivion washed over him.

"Where is the stone . . . ?"

"They took it . . . my hand . . ."

"You must retrieve it, Tarod. You must."

"I can't . . ."

"You must! So much depends on you. You must take it again, and wield it, and understand. If you die, there will be nothing. You must not die."

"I have no choice . . ."

"You have a choice. Take it. If you love this world, take it . . ."

Tarod's mind twisted in protest, and the sibilant, characterless voice faded away and was gone, leaving only the memory of its urgent words. Only the memory . . . it was nothing but a pain-dream, a delusion. It had no meaning . . . sighing silently, he let his consciousness sink down again into emptiness. . . .

"By the Will of Aeoris shall evil be bound!"
"Bound, by the Will of Aeoris!"
"By the Blood of Aeoris shall evil be scourged!"
"Scourged, by the Blood of Aeoris!"
"By the Sword of Aeoris shall evil be sundered!"
"Sundered, by the Sword of Aeoris!"
"By the Fire of Aeoris shall evil be destroyed!"
"Destroyed, by the Fire of Aeoris!"

The slow, grim chant rang through the unfathomable dimensions of the Marble Hall, the High Initiate's voice soaring in a trance-state to be answered by the descant of the Adepts. A strange, pale light glowed around Keridil; he felt the power at his command increasing like a surging tide as the inexorable chant continued, fed by the composite will of the Circle who now formed a complete ring around him and the massive blackwood altar. The sensation was dizzying, almost terrifying; and he felt as though the countless shades of his predecessors stood at his back, joining their ancient strength with his own. Greater though Tarod's powers might once have been, a spark of divinity seemed to possess Keridil now as the long-disused rite gathered momentum.

Tarod came up from the black vastness of unconsciousness with the sound of the Adepts' chant ringing chillingly in his ears. A searing, pulsing pain throbbed through his entire body and focused in his left hand; he couldn't move. . . . Straining, he half opened his eyes, and flinched from a blinding shaft of blue-white light that seemed to hang in mid-air before him. He felt the presence of something unhuman; something that filled the Hall with power, that held him, pinned him effortlessly to an iron-hard surface.

The shaft of light moved suddenly as the chant swelled to a crescendo, and he realized where he was. He lay face upwards on the altar, head hanging back over its edge, and the light was the brilliant radiance flickering along the length of a huge sword which Keridil Toln held upright in both hands. Tarod felt heat pulsating from the blade like a hellish breath on his forehead, saw the High Initiate's face illuminated by its glow, eyes closed, expression a mask of inspired concentration.

The rite had begun—and he was powerless to stop it. Already the forces conjured by the Circle held him fast; and now Keridil was beginning to chant the eerie, high-pitched Exhortation and Exorcism that would call down the Gods' damnation on their victim. Soon it would be done . . . and when the ceremony reached its frenzied climax, the High Initiate would summon the White Flame— the pure, supernatural fire that, legend had it, burned eternally in Aeoris's heart, and which alone could destroy the essence of a demon of Chaos.

Sweat broke out on Tarod's skin, as though his body already felt the White Flame's touch. *He didn't want to die* . . . and with that realization came a shock like a hammer-blow, as the fury pent inside him and kept at bay by Sister Erminet's drugs came flooding into his mind. Before they broke his hand to take the soul-stone from him, he'd cared nothing for his own fate. But now a new sensation was in him . . . a raging, savage *need* to hold to life, to defy and defeat the Circle, eclipsing all other desires. And some-thing else . . . something that only gradually dawned on his awakening senses.

The High Initiate still chanted, the Adepts almost howling their responses as they too were caught up by the incredible charge of power. But their voices washed over Tarod and left him unmoved. Carefully, he concentrated on the fire of pain that filled his body. It receded . . . He turned his mind towards his left hand, exerted just a little of his will. . . .

The pain vanished altogether. When, tentatively, he

flexed his fingers he knew that they were whole again, the damage inflicted by Keridil healed as though it had never existed. And he began to understand.

Keridil had taken the stone that contained his soul, but the High Initiate had reckoned without the effect such an action might have on his enemy. A mortal man, soulless, would be an empty husk—but Tarod wasn't entirely mortal. In losing the stone, he had lost his links with the full, awesome power of Chaos—but he had also gained something that neither he nor the Circle had foreseen. Power still remained to him—and it was a power stripped of all the taboos and constraints imposed by humanity; for he was no longer human.

He believed that that power was great enough to save him. The way was fraught with hazards beside which the Circle's death-rite would seem child's play, but now Tarod was incapable of knowing fear. Neither was he subject to pain or conscience—a coldness lodged at the core of his heart where before there had been the pitfalls of human emotion. Though he had fought to suppress the devastating forces which deep down he knew he could command if he chose, they were there, dormant, waiting. Now he would use them without compunction—and if that meant freeing the insane power of Chaos locked within him, then so be it. The Circle must take the consequences.

Above his head the huge sword hung, still pulsating with light that obliterated the shimmering mists of the Marble Hall. Keridil's voice rang shrieking, the Adepts half shouting, half singing a grim dirge in counterpoint. Slowly the blade's brilliance was increasing, and Tarod felt tremendous forces dragging him downwards, trying to pull his mind into the Circle's power. Silently he resisted, but even as the influence faded he knew that time was rapidly running out.

Time. It was as if a key had turned in his memory, unlocking a kernel of knowledge so old that he had been unaware of its existence. Yandros in his cryptic way had referred to it, but Tarod had never truly understood, until now. . . .

Long ago, when the Old Ones ruled, Time had been a

plaything of the Lords of Chaos. The unhuman minds behind the hands that shaped this Castle had chosen it as a focus for their manipulation of temporal forces, and that ancient property still lived on. The Circle had never been able to fathom its mysteries; as a Circle Adept Tarod had been as unenlightened as they. Now though, the secret lay open before him. . . .

The chant was a wall of sound battering against his senses as the ritual neared its climax. Tarod closed his eyes, shutting out the image of Keridil in his trance-state. A darkness hovered on the brink of his inner vision and he recognized it as emanating from a spot directly beneath where he lay; the black circle that marked the very center of the Marble Hall's peculiar dimensions. He let his mind follow it, felt it call to him . . . slowly the real world faded away, until his consciousness hung, alone and unsullied, in darkness. Beneath the closed lids his eyes glazed, and a trance far deeper than the High Initiate's took hold of him. . . .

A wall of sheer rock barred his path. Black basalt, glittering with razor-sharp facets of crystal embedded deep in its surface, it reared into a sulphurous sky and offered no passage. Tarod gathered his will, remembering, then raised his hand and spoke a single word.

A titanic *crack* rolled from the cliff face and it split, revealing a narrow fissure from which a deep green light glowed. Tarod moved forward, feeling the rock shroud him, and saw within the cliff a shaft that fell away into mind-bending nothingness. The green radiance filtered up from the shaft and he headed towards it—

Stay.

He stopped. The voice had spoken out of nowhere, and the green radiance began to quiver as though some unseen presence disturbed it. The tide of memory surged again, and Tarod formed a stern question in his mind.

Who thinks to command me?

The answer came back to him, ponderous and heavy. *The Guardian of this place.*

Tarod smiled. He raised his left hand, and beckoned. *Show yourself, Guardian.*

It formed slowly, taking its shape and substance from the living rock that surrounded him. Manlike, but hunched and ill-formed; a stocky dwarf with basalt eyes, crystal glittering in its throat as it opened an ugly but humorous mouth in a grin.

Welcome, traveller, it said, its voice like shale sliding on granite. *What is your business?*

It was half Tarod's height, but it had a strength and a stability which he knew he would find hard to combat. Nor did he wish to combat the Earth-Guardian. There were better ways . . . and older allegiances.

He said softly, *Do you know me, Guardian?*

The stone-dwarf frowned as memory stirred, and for a moment the basalt eyes flickered uncertainly. *You are a stranger, mortal . . . and yet not a stranger . . .*

Tarod's green eyes glowed, and his astral form shifted subtly, so that the dwarf's eyes widened in sudden recognition. The peculiar, squat figure went clumsily down on one knee and the Guardian murmured, *Master!*

Tarod laughed, softly but it was enough to awaken a thousand echoes in the rock all around him. *Old friend,* he said to the stone-dwarf, *ours were good days . . .*

The being raised its ugly head to regard him with something resembling affection. *The Earth does not forget.*

Then aid me.

Another grin split the pocked and jagged features. *Master . . . Earth is yours. Take what you will.*

Tarod drew breath. The dwarf's outlines wavered and he felt a sensation as though his own frame were turning to stone. Granite bones, basalt flesh, crystal skin . . . the essence of the earth-plane filled and strengthened him even as the squat Guardian's shape dissolved into nothing.

He had passed the first barrier . . . slowly, Tarod moved towards the yawning shaft and its shimmering green glow. Its radiance bathed him like cool rain; he gave himself up to it, let his consciousness sink down into its quietly shining depths . . .

He moved with the ease and grace of a fish, through a

world composed only of water. Strange, elemental shapes
flickered at the limits of his vision and a gentle murmuring
filled his mind, lending his thoughts a tranquility that he
had never before known. He absorbed the feeling, letting it
permeate his being, drawing more strength from it as he
felt his way steadily towards the third of the seven astral
planes.

And then suddenly he was in air. Air that screamed and
shrieked around him, buffeting and whirling with a vibrant
life of its own. A giddying sense of vertigo swamped
Tarod, and pale, lurid colors shot through with darker
veins danced before his eyes. He forged on, letting himself
become one with the wild gale, twisting and turning on the
air-currents, until—

Heat seared him. Sand burned under his feet and the sky
was crimson fire from horizon to horizon, a blaze far more
spectacular than any sunset. He might have been standing
at the very heart of the sun itself. A fireball blazed overhead in brief glory, and flames leapt like exotic trees from
the ground only inches away, to die back as their brief but
violent energy was expended. Tarod focused his mind and
drew on that energy—he had reached the fourth plane
now, and the exertion was telling on him despite the
strength he had taken from the three he had so far trav-
ersed. And impinging on his consciousness was the knowledge that, far away in another and more material dimension,
the death-rite of the Circle was drawing towards its grisly
conclusion. If Keridil summoned the White Flame before
he could reach his goal, then his mind would be snatched
back to the mortal realm, and he'd die screaming with his
task unfulfilled.

A geyser of white-hot fire erupted skywards only a pace
ahead of him, roaring like a furnace. Tarod's astral form
flickered as he launched towards it and it overwhelmed
him—fire flashed through his veins so that he became a
living flame, hurtling upwards, outwards, until he burst
into a realm of illusion.

Laughter rippled from hunched black rocks over which a
silver aura played deceptively. The ground shifted beneath
him and faces formed out of the air only to shiver and

vanish again before he could name them. But despite the
intangibility of this plane—which, so the Circle Adepts
believed, was the highest attainable by any human magician—
Tarod knew that he was drawing close to his objective. A
faint, regular pulsing throbbed through the very fabric of
the world, and though it was as yet far away it was a sure
sign that his instinct was guiding him well.

With a great effort he shook off the seductive illusions
and fantasies that urged him to turn aside and stay, and
launched his mind towards the sixth and penultimate plane.
He had never before dared to reach for such a goal—but
the barriers that might have existed for any purely mortal
man crashed around him, and he erupted into a place
where a single, gargantuan voice screamed on an endless
note. Rage, madness and an unholy delight mingled in the
deafening cacophony and Tarod recoiled from its onslaught,
all but losing control as the din threatened to push him
over the brink of insanity. He took a desperate grip on his
senses, knowing he dared not resist the voice but instead
must let it flood into and through him. . . .

With a small part of his mind that still clung desperately
to earthly reality he felt he was about to break apart under
the voice's screeching onslaught—but in the very moment
when it seemed it would overpower him, he exerted his
will in a last, defiant surge—

The universe crashed into utter silence.

Tarod felt as though he were back on the physical plane,
in his human body. Every muscle movement brought tearing pain and he felt bruised through to his bones, as
though he had crawled half alive from some insane battle.
But he had succeeded—he had broken through to the
seventh and highest plane. Only one barrier lay in his path
now—and that barrier hung before him.

It was a wall of utter darkness, with no limit in any
direction. Beyond it was the greatest and most deadly test
of all, and Tarod gathered all the strength he possessed to
face and challenge it. He needed to utter just one word for
the black wall to break down and allow him to pass . . .
but the mere thought of that word filled him with repul-
sion. Its language had been created when the fabric of the

universe was barely formed and it was so alien to human speech that he could hardly bear to consider it. Even now, as it formed in his mind, he wanted to turn and run. . . .

Tarod gasped, and his hands clenched savagely, straining. His lips parted and he uttered the word, holding tightly to the last tatters of his will, commanding himself to listen and absorb as the monstrous syllables filled his being.

The wall hurled itself at him, and he hung in the very midst of the darkness.

He had succeeded. He had broken through the gateway, and reached the bizarre multidimension that lay beyond all the seven planes—his final goal.

Unconsciously the knotted muscles of his astral body relaxed, and Tarod began to sway. The rhythm was absolutely perfect. And as he moved, he felt the change beginning. The deep throbbing that had hovered on the fringes of his consciousness drew closer until it became a gigantic heartbeat, echoing in the pulse that coursed through his veins. Currents flowed past him and through him, Time itself dancing and twisting and warping . . . and at last, shrouded in murky darkness, a monstrous shape appeared to him.

It was a vast Pendulum that moved in the gloom, swinging on a long arc that carried it through a myriad shifting dimensions in faultless rhythm with his swaying. Tarod felt a sense of awe at being in the presence of a power whose true nature was beyond even his comprehension. He knew that the image he faced was only a minute fraction of the Pendulum's true form—for this was the force that controlled all of Time, in all of the universe's countless planes and dimensions. But the Marble Hall was and had always been a gateway—for those with the skill to use it—through to that aspect of the Pendulum which encompassed the Castle's dimension. And here, in this dark moment, Tarod's destiny was inextricably linked with the titanic artifact as it marked out the movements of Time in his own world.

To save himself, he must stop the Pendulum.

If he could do it—if he could bring Time screaming to a

halt—then day and night would have no meaning, all movement would be arrested, and all living souls would cease to exist until Time should once again be set in motion. All living *souls* . . . Tarod smiled thinly. Soulless now, he alone would live on in the Castle, and could fulfill the quest to which he had pledged himself . . . though the nature of that quest now eluded him. No matter—with the stone once more in his possession, his will would prevail.

If he could stop the Pendulum . . .

He focused his concentration into a bright prism with the Pendulum of Time at its very center. Slowly, achingly slowly, the vast bob drew nearer, seeming to swell until its proportions filled the air and swamped Tarod's mind. He knew what must come, and braced himself in trepidation to receive the initial shock. When it came, at the moment when he and the Pendulum fused and became one, the pain that flooded him was far, far worse than he had expected. He had to fight desperately not to scream aloud—and the Pendulum was carrying him with it, the swing increasing in force. He couldn't hold out against it much longer; its strength would soon overcome him and then he would have no hope of controlling it—it would shatter and destroy him.

Tarod thought of the White Flame, which even now Keridil must be calling from its netherworld into manifestation. He drew breath as he swayed, as the Pendulum of Time swayed; and summoned every last dreg of his resources into a single bolt of pure power. The moment had to be perfect—

A cry that could never have been uttered by a human throat wailed through the dimension, and suddenly, violently, Tarod stopped.

It was as if he had been hurled into the epicenter of a gigantic earthquake. Shock upon shock roiled over him, racking and pounding and tearing; the darkness warped and shredded into a million fragments—as the Pendulum of Time screeched to a tortured halt.

As the massive swing was arrested in mid-motion, a shattering explosion smashed Tarod backwards. Unbearable light blazed in his head—then his body struck a hard and agonizingly physical surface, and he blacked out.

When he came to he was sprawled face down on stone, with dust clogging his mouth and nostrils. Coughing, his head spinning, he tried to raise himself and fell back with a gasp as pain shot through his left arm. The force that had hurled him back to the material world had slammed him against the floor with a terrible impact, and the bone was broken. For an instant he wanted to laugh—the Circle had seemingly come full turn, and for the second time in his life he had arrived at the Castle of the Star Peninsula as an injured and disoriented stranger.

But this time there were great differences . . . Tarod silently willed the bone to heal, and the pain flowed away into nothing. He flexed shoulder and wrist, and smiled grimly to himself. Whatever else he might have achieved, the power reawakened by his loss of humanity was undiminished. He lived, and he was free. What he would see when enough physical strength returned for him to rise and look about him, he didn't even try to imagine. All he knew was that the Circle had been thwarted, and the knowledge made him weak with relief.

He craved sleep. Despite his healing abilities, his soul—no, he corrected himself, his *mind*—ached with the titanic strain imposed by what he had done, and he could have simply rested his head on his arm and slept where he lay. But that must wait—he had to know the final outcome of what he had done.

Stiffly, he rose. The Marble Hall was dark, and that disconcerted him—the coruscating mists with their peculiar intrinsic light had vanished, and his senses warned him that he wasn't surrounded by a vast space, as he had expected, but by walls that were perhaps only a few handsbreadths away. . . .

Realization came with a sudden shock. He wasn't in the Marble Hall—this was the Castle library! Quickly Tarod attuned his green eyes to the darkness, and made out the dim silhouettes of shelves surrounding him on every side. Many had been splintered by the force of the upheaval, and the Castle's collection of books and manuscripts lay wildly scattered about his feet.

An unnatural stillness hung in the vault. Nothing moved. Tarod felt a foreboding growing in him, a certainty that something was wrong; and as the dread took a tighter hold he moved towards the open door that would lead him to the Marble Hall.

This time, there was no blinding silver light. The door of the Marble Hall glowed a sullen pewter, and even before he reached it Tarod's intuition forewarned him of what would happen. He reached out towards the door—and, three inches from its surface, his hand was stopped by an invisible barrier. He tried a second time, and a third; but the result was the same. And at last he realized the truth.

The forces that the Castle's unhuman architects had imbued in the Marble Hall were as capricious and devious as their creators. Oh, he had succeeded in halting the Pendulum of Time; the Castle and its inhabitants were caught and held in limbo, and he had gained a kind of immortality. But Time had shifted more subtly than Tarod had bargained for—the moment that held the Marble Hall was fractionally out of synchronization with that in which the Castle itself had been frozen, and thus the Hall was barred from his reach.

And the soul-stone was trapped, together with the Adepts of the Circle, like a fly in amber beyond that door. . . .

Tarod felt something akin to despair flower in him. To have achieved so much, only to be thwarted by a quirk of fate when everything seemed to be in his grasp, was a cruel irony. He raised his left hand, looking at the twisted silver base of the ring which still clung to the index finger. Without the stone he was at a hopeless impasse—he needed to retrieve it if he was to stand any hope of finally bringing about its destruction, and yet he couldn't possess it without bringing back time, and with it the full wrath of the Circle.

Slowly, he turned from the dully glowing door and retraced his steps to the library. For a while then he stood motionless among the scattered books, absorbing the dead and silent atmosphere. He was the only living thing here, now.

Now. Tarod smiled bleakly as he realized that the word
no longer held any meaning. What became of a world in
limbo? What became of its inhabitants? He felt no pity for
Keridil and the Circle, and very little anger or malice. The
bitter taste of betrayal was still there, but it no longer
gnawed at him; it was as if his heart had chilled within
him. By surrendering his humanity he had also surrendered
the emotions of a human being, and, detachedly, he reflected that it seemed a small price to pay.

At last Tarod left the library. Reaching the courtyard, he
paused to look up at the sky. A dark red, lurid glow
seemed to hover beyond the Castle's black walls, throwing
the four gigantic spires into brooding relief and casting an
eerie radiance over everything it touched. Tarod smiled at
this evidence of the sheer immensity of the forces that
must have been unleashed on this dimension at the moment when Time ceased. Beyond the Castle, beyond the
Maze and the stack, the world lived and breathed still; but
the Castle of the Star Peninsula was no longer a part of it.
Time had shattered and separated them; no one could
enter, he couldn't leave—he was caught in the trap that he
himself had created.

He turned and walked along the colonnaded avenue that
led to the Castle's main door. The crimson glow had
permeated inside, and glimmered beyond the open doors
like a distant hellfire. Climbing the steps, Tarod paused
before entering. There would have been activity within,
despite the grim ceremony taking place. Servants going
about their business even in darkness, a crowd in the
dining hall, gathered about the empty fireplace to whisper
and speculate and ease each other's fears. Somewhere
Sashka would have been sleeping, or keeping vigil for
Keridil's return. . . .

An echo of his lost humanity made Tarod shiver at the
thought of what he might see if he stepped through that
doorway. Silent statues, frozen in the midst of life? Ghosts?
He quelled the unease, and moved on into the Castle.

There was nothing. Silent corridors, empty rooms. Nothing. The dining hall greeted him, stark and lifeless and
inhabited only by shadows that lurked where the dim red

radiance couldn't reach. Wherever they were, whatever their fate, the Castle-dwellers had left no trace of their existence when Timelessness consigned them to limbo.

A sigh, so soft that he might have imagined it, whispered through the silent hall. Tarod turned. He thought he glimpsed the flick of a cloak-hem moving by one of the empty tables, and heard the faint echo of a woman's bright laughter from the gallery above the hearth, but they were gone before his senses could fully register them.

Ghosts of his own memories . . . deep down he felt a sensation that might have been loneliness or sadness, but it was vague, and quickly faded. He could learn to live with memories. . . .

Tarod turned his back on the silent dining hall. His face registered nothing, for there was no feeling within him. Returning to the great doorway, he stood staring across the courtyard to the massive double gates in the Castle's outer wall. Then, almost as a reflex, he raised his left hand and made a careless gesture. Thunder bawled overhead and a bolt of blood-red fire cracked the length of the courtyard, momentarily lighting it with a furious brilliance. The sense of his own power brought him some small comfort. While he wielded that power, hope remained. He had triumphed once—and despite his seemingly impossible predicament, he believed that he could do so again. There would be a way—there *had* to be a way—to retrieve the soul-stone. And he'd find it.

Tarod stared up at the black walls of the Castle which was now his prison, and almost laughed. Yes; he'd find the way. And he had all the Time in the world. . . .